DATE DUE

AGENT OF INFLUENCE

David Aaron

G. P. PUTNAM'S SONS
New York

To my friends on Wall Street,
who make too much money
and earn every cent.

G. P. Putnam's Sons
Publishers Since 1838
200 Madison Avenue
New York, NY 10016

Library of Congress Cataloging-in-Publication Data

Aaron, David.
    Agent of influence.

    I. Title.
PS3551.A6A74   1989   813'.54   88-29816
ISBN 0-399-13378-X

Printed in the United States of America
1   2   3   4   5   6   7   8   9   10

ACKNOWLEDGMENTS

I would like to thank the following people for their assistance in the preparation of this book:

Rodger Altman, The Blackstone Group
Jeffrey Beck, Drexel Burnham Lambert Incorporated
Norman Brown, Donaldson, Lufkin and Jenrette
Frank Dunlevy, The First Boston Corporation, San Francisco
Nathan Gantcher, Oppenheimer and Company
Kenneth Lipper, Lipper and Company
Victor Palmieri, Palmieri Company
Steven Robert, Oppenheimer and Company
Robert Rubin, Goldman Sachs and Company
John Sanzo, The First Boston Corporation
Robert Sind, Recovery Management
Andre Wormser, Wormser Frères, Paris

PROLOGUE
SHANGHAI 1949

The early morning sun seemed to scatter sequins on the surface of the water. For centuries, that was the time of day when the Chinese came to the promontory between the Huangpu and Wusong rivers to practice "white snake stretching its tongue" and "carrying tiger to the mountain" and "seeing fist under elbow" and the other gentle tortures of Tai Chi.

But for almost a hundred years the Chinese had been banned and the embankment made into a park reserved exclusively for foreigners. Western women found that hour the quietest time to stroll across the Garden Bridge, through the park and along the broad avenue called the Bund.

Now, the European ladies with their parasols and prams were also gone. The massive Western-style buildings along the Bund were cordoned off with concertina wire and the streets were blocked with tanks and armored cars. The glittering light on the water concealed the bobbing heads of the dead Communist and Nationalist troops whose bodies floated downstream from battles raging for control of the bridges in Kiangsu province.

The besieged Nationalist Chinese authorities in Shanghai also chose that hour to lift the round-the-clock curfew briefly so that the increasingly desperate populace could attempt to buy food. Kuomintang troops scoured the nearby countryside in search of farmers to be escorted into the city. Each day they found fewer and fewer farmers, and less and less food arrived in the markets.

Kang Sheng and a dozen farmers had been walking under guard along the railroad track for five hours. In the middle of the night, the Army had come to the house in Soochow near the old Imperial Canal. He had expected them, and had assembled as much rice as the local underground revolutionary committee could spare. He had been told that the most dangerous moment would come when the troops argued over whether to make him carry the rice, or simply to shoot him and keep it for themselves.

To Kang's surprise they negotiated a deal: to ease his burden, they would relieve him of half of the rice: he would carry the rest to the city. Even that had dwindled from thirty to ten pounds as the soldiers at each checkpoint helped themselves. He began to worry. A few more checkpoints and there would be none left. He would be turned back. He would miss his crucial rendezvous. The project would be endangered.

In the growing light at Chia-ting, Kang could see columns of smoke rising in the direction of the tracks' ahead. He and the others from Soochow were loaded onto a boat to be taken down the Wusong to the center of Shanghai. Because Soochow was the culinary capital of the region, Kang counted on being taken to the VIP market on the Bund where the foreigners, Nationalist politicians and prominent families would be the only ones allowed to shop. But when he looked at what the group carried, an ancient goose, a cage with three emaciated chickens, a string bag with a handful of eggs, a few baskets of rotting vegetables, a pole with two small fish, his half-sack of rice, he wondered why Generalissimo Chiang Kai-shek would waste the gasoline to get them there.

Passing through the industrial suburbs and sprawling slums, the river narrowed to a stench-filled creek. Kang could see hundreds of desiccated corpses stacked like cordwood along the embankment. Nationalist troops were tossing the bodies into the backs of trucks while wailing relatives sat by, too enfeebled to interfere. Suddenly, Kang Sheng realized the pall of smoke over the city might not be a sign of war but of famine.

Where the creek joined the Whangpoo, the trees in the Garden Park had been cut down for fuel and the flowers and bushes uprooted to grow vegetables. Rounding the point, Kang saw the line of tanks and armored cars barricading the Bund in front of the customshouse. A huge throng jammed the boulevard. Machine guns intermittently fired into the air and the crowd would surge backward. Kang could see people falling and being trampled underfoot as a path opened for a car to slip past the barrier and into the market.

The boat came alongside the pier, and Kang Sheng and the others were forced off and marched into the market. At gunpoint, he was ordered to sell his rice to a middleman. As he handed over the priceless rice for worthless Nationalist currency, he understood why the authorities had made such an effort; cameramen from the Kuomintang press agency swarmed to capture the scene. The photographs and film footage would be circulated throughout the United States as proof of the vitality of Chinese capitalism in the midst of the war against the Communists.

Once stripped of their food, the group was herded into a barbed-wire compound set up against the granite walls of the Hong Kong and Shanghai Bank. They were ordered to stay until they began the trek back to the countryside. Kang Sheng squatted down on his heels like the farmers and waited patiently.

Soon, a Chinese dressed in English clothes passed slowly by, carefully searching their faces. He stopped, then approached the guard, pointing to Kang Sheng. In minutes, the two of them were sipping tea in a plushly carpeted office within the bank building.

"You are three days late," the man said to Kang Sheng.

"Comrade, you criticize me for the inefficient foraging of Chiang's troops?"

"I know you've come a long way," the man conceded, "but as you can see, the situation here is disintegrating rapidly."

"That should enhance our prospects," Kang observed.

"For the revolution, yes," the banker said. "For our project, I am not so sure."

Kang looked at him sharply.

"We had three possibilities," he continued. "In the last few days, one of the families managed to get permission to leave. They were Jews. Another family, pure Russian, is still here, but unfortunately the son died. Malnutrition, thin blood, I don't know what. There is cholera. Random violence."

"And the one that's left?"

"If nothing has happened to them, you should see the mother and child soon. They come to the market at eleven o'clock each day."

Kang Sheng glanced at the ornate French clock sitting under glass on the marble mantelpiece. They had a few minutes to wait. His eyes took in the pale blue silk wall covering, the paintings of English sailing ships in thick gold frames, the heavy velvet drapes hanging from the richly carved moldings around the windows. He returned his gaze to his host, who sat across a vast mahogany desk. He knew the banker had been a secret member of the Communist Party most of his life, but Kang could not bring himself to trust him.

"Why do our Russian comrades want young children?" the banker asked.

"Boys, only boys," Kang corrected him.

"Boys then. Have they not orphans enough from the war?"

"I don't know their reasons," Kang replied, which was only partly true. "But we are getting great fraternal assistance in the supply of arms," which again was only partly true.

Responsible for scientific as well as other strategic intelligence in the Chinese Communist Party, Kang Sheng had long regarded Stalin's military aid as totally inadequate for the struggle against Chiang Kai-shek. Then suddenly the Soviets offered to cooperate on the most advanced arms—atomic weapons. But there were two conditions. Chinese physicists in America who were sympathetic to the revolution first had to go to the USSR to work on the urgent hydrogen-weapon project. Second, young male children, even infants, of Russian families that had fled to China after the Bolshevik Revolution had to be "repatriated" to the Soviet Union. Why, Kang Sheng did not bother to guess.

The sound of machine-gun fire began again in the street.

"Here comes her car," the banker announced. He was standing at the window peering through binoculars into the marketplace. "Look." He handed over the glasses. "Hers is the Daimler. The dark blue one with the sloping back," he added quickly, realizing his guest might have never seen one at party headquarters in the caves of Yenan.

Kang watched as the car pulled up to the middleman to whom he had been forced to sell his rice. The driver got out and opened the rear door. A young boy in shorts hopped down. He looks healthy enough, Kang thought. Then the driver helped the mother out. She was young, not yet thirty, but she used a cane and trembled with malnutrition.

"Her husband died six months ago," the banker explained. "The family fled to Shanghai when our forces took Tientsin. She knows almost no one here. He squandered his remaining fortune to buy her a few privileges, like shopping in this market."

The woman made her way to the small stall where the middleman sat on a grass mat behind a tiny lacquered table. He did not rise to greet her. The driver did the bargaining. Each time the middleman shook his head, she looked more anxiously at the driver. Finally he nodded, and the woman took off her pearl necklace, untied the clasp and removed a pearl. The vendor examined it carefully, then placed it in a leather pouch in his lap. He measured out a cup of rice onto a piece of newspaper, folded up the ends and handed it to her. She looked desperately at the driver as if to say, Is that all? He shrugged.

"She gives most of the food to her son," the banker said. "I don't think she can last more than a week." The driver was helping her back into the car.

"And the driver?" Kang Sheng asked.

"He is our contact."

"He looks well fed."

"Slowly he is taking most of her possessions."

Kang made a decision.

"We risk too much by waiting." His voice became authoritative. "Have him take the boy. She is too weak to resist."

The banker nodded obediently.

Kang Sheng paused to watch the limousine roll away. In his lifetime, he vowed, the revolution would eradicate hunger and privilege. It would sweep the world of capitalism.

"And when he hands over the child to us," Kang concluded, "have the driver liquidated."

PART I
NO BRAINER

1

"Money, money, money!"

Jayson Lyman's voice could be heard while he was still far down the long forty-fourth-floor corridor that separated the Merger Department from the rest of Gould Axewroth's investment banking offices at One New York Plaza.

"Bonus time's a'comin'! Let's close some deals!"

He appeared at the door, briefcase in his left hand, his suit jacket carefully folded over his right forearm, gripping a pink *Financial Times* like a swagger stick. Lyman had wary hazel eyes and a straight nose and mouth framed by dark eyebrows and a sharply chiseled chin. He was of medium height with a muscular build, which he maintained more with stress than with exercise.

Attempting to look casual, he wandered through the suite of offices, checking on who was in, who was out, and who was on the phone. Anyone caught reading was in trouble.

"You don't read in the office, Rankin!" he lectured one of a half-dozen junior associates crowded into a windowless cubicle jammed with computers. "Why do you think we let you go home at night?"

Lyman walked into a vacant office and began to flip through the date book on the desk. It was full of breakfasts, lunches, drinks and dinners.

"Bosworth! Where's Bosworth?"

Lyman was calling for Mark Bosworth, a three-time Connecticut Congressman who had recently quit Washington for Wall Street.

De Grazia, a senior M&A specialist, stuck his head out of his office. "Putzworth?" he said. "Putzworth's out making his first midget with a revolutionary new concept. It's called leveraging his stomach!"

Lyman looked at him disapprovingly. "He was an important man in Washington. It's not his fault if someone told him that investment banking was a dignified way to make money."

"Yeah," de Grazia replied, "but he fell for it."

Lyman turned and dropped his bulging black "doctor's bag" brief-case on his secretary's desk.

"There's a lot of work for you in there."

"I don't do socks," she said, peering inside.

"Send those to the cleaners. You know cashmere socks last only two or three wearings? What are my messages?"

Standing in the middle of his corner office, which overlooked the south bay of New York Harbor and the Statue of Liberty, Jayson Lyman thumbed a sheaf of yellow phone slips searching for something interesting. He was thirty-three, and in eight years he had built M&A, his mergers and acquisitions department, into the most lucrative profit center at Gould Axewroth and a force to be reckoned with on the Street.

On sheer brains and audacity he had beaten financial giants such as Merrill Lynch Capital Markets and with audacity outmaneuvered con-glomerates such as Shearson Lehman Brothers/American Express. Lacking the established corporate connections of Goldman Sachs or First Boston, Jay Lyman had driven Gould Axewroth to the top ranks of the deal makers by being aggressive to the point of overbearing, solicitous to the point of shamelessness, and attentive to the point of obsession. He worried each deal as if it were a fetus threatened with miscarriage, and when he gave birth, he sank into a slough of depres-sion. In the past year, his postpartums were lasting longer and longer.

Lyman sat down in a tall chair behind a broad, leather-covered Louis XV table, which served as his desk. It was bare, except for a thick red Economist Diary. He rotated around to check the gleaming green screen of his Quotron, which displayed the current market price of all the stocks he cared about plus a running financial news summary from the Dow Jones Wire. The market was off to a slow start. His universe of stocks was quiet.

He opened the Economist Diary and groaned. Meetings, one after the other. He had tried to staunch his growing restlessness and compensate for a zero personal life by overscheduling. He had succeeded brilliantly. Lunches and dinners with clients stretched through every page, with the occasional gap filled by fundraisers. Being relatively young, with no family connections in New York, he was forced to start out with rather obscure charities. Somehow he had come to specialize in arts organiza-tions for the handicapped, the Deaf Jazz Ensemble, the Blind Mime Troupe of TriBeCa and the Spastic Kabuki Theatre, among others. His life was now the envy of his age cohort in the investment banking world and a total nightmare.

"Jayson, I got three lines holding," his secretary called out, disdaining the intercom. "You landed back on oith?" Marlene had once nearly been Miss Staten Island. Standing five eight, with a thirty-seven-inch bust and a twenty-five-inch waist, she lifted weights with the devotion of the Sisters of Mary, and played basketball, baseball and volleyball. She also marched with a tuba in the Columbus Day parade. Behind her back, Jay Lyman referred to her as the best-looking guy in the office.

"Who are they?" he demanded.

"The Chairman of RATCO—"

"Scumbag."

"Mrs. Pierce from the Caldwell Galleries—"

"A felon."

"And some creepy guy named Mr. Malcom, who won't say what . . ."

"Oh shit, I've got to talk to him!"

"Line two."

He spun his chair around, punched the button on his telephone console and picked up the receiver. As he talked, Marshall Cooke, the young president of Gould Axewroth, came through the open door. He stood for a moment unnoticed, then took a seat on the velvet mohair couch under a huge super-realist painting of Jay Lyman's car sitting in the Louvre with the Winged Victory rising above it. Rankin and de Grazia appeared in the office doorway and hung there listening.

"I know it's short notice, Mr. Malcom," Jay Lyman was saying, "but it's really time to do something." He ran his fingers through his hair, which was beginning to curl over his collar.

"A week from Thursday. . . . Can't you do it any sooner?" He turned around to his desk to pick up his diary and was startled to see he had an audience. "Would this Thursday be possible, Mr. Malcom? Early in the morning? Eight thirty? Fine. That seems pretty steep. You should be able to give me a better price."

"Jesus, Jay," Cooke exclaimed, "you even turn a haircut into a negotiation."

"I'm in a position to send you a lot of business," Lyman continued.

"Everybody at Gould Axewroth will want their hair done by Mr. Malcom," Rankin sang out. "Can I also get my beard sucked?" de Grazia asked.

Lyman waved at them to get out. "That's a fair price," he concluded. "So then it's Thursday at eight thirty A.M. I'm very grateful." He hung up.

"Oh thank you, Mr. Malcom," de Grazia mimicked him. "Yes, Mr.

Malcom, you're so sweet to me!" Rankin echoed. They began to prance around the office.

Lyman was offended. "Excuse me, but Mr. Malcom is not a hairdresser."

"He makes designer condoms, silly," de Grazia explained to Rankin.

"It's a fitting for custom-made prophylactics! How chic!" Rankin added.

"He happens to run a funeral home."

They stopped and looked at him.

"And I happen to be arranging a memorial service for my mother."

"God, Jay, I had no idea." De Grazia was stricken.

"You mentioned she was sick," Rankin mumbled.

"But I didn't know she died," Cooke apologized.

"Well, she didn't," Lyman said.

His colleagues looked perplexed.

"But she will, sooner or later! And when she does, I probably won't have time to go to a memorial service. Have you seen my schedule?" He spread his diary out on the desk. "If we do it this Thursday at eight thirty in the morning, I can be there."

They just stared at him. Rankin and de Grazia began to back toward the outer office.

"Do you think I should invite her?"

More troubled silence followed.

"I'm sure your mother would find that very thoughtful, Jay," Cooke finally said in his most soothing voice. "But you won't be able to make that date either."

It was Lyman's turn to look concerned. "What now?"

"We need some privacy." Cooke closed the door in Rankin's face.

For a moment, Lyman thought that it might be the start of the annual bloodbath over bonuses. But November was still two months away and no one had yet started locking his desk at night. Bonuses did not explain why he would be tied up Thursday morning.

Cooke was taking his time, pacing the length of the office, his footsteps leaving imprints in the thick wool carpet that had been put down only the week before. Each time Lyman closed a major deal, he redecorated. The new floor covering and drapes were mauve, the walls a high-gloss maroon, the coffee table black marble with streaks of silver quartz. For the first time, Lyman realized that none of it went with his antique desk, nor the portrait of his automobile.

"It's an unprecedented opportunity for Gould Axewroth," Cooke finally said, stopping to gaze out the window.

Are we selling out? Lyman wondered. He hated the thought, but it made sense; the firm was an anachronism. It had grown to have so many prima donnas among the partners that critics called it "the Opera House." Wall Street had become polarized between the huge firms, often owned by insurance companies, industrial giants or commercial banks, and the smaller boutiques that had an exclusive niche such as managing money, or otherwise living by their wits. Caught in the middle, GA had grown to the point that it would make a satisfactory lunch for some financial service's Goliath.

Lyman had come to Wall Street as a newly-minted Stanford MBA in the late seventies, before the long Reagan boom made it the thing to do. Investment banking had become so unfashionable during the fifties and sixties that a huge age gap opened up and thirty-year-olds were replacing retiring senior partners of major firms. To Lyman, that was a leading indicator of opportunity. He talked his way into the training program at Salomon Brothers, starting first on the bond trading desk, then bootstrapped his way into corporate finance and ultimately into mergers. In a few short years he had become a player, but he longed to become a principal, running his own department, doing deals on his own.

Then he met the legendary Billy Gould. Founding chairman of Gould Axewroth and a noted collector of Egyptian antiquities, he was being honored by the Metropolitan Museum at a black-tie dinner in the vast room that housed the Temple of Dendur. At the end of the ceremony, fifteen hundred of New York's social elite gave Gould a standing ovation. Five minutes later, Gould was alone and the hall empty except for Jay Lyman, his date, and a bulimic in a Balenciaga who battled with a weightwatcher in a Lacroix over which of them would take home the only remaining floral arrangement.

Gould stood by the podium unsuccessfully trying to fit a silver tray into his briefcase. Lyman introduced himself and offered congratulations. Without acknowledging any compliment, the old man asked if he could help him put away his award. Lyman managed to do so by first removing a stack of prospectuses. Gould did not thank him. He asked if Lyman were looking for a job.

"I already have a job," Lyman protested, "with Solly."

"All right, a better job."

"I never turn down a job I haven't been offered." Lyman started to recover. "What do you have in mind?"

"Nothing. You approached me."

Gould snapped his briefcase shut, put the prospectuses under his arm, and turned to leave. Lyman felt opportunity slipping away. Gould suddenly stopped and looked back.

"What do you think of this temple?" he asked.

Lyman paused. He had not seen it before that evening. Covered with hieroglyphics, it rose on a stone mount above a broad reflecting pool. A special wing of the museum with a soaring glass wall provided the perfect site. It had knocked him out. But Gould asked not only as a connoisseur but as an expert in value. Lyman discarded the idea of bluffing.

"The room is very impressive, but I don't know anything about Egyptian antiquities."

"It's not an Egyptian antiquity. You're looking at a deal. You think it's four thousand years old? It's barely two thousand and built by Romans. It was a Christian church most of its life. The Egyptians palmed it off on the U.S. government as gratitude for $16 million worth of help in saving the Nubian monuments from the Aswan Dam. This museum got it because they could use it to raise $25 million."

He began to shuffle away. Lyman felt he had somehow failed a test. Then Gould spoke again without turning.

"You're right about the room. It's the genuine work of art. Kevin Roche. Worked with Saarinen. If you ever get an idea that can make us both a lot of money, let me know."

The next afternoon, Lyman messengered a copy of his B-school thesis to Gould with a two-page executive summary attached. It argued that with the Dow Jones Index at 750, most American businesses were deeply undervalued, particularly the conglomerates—mish-mash companies which sold everything from brassieres to insurance and rented cars on the side—Gulf and Western, Norton Simon, Esmark, ITT. They had been assembled during the go-go years of the 1960s, but by the early 1980s, investors could no longer figure out what business these conglomerates were in, and their stock was trading at a fraction of what the companies would be worth if they were broken up and the pieces sold off separately. Lyman concluded that such "restructuring" would be big business for investment bankers in the next decade.

The following day, Billy Gould gave Lyman a chance to prove his theory by offering him a phone and a desk and $100,000 for one year. It was touch and go. He found that every public company already had an investment banker. Business executives disdained merger advisors as high-priced real estate brokers. Besides, "restructuring" was distasteful, something bankrupt companies were forced to do by their creditors. If they had to, corporations could do their own deals; they saw nothing special in Jayson Lyman. He only managed to get Gould to extend his contract by taking a substantial cut in pay.

Ronald Reagan rode to the rescue by gutting antitrust enforcement. Suddenly, the one thing needed to validate Lyman's theory appeared— buyers.

Mergers became all the rage. Soon, buyers did not even care if top management wanted to sell. They went directly to the public shareholders. Bidding wars erupted between buyers. Almost everyone got rich: the takeover artists, lawyers, arbitrageurs, top executives, shareholders, and, in particular, the investment bankers like Jayson Lyman who would work either side of a deal. Nobody much cared what happened to the company, the workers and senior management in the process.

Now, Lyman thought, Gould Axewroth might be on the block, and with it, his department and his future.

Cooke had stopped pacing and stood at the window looking across the Hudson River at New Jersey. Only a few years older than Lyman, he had been surprised when Billy Gould, in failing health, picked him to run the firm. He was still as uneasy as Lyman was resentful.

To improve his executive skills, Cooke attended seminars on corporate leadership, where he was taught to speak slowly so as to capture people's attention and give his words weight. It merely drove Lyman crazy. His hyperactive mind scattered in a hundred directions each time Cooke went into a long pause. He once told Cooke he sounded like a recovering stutterer.

"I don't have to tell you how tough business is these days," Cooke said.

That means you'll tell me in excruciating detail, Lyman thought.

"Fresh flowers are disappearing from reception areas all over the Street. Morgan Stanley's the latest." He spoke as if he were talking about the black plague.

"Underwriting's been a shit business since shelf registration," Lyman responded.

Underwriting was what investment banks were supposed to be all about. They were not banks, and seldom made investments. Their basic business was to buy stock from issuing companies at a guaranteed price and then sell it in the market—at a profit. In theory, they took all the risk of the market going down. In fact, the issues were "presold" to insurance companies, mutual funds, pension funds and the like. Knowing what they would receive and what they would pay, investment bankers simply pocketed the difference.

Then the SEC changed the rules. Established companies could do their own paperwork, put stock issues "on the shelf," and force investment bankers to bid for the service of calling a few of their customers to sell it. Underwriting lost all of its mystery, and most of its profitability.

"So with the market in the toilet, what do those, those . . . those . . ." Cooke grasped for the right word. "Those ingrates in Congress do? Let the commercial banks sell stocks and do underwriting! After all the PAC money we put into political campaigns. Citibank's cutting our throat!"

Lyman had long argued that a truly free market was the enemy of the clubby world of investment banking. Lulled by the long Reagan bull market, however, many investment bankers failed to see that deregulation, tax reform and intensified competition would cause line after line of their business to evaporate.

"Political power is a commodity like any other," Lyman observed. "The commercial banks paid more."

Cooke was not listening. "And the trading desk's been whipsawed by the market. Arbitrage dropped a ton over the summer. I let 'em move the operation to Southampton on the grounds that they did all their business on the phone anyway. Then they lost twenty percent of their capital! When I asked why, you know what they said? 'Beach brain.' "

"Marshall," Lyman finally interrupted, "I get the picture. You want to sell the firm. But are you also telling me to expect a lousy price?"

Cooke looked stunned. "Who told you that? I'm not here to talk about selling out. I just wanted to emphasize how important your operation is to the profitability, even the viability, of the firm."

Lyman resisted the instinct to pat his wallet to make sure it was still there.

"That's a real morale booster, Marshall. Then what's this great opportunity?"

"I want you to take on an assignment. A challenge, but crucial to our cash flow."

Lyman never accepted assignments, at least not from Cooke. He liked to create his own deals. He rolled a gold Mark Cross pen between his fingers and waited for Cooke to say more.

"Our friends at News/Worldweek are going to get hit."

"Research has been saying that for weeks."

"I'm not talking some thumbsucking analyst's opinion," Cooke's control was finally wearing thin. "I'm talking real money."

"Who?"

"Les Éditions Bresson."

"The frogs?" Lyman was incredulous.

Cooke nodded.

"You mean foreigners, the French of all people, think they can take over the biggest media company in America? They'll get their butts kicked!"

"You'd know how to defend News/Worldweek?"

"No question!" He was getting excited despite himself. "We'd have defense in depth!"

He spun to face his Quotron and punched *CARS Mode,* then *QM/ #99.* Working through a series of menus, he finished with the symbol *NWC.*

"What've they got?" He was talking to himself now. "Over two hundred newspapers, the wire service, a dozen TV stations, three hundred cable outlets—they're virtually a fourth network—and Total News Service, that *is* a network, plus the baseball team, the record label, book publishing and of course *Worldweek* and the other magazines. What a restructuring!"

It was Lyman's turn to start pacing. "We'll have to go with whatever 'shark repellents' they've got in place. Sell off the crown jewels. If that doesn't ruin Bresson's appetite, go to scorched earth. Load the company with so much debt that nobody in their right mind would want to buy it!"

"And if that doesn't work?"

"We've always got the fact that they're foreigners. Raiding our biggest press empire. My God, they'd control the *Washington News!* That's like taking over part of the government!"

"Foreigners manipulating the minds of Americans! Congress should be outraged! Ditto the SEC, the FTC, the Justice Department. Hell, I'm outraged! The press is protected by the Constitution, for Christ's sake!" With that, Lyman was on top of the coffee table. "Is nothing sacred? Is the Bill of Rights for sale?"

Lyman was on a roll. "We can use the press itself! Who is this guy Bresson? News/Worldweek reporters can dig into his life, peel his skin off! Stir up the country! Fight back!"

"It's a big fee," Cooke was once again deliberate.

"Five million?"

"More. You want it?"

"Absolutely!"

"And you're confident you know how to defend News/Worldweek?" Cooke insisted.

"It's a no-brainer."

"I'm glad you feel that way, because you're going to represent the frogs."

As he struggled into the soft but narrow leather seat of the Air France Concorde, Lyman reminded himself to watch his diet: the collapsing time zones would tempt him to eat on both New York and Paris time. Since it was only 10:15 A.M., he found it easy to demonstrate resolve by declining the steward's offer of Moët et Chandon and sevruga caviar, but moments later, he guiltily succumbed to a sliver of fresh foie gras on toast.

The aircraft was filling fast with passengers. He had chosen an aisle seat to the rear of the mahogany-veneer bulkhead that divided the cabin into two small compartments. From previous flights, he had learned that nothing could be seen out of the monocle-sized windows, and sitting on the aisle eased the mild claustrophobia that came whenever he thought of rocketing at Mach 2 along the edge of the earth's atmosphere in a tube that felt only a little larger than a rolled-up French travel poster. He prayed the place next to him would remain vacant.

As if to stake a claim, he positioned his briefcase on the empty seat and proceeded to pull out several folders. Only in airplanes, strapped down and deprived of a phone, could Lyman read for sustained periods. He was anxious to concentrate on the file his staff had hastily assembled on Marcel Bresson so that he would have some idea whom he was meeting that afternoon in Paris.

One secret of Lyman's success was that he always knew his client inside and out. It was the only thing he ever acknowledged learning from his father, a wholesale hardware salesman who started out in life as a small-time magician. His father had admonished him, and now he admonished his more junior associates, "Get to know your rabbit!"

Lyman knew he would have to be a magician to get the News/Worldweek deal done. It would be the crowning achievement of his career. The deal would go for $6.5 to $7.5 billion. His firm would earn $50 to $60 million; his cut about $20 million, some of it shared with his staff. He could retire and do whatever he wanted, whatever that was.

But first he had to get the deal. The U.S. was the greatest single media market in the world. Foreigners had long sought to become major players but had had only moderate success. Beyond the legal obstacles, it was something that rubbed Americans the wrong way. Rupert Murdoch's acquisition of *TV Guide* had set off a storm of protest, even though he was just an Australian—and Americans like Australians. Electronic media were even more sensitive. Ted Turner, who was no foreigner, failed to gain control of CBS merely because he was from the South.

Now a Frenchman wanted to take over one of the two most important newspapers in the U.S., the most widely read newsmagazine, the sole surviving general news wire service, the only all-news television network, the fourth-largest book publisher, a major advertising agency that had a PR firm with one of the best lobbying records in Washington, and a whole lot more. Lyman's penchant for theatrics aside, controlling that much of the American press added up to a lot of political power. A foreigner would be deciding what more than half the country saw and read. France might be an ally of sorts, but it was still a little frightening, Lyman had to concede. The protectionists would have a field day. Bresson himself would become a major issue, just like Ted Turner.

If he was to make this deal happen, Lyman had to know everything about Marcel Bresson, business background, finances, personal history. But would he cooperate? Like many foreign raiders, Bresson had cultivated an enigmatic aura. Takeovers were fueled by fear and greed. American raiders, such as Sandy Sigaloff, who was known as "Ming the Merciless," usually promoted an image of ruthlessness. Foreigners, however, such as Bresson, Sir Robert Maxwell, Sir James Goldsmith and Robert Holmes à Court, exploited mystery to make themselves appear more dangerous and unpredictable.

Lyman knew that this did not always work in the United States. Maxwell, for example, reveled in rumors that he had been a spy in Central Europe for British intelligence before settling in England under the name of Maxwell. But in his battle to control the American publishing house Harcourt, Brace, Jovanovich in 1987, Maxwell's obscure origins proved a fatal weakness. Stockholders were mobilized against him by Jovanovich, who accused Maxwell of having "emerged from the mists of Ruthenia." Even Lyman's own firm, Gould Axewroth, backed out of a deal with Maxwell when Cooke learned that in London, Sir Robert was widely known as the "rubber Czech."

Marcel Bresson could not afford any such jokes.

The first thing Lyman wanted to know was how Bresson got started. That was the most difficult and unpredictable stage in any entrepreneur's career. It always revealed his character and shaped his later judgments. Second, Lyman was eager to learn how Bresson spent his money once he had plenty of it; that usually provided a clue to the personal demons that drove him onward. Lyman's file on Bresson painted an intriguing portrait that unfortunately left too much blank space.

A computer-generated summary from the Dow Jones Executive Search Data Base began with the basics: born Annecy, France, June 1943; service in the French Army, 1960–61; degree in humanities from the University of Grenoble, 1965. It then outlined how Bresson had assembled a European media empire by exploiting small opportunities. Starting out as a journalist with *Paris Match,* he soon turned to buying up family-owned regional newspapers such as *Nice Matin, Le Dauphiné Libéré* in Grenoble, *Progrès de Lyon* and *Nord Matin* in Lille. At the time, radio and television were state monopolies and off-limits to private investors in France and most of the rest of Europe. But Bresson managed to break into broadcasting by developing stations in pockets of free enterprise: Radio Andorra and Luxembourg's Eurokanal 1. Then, with the connivance of local Communist authorities in the tiny independent enclave of San Marino in Italy, he built Radio Mediterraneo into the most listened-to station from Barcelona to Beirut.

From there, he branched out into record and video distribution and even bought a film production facility in Munich. In recent years, Bresson had returned to publishing, emphasizing quality and clout. He acquired the prestigious German firm Deutsche Herausgeber, the Swedish publisher of the prominent Stockholm daily, *Svenska Dagblat,* as well as two highly regarded publishing houses in the Netherlands and Denmark.

Bresson's flagship was *France Hebdo,* an influential and somewhat long-winded moderate right-wing newsmagazine that he had saved from bankruptcy. But in Dow Jones's opinion, his real impact came from several conservative mass-circulation magazines in France, Germany and Italy. Jay Lyman recalled thumbing through them at airports. Regardless of language, they all seemed to follow the same formula each week: one crime exposé, one royal scandal, one new disease, lots of recipes and a cover showing a bare-breasted young woman.

Lyman set the report aside, dissatisfied. It described but did not explain how Bresson got started. It suggested that he was now focused on buying political influence, but provided no evidence he ever exercised it. The distinction could prove crucial to U.S. public acceptance of the News/Worldweek deal.

He looked at his watch. The plane was late in departing, but passengers had ceased boarding. Lyman tried to relax by spreading more material over the next seat. He was now looking for insights into Bresson the man.

A series of clippings from the London *Financial Times* chronicled Bresson's repeated failure to extend his empire to Fleet Street. In three separate forays to buy British publications, Bresson had been outmaneuvered by Sir Robert Maxwell, Sir James Goldsmith and Rupert Murdoch.

Lyman began to feel better. He thought he had discovered a clue to Bresson's ego and thus to his objectives; in corporate raiders, they usually amounted to the same thing. Bresson had been defeated by the London press lords. He wanted revenge. They had all made major acquisitions in the U.S., Murdoch even becoming a U.S. citizen to do so. Lyman concluded that Bresson planned to skip Britain, follow his rivals to America where the playing field was more level, and then pull off a deal that would make Maxwell, Goldsmith and Murdoch combined look like pikers.

But did he have the money? As with Maxwell and the others, it was difficult to figure out the extent of Bresson's wealth. They were all assumed to be rich because they bought expensive companies and lived in high style, but Lyman knew that few if any outsiders had ever been allowed to see their consolidated balance sheets or income statements. None of them showed up on *Forbes*'s annual "World's 500 Richest." That did not surprise Lyman. The *Forbes* lists were notoriously inaccurate, because they were based primarily on real estate holdings, which were more a matter of public record than stocks, bonds and cash.

But Lyman was interested to discover that Bresson owned no personal real estate at all. In fact, he had no fixed address, a trait he shared with Australian publisher Robert Holmes à Court. London's *Tattler* magazine described how Bresson lived in hotels as he moved restlessly around Europe. The closest he came to having a home was Monte Carlo, where he berthed a 325-foot yacht in the harbor and where he sometimes checked into a suite at the Hotel de Paris. Also like Holmes à Court, Bresson reportedly disappeared for long stretches. A man like that, Lyman thought glumly as he set aside the clipping, will not be thrilled at the prospect of sharing his most intimate secrets with the American public.

His growing irritation at the Concorde's unexplained departure delay was compounded by the difficulty of unearthing anything from the dossier that answered Lyman's most important questions—who were Bresson's financial partners? Which were his banks? What investment banker did his previous deals? Could Lazard Frères have missed such a client?

He rifled through the papers until he found extracts from the M&A Journal Deal Index that had been highlighted with a yellow marking pen. To Lyman's surprise, the Index showed no partners on Bresson's previous deals, nor any investment banker. Did he do his own transactions? That seemed unlikely. Data on international deals, Lyman knew, was often hard to develop. Foreign governments permitted far more corporate secrecy than the U.S., and Wall Street publications had not fully grasped that the merger business had become global. Lyman concluded that the Deal Index was simply incomplete.

But when he looked at the entry that reported Bresson's sources of financing, the enigma deepened. On every deal, the loans had come from the same institution. Even on his very first acquisition, the Swiss Bank Corporation had provided the money. Now that Bresson was a tycoon, that made perfect sense. But, Lyman wondered, when he was a young reporter fresh from the provinces, how did Bresson ever get in the door?

Lyman's curiosity was momentarily diverted by the satisfying lurch he felt as the aircraft began to move away from the gate. Before he could dig deeper into his files, he felt someone looming over him.

"You think you could move that stuff?"

Looking up, his heart fell. Another passenger had boarded at the last minute and wanted the seat next to him. Worse, it was a woman. Worse still, he was instantly attracted to her.

Heidi Bruce had steeled herself when she heard the news. The Chairman of the Senate Select Committee was going to *Face the Nation,* or, more ominously, face Leslie Stahl. That meant the committee staff director had to prepare the Chairman. That meant she would have to take his place at the conference in Paris. In truth, the Chairman did not really need his staff director to help him get ready for his TV appearance, but like most Senators, he liked to periodically remind his senior professional aides that they were body servants.

Normally, Heidi would have been thrilled to trade Washington's September heat for autumn in Paris. But to be told at four in the afternoon that she had to leave that evening! Of her two decent dresses, one was in the cleaners, and the other, along with much of the rest of her wardrobe, should have been. So she had rushed home to her basement apartment in Georgetown and was stuffing dirty clothes into her suit bag, praying the conference site had twenty-four-hour laundry service.

She also dreaded the flight. Working in the Senate, Heidi was a government employee and normally was required to fly economy class on an American carrier. As she once explained to her widowed mother, who still considered air travel an adventure, "These days, flying's romantic only if you're into S&M."

The airlines wasted no time in reinforcing her bad attitude. Before taking off, the Eastern Shuttle to La Guardia sat buttoned up on the runway with no air conditioning for forty-five minutes in one hundred-degree heat and humidity. Because of thundershowers, the plane circled for another half hour off the coast of New Jersey. The rain had caused an enormous traffic jam on the Van Wyck Expressway from La Guardia to JFK airports. She missed her connection with TWA at JFK by three minutes, then she had to plead with several taxi drivers before persuading one to accepting $25 to drive her and her luggage seven hundred yards to the Pan Am terminal so she could try to catch a flight leaving fifteen minutes later.

She seemed in luck. PA 106 was delayed; she had two hours until flight time. The nice clerk at the desk gave her a pass to the Pan Am lounge. Since it served no food, she had a dinner consisting of a dozen cocktail onions soaked in two Tanqueray gibsons. By 10:30 P.M., the lounge was almost empty. Adequately anesthetized, she decided it was time to make her way to the gate. No one was there.

Frantic, Heidi searched for an airline official. There were none. All the other gates were vacant except one where passengers were arriving. She raced back to the lounge and found it locked. After she pounded desperately on the doors, a busboy emerged. Speaking no known language, he was not much help.

At last, she found a guard dozing by an x-ray machine who directed her back to the entrance of the terminal and through a nondescript door. Inside, a large woman bulging out of her Pan Am uniform sat at a desk making random remarks into a microphone.

"PA 106? Canceled an hour ago. I made the announcement myself," the woman said.

"How could I have missed it?" Heidi was bewildered. "I was in the Pan Am lounge."

"A sign in the coat closet says quite clearly that departures are not announced in the lounge."

"But this was a cancellation!" Heidi was now on the verge of screaming.

"Hey, I'm trying to help you, lady."

Heidi forced herself to calm down. She asked about alternate flights.

"It's too late for that."

Accommodations for the night?

"Sorry, you're ticketed on TWA."

All the airport hotels were full. Heidi finally found a motel near the Belt Parkway that had bars on all the windows. Throughout the night, expensive sports cars roared up to the entrance, which was directly below her room, stopped for a few minutes, then raced away in a hail of shrieks and curses. At 9:10 A.M. the next day, a special dispensation arrived in the form of a phone call from the staff director. She had persuaded him, and he had convinced the Chairman, that if she failed to deliver the speech in Paris that evening, it would be an insult to the French government. The Chairman approved her taking the Concorde.

The crew had to reopen the door to let her on board. Heidi climbed over the man on the aisle without much noticing him and immediately fell asleep despite a monster roar from the four Rolls-Royce SNECMA Olympus 593 jet engines that launched the supersonic aircraft skyward.

Jay Lyman found the woman appealing even sleeping with her mouth hanging open, something he had never gotten accustomed to with his ex-wife. She had said it was another sign of his juvenile romanticism and his unwillingness to face the reality of intimacy. He just thought it was gross.

But he had been feeling so lonely the last few months that he was seriously considering calling her again to find out if they . . . well, he did not know what exactly. In the back of his mind he had thought of bringing her a special gift from this trip, maybe a diamond necklace from Cartier.

After his divorce, Lyman had chased around like a crazy person. Soon, however, he grew tired of taking lady lawyers to Lutèce to talk about torts. He also quickly lost interest in snuggling up with women securities traders to discuss selling short against the box.

So, like many of his single colleagues, he had fallen into the habit of dating those beautiful young women, mostly models, who were collectively known as "cucumbers" in recognition of the computing power of their central nervous systems. "Cucumbers" remained silent at business dinners and looked stunning at charity events. Lyman came to know what it was like to be surrounded by ocean and die of thirst.

He carefully examined the woman gently snoring next to him. She was fair, with traces of freckles and short, thick, dark hair brushed back. Her features were fine but not delicate, her mouth strong, her lips full and even, her lipstick, slightly askew, applied without a brush, possibly in haste. Slept too late? he wondered, or a sudden trip?

Lyman prided himself on being able to categorize women from their appearance, but he found her a puzzle. She was clearly a professional, not a tourist, but Alcott and Andrews suits were seldom seen on the Concorde. Was she an associate at an investment house? Since the crash of '87, junior staff did not travel supersonic to Europe. A lawyer? Possibly. The client would be paying. But where were the volumes of transcripts, depositions and contracts? She only carried a slim i Santi briefcase. Besides, she seemed too young, unless she were a show-biz lawyer, and they did not dress in chalk stripes, pale silk blouses with ties at the throat and pearls. Ditto advertising and public relations. Despite her apparent exhaustion, her nearly translucent skin had a healthy quality usually lacking in New York's executive women.

She turned in the seat and her leg fell against his. A jolt went through him. The second button from the top on her blouse was undone. He tried unsuccessfully not to look at the smooth swell of her breast. She wore no wedding ring, but that, Lyman knew, did not necessarily mean anything.

His analysis was leading him in a disappointing direction. An attractive professional woman in her late twenties, tastefully but inexpensively dressed except for her briefcase, which was probably a gift. Business would not have sent her on the Concorde, so there were only two likely alternatives: rich family or rich boyfriend. She would not dress for the office to visit mom and dad, but that would go for her boyfriend as well, unless . . . unless . . . Of course. Unless he were her boss.

I wonder if he's richer than I am, Jay Lyman thought, as he resigned himself to focusing on the mystery of Marcel Bresson and his finances.

Heidi only vaguely stirred when she heard the words, "Shall I wake Madame for lunch?" But when she heard a man's voice say, "Let's let her sleep," she became instantly awake.

"I hope you're not talking about me, I'm starving." She frowned at

Jay Lyman, and then looked at the stewardess hovering over her. "And if you are, it's Mademoiselle."

Jay retreated into an embarrassed silence. The stewardess spread a heavy Porthault linen cloth over the tray tables, placing a rosebud on each of them for decoration. She picked up the single blossom that had become the symbol of the antiabortion movement and said, "I guess it's reassuring to think that Air France is prolife."

Lyman was startled. "What?" he finally managed to respond.

Never try to make political jokes outside of Washington, Heidi reminded herself. Besides, she was not sure she wanted to strike up a conversation. "Oh, nothing," she replied.

He felt rejected, then chided himself for being childish.

She was deciding he definitely was not from Washington. His hair for example. Full and flecked with gray, it was long and loose but stopped just short of his collar. No one in the nation's capital had such a perfect haircut, except presidential candidates who flew hairdressers down specially from New York. Heidi once tried to persuade her Chairman to see a good barber before the start of televised committee hearings, but he refused. "The people of my state," the Senator explained, "like shitty haircuts."

Heidi concluded that her traveling companion had to be New York, and probably an investment banker. It was the details. His tailor-made suit was so conservative that he might have been an auditor, but what green eyeshade would pay good money just to have real buttonholes in the sleeves? Or he might might have been a high-priced corporate lawyer except for his shoes. Tasseled slip-ones that barely covered his toes, they could only come from Susan Bennis. Legal counsel was expected to be more substantially shod.

When Lyman bent down to tuck away his bag, Heidi could see the telltale three-button shirt cuff. Turnbull and Asser, Jermyn Street, London. His tie, an expensive paisley, had been formed into a tiny knot, possible only if it were unlined silk from Italy. Both were indications that he was on the international side of finance. She wondered if she could narrow it down further. His watch. It was not a Rolex, so he was not a broker or an arbitrageur. He was either corporate finance or mergers. Corporate finance would be handled out of London. That shifted the odds to mergers, and he was probably with a smaller firm or else he would be traveling with an entourage.

At several points, as the stewardess cleared the plates and served the hors d'ouevres, she saw that he wet his lips and turned as if he were about to speak. But he did not. Feeling mischievous, she decided to check her intuition.

"I didn't realize deal guys were so shy," she said, cutting into her crepes stuffed with crabmeat.

My God, Lyman recoiled, she must be from the SEC!

"Why are you going to Paris?" she continued.

"I thought that suspects always had their rights read to them before the ratatouille," he said, poking at the burnt umber mass clinging to his plate.

"Ugh! You like that stuff?" She made a childish face.

His heart lodged in his socks.

"Okay, I'll confess," he said. "I hate it. I ordered it to kill my appetite."

"So that's one count of assassination," she noted. "And the deal business?"

"Mergers and acquisitions," he admitted.

She flashed a triumphant smile. "And who are your targets?"

"With the dollar so cheap, it's mostly American companies being bought by foreigners."

"Ah, treason!"

Lyman bristled. "It sounds like you don't approve," he replied stiffly. Christ, you sound like a jerk, he told himself. Loosen up. She's just making jokes. But it got worse as he heard himself saying, "America's imported more goods than it exports for so long, that it finally has to sell its businesses to pay for it."

"Why?" She looked innocent. "Have the Japanese already bought all our real estate?" She picked up the airline magazine. "You know, I read somewhere that the Japanese control ten times more U.S. territory now than if they had captured Hawaii? Why did we go to war if we were willing to sell out?"

"Well, at least we're getting paid."

She looked at him as though his head were Steuben glass. He had to admit that it was not a very good reply. They fell silent as the stewardess served the main course. He had ordered sole Veronique and Perrier and frowned as she took several slices of chateaubriand and a glass of Cheval Blanc that he could smell as it went by.

Lyman wondered if it was his diet or his assignment that was making him so touchy. Maybe he was just unused to talking with grown-up women. He decided to try again on a topic that made him more comfortable.

"How did you know I was in the deal business?"

"You dress too well for your age."

"But I gave up suspenders!"

"Exactly."

She laughed and explained that her father had been a stockbroker on Wall Street for thirty years. He started to relax.

"And you?" he asked.

"Government. Dad raised me a contrarian. When I got out of school in '85, public service was in such bad odor that he convinced me I'd have a lot more opportunity in Washington. For women at least, he was right."

"So what do you do exactly?" Lyman's paranoia about the Securities and Exchange Commission had returned.

"Dissemble and dissimulate. I stop just short of deception and deceit."

"CIA?"

"Quite the opposite."

Jay looked baffled.

"Ask me to dinner in Paris," she said, "and I might tell all." Heidi immediately regretted being so impulsive.

A shot of excitement flashed through Lyman. He shut off the warning light that blinked on in his head. "Will you have dinner with me tonight?" he asked obediently.

"Can't, I'm busy."

"I'm going back tomorrow." He failed to keep the complaint out of his voice.

"Then it wouldn't have been much of a relationship anyway." She broke the top of her crème brulée.

Was she playing with him? he wondered. No, he had simply ignored the rule that everything was a negotiation. He waved away dessert and tried a counteroffer.

"But I might have to stay over." He attempted to sound not too eager.

She gave a noncommittal nod.

"How would I reach you?" he persisted.

"Call here." She relented and scribbled out the eight-digit Paris phone number on the menu. "Give them your name."

"It's Jay Lyman. Who do I ask for? I don't know your name."

"Just leave a message." She smiled sweetly. "I'll call you."

3

The Concorde's regular gate was under repair, so they docked at Charles de Gaulle's Aérogare Numéro 1. Packing up, Jay Lyman found that, as usual, the papers that had come out of his briefcase no longer fit back into it. Plus he had no room for the stack of recent Bresson publications which he had scavenged from the other passengers. He also wanted the copy of *France Hebdo* in Heidi Bruce's seat pocket, but he was reluctant to ask for it.

Since she had declined to tell him her name, he had stopped trying to make conversation. She concentrated on reading what seemed to him a speech, and he tried to focus on the spreadsheets on News/World-week. In reality, he had spent most of his mental energy persuading himself he should write her off.

The "mystery lady" routine galled him. It put him at a disadvantage, and he hated being at a disadvantage. Besides, she did not seem all that excited about him, and he had a tough assignment ahead of him. He hadn't thought through his approach to Bresson, let alone the deal. And who did she think she was? Probably a lingerie buyer who traded in years of Frequent Flyers for the Concorde. . . . His thoughts rambled on obsessively about her while the rest of the passengers disembarked.

Trapped in the inside seat, Heidi was impatient to leave. She looked at him staring at her magazine.

"Would you like to take this?" She offered her copy of *France Hebdo* to get him moving.

"Oh, sure." He snapped out of his fugue.

"You're going to read all that?" She pointed to the pile of periodicals that included a magazine on sewing, one on child care, two on women's fashion, another on do-it-yourself home decorating, as well as one on cooking microwave pastry.

"It's research," he mumbled, noticing uneasily that her look of curiosity intensified. Then she smiled at him as if he were the mystery.

Maybe I'm being unfair to her, Lyman thought. She had given him her number. They hadn't talked because she had a lot of work to do, too.

He followed her from the gate onto the moving sidewalk that took them to the main terminal. As it dove into a tunnel and under the airstrip, the sidewalk abruptly changed inclination and speed.

"Whoa!" she exclaimed. Jay took her arm to steady her. "I wonder how many elderly travelers they lose on that spot each year," she laughed. He held onto her a moment longer than he needed to. She did not seem to mind.

The two of them passed by the odd suspended spheres on which were projected pictures of perfume, cognac and cigarettes. "Those weird ads have been there as long as I can remember," Lyman remarked on the old and faded slides.

"I can't tell the perfume from the cognac," she said.

"They often taste the same, too."

Once in the main terminal, they transferred to a steep plastic tube walkway that carried them upward and across the open center of the building to the baggage-claim area at the top. Other tubes crisscrossed from floor to floor to no clear purpose. A light rain was falling. The tubes leaked. Lyman did not care. He was making plans.

She'll need help with her luggage. I'll do that. And I've got a car meeting me. I'll offer her a ride. Find out where she's staying. If not dinner, maybe a nightcap. His excitement grew as he rose higher and higher through the transparent tube. Lyman felt like some kind of homunculus in line for ejaculation. "You're really sick," he muttered.

The Concorde baggage received priority and was waiting when they arrived. Lyman was primed to make his move. He picked out his suitbag and turned to help his traveling companion. He found her walled off by three tough-looking men in raincoats.

Christ, he thought, I didn't know they made Frenchmen that big. He excused himself and tried to get through to her. Instead of yielding, one of them pushed Lyman backward into the crowd as the other two grabbed her bags. Before he could recover, they whisked her through customs. He cut into the front of the line attempting to catch up. But it was no use. Lyman saw only a glimpse of a smile that she seemed to cast toward him before vanishing through Passport Control. By the time he got outside to the curb, she was gone.

Heidi sat in the backseat of a spaceship-like Citroën CX as it floated down the *autoroute* from the airport at a hundred miles an hour. A pistol butt protruded from the shiny blue suit jacket of the security man beside her. The beefy young man next to the driver kept his right hand on a machine pistol holstered in the door. They were not talkative. She was not reassured. The butterflies had started.

Only recently promoted to deputy staff director of the Senate Intelligence Committee, Heidi now faced her most challenging assignment. She was to speak to a conference of the Quadripartite Intelligence Group—senior intelligence officials from France, West Germany, Great Britain and the United States who met semiannually to coordinate strategy. Her task: to alert the Allies to a new Soviet intelligence threat identified by her committee. She also hoped to persuade them to coordinate efforts to counter it.

Unfortunately, each clandestine service believed that the others were penetrated by Soviet spies, and since they did not trust one another, their collaboration was accordingly modest. Moreover, what minimal cooperation they had achieved over the years was now being jeopardized by rapidly warming relations between Washington and Moscow.

Individually and collectively, the Western intelligence services felt besieged. Politicians denounced them as anachronisms, and what was worse, Treasury Departments were cutting off their lifeblood—money. Some secret services resisted, insisting that the Soviet danger was as great as ever. Others had capitulated and even became spokesmen for collaboration with the USSR. Without a consensus enemy, the Allied intelligence community seemed lost. Past Quadripartite conferences focused on penetrating the KGB, or combating Soviet-sponsored terrorism. This one had the depressing title, "Defining a New Role for Intelligence in an Era of Improved East-West Relations."

Though nervous about appearing before such a distinguished gathering, Heidi was convinced she could make an important contribution to the conference. Never before had anyone from the Congress or any European parliament been invited to attend. She saw her participation as a singular honor, as well as an indication of how desperate the professional intelligence community had become.

At the end of the Autoroute du Nord, the car proceeded left on the Boulevard Periphérique, heading southeast through a wilderness of factories and railyards. At the Porte des Lilas the driver took the up ramp, turned right and then left onto the Boulevard Mortier. Just past the Stade Nautique, the black Citroën was brought to a halt by armed paratroopers at the gates to the *caserne Mortier*.

Built after the Franco-Prussian War as part of Paris's defensive perimeter, the nondescript stucco-covered barracks had served since

World War II as the headquarters for the *Deuxième Bureau,* the traditional name for the French secret intelligence service. Once past the gate, it looked to Heidi like any other military base, with one exception. At the center of the complex of barracks, garages, machine shops and storage buildings stood a classic but ominous-looking French château.

Any charm the building ever possessed had been lost to a century of military maintenance. The granite and brick walls had been painted gray. Bars covered the windows. Wire mesh wrapped the carved stonework over the entrance, apparently to keep away the pigeons. The steeply pitched mansard roof had large white boxes cut into it that served as platforms for a score of antennas and satellite dishes.

With a perfunctory *"Bon soir,"* Heidi's bodyguards handed her over to three young military men. They wore blue berets and matching ascots, but nothing on their uniforms to indicate rank. One of them spoke English.

"We will take you to your room, Mademoiselle," he said anxiously, hurrying her through a once-impressive foyer now divided into cubicles by green metal partitions. The same sick green color covered the walls and woodwork. It had the unclean texture of generations of fresh paint layered over chipped surfaces.

Everything changed when they entered the south wing of the building. Worn asphalt tile gave way to carefully waxed oak parquet floors in a herringbone pattern, covered with a carpet runner of burgundy wool. Heidi could see her reflection in the highly polished mahogany walls. But the corridor was so narrow, and the doors with their metal-lever handles were set so close together, that even with the ten-foot ceilings, Heidi had the peculiar sensation she might be on the Orient Express.

"We regret you have no time to rest," her guide continued briskly. "You are expected to speak in less than five minutes."

"But I'm supposed to talk after dinner," Heidi protested. "Are they already eating?" She looked at her watch and wondered if she had set it incorrectly.

"No, no. The plans, they change. You will speak now."

With that, he opened a heavy mahogany door outward into the hall, revealing another door that opened into a tiny room. It only had space for a single bed, a small desk, sink and watercloset. All mahogany and beautifully built-in, Heidi thought it looked like a cell for a Very Important Prisoner.

"I will attend you outside," the Frenchman said.

Intimidated and excited at the same time, she plowed through her luggage to find her cosmetics kit. Quickly cleaning her face with a cotton pad and astringent, she carefully avoided the eyeshadow, which still looked acceptable. Then she brushed her hair, cursing the bent strands that stuck out over her ear. She tried pasting them down with hairspray, hoping they would stay flat.

Her escort knocked on the door and asked her to hurry. She urgently applied another coat of lipstick. Standing back, she looked in the mirror. Her clothes looked like she had been sleeping on an airplane. Posture, she told herself, posture makes all the difference.

The guard rushed her to the end of the hall to a set of large double doors. Heidi stopped to get ready for her entrance. Then she realized that she had forgotten the speech.

Dashing back down the hall, she became confused over which was the right door. Her escort came to her rescue. She spilled the contents of her briefcase onto the bed. The clip holding her text together popped off. The speech scattered on the floor. Heidi, on her hands and knees, scooped up the pages while her military escort helped by hissing, *Vite, Mademoiselle! Vite!*

Again she paused at the double doors to compose herself. Dignity was important to an aura of authority. She was representing the United States Senate. After a deep breath, Heidi nodded to her escort that she was ready.

She entered a large darkened room. A dozen men sat around a white circular table lit by recessed spots in the low ceiling. A German was speaking. No one acknowledged her arrival.

Her escort said a few words to one of the men at the table. He rose and came toward her.

"D'Uberville," he whispered without greeting. "You are Mademoiselle Bruce?"

She nodded, noticing that the legendary head of French intelligence looked at her with a mixture of contempt for her presence and fascination with her breasts.

"You will speak as soon as the German has finished," he continued.

"But I thought it was after . . ."

"We gave that honor to Sir Charles." He gestured vaguely toward the Permanent Secretary of the British Cabinet Office, and left her standing alone in the dark.

Lyman sank into the back seat of a long black 1972 Mercedes-Benz 600, and tried to reassure himself that she had to be all right. Did she look like she was being kidnapped? No. Certainly, Customs and Passport Control wouldn't cooperate like that with terrorists! Besides, was he really worried about her, or wallowing in his sense of loss? He hated losing anything. Too often, he knew, that extended to things that were not his.

As the limo sped through the wheat fields along the Autoroute du Nord, he told himself to stop thinking about her. You're obsessed with this woman because you don't want to focus on the job ahead. He was to meet Bresson at the Bristol Hotel and he had neither a plan nor a strategy. In any deal, the first encounter with a client was always the most delicate step. He had to probe Bresson's intentions, make sure that he was a bona fide buyer, not just a window shopper who would waste everybody's time. Lyman also had to establish rapport with Bresson while, at the same time, creating a psychological climate that gave him control over his client's actions. Control. That was always the key to executing a successful transaction.

But how to gain such control? His mind stayed blank. He might have to walk right from the limo into the meeting with Bresson, and still his brain refused to think about it.

Suddenly, he could no longer tolerate the Vietnamese music whining out of the tape deck in the front seat and the rattle of a blue plastic fan that was attached to the dashboard. He tried to close the window to the driver's compartment. It was stuck.

"Could you turn the music down?" he asked in broken Berlitz French. There was no response. He tried again in English.

"You American?" the driver asked.

That was always a tricky question from a Vietnamese.

"Why?" he replied.

"You know I Corps? I come from I Corps. Binh Duc Tho."

"I was too young to be in Viet Nam," he said defensively.

"I pretty fucking young when you guys bug out. Come to France only fifteen, ten ounces gold up my ass." But he turned the radio down.

The *autoroute* had passed out of the golden countryside and into a long desolate alley of concrete office buildings interspersed with decaying villages caught up in suburban industrial sprawl. Again, Lyman tried to get his mind to focus on the deal. To no avail. He could only marvel at how Paris, the most beautiful city in the world, had evolved an entrance rivaled in ugliness only by the Van Wyck Expressway from JFK to Manhattan.

The limo swung off the Boulevard Periphérique at the Porte St-Ouen, on the back side of the Butte of Montmartre. The rundown neighborhood had become completely North African, part of the "couscous belt" that surrounded the central districts of Paris. Stalls full of cheap shoes, clothes, household goods and trinkets jammed the sidewalks. Lyman became enthralled by how the junked-up streets were made beautiful by the trees in fall foliage. An image of an aging tart in a couturier dress flashed through Lyman's mind. He wondered what was wrong with him.

The Vietnamese driver turned right at the Love Burger in the Place Clichy. As the car fought its way through the traffic of the 8me Arrondissement, the anxiety began to congeal in Lyman's stomach. That was some kind of progress. A block from the hotel, a gendarme halted the car so that a motorcade for the President of France could enter the Élysée Palace. Lyman wanted to get out and run. By the time they finally arrived at the Bristol Hotel on the rue du Faubourg-St-Honoré the tension felt like a block of ice. He did not know what he was going to say, but he was ready.

At the check-in counter, Lyman was informed that a message awaited him across the marble foyer at the concierge's desk. He tore open the heavy linen envelope and read the note inside with disappointment and relief. Bresson wanted to see him at 7:30. An assistant would come by his room. Lyman checked his watch. The next hour and ten minutes would be an exercise in tension management.

After the hall porter had hung up his suitbag and turned on the air conditioning, he reluctantly accepted a five-dollar tip and left Lyman alone. He opened the shutters to find that his fifth-floor room looked out on a grassy garden. A large fountain stood surrounded by tables where guests were enjoying an apéritif. Lyman rejected having a drink. He undressed, stepped into the marble shower and turned on the water. Multiple jets pounded him from a half-dozen nozzles. He slathered himself with *gel-douche,* rinsed and turned off the spigots. Wrapped in a heavy terrycloth robe provided by the hotel, he lay down on the bed and tried to ignore the air conditioning blowing down on him.

He had to trust his instincts. If he was reluctant to get into the deal, be reluctant, he told himself. Go with your feelings. Don't jump all over the deal. Play hard to get. An approach began to take shape in his mind.

First, he had to make Bresson understand that the deal was risky— almost impossible to pull off. Second, Bresson must accept full disclosure; he had to be willing to reveal everything about himself and his operations. Third, Lyman's first objective would be a big broken-deal fee. He was not going to work for nothing.

He got up and turned off the air conditioning, then rummaged through his briefcase for a travel clock, which he set for 7:15 P.M.

When it went off, he was still wide awake, running imaginary conversations with Bresson back and forth through his mind.

Lyman chose a dark single-breasted pinstripe suit from Paul Stuart and a blue button-down oxford cloth shirt. He picked a striped Bill Blass tie to go with it. He hated the look, but had learned from experience that it was important to foreign clients that he fit their image of an American.

The knock on the door came at precisely 7:30. He opened it to find a muscular young man in a striped T-shirt and sweat pants who introduced himself as Edouard. They took the cage-style elevator to the top floor and then followed the curving hallway to its end. Edouard opened the door and entered first. Jay Lyman followed him across the threshold and onto a late-nineteenth-century swimming barge floating off the Côte d'Azur.

Since there had been no seats at the table, Heidi Bruce found one against the wall. As her eyes became accustomed to the dim light, her spirits rose. Behind the American delegation, she spotted a man sitting in the last row like herself. It was Sean Gordon. He was a friend, a colleague, and more. He waved. She began to get her confidence back.

Heidi stood when introduced by d'Uberville. She was mentioned only briefly and identified as Senate "staff," a word he managed to inflect with disdain. Half of his remarks dwelt on what an unusual departure it was to invite someone from the U.S. Congress, while the other half stressed how disappointed they were that the Chairman of the Intelligence Committee did not attend. For the first time, Heidi realized that she was not only a substitute, she was a substitute substitute.

She approached the table and slowly looked at each of them. Their faces were glacial. She had a hard sell. Wetting her lips, she said, "Do you think you gentlemen could give me a seat?"

"Of course!"

"Mein Gott!"

"Bien sûr!"

They stumbled all over themselves to make room for her.

Sitting down, she smiled sweetly and began to ad-lib comments from her speech.

"Since everything's so informal, I thought I'd set aside the Chairman's prepared remarks. Perhaps," she looked at d'Uberville, "you could have copies made so that the group could study them later."

He replied with an irritated nod.

"The purpose of this meeting," Heidi began, "is to chart a new direction for the intelligence efforts of our respective governments. Many of you act as though improved East-West relations make you obsolete—except to spy on the poor and backward nations so we can defend ourselves against their terrorists. Others seem to believe that nothing has changed, and that all these summit meetings and arms-control agreements are a Soviet ruse. I've been asked to come here by my chairman and suggest a third alternative.

"Competition between East and West has not ended, but it has changed. The new focus of Soviet intelligence operations under Mikhail Gorbachev is in the field of economics. The threat is double-barreled. The USSR is using its intelligence resources to advance its economic interests at the expense of the West, and it is using its economic activities to pursue its long-term intelligence objectives against the West."

As Heidi paused to take a breath, she could hear muttering in the West German delegation. She pressed on.

"First, the KGB is using its massive technical intelligence capabilities to support the systematic manipulation of Western financial markets for the profit of the Soviet economy in ways that are entirely illegal.

"Second, Soviet scientific and industrial espionage is exploiting the new openness of the West to trade and business dealings with the USSR to make our controls on strategic technology a joke.

"Finally, and most ominously, the Soviet government, through the KGB, is translating its new economic presence in the West into political clout inside our parliaments and governments—"

"Mr. Chairman, Mr. Chairman!" It was the intelligence advisor to the German Chancellor's Office. "I do not wish to be rude, but I simply must object to these assertions."

"Surely, you have some evidence?" the British Cabinet Secretary added skeptically.

"Yes, Sir Robert," Heidi responded. "Let's take the Narodny Bank. It's chartered in London and wholly owned by the Soviet Government. Like any other bank, it's allowed to trade in stocks, bonds and commodities. Not long ago, our Securities and Exchange Commission stock watch group detected an important pattern of transactions that could only be inside trading in certain takeover stocks. The transactions were traced to the Narodny Bank. The National Security Agency determined that the information used by the Soviets comes from telephone conversations and computer links in New York and is collected by antennas on the roof of the Soviet Mission to the UN.

"A similar pattern of eavesdropping and inside trading has been found in bonds and commodity futures. In other words, the Soviets are tapping our phones and using the information to make hundreds of millions of dollars each year, if not more. And don't think this is just a U.S. problem. We've determined that similar Soviet actions are underway against the London exchanges and the Bourses in Paris, Vienna, Frankfurt and elsewhere in Europe."

The ensuing silence led Heidi to hope she was having an impact. Then d'Uberville spoke up.

"Larceny, my dear, even on a grand scale, is hardly a national security matter." He smiled indulgently. "As for the idea that the Soviets are circumventing our strategic controls, putting your Macintosh computers in their diplomatic pouches, that's nothing new. France has always been skeptical of such controls."

"But now we face a problem of a different order." Heidi stood fast. "The Russians don't even bother to sneak high-tech products back to the USSR. They simply ask that samples be sent to the new companies they're setting up in the West. Then they take the items apart, figure out how they work and how to copy them. Only the information is sent back to the Soviet Union. They don't need export licenses. Most of the engineers doing the work are our own nationals—Americans, British, French, Germans. The Soviets get the technology and often don't have to pay for the samples!"

The whispering had spread to the British and French delegations.

"Most important of all," Heidi continued, "and this is more ephemeral but no less vital, the USSR is exploiting its growing business relationships to influence policy and politics in the West—"

"This is typical American paranoia," the West German intelligence advisor broke in again. "You, my dear, are living in the past. The barriers between East and West are tumbling down."

"But not the barriers between the West and East." Heidi shot back. "Can we hop a plane to Minsk, start a business in forty-eight hours, and fill the office with intelligence agents within a week? How often have we been able to translate the sale of grain or semiconductors into influence on the Politburo?"

"We've had our little successes, actually." It was Sir Robert. "From time to time . . ." He trailed off. The group all laughed. It was a warning to Heidi to back off.

She refused. "How many Western businesses can hire PR firms and advertising agencies and lobbyists in Moscow," Heidi challenged him, "as the Soviets do in Paris, London, New York, Bonn—"

"When we invited your Chairman to speak to us," d'Uberville interrupted, "we thought he would talk about Congress and the American intelligence agencies. They haven't pressed these matters with us, have they?" He looked down the table at the representatives from the U.S. intelligence community. "Of what interest is all this to the Senate Select Committee?"

By this time, everyone in the room was acutely aware that the American delegation had not come to Heidi's defense. But she was encouraged that Sean Gordon was nodding his head.

"Oversight is not just keeping the CIA from doing something wrong or stupid like trading arms for hostages." Heidi was damned if she would shut up and eat her frogs' legs. "We try to get the intelligence community to focus on doing things they should do.

"You're all looking for a new role. Well, this is *the* intelligence challenge of the decade. But it's delicate, too. It involves free trade, open markets, civil liberties, privacy and the rule of law—values that make us different from the Soviets. The CIA and FBI need new charters that will allow them to tackle these threats effectively, along with additional safeguards to protect our liberties. There have to be new regulations requiring disclosure of international financial transactions and foreign businesses operating in the U.S. We've developed such legislation, but we've got to have similar action by your governments, too. Otherwise, tighter controls will only hurt American business and markets—"

"A typical American effort to control everything to your own advantage." The West German returned to the attack. "It has never worked. We believe business contacts with the USSR are good. Gorbachev is transforming Soviet society. They are moving toward democracy, and you would have us moving toward a police state!"

"Hear, hear." Sir Robert rapped the table.

"Well, on that note," d'Uberville intervened again, "perhaps we should move the discussion to drinks and then dinner."

Heidi had failed.

4

Lyman felt disoriented. He stood on a teak deck. Twenty meters away, several gentlemen in nautical caps and turn-of-the-century blazers and white flannel suits stared at him as if he were an intruder. Women posed invitingly in full length white muslin dresses. Crew members dressed like Edouard in white ducks and blue-and-white-striped shirts bent to various tasks. But nothing moved except a lone individual wearing a black bathing cap and tiny goggles who patiently stroked through the water.

Lyman blinked several times before he realized that what he was seeing was part real, part trompe l'oeil. The opposite wall was a life-size mural of Renoir-like figures on the deck of a swimming barge floating off the coast of Cap d'Antibes. To complete the illusion, the room had been furnished with chairs and tables in the same style as those in the painting. He assumed he was going to Bresson's suite, but this, he finally recognized, was the Bristol's indoor swimming pool. And the man in the water had to be Marcel Bresson.

Every time he approached his end of the pool, Lyman expected Bresson to stop and acknowledge his arrival. But each time he turned and swam back to the other end. After five minutes of standing at the edge in anticipation, Lyman's wool suit was getting damp and beginning to cling to his legs. With growing anger, he briefly considered going back to his room. But that would mean he had lost the game. Bresson was jerking him around, a common if amateurish strategy among prospective clients. The best reaction was no reaction. He would have plenty of opportunity to tell Bresson to stuff it, if it came to that. Better to do so once Bresson was hooked on the deal.

He decided to take a seat on a wicker couch next to the large stern gallery window that overlooked the city. It was almost dark and he could see the avenue of light rising into the sky from the buildings along the Champs-Élysées. As he gazed restlessly across the rooftops, he tried to empty his mind of all thoughts, but succeeded only in wondering where his seatmate from the Concorde might be at that moment.

A loud sound of rushing water prompted Lyman to turn and find Bresson climbing out of the pool. Stocky and powerfully built, he bore the tell-tale sign of someone who once had been much heavier. A flap of skin hung around his abdomen and hips, giving the strange impression that his torso could slip down over his legs. His black bikini cupped his private parts like a bag of marbles. Large vaccination marks pocked his upper arms. Edouard wrapped a towel around him and they moved into a solarium that overlooked the garden. He waved for Lyman to join them.

"Monsieur Bresson, Jayson Lyman." He held out his hand. Bresson shook it in the perfunctory European manner.

"Sorry not to greet you sooner, but I lose track of all but the laps," he said. The only trace of regret Lyman could detect was that he had to apologize. As he lay back on a chaise lounge, a woman in a white coat appeared with a footbath and began to give him a pedicure. Edouard turned on two banks of sunlamps and covered Bresson's eyes with damp cotton balls. Lyman perched on a small stool, wishing he had brought his dark glasses.

"Always take care of your feets," Bresson said. "People don't realize. When things get tough, the feets are more important than the brains."

Lyman could understand Bresson's English, even though he had a heavy and somewhat odd French accent.

"And always do the pedicure after the swim. It makes the skin soft."

"Could we talk about this transaction you have in mind?" Lyman gambled. Europeans either loved or hated Americans to be blunt.

He lost.

"Why should I discuss my business?" Bresson showed he could be equally direct. "I have not decided to hire you."

"If I were you, I wouldn't," Lyman doubled his bet.

"And why?" Bresson played along.

"Your regular French and British investment bankers will work for nothing except a transaction fee. And if the deal never happens, they'll write it off against other business they do with you. Me, I'm already costing you money just sitting here." A fragment of Bresson's toenail whizzed by his head.

"I do not have regular investment bankers."

That answered one of Lyman's questions, but raised larger ones about how Bresson had put his empire together.

"So why don't you go to one of the big blue-chip firms?" Lyman tried not to flinch each time the clippers snapped.

"I want to be your most important client." Bresson smiled for the first time. He had some remarkably bad dental work for a rich man. "You want me to convince you to take the assignment? Clever, but you are here to sell me!"

It was Lyman's turn to smile. "I can tell you why I shouldn't do it. First, the deal's tough, a long shot. Maybe impossible. And I don't even know if you're serious or just browsing. No matter how big a retainer or a busted-deal fee, I only make real money if the deal goes through."

"And why is the deal so difficult?"

"It comes down to one word."

Bresson waited.

"You," Lyman said.

"Why should that be?" He sat up and took the cotton balls off of his eyes. "Other foreigners own media companies in America."

"But not an empire like News/Worldweek with so much television. It's against the law for foreigners to own American TV stations. Rupert Murdoch became an American citizen to do it."

"You disappoint me." Bresson stared hard at Lyman. "I was told you were creative. I can put the TV stations in a special subsidiary . . ."

Lyman was impressed with Bresson's homework.

". . . And the Germans own cable stations—"

"That's legal because it's not broadcasting. Look, I'm not saying it's legally impossible. I'm saying this is a high-profile transaction. The media loves to talk about itself. You'll be the story of the year. What you're like. What your family's like, who your friends are. What you eat. What you do for grins. Who you're sleeping with. Girls, boys, furry animals." He paused for effect. "I don't mean to be impolite, but you ought to know what you're in for."

"What stupidity!" Bresson dismissed Lyman's lecture. He waved for Edouard to turn off the sunlamps. "Bertelsmann owns the Doubleday and the Dell publishers, the RCA records, the cable TV, the *Scientific American* magazine. What does anyone know about the Mohn family who controls it? They live in a town they have owned for two centuries—Gütersloh. Do you know what they do there, or even where that is? It is a hundred miles from the nearest airport. They did not have to become celebrities to make their investment in America."

"They aren't interested in political power," Lyman observed quietly, testing for a reaction.

"Neither am I," Bresson snapped. He sat up and pushed the pedicurist away. "Mr. Lyman, I understand the point. It will cost more money. That is no problem. I am accustomed to paying a premium to maintain my privacy."

"Yes, you'll have to pay more for News/Worldweek than a U.S. buyer. But I'm saying something else. There'll be no privacy at any price. And if you don't play by American rules, you may not get the deal."

"I was told you know how to rewrite the rules." A touch of supplication edged into his voice.

Lyman hated himself for being flattered.

Bresson abruptly stood. "I will think about what you have said. Maybe the whole thing is a bad idea."

Inside, Lyman tightened. Had he gone too far? "When should we plan to meet?" he asked, unable to conceal his concern.

"If we have need to talk, you will be contacted," Bresson said diffidently. "In the meantime, you should swim to relieve your tensions." He had taken command again. "Start with twenty laps," he said, disappearing through a door marked *Privé*. "Edouard will count."

"Actually," d'Uberville said, "we call this place the 'swimming pool.' " Having taught Heidi Bruce a lesson, he was trying to be charming. "We take the name of our headquarters from the neighbors next door, the Stade Nautique, a famous public swimming stadium here in Paris."

In fact, they stood in a Belle Époque dining room festooned with chandeliers. A long table was set with Limoges china bearing the initials *RF* for French Republic. A brace of dead pheasants surrounded by autumn wildflowers formed the centerpiece. "As a clandestine service," he concluded, "we are in the habit of misrepresentation."

A waiter in a military tuxedo served Heidi a scotch.

"I have arranged for us to sit together at dinner." D'Uberville squeezed her arm. "But now I must speak to my other guests." He left her alone trying to look interested in a painting of the battle of Austerlitz. Sean Gordon approached her.

"You kicked a little ass in there, dear." He smiled.

"Bastard," she replied. "Where have you been all these months?"

"You rejected me, remember?" He said it kindly, almost indulgently. Sean Gordon had been the CIA liaison to the Senate Intelligence Committee during an investigation of allegations of agency involvement with Central American drug trafficking. In his mid-forties, lean, weathered, with a full head of graying Irish hair, Heidi had found him extremely valuable, totally reliable and completely irresistible.

"I only said I didn't want to get married," she said. "Admit it, you were using me." The words were heavy but the tone was light.

"The evidence suggests you were using me," he replied evenly. "As soon as the investigation was over, you lost interest."

"Another lie," she said with a grin. "I did enjoy using you, though." Her voice dropped an octave.

He blushed. She liked that in a man.

"Surprised to see you here," she continued.

"Sort of an accident," he explained. "I've been assigned to the Inspector General's staff and was passing through Paris. For some reason, they thought I should come here as an observer."

"Probably to report on me."

"Probably."

"Well, you can tell them I bombed."

"Don't be too disappointed. What you're trying to do takes time. In every Western country, the intelligence and counterintelligence outfits always hate each other. You're suggesting that separate operations may be obsolete. These characters are all interested in a new role, but not at the price of being merged out of existence."

He paused. "Now, may we discuss something serious?"

She took a long, expectant pull on her scotch.

"Can I see you later?"

"Oh, Sean, do we really want to start again?" she asked, her voice solemn for the first time.

Before he could answer, the dinner bell rang and d'Uberville took her arm and led her to the center of the table. Sean Gordon found his name card at the far end, below the salt.

As they waded through eight courses (oysters, fish, game, sorbet, tournedos, salad, cheese and dessert), lubricated by carefully measured doses of Puligny-Montrachet and Château Margaux, d'Uberville regaled her with anecdotes of trying to maintain the family château in the Dordogne on a government salary. Then came the punchline. "You don't happen to know any wealthy Americans who might want to buy it?" he said in all seriousness.

She immediately thought of Jayson Lyman and tried not to laugh. She could picture him in his Paul Stuart corduroys and Land's End boat shoes shoveling a century of horse manure from a ballroom that had been used as a stable. "Maybe," she said.

D'Uberville warmed to her even more. "You know I actually

agree with what you said this afternoon," he confided, his voice, head and eyes cast down as if he were talking into her cleavage. "Soviet penetration has gone even further than you suggest. Their influence has reached the point that this government, a conservative government, won't let us pursue leads. . . . It's very delicate. Perhaps we could meet privately after the conference. A drink tonight? Lunch? Dinner tomorrow? We could also talk about your friend who wants a château . . ."

Heidi smiled noncomittally, as d'Uberville rose to introduce the dinner speaker. Sir Charles ruminated at length on what he regarded as the greatest threat to Western security—the propensity of legislatures and parliaments to stick their noses into the intelligence business. He stared at Heidi the whole time.

She tried to look back at him pleasantly in the English tradition of trading insults, and to avoid Sean Gordon's steady gaze. But her attention wandered. As Sir Charles was going into what everyone hoped was his concluding peroration—to that point Heidi had counted five "finallys" and four "lastlys"—an orderly handed d'Uberville a note. After a polite round of applause for Sir Charles, d'Uberville asked if anyone was expecting a call from a Mr. Jayson Lyman. Heidi took the message. Lyman asked her to call him at the Bristol at any hour. She looked up at an unhappy Comte d'Uberville, then down the table at Sean's disappointed face, and wondered what she should do.

He hated to admit it, but after almost drowning from the effort of twenty laps in the Bristol pool, Jay Lyman felt refreshed. By his biological clock, it was only 3:00 in the afternoon. He wanted some action. Figuring that nothing much more terrible could happen that day, he called, and left his name at the number the woman on the Concorde had scribbled on her menu. Then he called his office. Everyone was out except Rankin. Lyman told him to stop work on the News/Worldweek deal. Next he called Cooke, but he was in a meeting.

When no one had called back by 10:00 P.M., Lyman punched Paris into his Tele-Art credit-card-sized computer phone directory. He scrolled through a list of bankers and lawyers, finally stopping at the name of an old fraternity brother from UCLA. They had become close friends during their sophomore year when they had lived together in a room that was painted entirely black. Even the light bulbs had been painted black.

"Jayson in Parigi!" Dick Rensselaer's enthusiastic voice boomed out of the phone.

"I hope I'm not calling at an inconvenient time—"

"Well, I am in the middle of a blow job, but hey! I can do two things at once! Actually, I'm just sitting here grooving on the oldies-but-goodies."

One of Rensselaer's favorite pastimes was to listen to transcriptions of his old radio shows, recorded when he was a disc jockey for the Armed Forces Network in West Germany. A few years older than Lyman, he'd served two years in the Army before going on to college. After graduation, Rensselaer had spent a short stint in the U.S. Information Agency, which assigned him to Paris. When they wanted to transfer him to the African Eden of Upper Volta, he'd quit, stayed in Paris and started his own public relations firm. It was a hand-to-mouth existence, but he had gotten his hands on some pretty nice mouths.

They agreed to meet at the Alsace, a brasserie on the Ile St-Louis across from Notre-Dame. The night was balmy and the restaurant so full, even at that late hour, that they stood in the street drinking from litre steins of Mutzig beer.

"Are you gonna have to get shit-faced before you tell me why you're in town?" Rensselaer asked.

"Marcel Bresson. But I think the deal's gone before it started."

"Then you're lucky. He's a real killer."

"Aren't we all," Lyman said with a touch of pride.

"No, I mean like corpus delicti as a routine business practice. Maybe I exaggerate a tad, but folks who cross him seem to get their life insurance cashed by others."

"Give me a data point."

"The most famous case was about six years ago. Bresson invited a woman who was writing his biography onto his yacht for a sail in the Med. It was a chi-chi crowd that included Prince Andrew and Fergie. Well, off the coast of Malta, the woman disappears. Two weeks later her body washes ashore in Libya."

"Accidents happen," Lyman said.

The headwaiter called Rensselaer's name and they made their way into the jam-packed bar and through to the even more crowded dining room. Patrons sat cheek by jowl at eight long, paper-covered tables. Lyman and Rensselaer had to climb over a half-dozen people to arrive at their seats.

"If it was an accident," Rensselaer continued, "why did His Royal

Highness order up a helicopter from a British destroyer docked in Valletta to get him off the yacht even before the search began?"

"They're very sensitive to bad publicity," observed Lyman.

"Maybe they thought bad was gonna get worse," his friend responded.

Lyman noted that on his right, a French couple as usual ignored them. But the tourist to his left was trying to listen to them and talk to his wife at the same time. The result was a lot of cooked cabbage piling up in his lap.

Rensselaer pressed on with his story, "Anyway, the French consul from Bengazi who looks at the corpse reports that her head was caved in and that she had a rope around her leg. But the next day, the Libyans say she died by drowning. The death certificate makes no mention of any head wounds or ropes."

"Libya's a Third World country, what do they know?" Lyman noted. "If they suspected anything, the French could've examined the body themselves."

"That's the neat part. Before the family can get there, or the French consul can act, the Libyans burn the body—for sanitary reasons."

At this point, Lyman saw the tourists on his left lose their appetites. He ordered a cassoulet and a salade frisée lardon—spiky lettuce with chunks of bacon and a dressing made with hot bacon fat.

"What's the rumored motive?" Lyman sucked down half a glass of the house Côtes du Rhône.

"The woman's boyfriend made one statement about how your friend Bresson didn't like some of the things she put in the book, then he shut up." Rensselaer popped a morsel of preserved duck into his mouth.

"What about her editor?"

"Funny you should ask. Bresson bought the publishing company during the two weeks before her body was found."

"So, the book never came out."

"You got it."

After dinner, they took a Calvados on the deck of the Rhumerie overlooking the Boulevard St-Germain. Rensselaer studied his watch. "It's not too late. We can still get laid."

"I already made a feeble attempt once today . . ." Lyman's words faltered as he caught sight of a young woman walking arm in arm with two men. One of them was clearly French, older and seemingly uncomfortable with the situation. The other man was in his forties, probably

American, and looked pleased at the way the young woman squeezed his arm. It was her, Lyman realized, the nameless lady from the Concorde. No wonder she had not answered his telephone call.

"You've got to get right back up on the horse," Rensselaer continued to admonish him. "I'll take you to a place where your buddy Bresson used to hang out during his playboy days."

Lyman downed the Calvados in one gulp.

A *club privé,* Castel occupied five floors and two subbasements of a tiny townhouse on the rue Princesse. One glance at Rensselaer, and the girl guarding the door waved them through. An attractive couple behind them was turned away.

"I sort of live here," Rensselaer explained, "but I still can't tell you how they decide who gets in and who doesn't. But it's worked for a generation. My dad used to try to come here!"

They had passed a small and plain dining area on the left and were angling through the bar toward the steps that descended to pulsating music. "Twenty-five years ago, Françoise Sagan, Aristotle Onassis and Maria Callas would sit in here talking all night. Today this place is still the hottest ticket in town."

Descending the spiral staircase, they passed another bar that appeared to be dug out of the earth halfway down on the right.

"The old guy in the white hair, that's Jean Castel. The French are thinking of making room for him in the Panthéon. He's usually never here. His son runs the place. I met him skiing in Val d'Isère."

The discotheque itself was comfortable rather than flashy. Large plush circular sofas divided up the seating area. Pillars at each corner of the dance floor were clad as gilded palm trees. One wall held a floor-to-ceiling cabinet full of bottles of Johnnie Walker Black Label with little number tags around the necks. To Lyman that seemed a perfect example of the tight-assed French, until he ordered a drink and found it cost $30. The two of them took up places standing in the "watchers" section, between the dance floor and the D.J. in a glass booth.

The room was moderately full. The men came in two varieties, young and old; the women in only one—young. Everyone was fashionably dressed, the younger men in baggy suits from Daniel Hechter, T-shirts and loosely knotted ties, the older roués tending toward Savile Row. All the men appeared to be French.

The women, Lyman noted, were not all French. And while most of the men sat, they danced: a slinky Eurasian in a silk jumpsuit, a towering African in a white robe over shorts and a bikini top, a broad-shouldered Scandinavian whose full breasts slid around under a V-necked gray cashmere sweater, a French girl in a miniskirt with coltish legs bouncing up and down on thick platform wedgies.

"It's almost one in the morning on a weeknight." Lyman turned to Rensselaer. "Who are these people?"

"Not too many Bressons. Basically two types, *publicité*—you know, ad guys, show-biz, PR people like me. And then you have the *jeunesse dorée*—rich kids." He paused. "Strange company for a guy who started out as a business partner of the French Communist Party."

"Who? You?" Lyman was startled.

"No, I'm talking about Bresson."

"How so?"

"Hey, it was long before my time, but the story goes that he cut a deal with the unions to push these little family newspapers into bankruptcy and then he'd step in and buy 'em out."

"What did the Reds get out of it?"

"Fat union contracts."

"So how did he make money?"

Renssalaer shrugged.

"And how did he establish this relationship with the PCF?"

"His dad. He was a hero in the French Resistance during the Second World War. They were mostly commies, you know. He opened the doors, at least that's what they say."

"He could've just been opportunistic."

The D.J. segued into the Rolling Stones' classic "Let's Spend the Night Together." Rensselaer responded by heading toward the dance floor. Jay grabbed his arm.

"How does this work?" He pointed to the girls dancing alone or in groups.

"Just get out there and let your pheromones do the talking!"

5

He heard the phone, but Lyman did not want to give up his dream. It involved the woman from the Concorde, who was dancing in a gray cashmere sweater. The ringing insisted that he wake up.

"Monsieur Bresson would like to talk to you." It sounded like Edouard. "Be ready in forty-five minutes, please."

Downstairs, a limo was waiting. The driver was his old friend the Vietnamese. Edouard gave him an address at Maisons Lafitte.

"What's in Maisons Lafitte?" Lyman asked as they pulled away from the curb.

"Horses."

"You work for Bresson?" Lyman followed up.

Suddenly the Vietnamese seemed not to understand English. Lyman felt too tired to push it.

Light was just breaking over the city as they made their way up the Champs-Élysées, under the Arc de Triomphe and onto the Avenue de la Grande Armée. Crossing the Seine, they passed from ancient Paris to La Défense—a twenty-first-century complex of glass and steel towers wrapped in freeways, with buildings bearing corporate monograms such as EDF, UAP, ATO, IBM, ELF and GAN. With no place for pedestrians to stroll, it reminded Lyman more of downtown Houston or L.A. than of France. Then they once again crossed the Seine and the freeway abruptly dumped them onto a four-lane road. Gas stations, car repairs, tiny cement houses crowded close to the highway. The dirt shoulder made it look like a Third World country.

Lyman fought sleep. He was tired and mean and wanted to stay that way. Nothing he had learned about Bresson encouraged him. He was fed up with the rope-a-dope routine. Either Bresson made a commitment to move forward, or Lyman was on the noon Concorde back to New York. One of the hardest things in the M&A business was to remember that you did yourself and the client no favors by taking crap from him. Forget the $60 million fee. It was time to get tough.

The road suddenly came to a third bridge over the meandering Seine River. An arched, early-nineteenth-century stone structure, it served to frame a beautiful eighteenth-century château that stood at the top of the opposite bank.

"Maisons Lafitte," the driver announced, recovering his voice. He turned right past broad green practice fields where young horses were getting a morning workout. They then drove slowly around a long oval full of tangled wildflowers surrounding a statue of a young horse, as the driver tried to match a number on his clipboard with the blue and white ceramic address plaques on the walls of the stables. He finally paused before a huge wrought-iron gate that served as an entrance to a court-yard with half-timbered Norman-style stables on three sides. A man wiping a sweating horse said Bresson was not there.

"Fuck 'em. Let's go back to the hotel," Lyman said.

"*Un moment.*" The horse trainer stopped the driver. "*C'est un Américain?*" They exchanged what Lyman considered a series of groans, whines, moans and snorts.

"*Monsieur Bresson vous attend,*" the driver said. "We go."

They found him at the rail of an enormously wide grass practice track that ran along the banks of the Seine. A two-foot layer of ground fog clung to the river and the turf. From a distance, the horses looked like strange ships as they galloped toward them, their legs enveloped in mist.

"*Bonjour, Monsieur Lyman.* Thank you for getting up so early. It is beautiful here at this hour, no? Have you made up your mind?"

"I thought you wanted time." Lyman was on the defensive again.

"For me the decision is made." Bresson said cheerfully. He picked up his binoculars and peered through the haze at a colt pounding across the grass hurling divots in all directions. "Watch that horse," he ordered Lyman. "It will never run fast. It has no economy of motion. It thrashes."

"Why do you want this deal?" Lyman was not interested in lectures on horses.

"Robert Maxwell said it. By the year 2000 the world will be domina-ted by only a dozen media combines. But he is wrong to name himself the European one. There will be no European. We are too small and divided. Europe will be an appendage of America. I had the misfortune to start here. Now I go there."

"And have you got the resources for a deal this size?" Lyman was determined to cut to the bottom line even at the risk of being rude. But Bresson just smiled.

"You have to tell me how much I should pay."

"And you have to pay me to do it."

"How much?"

"Two million plus eight-tenths of a percent."

"Of four billion dollars." Bresson started shaking his head.

"The deal will cost you more than four billion," Lyman corrected him.

"So you know already how much!" Bresson jumped on him.

"Plus a bust-up fee, out of pocket and legal."

"How much?" He looked again through his binoculars.

"Five million," Lyman said as if it were nothing.

"Let us have breakfast."

Lyman took a sip of the freshly squeezed orange juice and made a face. "Why is the orange juice so sour in this country?"

"Because France is a sour country," Bresson replied. Lyman wondered if that was his way of being ingratiating.

They sat on the terrace of a yellow sandstone building with bright red awnings that looked like a hotel on the Riviera. From their table next to the railing, Lyman could look down on the practice tracks that ran down to the river. Through the trees he could see the greensward of the château of Maisons Lafitte next door.

"You know the history of Maisons Lafitte?" Bresson asked.

Lyman shook his head.

"It was the first of what you call the big real estate play. Jacques Lafitte, a famous banker, made the mistake of getting into politics, lost his position and found himself fifty million in debt. He had to subdivide the land. He even tore down racing monuments to get the stone to build the houses in the neighborhood."

"This happened after the war?"

"Which war do you mean? It was 1831."

"And what's this place?" Lyman asked, refusing to be intimidated by the "old Europe" ploy.

"A sanitarium. I come here to lose weight."

"You're not at the Bristol?" For effect, Lyman turned up the surprise in his voice.

"I moved last night," Bresson responded uncomfortably. "Tell me"—he clearly wanted to change the subject—"how you would approach the deal?"

"Are we working together?" Lyman asked warily.

"Naturally."

Lyman reached over the table and got a typical French handshake, so limp it felt like a lie.

"There's no way this can be a friendly deal," Lyman began. "Fifty-two percent of News/Worldweek stock is held by the public and the rest by family members or their trusts. The company hasn't done well for six quarters, but the family and the management get more than cash out of the business. With the prestige involved, neither will want to sell."

"What would be your strategy?"

"Accumulate as much stock as possible in the market, then go right to a tender. Nothing too creative. Make an all-cash offer for all the stock at, say, a fifty percent premium to the market price. If the family or management balks, as they probably will, a fifty percent premium will take out the public and force the trust managers to face up to their fiduciary responsibility. You might not get a hundred percent of the stock, but you'll get enough for control. In time, you can freeze out the rest."

"All cash is very expensive," he responded. "I have read of transactions in which one only pays cash to the first fifty-one percent of the people who come forward with their stocks. The rest are given paper—a note or the preferred stocks. That way we would force the stockholders to compete to get the cash."

"Worked wonders a few years ago, but now the courts have said such offers are coercive. The target can respond with discriminatory tactics against us."

"For instance?"

"Like News/Worldweek offering to buy back their stock at a higher price than you're paying, only leaving you out." Lyman was getting pumped up. "With those big family blocks, they could reduce the number of public shares and put themselves in a majority position again. They already have a poison pill."

"How does that work?"

"Their corporate bylaws include a rule that anytime a raider goes over twenty percent, all the others get the right to buy more stock at a fifty percent discount once the company is merged."

"I'd have to buy the company twice!"

"That's right."

"And that's legal in America?"

"If you try a coercive front-loaded tender offer."

"Could we raise the cash with junk bonds?"

"Junk bonds can't be rated 'investment grade' and a lot of institutions, like pension funds, can't buy them. So they've got to pay a prohibitive interest rate to attract buyers—currently twenty percent. It's better to go to the Mafia. You'd have to sell a third of the company to pay them off."

"But I want to keep it intact."

"Then a typical bust-up junk-bond takeover won't work."

"What's the alternative?"

"Bank debt. You can borrow against your holdings here in Europe."

Bresson did not respond.

"We can look at alternative structures," Lyman assured him. "Perhaps some mezzanine financing, maybe a little junk. But I don't think anyone could place several billion in this market. Junk bonds are in shit city these days."

"*Ville de merde! Mon dieu!*" Bresson looked at him askance.

"Sorry."

"*Il n'y a pas de quoi.* Don't be embarrassed," he said, rubbing it in. He took another helping of scrambled egg whites. "Tell me about the timing."

"Your greatest asset is surprise, time pressure. I say mug 'em. Hit on Friday at four oh five P.M. on a long weekend. Give the minimum, twenty days, to tender their stock. Management won't have time to react. They'll try lawsuits and other delaying tactics. But we'll have momentum, and moving fast will also minimize the time you'll be under the microscope."

"I still don't see why my personal life has to come into it."

Back to square one, Lyman thought.

"This is a hostile takeover." He decided to start at the beginning. "The target will use anything and everything it can against you. They'll sue just to get discovery."

Bresson looked blank.

"You don't know about 'discovery'?"

Bresson's shrug meant he did not.

"In America, if you sue somebody, you get the right to go into their files to prove your case. That's called 'discovery.' Impeding discovery is a criminal offense. When Sandoz, the Swiss drug company, tried to take over McCormack, they sued. Sandoz didn't want their business secrets exposed and backed off. Sterling Drug tried the same trick on Hoffman-La Roche."

"But in that case it didn't work," Bresson noted.

Lyman flushed. "Well, Kodak stepped in." Again he'd been sucked into underestimating Bresson. "The question is whether it would work against you!"

Bresson looked thoughtful.

"Look, in America we've had Presidents who were adulterers. First Ladies on drugs. They survived. What could be so bad about you? It doesn't matter anymore what you've done, it's how you handle it."

"You must understand I'm not trying to hide anything," Bresson insisted. "It's just a question of privacy."

They were silent for a moment. The distant sound of horses' hooves and barges on the Seine filled the air. Lyman thought he saw a cloud of uncertainty pass over Bresson's face.

"What kind of things would I have to deal with?" he finally asked.

Lyman decided to let it hang out. "Well, like what happened to that woman who fell off your boat?"

Bresson showed no surprise. His voice turned sorrowful. "Would I have to explain that we were . . . ?" He made an unmistakable gesture.

"I thought she had a boyfriend," Lyman said, slightly surprised.

"That is why he said stupid things about me."

"What about the French consul's report? The head injuries? The rope?" Lyman felt nervous repeating hearsay.

"She had been caught in the fisherman's net and hauled aboard a ship. It was horrible."

"I'm sorry." This time, Lyman meant it.

"So you looked into my past. What else have you found?"

"Your father. He was a Communist?"

"He is still. With a picture of Stalin over the bed. I have not talked to him since I was seventeen."

"Why?"

"I felt it was my patriotic duty to join the army and fight in Algeria. He said I had become a fascist."

"I'd heard he'd helped you with the unions."

"That old canard. Help me? He never forgave me! My enemies say that, because I have no strikes. I believe in good pay and working conditions. And I know how to talk to my employees. I don't apologize for that."

It was suddenly silent between them.

"Well, all that should be manageable, if there's nothing else," Lyman finally said. "I'll develop a detailed strategy paper and valuation. We'll work up alternative financing structures. You'll need topflight lawyers. A PR firm—McFadden Dworkin is good. We should set a target date. Start drafting all the filings for the SEC, Justice. We need to look at your financials—" Lyman's mind had gone into high-speed print mode.

Bresson interrupted him, "But I do not want a hostile takeover."

"What?" Lyman asked incredulously. "What have we been talking about?"

"We should try to be more friendly," said Bresson calmly. "Proceed step by step."

"Like what?"

"I want you to start gently. Meet with News/Worldweek. Talk with them."

"Really?" Lyman was ready to walk.

"Yes. Infect their minds with fear and greed."

"He's a piece of work!" Lyman was back in his room at the Bristol, complaining over the phone to Cooke in New York. "He wants me to go to Washington, see the chairman of News/Worldweek and offer his 'assistance.' First, I'm supposed to persuade Drew Richardson that he's a target. Then I tell him I've got a passive investor who'll give the family and management an unbreakable majority if they'll sell a big block of new stock. Bresson thinks he can start out as a 'White Squire,' then capture control for himself."

"What's wrong with that idea?" Cooke sounded distracted.

"Bresson won't even let me use his name, for shit's sake! I get to tell Richardson about a mystery man who'll save him from the big bad wolf. He'll probably respectfully suggest that I take a flying fuck!"

"That's good." Cooke definitely was not listening.

"Try to focus, damn it! This deal's about to hit the wall. Once I tell News/Worldweek there's a bear in the woods, they'll call Marty Lipton down from New York and start buckling on the antitakeover measures. We'll lose surprise! Time pressure will shift against us!"

Lyman could hear Cooke put his hand over the mouthpiece so he could talk to someone else. That was it.

"Hey! I don't want to take your time!" Lyman screamed into the phone. "Just don't count on any $60 million fees."

"What?" He finally got Cooke's attention.

"Plus which, he rejected the $5 million guarantee. He'll only sign up for a $2 million retainer."

"Why's he behaving this way?" Cooke sounded anxious.

"Only two answers. Either he hasn't got the money, or he's got something to hide and is afraid of all the disclosure in a hostile deal. Unfortunately, it could be both."

"But he'll still give us $2 million for you just to go to Washington and talk to Drew Richardson. That's something!"

"Yeah." Lyman was not interested.

"I'm sorry I sound so preoccupied," Cooke said, "but the *Journal*'s going to run a story tomorrow that we lost $26 million in the last quarter. Hit squads are forming in the trading room to come after the whole executive committee—including you. If we can get this takeover going, we can change the subject."

You incompetent jerk-off, Lyman thought, don't try to lay it on me. "I'll think about it on the plane."

"Wrap it up before you leave," Cooke pleaded. "Sure, Bresson's hard to handle, but you know the rule."

"Yeah?"

"All clients are assholes."

Lyman checked with the concierge, who got him a seat on the afternoon Concorde. He had to pack fast to make the plane. Bresson's magazines went in the trash basket.

On the way out, the concierge handed him a stack of messages. He went through them in the taxi: three calls from his secretary, two from de Grazia, one from Sidney Slez of RATCO, Emily Pierce from the gallery, somebody named Heidi Bruce, Mr. Malcom, his mother and a note from the Finnish girl in the cashmere sweater who he'd met at Castel, asking for help in getting a visa to the States. He stuffed them all in his suit pocket. They would have to wait until he got to the airport.

The traffic was impenetrable. He had no time to stop in the Concorde lounge to make calls, let alone shop in the Hermès boutique to stock up on scarves for his cucumbers. He would buy gifts on the plane. Only when he was strapped in and drinking a glass of Dom Perignon did he look at his messages. Again he came to Heidi Bruce. It was the eight-digit Paris number! That was her name! And she called back the night before at 10:15!

He jumped out of his seat and rushed off the plane through a gauntlet of protesting stewardesses to a telephone. A Frenchman answered and in broken English explained that the conference was over; Mademoiselle Bruce had returned to Washington, D.C.

Crushed, Lyman started slowly back toward the plane, urged along by the crew. Then he abruptly stopped. Washington! Why not? He turned back to the phone and got through to Marcel Bresson immediately. Without haggling, Lyman accepted the assignment. The $2 million would be just a bonus.

6

The white ball arched through the sky heading straight toward the pin. It dropped onto the lip of grass between the green and the bunker, gave a little bounce, then seemed almost to rest a moment before dribbling backward into the sand trap. Unfazed, Drew Richardson calmly handed the three wood back to the caddy. Such even temperament was not the hallmark of his character, as the rest of his foursome knew. His mind was simply elsewhere.

Richardson reserved his outbursts for the NEC P900 cellular telephone attached to his golf bag. The stream of calls had begun before the first tee. Each time he excused himself and made for the rough. There he could be seen, but not heard, as he kicked the bark off of trees or yanked clods of grass out of the ground while he talked into the handset. When he rejoined the others, he acted as if everything were normal, except that he was on the verge of doubling his handicap by the fifteenth hole.

Five other foursomes had asked to play through while Richardson talked on the phone, and the three Congressmen in his group began to worry about missing a 10:30 A.M. roll-call vote on the defense authorization bill. However, they were in no position to complain. As chairman and chief executive officer of News/Worldweek, Drew Richardson was the most powerful publishing executive in Washington, and probably in the United States. The Congressmen were not about to provoke a man who viewed himself as a senior statesman, second only to the President of the United States, even though he had never held public office. An invitation to join his regular Thursday-morning golf game at the Congressional Country Club, where Congressmen were seldom admitted as members, constituted a command performance.

Power was relatively new to Drew Richardson and he was inclined to use it clumsily. For twelve years he had labored meekly in corporate obscurity while Cornelia Nichols, the former CEO and wife of the founder of News/Worldweek made herself into a legend. During that time, not a day passed that he did not fear being summarily fired by her—as all his predecessors had been. And he had to bear the ceaseless barbs and intrigues of "Cornelia's darlings"—the managing editor of the *Washington News,* featured columnists at *Worldweek,* her Pulitzer Prize-winning reporters—people who considered themselves talent and whom Richardson regarded as commodities.

As soon as Cornelia retired from the board and Richardson was anointed chairman, he began to implement a long-planned three-phase strategy. First, he aggressively expanded the corporation into cable TV and other electronic media. Second, he retired or sacked all of Cornelia's darlings and minimized the remaining influence of the Nichols heirs by encouraging the placement of family stock into trusts. And now he was on the brink of his third and most important step, to make himself undisputed master of News/Worldweek and a multimillionaire at the same time.

Like most chief executives of major American corporations, Richardson, despite his stock options and seven-figure salary, was by no means wealthy. The *Washington News* itself had proclaimed that, since the Reagan tax reforms of the eighties, being truly wealthy required a net worth of at least $200 million. Richardson could not even come close.

A member of the Bohemian Club, the Business Round Table and the River Club in New York, among others, he was a well-known figure in business and social circles. Although he was ostensibly nonpartisan, his control of media outlets gave him enormous influence in both political parties. But he knew he would never achieve lasting respect or the recognition of history without real wealth.

Richardson was sick of going to receptions at the National Gallery for Paul Mellon, who acted as if he owned the place. Or the Hirshhorn Gallery on the mall. Who was Hirshhorn? Or Smithson, for that matter? One had been a switchboard operator and the other was illegitimate. But they had been rich! The names Ford and Rockefeller meant cheapskate until they endowed their great foundations with enough money to make their names immortal.

Drew Richardson knew that being a chief executive officer guaranteed nothing for the future. The golf links from Sea Island, Georgia, to Pebble Beach were littered with once-feared CEOs, now pensioned off, bereft of power and influence, their names forgotten almost as soon as they lost control of their corporate boardrooms. That would not happen to him. Wealth would ensure posterity to the name Richardson, and the best dinner parties from Palm Beach to Southampton, until the day they put him on a respirator.

Neither discrimination nor a deprived childhood stoked the fire in his belly. But Drew Richardson's burden felt heavy nonetheless. He came from a prosperous family in New Canaan, Connecticut, attended Choate and then Yale, where he was Skull and Bones. He knew privilege. And he also knew that it was enervating. Richardson became obsessed with proving that a white male Protestant with advantages could still make it in America.

The phone beeped again.

"Yes?" Richardson snatched it up. One of the Congressmen hit an airball.

"I don't know if this is part of what's been going on," his secretary said, "but you've just gotten a call from a Jayson Lyman at Gould Axewroth. He said he's an investment banker."

"Never heard of him." Richardson hung up.

However, on the eighteenth hole the CEO of News/Worldweek received another call from his secretary, together with a message from Jayson Lyman. He then missed a six-inch putt for a triple bogey.

It was Lyman's idea of controlling his temper. "That white-shoe ass-face . . . He doesn't *want* to talk to me? Or he just *can't?*"

"Richardson's doin' lawn work," Marlene shouted back from the outer office. "Ya know, at the golf course. But his secretary told me he don't wanna talk to no investment bankers."

"Is that what you said?" Lyman fumed. "That I'm an investment banker? Christ, no wonder! Every dip-shit stockbroker calls himself an investment banker these days! The guys who shine our shoes every afternoon probably call themselves investment bankers!" He wanted to bang his head on his desk.

"Jayson, calm down. It's not my fault that this guy's a putz. And it's not my fault you can't get no answer outa this number for Heidi Bruce, neither," she added, striking below the belt.

He slumped back in his chair. "Can you check Washington information again?" he said weakly. "Maybe Heidi is short for something."

"It's not short for anything. It's in a book, the number just doesn't answer. Now you're late for the executive committee meeting."

"That's a lynching. I want an excuse to stay out of it. Let me talk to Richardson's secretary."

She came on the line and was very pleasant and very firm. "He doesn't know you, Mr. Lyman, and therefore he doesn't want to talk to you."

"Would you give him a message?"

"That would probably be best."

"Tell Mr. Richardson that I want to see him this afternoon in Washington, that I'm head of the Merger Department at Gould Axewroth, where we do our little corporate takeovers, and that I represent a client with twice the financial assets of News/Worldweek." He paused. "You've got that?"

"Yes."

"Oh, and you might add something else."

"Go ahead."

"I'm his worst nightmare."

As the air shuttle from New York came in across the lower Potomac, Lyman could barely see the Capitol dome through the thick haze that usually forecast a late afternoon thunderstorm. He found the limo driver despite the usual misspelling of his name, and as soon as he got in the back seat, tried Heidi Bruce's telephone number again. And again, there was no answer.

The meeting was set for 3:30. Lyman told the driver to take it slow. He did not want to arrive until 3:35. Time to make Richardson sweat a little. Trouble was, Lyman was sweating too.

This was the part of the deal business he claimed to like best— creating the situation. Anybody could come busting in and lay a lot of cash on the table. Despite his misgivings, Lyman felt challenged by the task of igniting a transaction without making an offer or naming his client. But he forced himself to stop thinking about what he would say to Richardson. Credibility required spontaneity. He did not want to leave his game in the locker room.

The limo crossed the 14th Street Bridge, passed the Jefferson Memorial, and stopped at the light next to an old brick structure with strange Gothic towers and tall, narrow windows painted over from the inside, which were covered with rusty iron gratings. To Lyman, the building looked like a Civil War arms factory. He wondered why it still stood along the mall among the monuments. Then he noticed the line of tourists waiting to get inside and a small blue sign that announced, BUREAU OF PRINTING AND ENGRAVING. It shocked him to realize that he was looking at the center of the financial universe. Wall Street merely traded securities. The printing presses in that old ramshackle building produced tens of millions of dollars in real money every day.

Turning left on Independence Avenue and then right on 15th Street, Lyman asked the driver to stop. He got out of the car to get a better look at the Washington Monument. Though he spent most of his working life in towering skyscrapers, the simplicity of the soaring marble obelisk rising from the small hill surrounded by nothing but fifty American flags always filled Lyman with awe. Was this patriotism, he wondered? Or was he just grateful that with all the trash built in America, somehow our most important monument somehow had escaped getting junked up?

The driver opened the rear door to signal it was time.

He returned to the car, and they proceeded north into the newly redeveloped heart of Washington, D.C. As always, Lyman was surprised that the capital of the most powerful nation in the world could be such a small town. He could think of a dozen other American cities with more impressive downtown areas. Unlike most of the government buildings, which looked like they had been designed by the Federal Bureau of Prisons, the corporate headquarters of News/Worldweek at 16th and K Streets proved to be in the postmodern style which dominated Washington in the 1980s.

Until the Richardson regime, the corporate offices had been on the top floor of the nearby Washington News Building. But to emphasize the new and broader strategic thrust of the corporation, not to mention distinguishing himself from the mere print publishers who had preceded him, Drew Richardson had built a new structure on a site overlooking Farragut Square.

A mélange of columns, arches and pediments, it mixed glass brick with real brick, and turquoise mosaic from Miami in the thirties with slabs of pink marble à la Donald Trump. Here and there, fragments of old Victorian mansions which the Landmarks Commission would not let the builder tear down were randomly incorporated into the facade. The charitable said it looked like it had been designed by a committee. Lyman thought it looked like a merger from hell.

As he walked down the long eighth-floor corridor of executive power, Lyman felt depressed by the rigid sociology of corporate life. The scale of the offices grew in lockstep with the grandeur of the titles: Vice President, Senior Vice President, Group Vice President, Executive Vice President. Through an occasional open door he could see that the size of the desks also appeared to increase according to rank. The Senior

Executive Group Vice President seemed to be working off the deck of an aircraft carrier.

Drew Richardson's office carried the invidious ritual to its logical conclusion. He had no desk at all.

A secretary ushered Lyman into a room furnished in leather couches, overstuffed reading chairs, and book-lined walls. The potted palms and Oriental carpets made it look every inch a London men's club, except that the floor did not creak and everything appeared smartly new, not comfortably tatty. Only the multifunction AT&T 6300 telecomputer terminal on a table at Drew Richardson's side suggested that actual work might be done in the room.

Richardson rose and introduced the other half-dozen people in the room—assorted financial officers and lawyers, an executive assistant and even a PR woman. Lyman had expected to be outnumbered but not encircled. He would have to get aggressive. He shook their hands and then turned to Richardson.

"I suggest we speak in private."

"Anything you plan to say to me, you can say to them," Richardson waved a long patrician hand at the group.

"I don't doubt that," Lyman replied, "but if what I say leaks, it will be to my advantage, not yours."

For a moment, Richardson failed to understand. Then it dawned on him. Lyman could leak a merger offer to the press, create a furor in the stock market and blame it on the large number of people in the room.

"All right, Mr. Lyman," he conceded gracelessly, "but my chief financial officer stays." The rest were dismissed.

To Lyman, Richardson was the kind of guy he loved to hate. Tall, with a full head of hair appropriately graying at the temples, he radiated the arrogance and aplomb of an ambassador. And like ambassadors, who seldom acknowledged that they owed their position, power and prestige to the taxpayer, Richardson would never acknowledge that his self-importance was paid for by the corporate shareholders.

"You're under accumulation, Mr. Richardson," he said.

The News/Worldweek chief looked at his financial officer for a translation.

"He means somebody is buying our stock," explained the thin, nervous man who had remained behind.

"Somebodies," Lyman corrected him. "Somebodies are buying your stock."

Richardson felt a stab of anxiety. How could this young man know that?

"Your company is going nowhere. Your last three acquisitions diluted the stockholders' thirty-two percent. You've had six quarters in a row with negative growth in earnings. If you were the U.S. economy, you'd be in a recession and your editorial writers would be raising hell."

"I've explained all that to the financial community and I don't intend to explain it to you." Richardson decided to drop the polite act. "Our stock has been moving up in recent weeks." The finance officer nodded enthusiastically.

"That's because you're under accumulation." Lyman explained again. "Your stock has been trading at a forty percent discount to the net worth of the company. Every analyst on the Street thinks you're a target. The smart money is positioning itself in your stock. Even the more aggressive arbs are taking blocks. They figure it's just a matter of time until you get hit."

"Thanks for the warning," the corporate chief replied with a smile. "Now, do you actually have business to conduct?" Lyman had hoped to make him worried and was surprised that his assault seemed to make Richardson relax.

"I deserved that." Lyman laughed, trying a more friendly, self-deprecating tack. "I sometimes get carried away," Richardson said, also laughing. None of it was sincere. It did nothing to break the tension. Lyman did not like the way things were going.

"I represent a passive investor," Lyman said carefully, "who is prepared to take a significant block of new stock from the company in return for appropriate representation on the board. He's prepared to commit himself, insofar as the law allows, to vote with management."

"If he's so passive, why does he want seats on the board?" the financial type demanded.

"Insurance," Lyman responded. "And to prove his sincerity he's prepared to sign a standstill agreement not to buy any more News/Worldweek stock for an appropriate period."

"The details aren't important." Richardson held up his hands. "We're really not interested in White Knights, or White Squires, or what have you to protect us from a takeover. Much of the stock of this corporation is in family hands, and they're not about—"

"The public owns fifty-two percent." Lyman refused to yield. "The convertible debentures and the the warrants issued in your recent deals, when fully exercised, add ten percent more in public hands. That leaves thirty-eight percent with the family, but more than half of that is in various trusts, some run by the family, some not. I'd guess the family really *controls* only twenty-two percent of the stock of this corporation."

"That's really quite enough, when you consider that we're so big, no other media company in the country could buy us. The Justice Department would never give antitrust clearance. The Reagan days are over. Thank you, Mr. Lyman, for stopping by." He stood up.

"Don't you even want to know my client's name?" Lyman desperately played a card he did not have.

"No, and if I read it in the paper then I'll know who leaked it, won't I?" His smile was ice. "And don't think you can put this company in play with a few rumors. I do have some influence with my colleagues in the press." He showed Lyman the door without shaking hands.

"If he was playing hard to get, Richardson convinced me." Lyman was reporting to Marshall Cooke over the phone. "I'd say it was a blow-out. A kiss-off."

"Don't let this deal die," Cooke pleaded.

"Die? Are you listening? It's stillborn!"

"You've got to buy some time! Things are going crazy here! Bosworth resigned because of the rumors that the firm's about to go under. Your deal's the only thing that stands in the way of a partners' revolt."

"You told everybody about it?" Lyman was incredulous.

"I had to! But don't worry. I put News/Worldweek on the restricted list. Nobody can buy the stock."

"B.F.D. Nobody's supposed to know about it at all!" Lyman did not hold back his anger. "As soon as I get back to New York, you and I are taking a ride on the Governor's Island ferry and only one of us is coming back."

"You're right," he replied without listening. "We've got to talk. Strategize. But meanwhile, string Bresson along, play for time so we can cope with the situation. Gotta go."

He hung up. "So *we* can cope with the situation," Lyman thought furiously. He's used this transaction to make everyone at Gould Axewroth think I'm on his side. And if the deal collapses, he blames me for the firm coming apart!

Lyman stared morosely out of the window of the corner suite at the Four Seasons where he had booked a room for a few hours in order to make phone calls. The international operator was still trying to track down Bresson and Heidi Bruce's phone had not answered for two days. As Lyman watched the Rock Creek Parkway below, the first automobiles began to turn on their lights.

He tried Heidi's number again, but got no response.

So he settled for his mother.

Heidi had been waiting almost two days for the chance to report to the Chairman on her trip to Paris, and now she had been told the meeting was in five minutes. She jumped off the open wooden car at the Capitol end of the Senate subway and raced up the escalator. On the main floor, she dodged through a throng of tourists being herded out at closing time by Capitol police. She then raced down the central hall, stepped over a velvet rope, and crossed the rotunda to a small stainless-steel elevator door hidden discreetly behind one of the massive columns holding up the Capitol dome.

The elevator took her high up into the attic, where she stepped out into a low-ceilinged complex of rooms originally built for the now defunct Joint Committee on Atomic Energy. She showed her badge to the armed guard, who allowed her past the steel gate and into the hearing rooms, which were used for a variety of classified meetings, including those of the Senate Select Committee on Intelligence. Heidi was surprised to find that, in addition to the Chairman and the staff director, the vice chairman and minority counsel were also present and the meeting was already under way.

"The minority will not be able to support this bill unless our allies enact similar laws," the vice chairman was saying. "We already require our companies to discuss more about themselves than our allies do and the same goes for trade with the Soviet Bloc—"

The Chairman stopped him and welcomed Heidi. "Miss Bruce has just come back from meeting with some of the Allies. Tell us their reaction, my dear."

Heidi gave a faithful rendition of the controversy stimulated by her remarks at the Paris intelligence conference.

"I think that finishes it," the minority counsel responded when Heidi had ended.

"Wait a minute," the staff director said. "Most of this bill is about authorizing new economic targets for the CIA and NSA—"

"And establishing Soviet Bloc economic intelligence operations as legitimate counterintelligence targets," Heidi added, "along with safeguards to protect privacy and prevent interfering with the market."

"What's wrong with that?" the staff director asked. "It doesn't have anything to do with making companies reveal more."

"What's wrong is that it strongly implies the intelligence community hasn't been doing its job!" the minority counsel replied.

"They're not against it," Heidi said.

"But are they for it?" the minority counsel fired back. "No!"

"The intelligence community is only unhappy because they didn't think of it themselves," Heidi argued.

She saw the debate getting political.

"Strengthening economic intelligence is not a criticism of the administration." The staff director cut to the heart of the issue.

"Hold on." The Chairman finally got the drift of the debate. "Is this young fellow"—he pointed at the minority counsel—"accusing me of running this committee in a partisan manner?"

"Hold on yourself," the vice chairman responded. "No one's accusing you of anything, but the majority leadership's been hammering away at the President for failing to give priority to our economic problems."

"Gentlemen! This bill is about Russian economic penetration," Heidi protested.

"A subtlety lost on the American people, I assure you," the vice chairman said, scowling.

"I'm not going to turn this committee into a pit of partisan rancor," the Chairman said loftily. "We should talk more with our allies, develop more facts on the problem. Yes, in a situation like this, more facts often help. Perhaps a consensus will emerge," he concluded vaguely. The staff director shot Heidi a look of condolence.

Just like that, Heidi knew, her bill was dead. A year's work down the drain. As she returned down the elevator and through the subway to her cubbyhole in the Hart Senate Office Building, two words kept ricocheting through her mind: Stupid! Blind! Stupid! Blind! Stupid! She wanted to talk to Sean Gordon.

Lyman finally tracked Marcel Bresson to the Hotel Dolder Grand outside of Zurich. He kept his report factual and to the point, but he had thought of one more step. Maybe it would breathe life back into the deal.

"I don't think we should take no for an answer without talking to the family," he concluded. "Our research suggests that Holly and Raffy Nichols are the most important decision makers. They hold the bulk of the personal stock. He chairs a few of the trusts, and she votes her cousin's proxies. I'd like to talk to them."

"Do not bother," Bresson said flatly.

So that's it, Lyman thought. For some reason, he felt relieved. He had done all he could. Now he could go back to New York and have his showdown with Cooke.

"I want you to stay in Washington until tomorrow," Bresson continued.

"Why?"

"This is not the medium for discussion. I can only tell you there will be developments tomorrow."

"What?"

"It will become clear."

"How? Who?" The questions suddenly mushroomed in Lyman's mind. But the line had gone dead. He slammed the phone down.

Developments involving Bresson? Or was it about News/Worldweek? What could Bresson know that I don't know, he wondered. Could he have some inside information? The deal began to feel slimier by the minute.

He would give Heidi Bruce one more try, and if that did not work, he would turn on the pay TV and start systematically emptying all the tiny bottles in the room's little refrigerator.

"Thanks for letting me cry on your shoulder," Heidi said from her office phone.

"Am I going to see you tonight?" Sean Gordon replied.

She hesitated. Since returning from Paris, Heidi had spent the last two nights at his apartment. They were starting up again. Did she really want that?

"Sean, I haven't really been home at all."

"It feels very much like home when you're here."

"Yeah, I know." That was the awful part. "Let me just go home and water my plants. I have to turn on my answering machine. And I need to pick up some fresh clothes anyway."

"No pressure. Just call and let me know," he said.

He was sincere. He was trying to ease off. Then why did it make her so angry and guilty?

As she opened the door to her basement apartment, the phone was ringing. She did not want to pick it up. Sean would be calling to say again in his warm and reasonable voice that he understood if she just wanted to hole up by herself for a while. It had been a hard day. And the more reasonable he became, the worse she would feel and the more he would urge her not to be, going around and around . . .

"Hello." She gave in on the fifth ring.

"My God, it's really you!"

"Jay Lyman?" She suddenly smiled.

"Heidi Bruce, I love you."

She could tell he was at least half smashed.

At the stop light before the entrance to the Four Seasons, Heidi pulled off her scarf and checked in the rearview mirror of the Fiat Spyder convertible to see what the wind had done to her hair.

I can't believe I'm doing this, she said to herself. When I was eighteen, I swore I'd never go out with anybody who was already drunk!

She almost drove right past him. Lyman was wearing the doorman's hat and helping him park cars. He climbed into the seat next to her without opening the door. His smile was broad and warm and made her instantly feel as if they had known each other forever.

"I really don't have any idea who you are," she responded, shaking her head at herself.

"Who would you like me to be tonight?" he insinuated.

"Someone who knows how to take orders." She popped the clutch and squealed out of the driveway before he could lean over to kiss her.

The afternoon thunderstorm had failed to materialize, and the air felt heavy and tropical. Heidi raced across the M Street Bridge and down Pennsylvania Avenue.

"Where do you want to go?" Lyman shouted over the wind and whine of the engine.

"Away! As far as possible!" She downshifted into third and moved into the center lane to avoid a slowing cab.

"How about Brazil?"

"Perfect!"

"Then stop right here!" He pointed to a small café tucked between a string of bars and Southeast Asian restaurants. She made a U-turn and pulled into a red zone at the end of the block.

"I average four tickets a month, but it's cheaper than having some red-neck trucker back out my headlights."

Rhythmic music poured out of the Carioca Café and onto the sidewalk. Every table, inside and out, was filled. A smiling Brazilian gave her one of the two seats at the tiny bar near the kitchen, promising it would be only a few minutes for a place.

"You stop, and I'll catch up a little," she ordered. He asked the bartender to give her a *caipirinha*. That turned out to be a short little drink made from squashed limes and something she thought tasted like fusel oil. But it relaxed her enough to allow Jayson to join her in the second.

He took off his tie and hung his blazer on a hook on the wall. Waiters with large trays crashed past them every few seconds, forcing him to press close to her. She could feel his warmth against her thigh. She tried to think of something to talk about and failed. To avoid staring at the green flecks in his hazel eyes, Heidi watched a large round ceiling fan swing helplessly through the air. The whitewashed walls stenciled with primitive designs in primary colors vibrated to the disco upstairs. She drank in the strong smell of the cheroot that wafted over the soccer magazine being read by the heavyset man on the other stool.

Jayson had done the impossible; in a few short minutes she felt transported.

"On an impulse one afternoon," Lyman was saying, "I left work, went out to JFK, and after looking at all the flights on the Pan Am board, hopped a plane to Rio. From there I flew up to a little beach town, Búzios, and sat in the sun drinking *caipirinhas*. It means 'country bumpkin.' I stayed almost a week."

"Sounds wonderful." She could see herself on the beach with him.

"I was lonely as hell."

"I need to get away," Heidi said. "You know when you were a kid there was always a display at the museum explaining how fossils are formed. A cross section of the earth showing layer after geologic layer, the weight of whole mountains pressing down, turning flesh into stone."

"You feel like that?"

"That's Washington bureaucracy. Everything's immobile, heavy, torpid and lifeless. God! You could fuck your brains out in this town and never lose your virginity."

"Bad day?"

"The worst."

"Want to talk about it?"

"Absolutely not!"

"Then let's dance."

To Heidi, the dark upstairs room smelled like Africa. The pungent odor of grass-lined walls mingled with the sweat of the dancers. The rhythm of a dozen drums, gourds, single string basses, chimes, tin flutes and guitars filled her up, made her body move. The *cuica* insinuated, the *birimbau* insisted. Heidi found herself in motion without thinking. As she swayed under the swirling lights, her own eyes tightly shut, she began to perspire away the toxins of anger, disappointment and frustration. She caught Lyman staring at her undulating under the stiff linen skirt and blouse. She made her body work with his, using her clothes like a veil, hiding, yet suggesting and promising.

The music changed to Gilberto Gil's "Rains of March." Jay pulled Heidi to him. She could feel her nipples grow hard as her breasts pressed against him. It's been a long time, she thought, an awfully damn long time . . .

She did not know the Samba or whatever it was they danced, but his movements swept her along. Wherever he wanted to lead, she wanted to go. She could feel he had become aroused as he stepped between her legs, twirling her through the shafts of light from the ceiling. Heidi clung to him, the muscles in his back rippling under her hand. She felt dizzy and safe as if she had just escaped, but she did not know from what. From her rotten career? From Sean? How could she even think that about him. She wanted to cry, but only one tear reached the corner of her eye before Jay caught it and kissed it away. He then moved toward her lips.

What was she doing? She wasn't in Brazil. She was in downtown Washington D.C. and Sean Gordon's apartment was only six blocks away. She felt Jay's mouth on hers, and wanted to bite him, devour his tongue. Instead, she pushed him away.

Heidi shook her head violently. "Let's eat," she gasped. "I'm a little weak."

A table awaited them. He ordered Frango Gaucha, grilled chicken, with black beans and a chopped salad for both of them. They each drank crisp, sweet Brahma beer. She tried to come down to Earth. You don't permit this to happen, she lectured herself, with somebody you know nothing about. "We need to talk," she told him.

"You're right, I know almost nothing about you," he parried. "You wouldn't even tell me your name."

"I couldn't. I work for the Senate Intelligence Committee."

"You're a spy?"

"God, no! We monitor the spies, watch the watchers. But we have to use pseudonyms when we travel overseas on business. It's supposed to protect us from terrorists or something. I didn't want to use my funny name and then have to explain my real one. Heidi's real."

"She sure is."

She flushed. Stop acting like a teenager, she told herself, keep talking. "Don't you hate having to go through your past each time you meet someone you like?" she said. "Telling the same old stories. Covering up the gaps in time you don't want to talk about. Why can't we just get to know people from scratch? Everything comes out sooner or later."

"It's okay by me. I won't tell you why I'm divorced," Lyman said.

"Fine, and I won't explain why I'm not married."

"Then you won't hear how I grew up in Orange County, California, and how my mother sold our house out from under us every two years in a relentless effort to trade up socially."

"If that's the way you want it, then you'll hear nothing of my girlhood in Westport, Connecticut."

"Wait, that's going too far. You've got to tell me why Westport's considered artsy-craftsy when most of the residents are stockbrokers."

"You are naive." She stroked his cheek. " 'Artsy-craftsy' is Connecticut for Hebrew."

"How was I supposed to learn that at UCLA or Stanford B-School?"

"Is that why you came east?"

"No, I was a shitty surfer."

"And what have you done to compensate?"

"Misspent my youth making money."

"How?"

"Now that's a serious question"—he ordered two more beers—"and deserves a serious answer. By the instinctive ability to manipulate marginal personalities."

"Then I'm in trouble."

"I hope so. And now I get to ask you a question."

"Maybe."

"Who were the two guys you were walking with on the Boulevard St-Germain the night before last?"

"Oh!" she exclaimed in surprise. "You must be a spy yourself. One was French. He wants to meet you as a matter of fact. Owns a château in the Dordogne"—she knew she was rattling on—"says it would make a wonderful hotel, once it's restored."

"I'm a banker, not a philanthropist. And the other guy?" he pressed.

She hesitated, trying to find the right words. "An old friend," she finally said. "We worked together on the committee."

"Were you lovers?"

"You said one question," she replied with an edge.

"Sorry," he backed off.

"As a matter of fact, we still are."

Lyman looked like he had been punched in the stomach. "Like they say, there are no embarrassing questions. Only embarrassing answers." He tried to smile but failed.

Jesus, why did you do that? Heidi wondered. Because you want to talk to him about Sean. Because you're confused and you want him to understand. You want him to help you understand. She reached out and put her hand over his.

He withdrew it and stood up. Without another word he walked over to the bar, where she could see him paying the bill. He picked his jacket off the wall and returned to the table.

"You don't have to drive me back."

"Are you walking out?"

"No, I'll stay as long as you like."

"Can't we just be friends?"

"I am not a homosexual."

"We can still talk." She did not want the evening to end this way.

"About your work?"

"No, it's mostly classified," she admitted. "Your work?"

"No, that's inside information. I'd do more hard time revealing business secrets than you would for divulging national secrets."

She gave in. "All right, let's go."

"You sure you don't want coffee?"

"Yes."

They walked to the car in silence. She regretted what she had said, but could not tell him without explaining about Sean. And she couldn't explain. Sean had been so important to her and now Jay had come along. She felt like a slut.

"Look, I'm sorry," she said. "It's been a very bad day. I'd like to make it up to you somehow."

Lyman seemed hardly to hear her. He was lost in thought. Suddenly, he appeared to get an idea. "Yes." He acknowledged her offer. "No reason the evening should be a total waste. Could I ask a favor?"

"Sure."

"Can you get me the story on somebody?"

Heidi bristled. It was the worst fear of anyone with a top intelligence clearance. Was that why he had pursued her? "My job is to protect

Americans' privacy, not violate it," she said, trying not to sound as angry as she felt.

"It's not an American," Lyman persisted. "He's French. His name's Marcel Bresson."

I'm just a source of information to him, Heidi thought. She wanted to slap his face, but knew a better response.

"Is Bresson the man you met in Paris?"

She could see that Lyman immediately regretted mentioning his name. "You're right. It's a bad idea, forget it."

She opened the car door and got in without his help.

"Good night," she said.

"Good night."

She drove off. In the rearview mirror she could see him go back inside the Carioca Café.

7

Only two hours later, Lyman's phone rang.

Bresson is calling, reported a monitor somewhere in Lyman's unconscious brain. He was emerging from a deep cave. When he opened his eyes, they seemed covered with fur. His mouth felt like a thousand country bumpkins had marched through barefoot. He tried to talk, but found his lips were stuck together. His tongue was no help; it stuck to his lips. Isn't it wonderful, he thought as he picked up the phone, this is probably the best you're going to feel all day.

"I fear our deal is dead!" Bresson announced.

"What are you talking about?" Lyman mumbled.

"Have you read the *Journal?*"

"It's two in the morning."

"I have the *Financial Times.* I read you it. Headline, 'News/Worldweek Buyout.' "

"I'll be goddamned." Lyman was waking up fast.

"The article says, 'Drew Richardson, Chairman and Chief Executive Officer of News/Worldweek Inc., announced today in Washington D.C. that he heads a group of investors who will offer to buy the corporation's outstanding public shares and take the company private. The largest media conglomerate in the United States, News/Worldweek recently reported revenues of $7.8 thousand million for the fiscal year ending June thirty."

"No wonder he didn't want our help," Lyman muttered.

" 'The buyout group,' " Bresson continued, " 'known as N/W Holdings Two, will offer $36 per share, according to Mr. Richardson, who valued the total transaction at $6.3 thousand million.' "

"That's $6.3 billion," said Lyman.

" 'It is one of the largest buyouts this year,' " Bresson continued, " 'and the largest ever in the media industry. "We are offering a substantial premium to our shareholders, because we believe the market has not properly valued News/Worldweek for some time," Mr. Richardson said.'

" 'Yesterday the stock closed at $29.75 on the New York Stock Exchange. Members of the Nichols family, who own the largest blocks of stock, could not be reached for comment on the offer, and it is not known if they are part of the buyout group.'

" 'News/Worldweek owns—' *Alors,* you know the rest." Bresson stopped reading. "Our deal, it is finish?" His accent could not conceal his anxiety.

"Hell no! It's the best news we could get! He's trying to steal the company!"

"But he pays a substantial premium."

"Not in this market. Let's see," Lyman pulled an HP 270 calculator out of his briefcase. "Six dollars and change works out to only twenty percent over the market! And now we know why the company's been doing so poorly."

"Why?"

"Richardson's been running News/Worldweek into the ground. Half the management buyouts work that way. First the top executives let the company go to ruin to drive the stock down. Then they buy the company cheap, make a few fixes that they postponed all along, and surprise! They reissue stock at $40 or $50. Richardson will make a fortune for himself."

"How can you be so certain it will go up?"

"Marcel, I haven't been riding around in the back seat of my limo talking to my cigar. We've been crunching numbers on this deal. The asset value alone—you know, real estate, plant, equipment, cash reserves, receivables, overfunded pension plan, should be around $40 a share. This offer's a lowball."

"So, we have a chance?" Bresson still seemed uncertain.

"Absolutely. The company's in play."

"In play?"

Was this guy from the moon? Lyman wondered. "There's going to be some kind of transaction here. The arbs will rush to buy the stock—"

"Les arbres?" Bresson said in French.

"No, not trees," Lyman backed up. "Arbitrageurs. That's a French word, right?"

"No."

"Well, anyway, on Wall Street they make money by buying up the stock of companies that are takeover targets, hoping the deal goes through. By this time tomorrow the regular shareholders will have sold to the arbs and made a profit without waiting for Richardson's deal to close. Arbs aren't long-term investors: they'll want to get out as soon as possible and to the highest bidder. If they think Richardson's bid is too low, they could even bid the price up over his $36 offer, expecting someone else to come in at a higher price."

"Like us?"

"Not necessarily. Others could now come out of the weeds. You're going to have to move fast. Richardson will try to stampede the board. He's probably lined up key support. You've got to jump in now!"

"Perhaps," Bresson replied cautiously.

Lyman's spirit sank. Europeans. They were all pud-pounders at heart.

"I have another question first," Bresson said with deliberate calm. "Why would the Nichols family sell so cheaply?"

"They're probably part of the group," Lyman dismissed the question.

"If I were Monsieur Richardson, I would want that to be part of the announcement."

"You've got a point," Lyman said slowly. He hated himself when a client saw a crucial fact he had missed. It must be the hangover. Lyman tried to recover. "And if I were Richardson, would I go through all this trouble and still have the Nichols family on my back? He must be going for a freeze-out."

"So you talk to the Nichols, yes? Get them on our side. Then we meet."

"All right, I'll call you as soon—"

"No." Bresson cut him off. "You must minimize the telephone. We will meet."

"But the time factor—"

"I let you know where." The line went dead.

Lyman stared at the phone. He needed aspirin and water, but was afraid it might make him throw up. He thought of Heidi Bruce. It seemed to start so well, and then . . . Forget about her, he commanded, then rushed to the bathroom to drive the porcelain bus.

Lying back on the bed, Lyman tried to sleep, but questions circled endlessly through his mind. How was he to get the Nicholses "on our side"? What proposal was he supposed to make or even hint at? The

White Squire strategy had been dead on arrival. The prey turned out to be the hunter.

Baffled as to what he should do, Lyman sat up again and tried to call Bresson at the Dolder. The hotel operator in Zurich announced that he had checked out. No forwarding number. That sent another round of questions swirling through his head. How could Bresson do business this way? Why was he constantly moving? And how could he be so ignorant of some basic things, like the role of arbs, yet so in command of others? Like the fact that there were going to be "developments." That was classic inside information.

Nobody's perfect, Lyman reminded himself and lay back again. If Bresson knew everything, he wouldn't need you. So he wasn't familiar with the Anglo-American way of doing things. The financiers of continental Europe lived in a gentler world than their New York and London colleagues. The stock exchanges were smaller, less liquid, the financial instruments less varied and complex, the opportunities for takeovers far more rare. And, Lyman reminded himself, Bresson had failed when he tried to play the game in London. He managed to find some excuse for all of Bresson's peculiarities except how he got wind of the News/Worldweek buyout yesterday.

Just as he had drifted off to sleep, a thunderclap from a sudden storm outside his window made Lyman sit up. How was he going to get in touch with the Nichols family? He got up and thumbed through the Washington-area phone books. Plenty of Nicholses. None appeared to be the ones he wanted, Raphael Nichols or his sister Holly. She was a socialite and sometime political activist. "Raffy," as he was called by the press, was an artist who devoted his time to making papier-mâché animals. Neither of them took much interest in the company. Lyman was not sure they even spent full time in Washington.

He picked up the phone and called his office. A woman's tired voice answered.

"M and A."

"Jay here. How's it going?"

"It's quick and dirty, but we'll have an envelope of values by noon tomorrow."

"Great, only make that eight A.M. They don't have to be in stone. I only need talking numbers. Give me Rankin."

"He went home a couple hours ago."

"Chicken shit!" Lyman hung up and dialed Rankin's Greenwich, Connecticut number.

"Christ, I just got home!" Rankin protested. "It's almost three in the morning!"

"Goddamn it, this is crucial! You've got to go in and get the unlisted phone number book from retail sales. If it's locked away, wake up whoever. I need numbers for Holly and Raffy Nichols, by no later than seven."

"So I can sleep first and go in later."

"No! I also need you to monitor News/Worldweek's price on the London Exchange and let me know if it tops $36."

"Thirty-six dollars! What happened?"

"You assholes haven't been watching the ticker? Richardson's trying a self-tender. I want all wire stories faxed to me immediately here at the Four Seasons."

"What are you going to do?" Rankin had stopped complaining. He knew the fight was on.

"I wish I knew," Lyman answered honestly.

The Unlisted Telephone Number Book was a perfect invention of the information age. It had made a fortune for its creator, a stockbroker at E. F. Hutton who specialized in rich clients. He realized that almost all of his customers had unlisted numbers and that this must be true for other big-ticket brokers. If the private numbers of rich people were valuable to him, they would be valuable to others. So, together with colleagues on the Street, he put together the first unlisted number book, giving each source a piece of the action. The books were now sold by subscription, with quarterly updates on people who changed numbers in a futile effort to protect their privacy. The enterprise had grown to the point that it employed a dozen staff researchers, prying numbers out of NYNEX, AT&T, credit card companies, private clubs and other sources. The broker who started it now managed the effort full time and made more money than he ever did as a stock salesman.

Rankin found both Holly's and Raffy's unlisted numbers promptly and passed them to Lyman. He waited until 7:30 A.M. and then started dialing.

Holly proved hard to locate. A maid in Washington said to try her New York apartment. A maid in New York said to try her villa in Palm Beach. A maid in Palm Beach refused to say whether she was there, but informed him that she never answered phone calls before noon. If the matter was social, her secretary would be in at 10:30. If it was business, he should call Julian Alexander in Washington.

Raffy proved to be an easier case, but no more successful. The butler simply refused all calls.

"Mr. Nichols is taking none of your messages," he proclaimed.

None of them? Lyman wondered. "Who else has called?"

"Really, sir, you investment bankers are worse than the press. I've been instructed to tell you all to contact Julian Alexander."

So the sharks were circling. Other investment bankers had spotted the fact that the Nicholses were not mentioned and were trying to squeeze into the deal. Lyman checked his watch: it was shortly after 8 A.M. He called Alexander's office.

Lyman felt slightly intimidated, Julian Alexander was one of the most prominent lawyers in Washington. But he seldom tried cases, unless it were a special appeal to the Supreme Court. Having served off and on as a cabinet member in Republican as well as Democratic administrations for over thirty years, Alexander was no run-of-the-mill "fixer" either. He confined his practice to the delicate art of putting his clients in touch with those who were fixers. Washington had become so complex that influence peddlers had to specialize. It was not enough to know the right decision-maker, one had to know how to push his button. In short, Alexander sold access to those with access. His legal skills focused on keeping his own skirts clean.

The phone rang several times, then Lyman got a recording. At 8:30 he called again and reached a secretary.

"Mr. Alexander won't be in this morning," she explained. "No, he's not free for lunch either."

"It's extremely important. Can I make an appointment to see him this afternoon?"

"I'm afraid not. He's going straight out to Middleburg from the board meeting."

"The board meeting of News/Worldweek?" Lyman made a stab in the dark.

"What did you say your name was?" She suddenly became wary. He hung up.

Richardson's no fool, Lyman thought as he looked out on the growing volume of traffic on Rock Creek Parkway. He's making a losing bid and wants to lock up the board before anyone else has a chance to react. And what's to stop him?

He went into the bathroom and splashed cold water on his face.

Staring into the mirror, he saw a hungover, sleepless mess. If I could just get into the board meeting, Lyman decided, I could breathe on Richardson and maybe he'd die.

Heidi Bruce wanted to call in sick. But she knew the minority counsel and his friends would think it was because her project had been killed, and she would never give him that satisfaction. Besides, she was not ill, she was angry—not only about her work, but at herself.

She had been awful to Jay Lyman, had compounded it by turning paranoid when he'd asked for a simple favor. Heidi knew from her father that while Wall Streeters cursed Washington, they often blithely assumed the government should help them any way it could. And they had no sense of propriety when it came to money. Lyman hadn't planned to exploit her. He didn't even know she worked on intelligence until last night. He merely asked for information and she treated it like date rape.

Her life got worse as soon as she walked out of her basement apartment. She had forgotten to put the top up on the Fiat. The overnight thunderstorm had left it full of water. Her mood darkened further as she had to stand on Wisconsin Avenue for twenty minutes before catching a taxi. The driver managed to pick up three other passengers and detour through most of downtown Washington before dropping her at the Hart Senate Office Building.

She made her way up to the second-floor balcony overlooking the atrium, to room 211. The staff offices of the Senate Intelligence Committee consisted of "interior landscaping"—a series of cloth-covered partitions dividing up a long narrow room closed at the far end by a large vault. Heidi's cubicle was near the entrance where the staff director could keep an eye on her.

She sat down at a metal desk already covered with yellow phone slips. She didn't want to return the calls. They would all ask what happened to her Soviet economic counterintelligence bill. She had nothing to do except work on Terrorism IV. The staff had started numbering the hearings on terrorism like Rambo movies. They were produced as frequently and had as much impact on the real world.

Heidi thought about phoning Jay Lyman. But he probably had checked out. Why did she like him? Sean Gordon was mysterious and often remote, but he knew who he was. That strength made it hard for Heidi to stay away from him. Jayson was the opposite. He was needy, somehow unformed and still incomplete. She was drawn to him out of a feeling that she might make a difference in his life.

Then why had she treated him so badly, she wondered. And why was she treating Sean so badly? And why was everyone treating her so badly?

The phone rang. It was Sean.

"I just wanted to find out how you were," he said.

"I'm perfectly fine," she snapped.

"Don't take it out on me," he said evenly.

"Take out what?" she demanded.

"I don't know. I'm just trying to be your friend."

"Then why do I feel so claustrophobic?"

"Would you like me to stop asking to see you?"

"No."

"Heidi, what would you like me to do?"

She paused. "Find out all you can about Marcel Bresson."

Lyman easily swept past the guard at the News/Worldweek corporate offices by saying he was attending the board meeting. But the young executive-suite receptionist on the ninth floor proved more tenacious.

"Is Mr. Richardson expecting you?" she asked.

"I'm here for the board meeting," Lyman said, covering his nervousness with his most officious air.

She looked at a sheet of paper. "I don't see your name. What is your affiliation?"

"Gould Axewroth," he said, his tension growing. "Investment banker."

"Then you must be with the group in Conference Room C," she said, relieved that she did not have to challenge anyone who looked so rich and mean. "Down the corridor to the right," she directed. "Conference Room C."

One step at a time, Lyman cautioned himself, wondering where he was headed. He paused before the heavy walnut door marked with a carefully polished brass *C* and strained to hear what was happening on the other side. Would he be walking into the middle of the board meeting? What would he say then? No sound came to him. He grasped the large brass knob and opened the door.

It could have been a closing dinner at Christ Cella restaurant in New York. He knew almost every investment banker and lawyer in the room. Gathered in conspiratorial groups or sitting on the long rosewood table nibbling cheese danish, they waited to be called before the board to render advice. This was the holding pen for the financial and legal hired guns. They were all surprised to see him.

"What brings you here, Jay? If you're looking for a job, the Want Ad section's over on 15th Street." The greeting came from a managing partner of Kidder-Bache, News/Worldweek's traditional investment bankers.

"I heard you were here and dropped in to get my rocket polished," Lyman replied. "You in charge of this freak show?"

"Up to a point. We represent the company, as usual. Drexel-Stearns has Richardson and the buyout group." He gestured toward Blackford "Blackie" Muldoon, a sallow-faced young man with oily hair slicked straight back. "And the guys at Shearson-First Jersey are here for the outside directors. Who do you represent?"

"Bad news for Blackie." Lyman smiled at Richardson's investment banker. "And good news," Lyman continued, "for the shareholders."

"You've got a better offer?" Blackie challenged him. He had the desiccated look of someone who jogged too much.

"We think Richardson's offer is fair," chimed in the managing partner of Shearson Lehman Hutton First Jersey. As advisor to the outside directors, he was supposed to protect the interests of the shareholders.

"Was it your firm that wrote the fairness opinion in the Gibson Greeting Card deal? You told the Directors of RCA that $80 million was a fair price for selling the greeting-card company. Then a year later the buyers turned around and sold it to the public for how much? A hundred forty-five million? Are you going to write another fairness opinion like that on this deal?"

They had all gathered around him. "What do you want?" several said at once.

"To talk to the board. I have a client who is also interested in acquiring News/Worldweek."

"You're too late," Blackie smiled. "We've already made our presentation and the board's discussing it."

"If you refuse to hear from another bidder"—he turned to the lawyers—"you've got a sure-fire lawsuit on your hands." With no bid in his pocket, Lyman knew he was hovering on the margins of fraud himself. But he was getting their attention. "Not hearing me out would be negligence," he insisted. "Don't think your indemnification arrangements will protect you."

Everyone in the room knew that most mergers, buyouts and takeovers were accompanied by a blizzard of lawsuits. Investment banks, whose net worth was often only a fraction of the size of the deals, protected themselves by having the clients assume responsibility for any legal claims and damages. Except for gross negligence.

"He's got a point." One of the lawyers spoke up. The other legal advisors began to nod in agreement. One of them picked up a phone and dialed an extension. Lyman could not hear the conversation but he could tell it was heated. The man hung up, and then introduced himself as News/Worldweek's Washington counsel.

"The board will be happy to talk to you," he reported.

As the lawyer led Lyman out the door and down the hall, Blackie shouted after him. "Jay, you'd better have something in your briefcase besides your lunch."

They were not buying it. Lyman could feel the hostility and resentment before he started to speak, and it went downhill from there. He told them that the buyout offer had a lower premium than any acquisition in the media industry in the last ten years. There was no response. He claimed that the News/Worldweek shareholders would be receiving less, for each dollar of sales or profit, than the shareholders of any other Fortune 500 company sold in the last year. No response. He pointed out that Richardson's price was less than the asset value of the company. He aimed that argument directly at Julian Alexander, who represented the Nichols family interests.

Alexander responded. "We know we could get a higher price for the company's assets if we broke it up, if we liquidated. But why would we want to destroy a great American corporation? We have an obligation to the stockholders, to be sure, but also to our employees and the communities in which we operate and those which we serve. Indeed,"—Alexander rolled out his hypnotizing cadences—"we have an obligation, as a member of the free press in a free society, that goes beyond our stockholders to the entire American people! We do not have to dismember this fine institution in order to grub for the last dollar."

There were assents all around.

"But my client has no intention of breaking up the company," Lyman protested.

"And just who is your client?" the vice chairman demanded.

"I'm not at liberty to say, unless the board is prepared to consider our offer."

"Then what is your offer?"

"I approached Mr. Richardson yesterday. He gave me no indication that he planned his own bid in the afternoon. Nor did he say there would be a meeting today to consider it. We want an opportunity to make an orderly presentation to the board early next week."

Richardson finally spoke up. "So, you want this board to delay action on a bona fide offer when there's no buyer? And no other bid?"

"When your price falls far short of the value of this company, yes."

"But you've no offer that proves that, do you?" Richardson gave him an indulgent smile.

"I suggest we waste no more time on this matter," the vice chairman said. "Good day, Mr. Lyman."

He stood there awkwardly for a moment, then had no choice except to leave. Can't beat something with nothing, he tried to console himself as he walked back down the corridor to the receptionist's desk.

She smiled brightly and handed him a telephone message. It was from Rankin. Lyman read it, turned sharply around, and dashed back toward the boardroom. He did not bother to knock.

"Gentlemen," Lyman announced. The directors spun around in their chairs. "Mr. Richardson asked for a higher price. Well in London, News/Worldweek stock has edged past his offer of $36, proving that the market believes in a higher bid!"

"Wait a minute, what's the dollar doing in London today?" the chief financial officer asked.

"I don't know," Lyman admitted.

"Then it's probably a foreign exchange arbitrage."

Most of the board looked baffled.

"Okay, let's make it simple." Lyman snapped open his briefcase. "The New York Stock Exchange opens in less than ten minutes." He took out a small black device that looked like a hand-held portable radio. "I'll leave my Quotrek right here." He pulled up the antenna and set the machine on the table. "If News/Worldweek's stock doesn't open above Mr. Richardson's $36-a-share offer, I apologize for bothering you. If it goes over $36, the market's saying this is a punk deal, and I want the chance to make another offer by Wednesday."

Lyman took a seat out by the receptionist where he could see down the corridor. He tried to relax. He had done all he could. Unbuttoning his jacket, he straightened his tie, then pulled at his pants leg to ease the pressure on the crease. He checked his watch. Only two minutes had elapsed. He tried again to relax. It didn't work. Maybe he should check with Rankin. What if the chief financial officer was right? If Rankin used the wrong exchange rate, the stock, which was quoted in pounds in London, might not convert to more than $36. He jumped up and asked the receptionist if he could use the phone.

"Is it a local call?"

"No."

"Sorry, it's against company policy."

"But this is important!" Lyman tried not to shout.

"I'm sure it is, sir. But these phones won't take outgoing long-distance. There's a pay phone by the candy stand on the first floor."

He sat down again and stared at his watch. It read ten o'clock. But he always set it fast, and then forgot by how much. The receptionist said it was around ten.

Suddenly, at six minutes after ten, the entire mass of financial and legal advisors poured out of Conference Room C and into the board room. Lyman's heart leapt. Something had happened. But as the minutes dragged by, he began to fear that the market had failed him. Then he got another signal. A black man in a white serving jacket came down the hall and removed a sign from the receptionist's desk that read BOARD LUNCHEON IN CONFERENCE ROOM B. They had canceled the lunch! Was that good news or bad? Two minutes later, the boardroom disgorged its assembled directors, investment bankers, attorneys, and executives.

The departing members of the board filed past Lyman without looking at him, except Julian Alexander, who smiled courteously. Did that mean he had lost? Had the board voted to accept Richardson's offer? Lyman was starting to feel slightly desperate. Then Blackie shouted down the hall, "Okay, Jayson, you get your meeting!"

"Where did the stock open?" he called back in triumph, but Blackie had disappeared into the recesses of the executive suite.

The chief financial officer appeared beside him and handed back his Quotrek machine.

"The stock's at $38 and rising."

"Let's have a picnic."

"Sean, that's very sweet, but . . ."

"It will get you out of that cave you work in and ease your claustrophobia."

"I'm just not in the mood," Heidi said.

"I've got something to tell you," Sean Gordon insisted.

They met in the parking lot between the Tidal Basin and the National Library of Annals—flower beds of every variety that were planted on the gentle slope that ran down from Independence Avenue. Sean had brought sandwiches from the French Market in Georgetown, Heidi, a cooler containing four cold bottles of Clausthaler, a nonalcoholic beer. Long ago they had agreed not to drink at lunch unless they could go to bed afterward.

"Let's rent a paddle boat," Sean said, pointing to the boat house on the Tidal Basin.

"You must have some very interesting information," Heidi noted. To the eye, the Tidal Basin sits in a bucolic setting of river and parkland. But to the ear, it is one of the noisiest spots in Washington. Bordered on one side by I-95, the terminus of three bridges over the Potomac, and square in the traffic pattern of National Airport, the Tidal Basin was renowned as a place to hold an open-air conversation without fear of being monitored.

They got on the paddle boat and spread the lunch on the console between them. Sean steered the boat toward the Jefferson Memorial on the opposite shore.

"Why do you want to know about Marcel Bresson?" he asked, bringing the boat to a halt in the middle of the Basin.

"And why do you want to know why?" She took a bite out of her paté sandwich.

"You didn't exactly go through channels, Heidi. I think I deserve some explanation for sticking my neck out." He opened the Clausthaler.

"A friend of mine needs to know."

"So it's not a committee inquiry."

"God! You're so bureaucratic all of a sudden!"

"Do I know this 'friend'?" Sean pressed.

"He's someone I met recently. A buddy, and that's all."

Sean looked like he did not believe her. "I'm not asking you because I'm jealous."

It was Heidi's turn to look skeptical.

"I'm just trying to protect you." His tone had turned professional: quiet, soft and deadly.

She knew he was serious. "My friend, he's thinking of doing some business with Bresson," she explained. "I can't tell you more."

"Well, he ought to forget it. And don't ask me why. I can't tell you either."

"Why?" she asked anyway, her concern growing.

"Because I don't know any of the specifics."

"Sean, you've never played games. You always level. What is this?"

"All I know is that his name is tagged in the central files," Gordon relented.

"That could mean anything. It doesn't have to be bad. What does his dossier say?"

"There isn't any."

Heidi stopped eating as she tried to fathom what that meant.

"All his files are held by the operating desks," he added.

"You could look at them."

"I don't know what offices hold them." Exasperation was creeping into his voice. "I don't have clearance to find out. And if you asked for his file officially, they'd probably send you a folder full of newspaper clippings and deny the existence of anything else. Your only chance would be a committee subpoena. Even then . . ." He paused, "Heidi, I don't know who he is, but this guy's hot."

She started pushing hard on the pedals. "Come on, help me," she pleaded. "I've got to get to a phone."

"It's the old Wall Street story," Lyman was lecturing Rankin. "Bulls make money. Bears make money. Pigs get nothing." He stood in the aisle of the Pan Am Shuttle talking into the airphone. He was still high from his performance at the News/Worldweek board meeting. Rankin used the speakerphone so the whole office could hear Lyman's report.

"I'm beat," he continued. "As soon as I land, I'm going straight to my apartment, run around the Reservoir a couple times and hit the sack. Don't wake me unless Bresson calls."

Lyman could make out the voice of his secretary shouting in the background, "He's on the other line now."

"Put us together."

"I don't know if I can do that," Rankin said. "The phones can't—"

"Over a million goddamn dollars for telephones and you can't put two calls together." Lyman had attracted the attention of the passengers in the seats around him as well as the stewardess. She asked him to sit down.

"Relax, Jayson," his secretary came on the line. "We'll call him back. Hold on."

Lyman bit into the bagel he had been served as a snack. A trace of blood was left on the crust. My God, my gums are bleeding, he thought. I'm going to lose all my teeth.

"Jayson, you have the news from the persons you were to contact?" Bresson started right in as usual.

He's talking about the Nicholses, Lyman realized. "No, no, I didn't have time—"

"When you work for me, you find the time."

Fuckhead, Lyman thought, but he got paid not to get angry. "That's all obsolete, overtaken by events." He then explained what happened at the board meeting, with neither comment nor compliments from his client.

"I saved the deal," Lyman emphasized. Bresson still did not react. "We've got until Wednesday. As soon as I'm on the ground, I'll start—"

"Where are you?" Bresson demanded.

"I'm calling from a plane."

"Are you mad? The whole world listens to us! Come here at once."

"Where's that?"

"Bürgenstock." He hung up.

Rankin was still on the line. "A real sweetheart," he said.

"Well, you're going to grow to love him. Meet me at the JFK helipad with tickets to wherever the hell Bürgenstock is. Bring all your analyses."

"You also got hot calls from Heidi Bruce and Cooke," his secretary added.

So she was still on the hook after all! He felt another surge of triumph. But this time, he would be the one who was hard to get. "Get back to her and say I'll call from the airport, or Europe or somewhere."

"What about Cooke? He said things are comin' apart. He's about to be stabbed inna back."

"Tell him to hold this shit-eating firm together until I get the deal done. Think you can say that?"

"Sure." She seemed positively eager.

"An' explain to him something else." Lyman adopted her accent. "On Wall Street, bein' stabbed inna back is death by natural causes."

9

"That's Bürgenstock," Rankin said, startling Lyman who had been dozing fitfully in the back seat of the rented Mercedes-Benz 560 SEL. "There's supposed to be three hotels up on top."

Lyman caught only a glimpse of a massive granite slab rising ominously more than two thousand feet above the south shore of the lake before the divided highway plunged into a long tunnel that ran under the city of Lucerne. He had refused Bresson's offer of a helicopter from the Zurich airport, hoping to get a couple of hours sleep on the road. But he was so keyed up, his mind refused to stop churning.

Somehow the News/Worldweek takeover had become the fulcrum of his future. Lyman now wanted to do the deal; thwarting Richardson put a taste of blood in his mouth. And Rankin's numbers showed the deal was doable. Moreover, as much as he hated to admit it, Cooke had maneuvered him into a tough spot. His reputation could be wrecked if Gould Axewroth collapsed because his transaction fell apart. Lyman was proud of living on his wits, but one of the problems, he knew, is that you're only as good as your last deal.

Or your last client. Lyman realized that his eagerness to do the deal put him at a disadvantage with Bresson. And whether he was crashing down from his success in Washington, or suffering normal jet-lag depression, Lyman faced this second meeting with Bresson with a sense of foreboding.

What surprises would he have in store? Could Lyman convince him to open up his books? Would he agree on strategy, tactics, and above all, price? Even more important, did he have the credit to complete the transaction? Finally, Lyman would insist Bresson pay his firm a lot more money, but would he? Lyman had proven himself; now, he decided, it was Bresson's turn.

The car burst out of the tunnel into the blazing alpine morning. Towering mountains surrounded them on three sides.

"Kind of teaches a man humility, doesn't it?" Rankin said in awe.

Lyman liked Rankin, but sometimes he seemed too nice for the deal business. "Maybe," he replied. "But in the Swiss, humility usually comes out as small-mindedness."

As the car turned off the *autoroute* and climbed the switchbacks past the farms that dotted the hillsides behind Bürgenstock, Lyman wondered why the Swiss were so highly regarded for hygiene. They were the only civilized country where people and livestock still lived under one roof.

The three nineteenth-century hotels that lined the top of the mountain were a world away from the farmers' *schali* below. The Grand, the Ritz and the Excelsior were survivors of Europe's golden age. The lobby of the Grand displayed ornate crystal chandeliers, gilded moldings complete with cherubs, trompe l'oeil ceiling paintings, walls covered with tapestry, broad oriental carpets on marble floors and furniture upholstered in petit point. The place made Lyman sneeze.

"This is really something," Rankin exclaimed.

"Yeah, it's not often you get to see what caused most of the revolutions of the twentieth century."

Edouard was waiting for them. While the bellman took the luggage to their rooms, he escorted Lyman and Rankin to the Spa Club next door for a meeting with Marcel Bresson. The spa proved to be a touch of Las Vegas in the Alps. Edouard led them through a tunnel lined with pink stucco illuminated by off-yellow sconces. As a chrome and brass high-speed elevator propelled them up through hundreds of feet of rock, Lyman took an inventory. He felt anxious, depressed and hyper—just right, he judged, for an encounter with Bresson.

They stepped out onto a terrace restaurant. To one side, a huge swimming pool complete with its own island looked out over tranquil cow pastures and in the distance, a forested mountainside. On the other, half of Switzerland seemed spread out before them, the fingers of Lake Lucerne forming a series of bays and peninsulas, the white wake of ferry boats pointing the way from Vitznau to Weggis and from Merlischachen to Lucerne. On the horizon, Lyman saw the glint of the Zugersee and the haze that shrouded Zurich.

Bresson was dangerously cheerful as he waved them over with his pink *Financial Times.* "You have read the statement of the News/Worldweek?" he smiled.

Lyman shook his head.

" 'A spokesman for the board,' " Bresson began to read, " 'said that in view of the unsettled market for the company's stock, they would postpone consideration of Mr. Richardson's proposal until next week. Mr. Richardson was reported to be revising his offer.' Not a mention of us." He almost beamed.

"We were lucky," Lyman cautioned him. "It's not often the arbs overbid an offer, even a fraud like this one."

"It was not luck, *au contraire!*" Bresson exclaimed. "I bought four and a half million shares at the opening bell in London and another ten million in New York!"

Lyman blinked twice. When would he stop underestimating this man? "Then I guess the Jews are fat."

Bresson looked baffled, then snorted, *"Les jeux sont faits!* Exactly. The bets are down!"

As the waiter served lunch, Lyman introduced Rankin and outlined his plans. Bresson took no interest in Rankin and seemed to disagree with everything Lyman proposed.

"Why do we make a presentation? I do not want to appear before that board until it is mine," Bresson said.

"I thought I would do it."

"You think they like you so much after ruining their plans? No," Bresson said flatly. "I see no reason to subject our offer to the cross-examinations of corporate bureaucrats. And why do we wait until Wednesday?" Bresson demanded. "That is what News/Worldweek expects!"

"There's a lot of work involved—" Lyman tried to explain.

"We attack on Monday!"

"Will you have time to work the details with us?"

"Of course. Rest assured."

But by the time the wild strawberries arrived for dessert, they had agreed on nothing else, and Bresson dismissed further discussion of strategy and tactics by proclaiming, "All that should be addressed with my staff."

Lyman decided to change his approach. As the coffee was served, he asked "Marcel, when do we get into the fun part and start talking numbers?"

"You mean the price I will pay? I assume you have a recommendation."

Lyman nodded slowly, silently rehearsing how he would present the $7.4 billion valuation Rankin had developed.

"Good," said Bresson simply. "Discuss it also with my staff." He rose to leave.

"One more thing," Lyman added quickly, his frustration evident. "We need to look at your books."

Bresson sat down again.

"We've got to file a lot of documents with the SEC, the FTC and the Justice Department. We won't put in anything that you don't want, but we've got to exercise some due diligence."

"What is that?" His tone was skeptical, unyielding.

"The filings have to describe your business, and we've got to be able to stand behind those statements," he said firmly. "Richardson will probably sue both of us."

"What do you need to see?"

"I could start with your consolidated financial statements"—Rankin spoke for the first time—"and if I have any questions, I can dig deeper."

Bresson and Lyman both looked at him sharply.

"But it's not an audit or anything," Rankin quickly added.

Bresson sighed. The wind had picked up. It was blowing down from the mountain toward the lake, carrying the smell of cow manure. "I do not have what you call the consolidated financial statement for my companies," he explained.

Rankin shot Lyman a worried look that said, don't give up on this one.

"But I have records," Bresson admitted at last. "They are either here or can be accessed by the computer. *Bon appétit.*"

Lyman felt a wave of relief.

"When can we start?" Rankin asked eagerly.

"We thought you were to arrive by helicopter. My staff has awaited you in the salon of the hotel," he checked his watch, "for three hours. They are still there." He rose again to leave.

Under the circumstances, Lyman decided that was not the opportune moment to raise the idea of increasing his fee. But for the first time Lyman began to feel good about the deal. He could work with Bresson.

That judgment proved premature, at least as far as Bresson's staff was concerned. They all had inexplicable and fancy titles like Director of Planification and Chief of Executive Direction or Manager of Financial Administration, but they all seemed to defer to the accountant named Maurice, who looked like a dog-faced gangster. As soon as New York was awake, Maurice allowed Lyman to hire Skadden Fried to be their lawyers and McFadden Dworkin to do their public relations, but that was where cooperation stopped.

The staff wasted hours pondering theoretical moves by Richardson and the board of directors that were unlikely to happen. No detail was too small to provoke intense debate, the language of the letter of offer, whether there should be outs or deadlines, the specifics of all the filing material, the points to emphasize in the press release. All chance of systematic deliberation was destroyed by repeated conference calls with the lawyers and PR types in New York. Drafts of the letter and press release along with backup material for the spokesman at McFadden Dworkin flashed back and forth across the Atlantic via modems and fax machines. Lyman found himself holding three negotiations at once. All to little result.

Despite his promise, Bresson was generally unavailable, having left Bürgenstock to spend Saturday night in Zurich at the Hotel Baur au Lac. The only time Lyman managed to get through was to persuade him to give Rankin access to more files. In his absence, Lyman tried to get as much consensus as possible, while leaving open anything with which he disagreed until Bresson returned Sunday night. That strategy seldom worked.

Bresson's people did not shrink from exercising judgment in matters about which they were completely ignorant. At one point, the law firm, Skadden Fried, raised the possibility of seeking an injunction to bar any News/Worldweek company from printing stories about Marcel Bresson on the grounds that it would be prejudicial to the transaction. The PR firm strongly opposed the idea because it would make Bresson look like an enemy of a free press and guarantee bad stories in other American media. Lyman sided with the PR people, but Maurice, the accountant, overruled him.

The most serious argument centered on the price and structure of the deal. Bresson's staff challenged Lyman's assumptions. They questioned his projections. They criticized his models and rejected his analysis. After six hours, Lyman had had enough.

"Look," he said bluntly to Maurice the accountant, "do you guys have some other numbers?"

He said nothing. The others also remained silent.

"Then if you can't accept my price," Lyman added, "I can only conclude one thing."

"What is that?" Maurice said slowly.

"You haven't got the money."

That shut them up. But it was only temporary, Lyman knew. The showdown would come in the final meeting with Bresson.

If Lyman was frustrated with Bresson's staff, he was impressed with his facilities. He had taken over both the Spa and the Grand Hotel, turning several of its public rooms into offices. The solarium, where gentle ladies usually sipped afternoon tea, had been reconfigured into a conference room equipped with giant screens and speakers for Mitsubishi audio and video teleconferencing. The bar had become the computer room and communications center. Four terminals were tied into an IBM 350. Rank Xerox had installed two X-2160 publishing stations. Thompson CSF had provided their Zeus system, AT&T-compatible with 150 channels for voice, data and video. These lines also supported a half-dozen Quotrons, the Reuters News Service, the Dow Jones Wire, AP, UPI, and Agence France Presse.

TV sets in every room were tuned to either CNN Europe or the Continental Edition of the Financial News Network. The road outside the hotel was partially blocked by three huge trailers crammed with electronic gear and sprouting antennas. One had been leased from the Swiss postal authorities, another was Bresson's own telecommunications van, and the third, Lyman had been informed, was for "backup." A battery of secretaries speaking three languages attended their every need except one, and Lyman was too exhausted for that.

He tried to nap in the sauna or under the prying fingers of the masseur, but his only real sleep came in the spa when he took an herbal wrap. Lyman was wound tightly in twenty yards of hot wet muslin that had been soaked in a broth of Ceylonese tea, hibiscus flowers, rose hips, chicory root and blackberry leaves. Then he was tucked away in a dark damp room for an hour. He dreamed of being reborn as a plant.

By early Sunday night, the preparations had deadlocked. Lyman was convinced that unless Bresson took firm decisions at the evening meeting, there would be no takeover. And unless the right decisions were made, Lyman vowed, they could launch the deal without him.

When Bresson and an entirely new retinue swept into the hotel at 8:15 P.M., Lyman finally figured out the game. Bresson had turned him into staff. He had established his superiority and exercised control by being absent. He made Lyman run the gauntlet of his junior staff, and now, Bresson and his senior associates would deign to consider their differences.

The meeting was arranged as a formal dinner in the Edouard VII Room. Bresson took the head of the table with Lyman on his left. A Herr Doktor Sperile Beck sat on Bresson's right. Lyman did not try to remember the names of the other new faces.

White-gloved waiters in livery stood at the ready behind each guest. The table service was gold, as were the battery of knives, forks and spoons that flanked each place setting. Portraits of William Tell, Bruder Klaus, Kaiser Wilhelm, Queen Victoria and Edward VII gazed down on them as the waiters served a half-dozen courses, three wines and champagne. Lyman refused the wine, and hardly noticed the food. For him the deal was the meal.

After dessert, Bresson asked him to begin. Lyman paused to accept a torpedo-shaped cigar. He clipped off the point, and held the fat end over a candle as he started his presentation.

"We've prepared a letter of offer and a press release. The bid can be in Richardson's hands tomorrow morning if we can agree tonight"—he stopped to take several quick puffs on his cigar—"on the price.

"At the same time," Lyman continued, "a 13D would be filed with the Securities and Exchange Commission revealing that you hold 8.3 percent of News/Worldweek stock. That'll show you're serious, and it's required by law anyway. Our lawyers have prepared a suit to enjoin Richardson's revised buyout whenever it's offered. They also are positioned to enjoin News/Worldweek from writing about you, but I think we need to talk about that further. My staff's at work on the Hart-Scott-Rodino filings with the goal of announcing a tender offer, if necessary, by the middle of the week." Lyman was amazed that he had not yet been interrupted.

"It'll be a classic 'swipe.' Our strategy will be a bear hug." He started to become expansive. "We'll offer to buy News/Worldweek on a friendly basis. If they don't go for it, we make clear we'll hit with an all-cash tender offer."

That's as far as Lyman got.

"Why don't we wage a proxy fight?" One of the unknowns challenged him. He had a vaguely Scandinavian accent. "That's a much less expensive way to gain control of the board than buying all the stock."

"True. That's why they've become popular again. But there's a low success rate. Most raiders do it to harass the management into buying back their stock at a premium. Besides, a proxy contest is a political battle. With all due respect, Drew Richardson will hold the advantage, including the Nichols family blocks, if this deal degenerates into a political fight."

Bresson looked around the table. No one else had more to say. He nodded almost imperceptibly. Lyman had won the first round.

But that was the easy one. Now he turned to the question of price.

"We have evaluated News/Worldweek from every conceivable

angle, bearing in mind," he stressed, "that we don't have access to their inside numbers."

Lyman motioned to the waiters to hand out the four-inch black binders stacked on a table at the end of the room. He had ordered Rankin to stuff them with every scrap of paper even remotely related to the deal. There were fifty pages of meaningless graphs charting the historical price movements of the stocks of companies used as comparisons with News/Worldweek. There were yards of fold-out spreadsheets projecting different cash flows based on alternative assumptions. Half of each book consisted of virtually unreadable photocopies of publicly available corporate documents, the 10K, the 10Q, the annual report, the last proxy statement, the most recent shelf registration filing, notice of shareholders meetings, and other irrelevancies. The binders looked impressive, and Lyman was betting that no one would try to read them at the table. No one did.

But that did not save him from Maurice the accountant.

Lyman was in the midst of dazzling them with the sophistication and complexity of the computer analysis, when Maurice interrupted in his brandy-soaked voice. "Why don't you just tell them the number?"

The entire group looked at him expectantly.

"Seven point four billion."

"*Mon Dieu!*"

"*Gott im Himmel!*"

"Impossible!"

"That includes the $600 million you've already spent," Lyman added.

All those at the table began muttering and shaking their heads, except, Lyman noted, Bresson and Herr Doktor Beck.

For the next twenty minutes, he fielded a barrage of questions.

"How can you compare News/Worldweek with other companies," someone asked, "when there are none like it?"

"It's a question of size," Lyman replied. "We found other companies with a similar mix of businesses and scaled them up. We also took News/Worldweek apart and priced each business, both according to market and cash flow."

"But we do not want to take it apart, the company," another said.

"That was a test," Lyman said with forced patience, "to make sure we were within the envelope. The $7.4 billion is well inside."

They continued to peck away. "What if there's a recession? What happens to your projections?"

"We looked at the firm's relative performance in other downturns." And it went on.

"How can your valuation be so different from Richardson's price?"

"I am not a crook."

"How do we know the company hasn't got some big problem we don't know about?"

"We don't. But with Richardson trying to buy it, a hidden asset's more likely." Out of the corner of his eye, Lyman saw Herr Doktor Beck nod and Bresson smile.

Then Maurice the accountant rose to his feet to ask a question. "When you discounted back the cash flow to get a present value, how did you derive your interest rate assumptions?"

Lyman turned to Bresson. "Marcel, I have been through all of these issues, and more, with your staff. Several times. If you want to accept their analysis, be my guest. Your only problem is that you'll end up offering *less* than Richardson. Innovative, I admit. Sure to sow confusion."

"What is your price?" Bresson asked.

"Forty-two fifty a share," he replied coolly. "And that brings me to a question I have for you. How do you plan to pay for this acquisition?"

For the first time, Lyman heard Bresson laugh. It sounded like a dog bark. "Beck," he gasped, "answer him."

The Herr Doktor did not seem to see any joke. "The Swiss Bank Corporation guarantees the financing."

"At what interest rate?" Lyman insisted. "We've assumed one point over LIBOR. But is it two? That's the key to whether you'll beat Richardson. If your money's cheaper than his, you can pay more." Lyman stopped to crush out his cigar. "Marcel, this is your first hostile deal, so let me explain what's going to happen. In the next several weeks, we'll all go through the wringer. We'll change strategy and tactics a dozen times. We'll maneuver in the courts and fight in the financial pages. We'll try every trick we can think of. But in the end, winning will come down to one thing."

"And what is that?" Bresson asked.

"Money. Will you pay the highest price?"

"Forty-two dollars and fifty cents per share is acceptable," Sperile Beck said. "And if Monsieur Bresson must raise his offer, the Swiss Bank Corporation will guarantee whatever he needs."

10

The polite applause and extra round of brandy did not permit Lyman to relax. Even as Bresson signed the letter of offer with a flourish of his fat Mont Blanc pen, Lyman was readying himself for his toughest test.

"Could we speak privately for a moment," Lyman asked Bresson as he handed the letter to a secretary to fill in the numbers. She would give it to a Eurocourier messenger, and by 9:00 A.M. Washington time, the letter would be on Richardson's desk.

Bresson wanted Lyman to step out onto the balcony. The night was clear with a slight breeze. A necklace of lights outlined the contour of the lake. The bright moon illuminated the rocky peaks of the Alps to the left and right. As Lyman looked down, the cliff seemed to drop straight to the black water a quarter-mile below.

"It's a good package, Marcel."

"Yes, I am content with it."

"But it's not the deal you hired me to do."

"You want what you asked for in Paris? *Très bien,* prepare the document for my signing."

"I've taken the liberty . . ." Lyman pulled a three-page letter from his jacket and passed it to him. Bresson held it out at arm's length and drew out his glasses, tilting them so he could see better in the dim light. The breeze picked up and ruffled the pages. Lyman could imagine his $60 million engagement letter floating down into Lake Lucerne.

"And everything is finished?"

"Not everything. Rankin's still working on some of the filings. We won't need them for a few days. And of course we don't have a deal."

Bresson stopped reading, distracted by dinner guests preparing to depart. "I'll look at it, but excuse me. I have to say good-bye to Herr Beck." He folded the letter haphazardly and stuffed it into his pocket.

Lyman stood alone on the balcony. Seething. He had made a beginner's blunder. How often had he told his junior associates always get the client to sign the fee letter first.

Sitting in his underwear on the edge of the huge Biedermeier bed, Lyman fought against the paranoia that came with exhaustion. Of course Bresson would sign the contract. He needed Lyman to execute the deal. Having not been in a bed for three days, Lyman realized that fatigue was clouding his judgment. He had reached the point where he could make deal-breaking mistakes.

He should sleep. But instead, he wanted to call Heidi Bruce. Hadn't he played hard-to-get long enough? Typical, he admonished himself, you've been submerged in the deal, and now, when you think something's gone wrong, you want to talk to her. But she called urgently last week! All right, he conceded, if you must call, go ahead. But do yourself a favor. Don't let her know that you need her.

On the third ring, a man answered.

"No, it's not a wrong number," he said. "Heidi, it's for you."

"Hello."

"Who's that guy?" Lyman demanded.

"Jay, it's you, thank God!"

"That's your boyfriend!"

"I really need to talk to you," she continued.

"I hope I didn't interrupt anything."

"Don't be silly," she said. "I wanted to tell you about Bresson."

Lyman's stomach turned cold. "What about him?"

"Don't have anything to do with him."

"Great! That's all I needed to hear. Why?"

"You just have to trust me," Heidi insisted.

"And where did you get this bit of inside information?" he retreated into sarcasm. "From your boyfriend?"

"I can't tell you."

"Thanks for trusting me," he said bitterly. "Do you really think I'm going to crater a deal that might save my firm, that's worth almost $20 million to me *personally* because of some vague stuff coming from a man who has every incentive to cut my throat?"

"Jay, it's coming from me."

"And where are you at six thirty in the morning? I'm sorry if I woke the two of you up!"

"It's six thirty in the *evening,* Jayson! Sean's just helping me carry in groceries from the car. And it's none of your damned business."

"Oh," he said mortified. "I'm sorry. Really. Forgive me. I'm burned out and this isn't exactly good news."

She melted, a sucker for a man who knew how to apologize.

"Never mind that, just take it seriously."

"We'll talk about it. I'll be back in New York tomorrow. Can you fly up for dinner?"

Lyman heard her cover up the mouthpiece and exchange words with Sean.

"I've made some commitments," she said, coming back on the line.

"Heidi, I need more to go on. I've already gone pretty far here." He stopped just short of pleading.

"I'll see what I can do," she said. "Call me when you land."

Inside the backup van in the hotel driveway one of the young secretaries who had been helping Lyman removed a set of earphones, swiveled her chair to the typewriter and propped up her dictation notebook beside it. She began to type.

Sunday: 00:23 hrs.
Call placed by Jayson Lyman to the United States (202) 555-6053.
    Man's Voice: Hello.
    M. Lyman: I must have the wrong number.
    Man's Voice: No, it's not a wrong number. Heidi, it's for you . . .

Five minutes later, she finished the transcript, placed it in an envelope and handed it to Edouard.

Lyman slept like a stone. The only thing good about his dreams was that he could not remember them when the phone rang at 7:30 the next morning. It was Rankin.

"We gotta talk."

"I'm asleep."

"Then wake up. It's serious."

"What, what, what!" he had not slept off his anger at Bresson.

"I've managed to consolidate all of Bresson's balance sheets and income statements."

"I'm proud of you," Lyman said on the verge of sleep again. "You get the Raccoon of the Year award." Lyman called his analysts raccoons because they all had circles under their eyes and only came out at night. "So?"

"So this guy doesn't make any money," Rankin said flatly.

"You're hallucinating." Lyman was coming awake. "You need sleep."

"Right. But that won't change the numbers in my trusty Compaq. I've checked 'em backwards and forwards."

"You mean just this last year, he didn't make money. That's not so bad. A lot of firms had trouble—"

"I mean," Rankin stopped him, "he hasn't made any money—ever."

Lyman told Rankin to print out his analysis on his portable Diconix. He would be right down.

After putting on the same shirt and suit he had worn for three days, Lyman was about to leave the room when there was a knock on the door. It was Edouard. Bresson wanted him to come to his room for breakfast to discuss the fee letter. Lyman grabbed a tie. He looked in the mirror and decided the wrinkles would conceal the spots.

Bresson had a full-sized apartment on the top floor of the hotel. The breakfast nook looked out over the lake. Bresson was already at the table talking on the phone. He looked up and smiled.

"It is Monsieur Cooke, I am giving him the good news." He handed the receiver to Lyman.

"Dynamite work, Jayson," Cooke gushed, "Dynamite work! Bresson told me the offer's launched today and that he's signed our fee letter for $60 million!"

"That's terrific," he said, a little uncertain.

"You're a hero, and I for one won't forget it!"

That sounds ominous, Lyman thought. "We've got a long way to go. The deal's only started."

"But if he doesn't do this one, he'll do another. He's a solid client. We're in the big time. Say good-bye to Marcel for me."

So now it's Marcel, Lyman noted. He did not like links over his head between his client and his boss. They could wind up operating behind his back.

"I look upon this as the beginning of an enduring business and, I dare hope, personal partnership." Bresson handed him two signed copies of the contract. "I had a second one made so that we both could have copies with each others' signatures." He then handed Lyman a pen.

"Of course. That's customary," Lyman allowed.

Suddenly, Lyman felt rushed. Heidi's call. Then Rankin's. Now he was committing himself to do this man's bidding. He would be his agent, spokesman. Codefendant in all likelihood. And what did he really know about Marcel Bresson? Nothing good.

"There is a problem?" Bresson looked at him.

"No, no. I'm just a little worried about something."

"What could that be?" Bresson did not seem concerned.

"Some of our preliminary analysis suggests you may have a cash-flow problem." "Poor cash flow" was always more tactful than saying you're losing your ass, just as "lack of liquidity" was the polite substitute for being broke.

"It is easy for you to make that mistake." He dug into his Bircher Muesli, a Swiss cereal concoction of grains and nuts that Lyman considered more suited to rodents. "There are many conflicting tax and accounting rules in Europe despite our Common Market. And my companies have a very complex structure. Not to mention that I do not maximize apparent income for tax purposes. I take the long view. Research and development. Investment. Aggressive pricing to secure market share. I'm not interested in short-term profit."

Suddenly a voice called through the window. Bresson caught Lyman's puzzled look.

"Yodelers. Wonderful, no? When the wind is right, you can hear many of them calling at this hour of the morning. But do not be worried." He returned to Lyman's questions. "I am certain we can assure your analysts that we are solvent. The Swiss Bank Corporation would not support me if that were not so."

Lyman wanted to believe him. Involvement by the Swiss Bank Corporation was a clear vote of confidence. The largest bank in Switzerland, it had been in Bresson's pants from the beginning. They would know if something were wrong. He told himself to relax.

Lyman cleared a space between a bowl of raspberries and the basket of rolls and spread out the contract. He had no alternative. He signed it.

The pop of a champagne cork startled him. This was pouring it on a little thick, he thought, as a crown of foam climbed the narrow glass and slid over the edge and down onto the heavy linen tablecloth.

"To our partnership!" Bresson exclaimed, filling a glass for himself. "With the money you make on this transaction you can start to become a significant person." He clinked glasses and drank his down in one gulp. "Create your own deals. Buy and sell companies." He paused to belch. "I can introduce you to new sources of capital. You help me in America! I help you in Europe! In a few years you will be worth hundreds of millions, have access to billions. When you command such capital, Jayson, it is like being lifted off the Earth. Your perspective changes. Politics, nations, powerful people suddenly become insignificant. You can literally get away with murder."

Lyman suppressed a shudder. Bresson refilled their champagne glasses. "And you won't have to work for a *con* like Cooke any longer." He laughed his barking laugh at Lyman's surprise.

If he's got Cooke's number, Lyman thought, Bresson can't be all bad. "I'm looking forward to working together, too," he said as genuinely as he could manage.

They spent the rest of the breakfast pleasantly, discussing corporate developments in Europe that Lyman filed in the corner of his brain marked investment opportunities. By the time he got back to his room, he was a little high from the money massage and the champagne. He had completely forgotten that he was supposed to meet with Rankin. Then he saw the note he had scribbled on the pad next to the phone— the word "ever" followed by three question marks.

Rankin did not answer Lyman's knock, but the door was not locked.

"Rankin!" he called thinking he might be in the bathroom. There was no response.

The bed, covered with file folders, had not been slept in. The floor was a minefield of room service trays camouflaged by dirty clothes. Fanfolded computer paper was draped all over the furniture. The Diconix printer sat on the coffee table and was still turned on. The doors to the balcony swayed back and forth in the breeze from the lake, the sheer white curtains blowing into the room. Lyman stepped outside.

It was a narrow balcony with a small table and two chairs. A coffee cup, a few torn sugar packets and several pencils littered the table top. But Lyman's attention was drawn to the several sheets of paper scattered on the floor of the balcony, a few of them stuck between the railing supports. He looked out and saw a morning thundercloud trailing a veil of rain across the lake. Below, more papers littered the steep slope that fell away from the hotel toward the cliff. And three hundred feet down, at a line of small trees that marked the point where the rock face of Bürgenstock plunged out of sight, Lyman saw something else: the figure of a man crumpled in his pajamas.

PART II
DUE DILIGENCE

KOMSOMOL CAMP 708, NASHEM GODOY, KAMCHATKA—

1954

Forty-foot sand dunes protected the yellow wooden barracks from the wind that blew constantly from the Sea of Okhotsk. The camp sat on the edge of a brackish pond that in summer provided a breeding ground for huge mosquitoes but which in the spring and fall offered great shooting and plentiful supplies of Siberian goose. Winters lasted six months but because of the sea the thermometer rarely dipped under ten degrees below freezing. The rest of the year the days were mostly overcast, with frequent rain. The pine-clad mountains of the interior could be glimpsed only when the clouds lifted. The treeless coast was given over to scrub, occasional grasses and rock.

Almost entirely self-contained, Komsomol Camp 708 had three auditoriums, two gymnasiums, an indoor swimming pool, a shooting range, an obstacle course, a soccer field, a mess hall and a score of classrooms and dormitories. Not counting a handful of menial workers from the nearby village of Nashem Godoy, the population of the camp was less than one hundred—thirty-five teachers and administrators for forty-six children, all boys under the age of fifteen.

The regimen for the children was rigorous. Up at 5:30 A.M. Regardless of the weather, a two-and-a-half-mile walk on the beach before breakfast—difficult for the smaller ones in the frequent blizzards. The afternoons and evenings were spent in regular school work, indoctrination, sports and military training. The prime morning hours of the day were devoted to language training.

Most of the boys learned English. Another large group studied German. A smaller contingent of swarthy youngsters from the Trans-Caucasus had been assigned Spanish. Only two boys studied French.

That made things difficult for Misha and Vladimir. The other groups were big enough to play games in their languages. They acted out the routines of daily life: going to the store, having a bicycle fixed, getting a haircut. The English-language group was big enough to divide into

American- and British-accented groups and to form teams to play baseball and cricket. The American house even had a football team.

Misha and Vlad had to make do with secondhand experience—books, magazines and films. While the other groups would be sliding around the muddy parade ground trying to imitate the World Cup soccer matches, the two students of French would be confined to watching Renoir's *Les Règles du Jeu.*

That suited Misha just fine, but Vlad chafed under the isolation. He was big and strong for a thirteen-year-old, and hated the word games that dominated play time in the French house. Boxing had earned him the camp silver medal two years in a row. He continually pestered Yuli Byrakoff, proctor of the French house, to transfer him to the American house so he could play football or at least let him be on the team. Vlad took every opportunity to make clear to Misha that he considered him a sissy. The rumor, which Vladimir helped spread about himself, was that he was found in the forest being cared for by wolves. In fact, he could remember nothing of his life before the age of seven.

Misha was the camp fat boy. Yuli Byrakoff had put him on a restricted diet, but to no avail. He had already learned how to hoard food and to swap favors with other cadets, like shining boots for extra cake and cookies. He volunteered for work in the kitchen and for the heavy duty of carting wood from the village so he could bargain stolen tinned vegetables for local sausages.

But as Misha entered puberty his weight problem and the taunting grew more severe. "He's got a *huyochik,* a baby's pecker," Vlad pointed out in the shower one day, and from that day forward, Misha was known as "Huyochik." He was also ridiculed for his obsessive attachment to an old shoe that he had worn when first arriving at the camp. Misha slept with it under his pillow, carried it in his school bag, and even took it with him on bivouac.

Misha's status in the camp abruptly changed the day he obtained a stack of French movie magazines, one of which contained an issue devoted exclusively to Brigitte Bardot and the film *The Girl in the Bikini.* His small food-trading enterprise blossomed into a major business with the addition of a new product line—sex. He rented out the Bardot magazine in five-minute stretches. He combed other magazines for provocative female photos, often surprised at what some of the boys considered erotic. When a few boys showed interest in magazines with pictures of men, he also became a trader in information.

These entrepreneurial activities often freed Misha from his camp chores and led to increasing resentment on the part of the others, particularly Vladimir. One day while Misha was taking the compulsory weekly shower, Vlad arranged to remove his precious shoe from his locker. Misha flew into a rage, accusing Vlad of theft and ransacking his room in an effort to find it. The next day, Misha was summoned before the cadet disciplinary committee where Vlad charged him with "opportunism and deviationist tendencies including the conduct of unauthorized commercial activity and a decadent attachment to personal property." Several of his magazines and the shoe were introduced as evidence against him. The committee ordered him to serve double guard duty and burn everything in front of an assembly of the entire camp. As he stood in front of the bonfire made from his invaluable magazines, he was handed the shoe. Before tossing it into the flames, Misha tore off the heel. It was hollow, and as he feared, empty.

Several days later, in his third stint of guard duty that week, Misha and Vlad were patrolling the north sector of the beach. The wind came straight off the water at near gale force. Flecks of foam clung to their gray slickers like leeches. Misha felt like digging a hole in the snow-covered sand, but to ensure that they actually walked the beach, the boys were required to trade a pile of red painted rocks at one end for blue rocks at the far end.

At about 5 P.M., the two of them stopped to rest in the gathering gloom. Suddenly, bright flashes illuminated the sky and streaks of flame burst down out of the clouds, disappearing almost instantly behind the outline of the nearby mountains.

"What was that?" Vlad exclaimed. "Lightning?"

"I don't think so," said Misha. "I've seen it before when there were no clouds, and I couldn't sleep."

"You're sure it's not one of your dreams?" Vlad tried to provoke him.

"I don't have those anymore," he insisted angrily. "Other kids have seen them too. I think they're rockets."

"Rockets go up, stupid, not down like these."

"Yuli Byrakoff talked about a military base on the other side of the mountains. Maybe it's a target range, and we're seeing the rockets they shoot at it."

They trudged along together in silence for a while, both filled with awe of a mysterious new experience.

"You ever think why we're here?" Misha finally spoke.

"I don't go in for that philosophical junk," Vlad said, shifting the stone from his right to his left hand and his heavy Kalashnikov assault rifle to his opposite shoulder.

"I don't mean that. I mean why we're in this camp, learning French."

"Sure, we're supposed to be translators someday, go to university."

"But why here, away from everything? We've only seen pictures of our motherland in books."

"We're orphans," Vlad said as if that explained everything. He shifted the rock and the rifle again. Then he sat down in the sand. "Misha, do me a favor. I'm tired. It's only three hundred more yards. You carry my rock."

"Why would I do that for you?"

"Because, if you don't I'll tell the committee you asked me to do your patrol. I also know where you've hidden some candy."

Misha wanted to punch him in the face, but knew he would get beaten up. He tried negotiation. "All right, but you keep my rifle."

"No, I can't do that," Vlad laughed at him. "That would be against the rules."

Furious, Misha struggled over the dune, the butt of his Kalashnikov trailing in the sand. He had only gone about a hundred yards when he heard Vlad shouting.

"Come back! Quick! Misha! Look!" The rest was indistinct.

Misha kept trudging across the beach. He figured it was a trick to make him retrace his steps. Then he heard a shot. It sounded like Vladimir's gun! That was followed by more shots from another weapon. Misha dropped the rocks and struggled to run back in his heavy boots through the sand and snow.

When he regained the top of the dune, Misha could see Vlad down on the beach behind a driftwood log exchanging fire with someone in a black boat bobbing just beyond the surf. In the distance, out at sea, he could see the outline of a submarine. Only a hundred yards away, two figures in black emerged from the dunes carrying a large metal box. Misha tried to shout a warning, but he was too out of breath. They opened up on Vlad, forcing him to dive behind the log.

Under the cover of their fire, the boat raced onto the shore. The two tossed the box into the boat and climbed in after it. The outboard engine coughed and sputtered. Vlad stood up and started firing again. Finally, the motor caught, but as the boat started up the face of a crashing wave, one of the figures bounced overboard. As he stumbled around in the water, falling down with each surge of surf, the boat tried to circle to pick him up. Misha started down the hill firing his Kalashnikov. One of the men fell back in the boat, the other returned fire but the shots scattered across the beach. Misha reloaded and fired again. The boat turned, leapt skyward over the waves and headed for deeper water.

Vlad had plunged into the surf to pull the man from the water. As Misha approached, Vlad stood triumphant over a prostrate figure that lay on the beach gasping for breath. Suddenly he grabbed Vlad's leg and flipped him onto his back. He yanked the rifle out of Vlad's hand and jammed the barrel into his mouth.

"Don't come any closer," the man shouted at Misha in strange and clumsy Russian. "Throw down your gun!"

The man was only ten yards away and Misha's Kalashnikov was on full automatic. He could not miss.

"Don't be stupid!" He jammed the barrel further down into the boy's throat, causing a strangled cry as he bucked and thrashed on the sand. Vlad's eyes rolled wildly from Misha to the man and back again, begging both of them not to shoot. Out of the corner of his eye, Misha could see the rubber boat circling just beyond the breakers. He smiled at Vlad, nodded slowly at the man, then emptied the clip into him.

He jerked backward, yanking the rifle out of Vlad's mouth, but not before his reflexes pulled the trigger and blew out the back of the boy's head. The boat circled twice more, then headed out toward the waiting submarine.

Misha ignored the dead man. He bent down and unzipped Vladimir's parka. Slowly and carefully he went through his clothes. In the left front pocket of his pants he found what Vlad had stolen from him. His mother had put it into the hollow heel of his shoe just before they took her away. Misha could not remember her face, only her gray eyes and the fact that it was her last pearl.

Three days later, there was a funeral for Vladimir. Afterward, on the frozen parade ground where he had been humiliated the week before, Misha accepted medals of heroism for both of them. The man he had killed was an American spy. That afternoon the camp commander even invited him for tea.

"You have brought honor on Komsomol 708. You made the right decision in shooting the American spy. He would have killed you both."

"Yes, sir," Misha said.

The commandant held up his hand to silence him. "Unfortunately, we will be losing you anyway. You are to be immediately transferred."

"Why? To where?" The fear showed on Misha's voice. "I've been here almost as long as I can remember—"

Again the commandant raised his hand. "You are being honored by admission to a special school run by the Committee for State Security. In six months, a year, you should be ready."

"For what?" the boy asked.

"Your assignment to France." The camp commander smiled.

Misha sat stunned while pictures from his magazines flooded his mind. "Do not be afraid. You will be accompanied by your instructor, Comrade Byrakoff. He will always be available to provide guidance. You will be given a new name and family," the commander concluded, "but you will always serve the Soviet State."

The commandant stood up. "They have very special plans for you, Misha. You have proven you are ready," he said, fingering the award for heroism newly pinned to the boy's chest. "Do you want to donate Vladimir's medal to the camp?"

"No," Misha replied. "I want to keep it."

11

Drew Richardson loathed breakfast. Sweet rolls, jams, jellies, it was like starting the day with dessert, or worse, taking a shot of cholesterol straight into his aorta. When he did not play golf for breakfast, he held business meetings.

Monday was usually golf. But that morning, Richardson was having a council of war with Blackie Muldoon and other members of the buyout team in a private room at Washington, D.C.'s Metropolitan Club. While they debated how to meet Bresson's threat, black waiters with gray hair and white coats moved expertly and unobtrusively around the table.

"What about using our own media?" the head of the Publishing Division was saying. "We ought to kick this guy's ass. Get our own people to write some stories about him."

"That will look self-serving," the PR woman said, "maybe even create a backlash for him."

Richardson's lawyer agreed. "We could end up with injunctions against us, prejudice our own lawsuits."

"What suits?" Richardson asked.

"We'll need to sue to put Bresson off balance," said Muldoon.

"We can tear him apart in the courtroom first," the lawyer said, "and then throw the pieces to the press. He's probably not used to the American system of justice."

"What are the grounds?" Richardson asked.

"We'll charge that Bresson's filings with the SEC contain false and misleading information and that Bresson's sources of financing are inadequate."

"But we won't see his offer until Wednesday," noted the PR woman.

The lawyer shot her a withering glance. "We always sue on those grounds."

"We won't have to wait that long," the chief financial officer announced as he entered the room waving a Eurocourier envelope. "This was with the guard when I stopped by the office. It's Bresson's offer."

"Deceitful bastard!" Richardson said, surprised. He took the letter and started reading it. "Forty-two dollars and fifty cents a share! All cash!" he exclaimed, "That's what our internal numbers say! Has that son of a bitch got a spy in the company?"

"No," Muldoon said, "Just good investment bankers."

"How comforting," Richardson snapped. "And what's this? 'In the event the board does not respond favorably to this offer, we reserve the right to approach the stockholders directly.' "

"That's a tender offer," Blackie said. "They're threatening to buy shares directly from the public."

"They already have," the CFO added. "The letter says they're filing a 13D reporting that Bresson already has 8.3 percent of our shares."

"That's more than ten times what I own!" Richardson was outraged.

"He's serious," Blackie Muldoon emphasized. As Richardson's investment banker, his responsibility was to try to get the lowest price and best terms. In fact, however, his main goal was to get the deal done and earn the $60 million fee. He did not mind putting pressure on Richardson to raise his offer.

"Can't we do something?" Richardson demanded. "What about the poison pill?"

"It only comes into play in a two-step offer," Muldoon explained. "If Bresson were offering cash for just the first fifty-one percent of the stock and planning to pay for the remaining forty-nine percent with some kind of IOU at a lower price, then the pill would kick in. But Bresson's offering all cash."

"So am I!" Richardson said petulantly.

"But not enough now."

"Will our people come up with more money?"

"Yes, I've been talking to the Zeebergs in Toronto and Jerry Ostrogoth in Chicago. I'm sure they'll boost their participation in the mezzanine portion of the financing."

"More damned debt," Richardson shook his head. "I don't think the company can handle it."

"You may have to sell some assets to pay it down once you control the company," Muldoon noted.

"You know I don't want to do that!" Richardson stared out the third floor window at the gray-suited bureaucrats rushing to work at the New Executive Office Building across the street. Every two weeks, for the rest of their lives, they would get a nice green check from the government. For a brief moment he wished he were one of them.

"What does the letter say about Bresson's financing?" Blackie wanted to know.

"The Swiss Bank Corporation," the chief financial officer read, "is confident that it can raise the required financing to effect the transaction."

A broad smile broke out simultaneously on the faces of the lawyer and Blackie Muldoon.

"We've got him!" the lawyer cried.

Richardson looked baffled.

"They're only 'confident.' That means they haven't lined up the money," Muldoon explained. "If they had the commitments, they'd say 'highly confident.' "

"That's all we need to put Bresson through the wringer," the lawyer gloated.

"But we can't beat him with depositions," Muldoon warned. "It'll still take more money, and other things."

"Like what other things?" Richardson asked warily.

"Get the board to give you an option to buy the company's crown jewels—the TV stations and the *Washington News*—if Bresson gets the deal. Also ask for a one percent fee for any offer they accept from Bresson."

"What would justify that?" the CFO asked.

"Drew's offer stimulated Bresson's higher one," Muldoon explained, as if to a simpleton. "It also would help you pay for the crown jewels."

"That would look like I'm conceding that he'll win," Richardson protested. "Goddammit, he won't!"

"No, no." Muldoon tried to pacify him. "It'll make it harder for Bresson to do the deal if you lock up the best parts!"

"But by law Bresson can't own the TV stations anyway," the chief financial officer pointed out. "We'll be helping him solve a problem—"

Muldoon impatiently cut him off. "The point is, if we own the stations, he can't sell them to pay down the ton of debt he would accumulate! So it's harder for him to pay as much as we can to begin with."

Richardson looked uncertain. Sounds of Washington's rush hour traffic filtered through the windows. "What's all this going to do to my reputation, dismantling the company, paying myself to buy the crown jewels?"

"If you lose," Blackie pointed out, "you won't have a reputation to worry about."

Shopping was not one of Heidi Bruce's strong points. She enjoyed looking but not buying, and the greater the choice the less likely she was to purchase anything at all. But today she had to.

She left early for lunch, picking up her car from the parking lot near the train station. Capitol Hill had no place to shop, unless one wanted antiques of uncertain vintage sold by shopkeepers of uncertain sexual orientation. Heidi drove downtown.

She had put the top down to help rid the car of the dampness that still exuded from the carpets. A news junkie, she turned on the radio and punched in an all-news/talk station. At Pennsylvania Avenue and 10th Street, she finally focused on what someone on a call-in show was saying.

". . . just don't think we should let all these foreigners buy up everything in America. I mean, we got this weird Korean minister, the Reverend Moon, who owns one newspaper in Washington already. And he's an ex-con! Now we get a Frenchman buying the *Washington News*. Where does it stop?"

What Frenchman were they talking about? Heidi turned up the volume, but the next caller wanted to argue that Reverend Moon was not weird.

The parking garage across from Garfinkel's had space. She left the Fiat for the attendant and crossed the street in the center of the block. In front of the main entrance stood several newspaper vending machines. Ignoring the *News* and *USA Today,* which she had read in the office, she glanced at the *Washington Times.* An afternoon paper owned by the Reverend Sun Myung Moon, for years it had been struggling in vain for readers and respectability. But because it started printing its first issue at ten in the morning, Heidi checked its headlines every day looking for breaking news. One glance and Heidi dropped her quarter in the slot. A banner headline gloated, WASH NEWS HIT BY TAKEOVER BID.

The subhead proclaimed, FRENCH TYCOON MAKES OFFER. And in the second paragraph she found what she was looking for.

"The offer was made by French publishing magnate Marcel Bresson . . ."

Then her eye was drawn to a boldface box beside the story with the caption, "U.S. Banker Dies in Alps." She read it with growing alarm.

A U.S. investment banker involved in the preparations of Les Éditions Bresson to buy News/Worldweek was found dead this morning, apparently having fallen from his balcony at the Grand Hotel in Bürgenstock, Switzerland. The banker, who worked with Gould Axewroth in New York, was found dead in his pajamas on a ledge 200 feet below the hotel.

Heidi put the paper down, afraid to continue. A woman coming out of the department store asked if she was all right. She nodded yes and continued reading.

A spokesman for Marcel Bresson said it was a tragic accident, but sources close to the Swiss police said they were not ruling out suicide. The man, Charles Rankin, was 28 years old and lived in Greenwich, Connecticut.

Tears of relief welled up in her eyes. She stood there a moment dabbing her cheeks with her handkerchief, before realizing she had a lot of work to do. Dashing back across the street to the garage, she found her car still sitting in the driveway.

As soon as she reached her office, Heidi called the director of the CIA's congressional liaison office.

"You've heard about this Frenchman, Marcel Bresson, buying the *News?*"

"Not really," he replied.

"Well he is, and we want everything you have on him by COB today."

"We?" he said calmly. "We the staff, or we the committee?" Professionally laconic, it was his job to make espionage, betrayal, bribery, murder and secret wars sound routine.

"This is a staff request, but we're preparing to brief the Chairman."

"No problem."

That indicated it would be a problem. She hung up and called the FBI, the Defense Intelligence Agency and the National Security Agency. Occasionally, intelligence held tightly by one agency could be squeezed out of another who considered it less important. And, since each agency had its own collection effort, one often uncovered secrets that another tried to conceal.

Finally, she called Sean Gordon. She did not have to brief him.

"Was Rankin your 'friend?' " he asked.

"No, thank God!" Her voice told him more than she wanted to admit about how she felt towards Jay Lyman. "He's flying back today. I've got to see him," she continued.

"You already warned him and he went ahead."

"But now he's got to see what a bad situation he's in."

"It could have been an accident, like the paper said."

"Even so, he'll be a wreck." Why hide it, she decided.

"And will he like the fact that you're trying to start an investigation of Bresson?"

So he already had heard of her call to the CIA liaison chief.

"That's another reason why I've got to see him tonight. I'm sorry, Sean, I'll make it up to you."

"When you get to be my age, you don't mind postponing your birthday," he replied.

Oh God, she thought, and I even forgot to buy his present.

When the President of the United States saw the headline about the News/Worldweek takeover, he laughed. The paper lay on the secretary's desk in the small reception area between the Oval Office and the Cabinet Room where the President was about to meet with the board of the National Association of Securities Dealers.

"Well, I see that President Richardson just might get voted out of office by his shareholders," the President said as his press secretary joined him. He always referred to Drew Richardson as "President" since hearing how Richardson often remarked at Georgetown parties that several people in Washington, including himself, were better qualified to run the country.

"This French offer to buy News/Worldweek is raising a storm on Capitol Hill," his press aide said. "You could get a question from reporters when you go in the Cabinet Room."

"What kind of question?"

"Under the 1988 Trade Act, you can veto a foreign takeover if it threatens national security."

"National security?" the President scoffed. "With all the leaks printed in the *News?* If someone responsible takes over, that would *improve* the national security!"

On the long airplane flight from Zurich, Lyman tried to sleep, but it was no use. He put on the earphones and tried to watch the movie. An endless series of car crashes alternated with other forms of violent death. It did not help him blot out the horror of that morning.

The police had questioned him for over an hour while they used a crane to lift Rankin's body from the lip of the cliff. At first, the Swiss investigators seemed to think Lyman had pushed him off the balcony, taking the mess in Rankin's room as signs of a struggle. Later they developed the theory that he had fallen accidentally, that a wind had blown his papers off the balcony table, causing him to panic and reach out too far to retrieve them. However, one of the police investigators kept pressing Lyman about the possibility of suicide, focusing on why the bed had not been slept in. He bluntly suggested that Lyman had driven Rankin to jump by working him too hard.

Lyman told them everything, including having heard yodeling, but he left one thing out: Rankin's claim that Bresson had never made any money. That information, Lyman told himself, was privileged between himself and his client. Moreover, he had no proof it was true.

No sign of Rankin's consolidated balance sheets could be found in the room. The yards of computer printouts were drafts of the SEC filings. The papers scattered about on the balcony and down the hill proved to contain figures on some of Bresson's companies, but no consolidated balance sheet. The hard disk on Rankin's Toshiba 3500 laptop computer contained data on News/Worldweek, but nothing on Les Éditions Bresson.

The Swiss police let Lyman go after telling him that he might have to return for the inquest. Bresson offered his helicopter to the Zurich airport. While waiting restlessly for it to arrive, Lyman took a walk along the escarpment overlooking the lake.

The day was cool, autumnal, with a hint of winter when the wind picked up. A few hundred yards from the hotel, Lyman found a station for the cog railway that descended the face of the Bürgenstock. Along with a handful of Japanese tourists, he bought a trip ticket and climbed on board.

As the car ratcheted down the face of the mountain, the operator spoke to him. *"Sommer ist vorbei."*

Looking out at the clouds gathering over the lake and hearing the wind rising around the cabin as it descended, Lyman nodded in agreement.

Then he said something in Swiss-German dialect that Lyman could not understand. He switched into a broken English. "Man fall this morning? *Von* hotel?"

"Yes," Lyman answered. "Did you see anything?"

The operator got a blank look on his face, and Lyman thought he did not understand. So he repeated the question more slowly.

"*Ja, verstehe Ich.*" He understood. Finally he replied. "I do not know."

It was Lyman's turn to looked perplexed. "What did you see?"

"Man not fall all way down?"

"No."

"I see something go all down."

They reached the bottom. To Lyman's surprise, the rock face did not plunge directly into the lake. A flat area fifty to a hundred yards wide bordered the lake with a narrow road running along the base of the cliff. Lyman decided to take a short walk to try and discover what the man had seen. He passed boat houses, a boarded-up summer restaurant, several farms and cottages, and open pasture with black and white cows crowded around a salt lick. He walked for about two hundred yards, then stopped and looked up, figuring that he had come to the spot where Rankin would have fallen had he not been stopped by the trees. From below, the rock was not a sheer vertical drop, but a steep slope with protruding boulders. Lyman then started walking in circles. The fine glass scattered all over the road confirmed his suspicion. Then, here and there, he began to find larger pieces of machinery but let them lay. Finally, over by the salt lick, half buried in the soft turf, he had discovered what he was looking for.

The Fasten Seat Belts sign flashed on and Lyman looked out his window to see the twin forks of eastern Long Island with Shelter Island nestled in between. Within a few minutes, the plane was on the ground. Lyman was the first to disembark, and, carrying only a suit bag and briefcase, the first to get through customs.

As the doors of the international arrivals section swung open, Lyman looked for his driver. Instead, he found Heidi Bruce.

"Are you all right?" She rushed to him. "God, at first I thought it was you."

He dropped his bags and gathered her up. She resisted only a moment before kissing him eagerly. They stood locked together until they realized the crowd around them was applauding.

Andy, his driver, had picked up his bags. They followed him to the curb where the gray Mercedes 450 waited. In the back seat, they kissed again, this time slowly exploring each other with building excitement.

Heidi pulled away, breathing heavily, her eyes bright. "You *are* all right!"

"Inside, I'm a disaster area." A look of gloom came over him. "Tell me."

He shook his head. "Did you ever have to tell someone that her husband died unexpectedly? It's just as awful as you can possibly imagine. How do you begin? I told Carol Rankin that there had been an accident. That Charles had fallen several hundred feet. You know what she said?"

Heidi gripped his hands tightly.

"Carol said, 'Will he be all right?' "

"And you know what I said?" Heidi pulled his head down onto her shoulder. "I said, 'no, not really.' " Tears came to his eyes. "What the hell kind of thing is that to say?"

They rode in silence for a while.

"When my father died suddenly at work," Heidi said finally, "I got a call from his secretary. I can't remember anything she said."

Again they were silent for a while, then Lyman sat up. "That's not the worst part. The Swiss police pretty much accepted the theory that it was an accident. That he leaned too far out to try to save some papers that had blown off the balcony. Well, I went to the bottom of the cliff and found this."

Lyman opened up his briefcase and pulled out a piece of metal that looked like several disks welded together.

"What is it?"

"The hard drive from Rankin's other computer, his Compaq. When we searched his room and found the Toshiba, I had forgotten that he always traveled with two computers, 'In case one craps out,' he used to say."

"I don't understand."

"If you're leaning over a balcony reaching for a piece of paper floating in the air, you don't hold a twenty-five-pound computer in your other hand. The wind didn't blow the computer off the table!"

"What are you saying? That somebody . . ."

"I'm saying that it's my fault, Heidi. I pushed him and pushed him. He didn't sleep for days. Sometimes I was rude, maybe even mean. I was pretty damn tired myself. When he asked to see me, I said I'd be right down. And then I left him sitting there for hours. In effect, I pushed him right over the cliff!"

She pulled away and looked at him. "How much sleep have you had?"

"Not much."

"It shows. You think that . . ." She paused. "How long had he worked for you?"

"Three years."

"And suddenly he becomes so freaked by the way you normally treat him. . . . It is normal, isn't it? The abuse? The lack of sleep?"

"Yes," Lyman admitted, "but it could have been the last straw."

"So freaked," she continued, "that he jumps off the balcony clutching his computer?"

Lyman looked out of the car at the old World's Fair buildings along Grand Central Parkway.

"He was probably mad and threw the computer off the balcony first," he finally said.

"Jayson, angry people don't kill themselves."

"Then what's your theory?" he asked irritably.

"It's understandable that you'd blame yourself. You feel responsible. But have you thought about Bresson? Did he have reason . . . ?"

The look on Lyman's face changed abruptly from self-pity to worry.

"What is it?" she pressed.

"I'm not sure it's relevant."

"Tell me."

"I don't know if it's true, and it's privileged information."

"I've got clearances," she insisted.

"Privileged between me and my client."

"Jayson, you should understand something. I'm going after Bresson."

"You can't! You'll screw up my deal!" he protested.

"Your deal? Your partner's dead! Bresson could be involved. The CIA holds files on Bresson that are so sensitive they won't even admit their existence. You know something you won't tell me, and all you can think about is your deal! What about your self-respect? What about your country?"

"Get real. You see the chance to create a Federal case. You want me to sacrifice my job to help your job!"

"So it's just ambition against ambition?"

Lyman clenched his teeth and said nothing.

"Andy," she said to the driver, "please let me off at LaGuardia. The shuttle will be fine." They had just passed Shea Stadium.

"What about dinner?" he protested.

"You're too cranky to have dinner. It's obviously past your bedtime."

"You're going back to Washington?" He could not believe she was serious.

"After a good night's sleep," she said, "you can call me to apologize." They pulled up to the Eastern terminal and she got out without saying good-bye.

"Where to, Mr. Lyman?" Andy asked. "Still want to go home?"

Still stunned, he took a moment to reply.

"You might as well make it the office."

By the time they arrived at the Battery, the sun was setting over New Jersey. Crowds of secretaries clogged the street in their rush to South Ferry to catch the boat to Staten Island. In his dark mood, Lyman was struck by their faces, many as haggard and worn as any he had seen at industrial plants in Ohio or mining towns in West Virginia. They only dressed better.

The driver dropped him off on the Whitehall side of One New York Plaza, then disappeared into the garage. Wearily, climbing the steps, Lyman made his way through the two-story lobby of gray and black marble. The young stock salesmen exiting the building seemed keyed up at the end of the trading day, but the brokers over thirty looked like they had high blood pressure and wore the furtive expression of race track touts.

When he arrived at the M&A offices, Lyman found most of the staff crowded into his room watching the television set. They apologized and started to leave, but he asked that they stay. Tom Brokaw was just leading into the News/Worldweek story.

"Wall Street was not surprised today when another bidder emerged for the News/Worldweek organization, the nation's largest publishing and communications empire. But they were surprised at who the new buyer turned out to be. Chris Wallace has the story from Washington."

The picture cut to Wallace standing in front of the Capitol.

"Americans are accustomed to foreign companies buying U.S. real estate, factories, advertising agencies, even Wall Street investment banks, but today a storm of controversy greeted the announcement that a French firm, owned by publishing magnate Marcel Bresson, is seeking to acquire News/Worldweek, publisher of the prestigious and influential *Washington News.*"

Several different members of the House and Senate appeared on screen asking if there were no limit to what one called the "foreign takeover binge." Only the Senate minority leader pointed out that U.S. corporations had been buying foreign companies for years. "We own more businesses abroad than foreigners own here," he added.

Wallace returned. "The White House, which has in the past clashed with News/Worldweek chairman Drew Richardson, did not seem as disturbed as Congress about the possible transaction. Asked whether the President favored Bresson, the Frenchman, or Richardson, who is making his own bid for the company, the press spokesman only said, "It's a free country, and a free press, if you can afford it."

Tom Brokaw reappeared and added:

"In a tragic sidelight to this story, a young American who was working on this transaction for the French company fell to his death in the Alps early today. A spokesman for Bresson called it an accident, but Swiss authorities refused to rule out suicide." NBC switched to a Dentucream commercial, and one of the raccoons muttered, "They didn't even mention his name." Another said, "Not even famous for fifteen seconds."

Lyman asked them to join him in the large conference room. He took a seat at the head of the table. Behind him, the wall was covered with "tombstones," facsimiles of the black-bordered formal press notices that announced their successful deals. The other wall was glass and looked out on the darkening south harbor, Governors Island and the Statue of Liberty.

"I can't add much to the news report you just saw. It was a total surprise and shock. We're all hard on each other in this business, and we always try to show how tough we are. Expressing affection doesn't come easy. But I'm going to miss him, and I expect all of you are, too."

"I don't believe that stuff about suicide," said Karen Kobyashi, a recent addition to the M&A associates from UC Berkeley. She had tears in her eyes.

"Neither do I," said de Grazia.

The phone rang on the side table. Lyman's secretary announced that Cooke insisted on speaking to him. When the president of Gould Axewroth came on the line, Lyman could hear that he was using a speaker phone. Lyman also switched to the speaker so his whole staff could hear the conversation.

"We're off to a great start," Cooke said. "Do you think the political reaction could stuff the deal?"

"I don't know," Lyman responded.

"Anyway, I want you to be at the executive meeting tomorrow. Explain what you're doing, pump up morale—"

"Marshall, I'm in the middle of talking to my staff about Rankin's death."

"Oh yeah. That was tough."

"Have you talked with his wife?"

"Not yet," Cooke said, "I should do that."

"I want a special compensation package for his family."

"Hey, wait. He's got an IRA. This isn't the army. You want combat pay?"

"Goddamn right!" Lyman shouted.

"We don't have the money—"

Lyman snatched up the receiver, cutting his staff off from hearing Cooke complain about the disastrous shape of the company.

"Well, find the money," Lyman declared. "Give his family a piece of this deal if we have to." He hung up and then saw the look of respect on the faces of his staff members. He felt like a grandstanding asshole.

"We've also got a lot more work to do. We're going to have to develop a full set of financials on Éditions Bresson. I've got some early bits and pieces he developed in Switzerland. Most of it was lost when Rankin"—he hunted for the right words—"had his accident."

"Don't worry," said Karen Kobyashi, "he sent all the data by modem. I've got the latest printout of the SEC filings on my desk."

"Did he send everything that way?" he asked, trying not to hope that she might have the missing consolidated statements.

"Sure. He was very good about backing up every file on diskette and if he was traveling, he always sent files in by modem to be doubly safe."

Just like he always carried two computers, Lyman thought to himself. "Can you show me the files?" he asked eagerly.

They adjourned to a small windowless room filled with a half dozen IBM PS-2 60s linked together in a local area network. Lyman asked that the others give them some privacy.

She turned on her terminal and logged in her password, *NETSUKE.*

"What's that?" Lyman asked.

"Netsuke are little carved Japanese buttons. Animals. People. Very beautiful. Museums collect them now. Very expensive."

A *C>* appeared on the screen. She typed in *cd\NW* to change to that part of the computer memory storing all the files on News/Worldweek. The prompt changed to *NW>*.

"Did he send back a consolidated financial statement for Éditions Bresson?" Lyman asked, trying to sound matter-of-fact.

"I think so. He had a balance sheet, a flow of funds and historicals."

"Let's look at them."

She typed in *CONBAL*. The screen flashed *Bad command or file-name*. She frowned and typed *CONFLO*. Again the screen reported *Bad command or filename*. Then she tried *CONHIST*. She got the same result.

"Maybe you haven't got the right filename," Lyman suggested anxiously.

She gave him an impatient look and typed in *DIR*. The screen changed to:

NW > DIR
Volume has no label:
Directory: NW
Files: BRESCOM   365,000 bytes

"What does that mean?"

"The files are gone!" she exclaimed.

"The consolidated financials?"

"Those and everything else!" She was stunned. "The draft 10K, the letter of offer, the press release, all the analysis on News/Worldweek. Thank God, I've got printouts of most of it."

"Including Bresson's financials?" Lyman dared hope.

"No. He didn't ask us to work on those, so—"

"Shit! How could this happen?"

"I don't know," she looked about to cry again.

"What's BRESCOM?" he demanded. "It's the only thing in there."

"That must be what those guys installed this afternoon."

"What guys?"

"They said Bresson sent them to put in a new software package that lets us talk directly with his computers. Maybe they accidentally erased everything else."

"Accidentally?"

"Maybe I can recover it. Usually files aren't really erased. Markers just go on the file allowing the computer to write over it." She switched to another directory labeled *Utilities* and typed *Norton*, then *Recover*. After a series of steps that Lyman could not follow, the computer flashed *Please Wait*. A few minutes later another message appeared: *No files found*.

"Wow, they've been totally deleted," she exclaimed.

"Could that have been an accident?"

Karen Kobyashi shrugged and shook her head, "I don't know."

Lyman returned to his office and dialed Heidi Bruce's number. He got the answering machine and hung up. After a few minutes, he dialed again. At the beep he said:

"This is Jay. I'm already sorry for my reaction this afternoon. Do what you have to do. Try to understand that I also have an obligation to my firm and to my client. Until one of us finds solid evidence of wrongdoing, there's a limit to what I can do to help. If you're going hunting, I've got a name in Paris that might be useful. And for God's sake, be careful."

12

"He won't go for it," the staff director told her. "It's too controversial."

"But it's a clear case of the CIA thumbing its nose at us," Heidi argued. "Look how they responded to my request." She pulled a thin sheaf of files from her briefcase and put them on the table.

"My God!" he whispered, "You're not supposed to have those outside the committee vault!"

Hundreds of conventiongoers milled around them as they sat in the International Café in the sunken lobby of the Capitol Hill Hyatt Hotel.

"You're the one who insisted we meet for breakfast," she pointed out. "Besides, there's nothing classified in these files, I assure you."

He started flipping through them. The file from the CIA contained a single sheet of paper, a one-sentence letter that said, "The Agency's registry contains nothing responsive to Ms. Bruce's inquiry." The Defense Intelligence Agency file, like that of the FBI, merely held clippings of French and American news stories about Bresson. The State Department Biographic Registry file had several reports, the earliest going back to a dispatch written by the U.S. consul in Lyon recommending Bresson for a Future Leader Grant to visit the United States. The National Security Agency's response was a terse memo that said, "All requests for information re. subject should be directed to the Central Intelligence Agency." "I don't see anything earth-shattering here," said the staff director. "Where's the case for starting a committee investigation?"

"Right there!" She took back the files. "Look, the CIA says it hasn't any files and the NSA says that's where we have to go to get them! Since when does CIA establish 'protect' arrangements for files it doesn't have?"

"That's still pretty thin, Heidi."

"But I know for a *fact* that the CIA has files on Bresson!"

"Your special source again?" he said wryly. "Will he give sworn testimony before the committee?"

She flushed.

"Let me explain the politics of this," he continued. "The Chairman is up for reelection next year. For the first time in a quarter century he'll be opposed in the primary. Scooter Farber in the House is coming after him. News/Worldweek has ten, count 'em, ten media outlets in his state. He can't afford to make enemies."

"But he'd be helping News/Worldweek's management. Richardson would be grateful."

"If he wins. But if he doesn't, this guy Bresson could break his balls. Look, not even the President wants to get involved with the issue of who should run News/Worldweek."

"It's our job to make the chairman get involved!" she said defiantly.

"Sorry."

Heidi looked at the staff director, his thin blond hair carefully combed over his balding head. He had always been her strongest supporter, but in recent months the fire had seemed to go out of him.

"What are you doing over here at the Hyatt all day?" She changed the subject to cover her disappointment.

"Oh, just a seminar," he said uneasily.

"On what?" She smelled blood.

"Just some personnel stuff." He reached for the check.

She stopped pressing, but on her way toward the escalator to the street, she checked the meetings board in the lobby. The only seminar on the schedule was "Opportunities in the Private Sector: Capitalizing on Government Service."

By removing all the partitions, the Executive Dining Room at Gould Axeworth had been turned into the Partners Conference Room. A long table filled the center and additional chairs had been placed against the walls to accommodate the forty-six junior and senior partners. A wall of windows looked north over the New York Stock Exchange toward midtown Manhattan. The opposite wall was decorated with several nineteenth-century American landscape paintings by Thomas Hill, William Keith and Cleveland Rockwell. Above the head of the table, a young Billy Gould peered down from a full-length portrait. Beneath it, Marshall Cooke tried to control the meeting. Lyman sat behind him, not wanting to be there.

"The capital of this firm has shrunk almost thirty percent in three months!" the managing director of corporate finance bellowed. "That's our money. I've had to turn down business because we didn't have the capital to handle it! There's got to be changes around here!"

"Don't blame my shop," the head of Trading spoke out. "The whole thing started when you mispriced that stock offering—"

"On your advice about the market."

"How could I know it would turn that day? Research didn't tell us about the prime rate going up."

As they bickered back and forth Lyman could see how Cooke had managed to maintain himself—by putting the partners at each others' throats. Cooke rapped for order.

"The purpose of this meeting is not to rehash our problems. I wanted you to hear about one of our important opportunities. Jay?" He turned to Lyman.

Lyman moved to the table, and looked around. Seldom had he seen such a group of unhappy campers.

"I don't have to tell you how unusual it is to be discussing a deal while it's still in progress," he began, "but I'm doing it because Marshall Cooke asked, and because you all have a financial stake in the outcome. I'm sure you've read about our representation of Les Éditions Bresson in the News/Worldweek transaction. If we are successful, the firm stands to earn $60 million in fees. I think we are in a strong position to win, especially on the financial front with the support of the Swiss Bank Corporation. But the deal has kicked a storm in the press and in Washington, so the outcome may turn on factors other than economics. Like any deal, it's not over till it's over."

The head of Corporate Finance interrupted, "Are you saying that we'd all be making a mistake to count on this transaction to save the firm?"

Cooke shot him a dark look.

Lyman nodded. "We all bear some responsibility for the firm's financial situation. Trading losses, mistiming the market, is only part of it. Overhead has grown forty percent in the last three years. Nobody's entirely blameless, I'm sure you can think back to times when you made mistakes that cost us all money. That's because this is a business where we take risks.

"Looking at where we stand now, we only have three basic choices. We can shrink the business. We can raise more capital and try to compete with the big boys across the board. Or we can sell.

"Any of these choices will require careful analysis and a consensus decision. Our most important capital is not financial. It is human. And this firm won't be worth anything if we don't pull together. That's tough for the prima donnas in this outfit, including me. But we have a common asset here worth protecting."

There was no response from the group except to look at Cooke. He didn't seem to like the way the wind was blowing.

"Thanks, Jay, for those words of wisdom," he said with a touch of sarcasm. "We're all busy, so if anybody has any specific questions on the News/Worldweek deal you can talk to Jay directly. Without objection, we're adjourned." He got up and fled through the nearest door.

Lyman stood with the heads of Trading and Corporate Finance who had been feuding earlier.

"What was that all about?" Lyman asked. "Why did he want me here?"

"He didn't," the Corporate Finance chief said.

"We did," said the chief trader.

"But why?"

"Because"—the two vied to speak first—"we want you to take control of the firm."

As she sat at her desk, Heidi Bruce had to admit that by any measure, it had been a bad twenty-four hours. Not only had the staff director dumped on her Bresson investigation, her personal life was a mess, something she only thought about when her professional life was a mess, too.

On her way back to Washington the night before, she had decided to surprise Sean. It was only 6:30 P.M. The taxi took her directly to his apartment on the Georgetown waterfront. He was not there. She knew the security codes and had a key to let herself in. Assuming that he was on his way home from the Agency, she ransacked the cupboards and refrigerator to find something suitable for a birthday dinner. She found squabs in the freezer and enough unwilted lettuce leaves for a small salad. She made a sauce from chicken bouillon to go with some wild rice she located on a back shelf. Heidi even managed to put together a vanilla cake from scratch. By 8:30 everything was done, except the cake. By nine, the cake was cooling and she had decided on a second gimlet, hoping he was also having a drink someplace with the boys. But by ten, everything was either cold or overdone.

Heidi had been torn between taking a nap or going home. But she decided that she had done enough walking out on people that day. She lay on the couch, feeling alternately guilty and angry for another twenty minutes, when it suddenly dawned on her that he might come home with another woman. She jumped up and rushed to the closet for her jacket. Only then did she realize that both his overcoat and raincoat were gone. She dashed into the bedroom and opened his closets. Half of his clothes were missing too. And all of his luggage. She ate the birthday cake by herself and went home.

Finding Lyman's message on her machine had helped a little, but she had not wanted to call him back until her investigation of Bresson was approved. Now, with the project quashed, what could she say to him? My staff director agrees with you, and by the way, he wants a job? She watched morosely as two tablets of saccharin fizzed across the top of her coffee—Alka-Seltzer for dieting depressives. She was so bored she began to skim the *Congressional Record*.

Despite the fact that the *Record* was delivered to the desk of every Congressional staffer each morning, no one read it. Originally created to document the debate in the Senate and House of Representatives, the *Record* had become incomprehensible and useless as a guide to what actually happened in each Congressional chamber. Members were allowed to insert additional material after the fact, often right into the middle of statements made on the floor. An eloquent speech in the Senate on the protection of endangered insects had probably never been delivered at all. If a Representative wanted to insert the Manhattan telephone directory into the *Congressional Record,* he could do so, and it would be faithfully reproduced for all his colleagues to read the next morning.

Heidi was browsing through the comments made the previous day about Bresson's bid for News/Worldweek. The reaction did not break down along traditional liberal/conservative, Republican/Democratic lines. Flag-waving conservatives denounced it; free market conservatives argued "hands off." Liberal Wall Street bashers attacked the deal, civil liberties advocates insisted that it was protected by the Bill of Rights.

In the section of the *Record* devoted to the House of Representatives, Heidi came across a speech about the News/Worldweek deal that set her thinking. If what it said were true, she just might have the lever to get an investigation going against Bresson after all.

Her first call went to the House Subcommittee on Telecommunications. The staff director was too busy to talk, but the general counsel bragged to her for fifteen minutes, confirming and expanding on information she had read in the *Record.*

Next she had to decide how to proceed. She was not senior enough to pick up the phone and call her Chairman. She needed an intermediary. Her own staff director was obviously no help, but his absence allowed her to deal directly with the Chairman's personal staff, a power prerogative usually denied her. The line between committee staff and personal staff was a delicate one on Capitol Hill. Committee staffers considered themselves experts. They looked down on personal staffers as political hacks. But in a showdown over what a Senator or Congressman should do, the hacks always won.

Heidi decided to contact the Chairman's top aide, his administrative assistant. The AA was a well-known snake who would appreciate what she had discovered. When he came on the line, she said, "I need to talk to the Chairman about something that could have a big impact on his race against Scooter Farber."

"You gonna do it?" de Grazia asked Lyman as he returned to his office from the board meeting.

"Do what?"

"Take over the company."

"News/Worldweek?"

"No, for Christ's sake. Our firm!"

"I can only take over one company at a time."

"But we need you," de Grazia insisted.

"If I help take over News/Worldweek, I get $30 million in cash," Lyman said with forced patience. "I take over Gould Axewroth, I get $100 million in liabilities."

"You've got a majority on the partnership committee."

"Are you part of this craziness?" Lyman demanded. "Well, I'd like to point out that you fuckwits haven't even talked to Billy Gould. He just happens to own the bulk of the voting stock."

"You don't appreciate anything people try to do for you." De Grazia turned angry.

"What you've done is drive a wedge between me and Cooke. You think he doesn't know about these plots? He won't trust a goddamn thing I do now!"

Lyman closed his office door on him. The last thing Lyman wanted to explain was how Cooke could use his own channels to Bresson to knock him out of the deal, and why Bresson could have a powerful incentive to get rid of him, too—quite literally.

He slumped behind his desk. He would have to get Bresson first. That meant finding out whether Rankin was right.

But how? One of his raccoons could go through all the data again. Unfortunately, any new numbers from Maurice the accountant would be pre-massaged. Bresson would not make the same mistake twice.

Lyman stared at his reflection in the window. He had a trick when stymied: turn the problem around. Start by assuming Bresson had never made any money. Where would the money come from to cover the deficit? The answer seemed obvious. Only two vast pools of capital in the world were prepared to sustain endless losses. The drug cartel and the Mafia. They could afford to take a fifty percent haircut just to launder their cash. It even made sense for them to be silent partners in the publishing business!

How to establish that? Not easy, Lyman knew. But he had the best resource on Wall Street right downstairs in the retail sales department. He reached for the phone and pushed the intercom, "Get me Maximilian."

Everyone called him "Max the Saint." His specialty was cultivating the world's richest scumbags.

A yellow phone message awaited Heidi Bruce when she got back from lunch. The Chairman urgently wanted to see her. She glanced up at the wall clock. Two orange lights were lit on the face. Tied into a system of bells that rang in every corner of the Capitol, the lights on the clock signaled that a vote was in progress, and told her that the Chairman would be on the Senate floor. Politicians who sought a seat in Congress anticipating that they would wield great power were always shocked to find their lives as regulated by lights and bells as laboratory dogs.

The foyer outside the Senate chamber was full of lobbyists and staff members waiting to grab Senators as they arrived to vote. Heidi showed her badge to the Sergeant at Arms. He admitted her to an anteroom that ran the width of the chamber behind the President's podium. A porter inside took her message to the Chairman while she sat and waited on a hard upholstered bench, staring up at the marble busts and dark paintings of obscure Senators.

After a few minutes, the porter returned and asked that she follow him. He took her the length of the anteroom to another hallway. They turned left and, passing under a heavily vaulted ceiling, came to a door hung with thick maroon drapes which led back toward the Senate chamber. Once inside, Heidi realized that in her seven years on Capitol Hill she had never before seen that room. It was the inner sanctum, the Senate Cloakroom.

She was, surprisingly, disappointed. The Cloakroom consisted of a series of rooms filled with overstuffed brown leather chairs and couches, some so beat-up they looked like they had been scavenged from the front steps of tenements in northeast Washington. The walls were a brownish yellow, due either to decades of cigar smoke or because they had been painted to resemble the same. The only decor consisted of highly polished spittoons and paintings so covered with filth as to be unrecognizable. Newspapers were piled everywhere.

The Chairman sat with a group of three other Senators. He motioned for her to stay away. Another dozen or so Senators lounged about reading, talking on the phone, or both.

The roll-call vote was concluding, and the three Senators left the Chairman to go on the floor and vote. He waved her over.

"Thank you for coming, my dear," he said in his most courtly manner. "I understand you have something urgent?"

"I don't want you to miss the vote." She knew the Chairman was extremely proud of his 99-percent-plus voting record, the best in the Senate.

"I'm just waiting for the results, to know which way to go."

Heidi looked taken aback.

"I'm in favor of this bill," he explained, "but my constituents are against it. If it's going to pass anyway, I'll do what my constituents would prefer."

She smiled as if she appreciated his courage.

"Now what's this about investigating the News/Worldweek imbroglio? That's hardly a matter for the Intelligence Committee."

"What if the CIA is concealing information about Marcel Bresson, the Frenchman who's conducting the takeover? I have a reliable source." She decided not to mention Rankin's death. It might sound like she was stretching things to make a case.

"That's not enough for a subpoena," the Chairman said. "They'd scream that I'm on a fishing expedition."

"Granted. That's why I want to develop as much information as I can on my own. Then we can target our demands."

"Ms. Bruce, I don't make it a practice to get involved in cat fights with cats that are bigger than I am."

"Even if it affected your campaign against Scooter Farber?"

"How does that figure in?" His interest sharpened.

"Yesterday, he announced that his House Subcommittee on Telecommunications would have hearings on the News/Worldweek deal. His general counsel told me Scooter plans to hold them in the state."

The Chairman's eyes flickered at that point, absorbing the political impact of such a move.

"They're going into every media market where News/Worldweek has an outlet. I understand there's five or six in all."

"That's a lot of free TV!" the Chairman acknowledged.

"I thought we might need to fight fire with fire."

"What's your strategy?"

"Dig up as much as I can on Bresson. Confront the agency with it and make them spill their files. At that point we can decide how to proceed, but I think we should be aiming for hearings with Bresson under oath."

"If we can reveal some secrets, we'll get a lot more tube time than Scooter . . ."

He paused and seemed to go dormant for a minute. "Or maybe I should take the opposite side, support this here takeover."

Heidi held her breath.

"No," he sighed, "no votes in that." He looked at her carefully. "And if I authorized your investigation, you think we'd get some TV?"

"My judgment," she said candidly, "is that either I'll find nothing, or we'll have a blockbuster on our hands."

"I'd have to check with the minority."

"That'll get right back to CIA. Maybe even into the press."

The Chairman looked deeply pained, then leaned close to her in a gesture of confidentiality she had seen him use a thousand times.

"My dear," he said, "there's going to be some important changes in the staff of the committee. As you may know, the position of director is going to become open. That belongs to the majority, but the person who takes it has to have the confidence of the minority as well."

Heidi could hardly believe what she was hearing. Was she a candidate for staff director?

"I'm going to leave the decision on this investigation to you. If the minority finds out about it, they'll bitterly resent being cut out. If you succeed, they'll want your head. Either way, your chance to become staff director . . ." He did not need to finish the sentence.

She sat there a moment while a porter whispered in the Chairman's ear. Heidi was pretending to think about it to preserve her reputation as a serious person. In fact, the choice was obvious. She had not come to Washington merely to hold power. She wanted to do something with it.

"I think the investigation is important. I want to pursue it."

"By yourself?"

She nodded.

"All right," he pushed himself to his feet. "Now if you'll excuse me, I've got to go vote against this bill."

"It's passing?"

"No. Unfortunately, my vote will make it lose. But I only allow myself one politically foolish act per day."

"Max is in the gym," Marlene explained.

"He never worked out in his life!" Lyman scoffed.

"He's gettin' a massage," she elaborated.

"Gettin' a hand job's more like it," de Grazia chimed in.

"They don't have no masseuses up there no more," Marlene pointed out.

"That wouldn't make any difference to Max," said Lyman as he put on his jacket and headed for the elevator.

The Gould Axewroth gym looked out over New Jersey from the forty-ninth floor. Along a wall of glass, a half-dozen stair-climbing machines flanked an equal number of stationary bicycles, all facing Hoboken. When the gym had first been installed, it boasted a half-dozen TV sets tuned to the Financial News Network and running displays of the tickers from the New York Stock Exchange, the Amex, Comex and several other exchanges, just like the trading floor. Billy Gould took one look at the setup and had it ripped out. He replaced it with a public-address system so he could call people back to the office. "When these jerks are up there screwing around," he explained, "I don't want them to think they're working."

Lyman found the facility almost empty as usual. Two women, in skin-tight body stockings that provided less privacy than a string bikini, worked out by trying to climb a five-step escalator that kept moving down. To Lyman, that had to be the ultimate New York exercise machine.

An attendant said Max was in the massage room with his personal trainer. Lyman found him lying on his back, a big cigar sticking straight up out of his mouth, while an attractive thirtyish woman with strong arms worked on his fat legs.

"Come on in, Jayson," Max greeted him, "but I charge to let people watch."

"I want to talk," Lyman said, "privately."

Max gestured for the woman to leave.

"Pretty good, Max," Lyman observed. "The executive committee bans masseuses, you get a personal trainer."

"Yeah, we're working on my flexibility. Hey, I got a joke for you." He sat up. "This Jewish guy, an *alter cocker* eighty-one years old, starts to get the drip in his *schwantz.* So he goes to the doctor, who's a little surprised, given his age. The doc takes a sample, spreads it on a slide and puts it under a microscope. He's stunned at what he finds.

" 'Do you have a girlfriend?' he asks.

"The old man nods.

" 'Did you have sex with her recently?'

" 'Two weeks ago,' he admits.

" 'Well, you better get over to see her right away,' the doc tells him.

" 'Is there something wrong?' the old guy asks.

" 'No,' says the doc. 'You're finally coming!' "

Max launched into a deep, raucous laugh which Lyman did his best to join. An old friend of Billy Gould, his real name was Maximilian Santo di Fazenda. Max bragged that as kids they put rocks in snowballs together. Always a smile on his face, and frequently a vulgar joke on his lips, he could also be charming and sophisticated. Even those who belittled him often liked him.

His niche in the investment banking business was positioning. He liked to compare himself with socialites like Alex Papamarkou, who boasted the King of Spain as a money management client, except that Max was a few rungs further down the ladder. A graduate of Bronx Science and Columbia University, he had his quota of New York and Hollywood celebrity clients, along with some no-account European nobility. But his principal stock-in-trade lay with the new money that others scorned as déclassé—waste management tycoons, suburban real estate developers, video chain store entrepreneurs, nursing home operators and chairmen of Florida savings and loan associations. His business technique consisted of providing services to his client—across the board. Gould Axewroth handled the money management, brokerage, pension fund accounts and stock offerings. Max took care of the other essential matters: the best tables in New York restaurants, the finest suites in hotels around the world, introductions to the fanciest hairdressers and tailors in New York, London and Rome, tickets to Broadway and West End theaters that were fully booked. People who suddenly became rich were always surprised to find they needed connections to spend their money. Max the Saint was their connection.

Less salubrious was Max's willingness to provide more intimate services, such as female, or even male, companionship. One demanding auto parts magnate insisted on mother/daughter combinations to help him through stressful nights in New York, and Max always obliged. He drew the line at drugs, but only after his own son wound up in rehabilitation. Then Max added clinics to his list of discreet services, along with helping sons and daughters of clients get into Ivy League schools despite inadequate SATs.

Max's generosity was legendary. He never forgot a client's birthday or anniversary. Twice a year, he took groups of clients on trips, up the Nile, across the Serengeti, through Europe on the Orient Express. Always, he mixed in a few celebrities, business contacts and political figures to add dignity to what was in essence a massive exercise in bribery and kickbacks. When his clients went to jail, as they routinely did, he helped get them assigned to the most comfortable rooms at Allenwood or Lompoc penitentiaries, as well as the best tennis instructors the federal prison system had to offer.

When Lyman became a member of the executive committee, he had tried to get Max moved out of the firm. His effort failed when Cooke pointed out that he was responsible for bringing in $15 million a year in brokerage fees and $1 billion in pension funds.

"You want my support to take over the firm?" Max asked with his usual smile. "I'm not even on the board!"

"If I was running, I'd want your help," Lyman said, "but this is more important."

"Must be money."

"More precisely, where it comes from."

Max inhaled on his cigar.

Lyman continued. "What do you know about Marcel Bresson?"

"Your new client?" He looked surprised. "I probably know some people who know some people."

"Could you ask around?"

"What if you don't like the answers? I want to be protected."

"I just want a lead. I promise not to do anything without information from other sources."

As he thought about it, the smile faded from Max's face. Cigar smoke swirled around his head. "Okay," he finally said. "But on one . . . no, make that two conditions."

Lyman waited.

"First, you agree to take over the firm."

"What for?" Lyman was surprised.

"Second, you put me on the executive committee."

"Why would you want that?" Lyman felt ill. "You always call us *schmucks!*"

"It's getting harder and harder to explain to my clients why I'm not on it."

Lyman had no choice if he wanted Max's help. "All right, I'll get you on the committee."

"And one more thing."

"What?" Lyman said warily. No deal was ever final with Max.

"Tell me what you think of this story. This guy is so proud that his son is going to join the family firm after graduating from Harvard Business School that after the ceremony he announces that he put half the company stock in the kid's name. The kid's excited and they start talking about where he'll start in the business.

"His dad suggests the mail room. The kid goes along, but points out that the dust could be bad for his asthma.

"So then the old man says accounting. His son says fine, but that was his worst subject. He wouldn't want to make a mistake and cost the firm a lot of money—"

Suddenly the loudspeaker in the gym barked, "Jayson Lyman, Jayson Lyman. Please call your office."

"You can use mine." Max pointed to the phone on the wall.

Lyman got through to his secretary.

"You got four calls from Bresson, three from Heidi Bruce, one from the *Wall Street Journal* and your mother wants to know when you're pickin' her up for lunch."

"What did the *Journal* want?"

"He said that News/Worldweek has issued a statement. I got somebody hangin' over the ticker right now."

"I'll be right down. Call my mother and make my apologies, okay?"

"I thought she was deathly ill!"

"Turned out she was just bored."

Now what do I do, Heidi Bruce wondered, I can't even use the professional investigators on the staff! She decided to call Sean Gordon.

"Three two one four," Gordon's secretary responded, giving only his extension number. All the secretaries in the CIA were trained to do the same. The theory was that since the person calling knew the number, no one would be giving away any big secrets.

"It's Heidi. Can I talk to Sean?"

"Miss Bruce, Mr. Gordon's on TDY."

Temporary duty. He was traveling. She remembered his clothes missing from the closet. Was that only last night?

"Is there someplace I can reach him?"

"I'm sorry, I can't give out that information."

"Well, how long will he be gone?"

"I really can't say, Miss Bruce." There was a trace of pleasure in her reply.

"Can you get a message to him?"

"If he calls in."

"Tell him I need to speak with him as soon as possible."

"Maybe someone else in the office could help you," she offered, rubbing it in.

"No, thanks." Heidi hung up and called Jayson Lyman. He was on an overseas call.

Stop it, she told herself. You don't need a man to tell you what to do! Make a list!

When she was done, it had twenty-seven items. The first was to get together with her personal assistant and her intern, the only two people on the staff of sixty-five who actually worked for her. To avoid the curiosity of the rest of the staff, they walked around the block as she gave each of them assignments and swore them to secrecy. They were to meet in room BB-217 in the Capitol at 4:00 P.M. for a follow-up session. From the street she called Jayson Lyman again. He was still "unavailable." Heidi then went home to pack. It was essential that she get out of town before the staff director returned from his seminar.

Room BB-217 was the Chairman's "hideaway" office in the Senate wing of the Capitol building. Every Senator was entitled to one, and, given the Chairman's seniority, his should have been sumptuous. However, he had backed the wrong candidate for majority leader when Senator Robert Byrd retired. As a result, he was given a dank and windowless cubicle in the second sub-basement. The walls were covered with a padded canvas that, when pressed, felt like it must harbor burrowing creatures. Heidi had once tried to estimate the location of the office and came to the conclusion that it was not within the Capitol building at all, but rather under one of the front terraces. The Chairman never went there.

"I didn't have a chance to send your 'funny' passport back to the State Department," Heidi's assistant began, "so you can still use it. And here's what the CRS sent over on Marcel Bresson." She hoisted an eight-inch stack of clippings onto the desk.

The Congressional Reference Service of the Library of Congress was one of the unheralded intelligence resources of the federal government. Frequently, it had information found nowhere else in Washington, simply because nothing on file was classified. But the CRS also had no sense of where to stop.

"They apologized for sending over such an undigested mass," her assistant continued, "but they didn't know exactly what we're looking for."

"I wish I knew myself," Heidi admitted. "It seems to me I can start in one of two places, either Monte Carlo, where Bresson has his principal offices, or Paris, where his main publications are located."

"I'd vote for Monte Carlo," her assistant said. "It's a small town and the closest thing he has to a permanent residence."

"I disagree," said her intern. "Paris has more information resources, the American Chamber of Commerce, rival press organizations and so forth that might give you leads."

"I think Paris," Heidi said, thinking of Lyman's offer of help even though she still had not reached him. "See if I can get a reservation on a flight tonight."

"I've already made one to Nice," her assistant said. "You can postpone the Paris-Nice portion."

"And what's my cover story?" Heidi asked.

"I think you should pretend to be a journalist," the intern responded. "It gives you a reason to be asking questions. Bresson's a big story."

"That's against the law." Heidi shook her head. "What do they teach you at Harvard Law School?"

"To read the law very carefully. It only applies to the executive branch. It's illegal for the CIA to pretend its spies are American journalists, but the law doesn't say anything about the Congress."

"And what publication do I work for?" she asked skeptically.

"Well, the *Harvard Crimson* and the *Lampoon* probably wouldn't get you very far. So I managed to put together this." He handed her a letter. "I got the stationery from another intern who works on the Commerce Committee."

Heidi thought both Sean and Jayson would approve. The letter announced that she was under contract for an article on Marcel Bresson and Les Éditions Bresson. The letterhead was from the *Harvard Business Review.*

"Bresson's coming on!"

"I've got it." Lyman picked up his phone but no one was on the line.

"It's that green thing," Marlene reminded him. "The secure phone."

Lyman lifted the receiver sitting on top of a large green box on his credenza. A fat cable led across the carpet, out the door and down the hall to the computer where the voices were scrambled and unscrambled.

"Why have they rejected my offer?" Bresson demanded.

"You've heard already?"

"You said it was a generous offer. They say it is inadequate!"

"Don't be offended Marcel, it's a negotiation." Dealmaking, Lyman thought, was 95 percent psychotherapy. "This is good news."

"Do not treat me like a fool!"

"Hear me out," Lyman said patiently. "The message from the board is negative, I grant you, but not unexpected, right?"

Bresson said nothing.

"And the timing of their response is positive from our standpoint."

"Why?"

"I thought they might wait until they got another offer from Richardson. Then they could not only reject yours but accept his, locking you out. By just rejecting yours, they're saying publicly to Richardson that he has to have a higher bid. No more inside baseball. Richardson's getting the same arm's-length treatment you are; he no longer controls the board. They've decided to hold a real auction."

"Then we go now with the tender offer." Bresson did not say it was a question.

"No, that wouldn't be wise." A tender was the last thing Lyman wanted, now that he was digging into Bresson's connections. It would set things on automatic pilot. Twenty business days and the deal could be over; the public either tendered their stock or not. Launching a tender offer would reduce his control over the deal—especially, his ability to abort it.

"But we plan that as the next step!" Bresson insisted.

"We've got to be flexible, too." Lyman was searching for excuses. "For one thing, we don't have the documents ready."

"Why not?" Bresson demanded.

"We still need to put together some consolidated financials on your company." He could not help thinking of Rankin.

"Don't worry about that. Maurice has done it. He will be sending you the numbers today."

"That's great." At the mention of Maurice's numbers, Lyman could feel the handcuffs going over his wrists. "But there's another reason to hold up on the tender." Lyman had a new thought. "The family block. The board's shifting. We should follow up on your idea and try to get the family on our side."

"Heidi on line one," Marlene called out.

Lyman covered the mouthpiece, "Tell her to hang on!"

". . . tell me again how that would help," Bresson was saying. More of his deliberately dumb act, Lyman thought.

"You might get a friendly deal! No matter what, it's an advantage to have twenty-two percent more stock in our pocket, particularly from the distinguished family that started the business."

Lyman did not want to get into an academic discussion of takeover tactics. The more ignorant Bresson was, the better. "Listen, Marcel, I've got a call coming in from Washington. Could be important. I'll get right back to you."

He picked up line one. "Heidi! Sorry you had to wait."

"I got your message on my answering machine and I would appreciate any help you can give me," she said, her voice even.

Lyman could tell that she was still wary. "I'm genuinely sorry for what I said or didn't say." He wanted to be conciliatory but not capitulate. "This is a very confusing situation."

"I'm going to try to make it clearer," she replied.

"Well if you need anything in Paris, call Dick Rensselaer, 781 44 691. He's plugged in all over town and has some stories you might find interesting. What are you going to do?"

"I'm leaving tonight. I don't think I should say more over the phone."

"How will you keep me informed of what you've found?"

"I don't intend to." Her voice was firm. "You should be keeping me informed."

"I can't. You know that."

"So we're still not allies." She said it as a fact.

"Let's say we're working parallel at this point. But we should stay in contact."

Heidi did not respond.

"I'll worry about you," he finally admitted.

"I don't know," she said softly. He had gotten through. "We'd need a way that's hard to monitor . . ."

"I've got an idea. What's your airline?"

"TWA."

"Look for a message at the desk."

Dulles International, forty minutes from Washington, D.C., was Heidi's favorite airport in the United States. Designed by Eero Saarinen and Charles Eames, the soaring glass-and-concrete structure evoked the feeling of flight, while also providing convenience to passengers. Instead of miles of corridors and moving sidewalks, special buses effortlessly carried passengers from the terminal to the doors of the airplanes. The Federal Aviation Administration had constantly tried to improve Dulles to the point of breakdown, but so far, it still worked.

Heidi Bruce picked up Jayson Lyman's message at the TWA counter. It read, "Leave messages at (212) 555-7971, Mrs. Harold Lyman. Good luck, be careful. Jay."

Mrs. Harold Lyman! That must be his mother, she thought. Jayson was introducing her to his mother! She was irritated that the thought gave her an extra shot of confidence.

Heidi showed her "funny" passport to the ticket agent, handed over her suitcase and collected her boarding pass. She then pushed her briefcase and light suitbag through the x-ray machine and got in the line for the bus. Just as she was about to board, she heard the public-address system call out a name that seemed familiar. It was her name, she suddenly realized. Not her real name, but her fake name! She rushed to a white courtesy telephone.

Sean Gordon was on the line. In a rush, she explained what she was doing, her eyes nervously fixed on the blinking boarding sign. He told her she was going about it all wrong.

"Terrific!" she said angrily. "You're some goddamned place else when I need you, as usual, and your only advice wrecks my plans!"

She listened to him for another minute and the hostility drained away.

"Of course you're right," she conceded. "But I can't talk. I've got only a few minutes to make the change. How are you? Good, I hope. . . . Happy Birthday."

Rushing back to the TWA counter, she frantically waved down a supervisor. He endorsed her coupon and sent her to Pan Am to change her flight. They had room on a plane leaving in twenty minutes, but could not guarantee her baggage would arrive in Geneva with her.

Geneva, Switzerland. From there, she would take a car to Annecy in nearby France, where Marcel Bresson had been born. Sean Gordon's advice had been impeccably professional. "When establishing some-one's identity," he told her, "always start at the beginning."

13

Heidi's guidebook described Annecy as "a little bourgeois secret," "a jewellike vacation town on the shores of an Alpine lake, surrounded by the spectacular mountains of the Haute Savoie." But coming off of the *autoroute* from Geneva, Annecy looked like any of a thousand small industrial towns scattered across the map of France by the official policy of decentralization: keeping industry away from Paris. Low-rise, blank-walled factories spread in every direction, relieved only by equally bleak high-rise working-class housing projects.

Heidi felt tired from the flight, and the desolate streets made her depressed. Following the signs to the lake, however, she soon found herself in a bustling commercial center with a faintly Mediterranean air. At the lake front, her spirits rose. Five-thousand-foot mountain peaks on each side cupped the deep blue waters that stretched to the horizon. Sailboats darted around a stately white lake steamer, while small bright clouds floated overhead. A broad grass promenade swept around the shore, offering space for townspeople and tourists to stroll and picnic to the music of a tiny gilded carousel.

Heidi left her car in a public parking area, and, directed by the map in her guide book, plunged into the labyrinth of medieval streets and narrow canals that formed the ancient heart of Annecy. Briefcase and suitbag in hand, she followed along beside the river Thiou, which rushed from the lake and flowed around a tiny island built over with a pocket fortress. There she found the Place St-François and, next to a church, the Hôtel de Savoie. Unfortunately, she could not figure out how to get inside. The hotel seemed to have no entrance.

She stared at the hotel building for several minutes, thinking that this was not a propitious beginning to her investigation. Just as she was about to seek help from somebody sitting in one of the cafés lining the square, Heidi realized that she had been looking in the wrong place. The hotel entrance was actually in the facade of the church next door. A small stone doorway led to a winding passageway that took her to the hotel reception area.

Her room proved small but tastefully furnished in French Alpine antiques. She sat on the bed and desperately wanted a nap. Instead, she got up and splashed water on her face from a sink in the corner. Then she hung up her suitbag, took a notebook, tape recorder, and Minox camera from her briefcase, and set out to find the Hôtel de Ville—City Hall.

A salmon-colored neo-classic building situated in a park on the lake front, the Hôtel de Ville was flanked on both sides by small, tree-shaded harbors, one for the lake steamers and the other for sailboats. On the ground floor, just inside the courtyard, Heidi found the *Bureau d'Accueil et Renseignements*—an information office. Having trekked through the wilderness of Washington's bureaucracy, Heidi was amazed and delighted that the French had a system to help people find what they needed from their government. The only problem was that the bureau was closed.

She climbed a broad stone staircase lined with geraniums and potted plants in search of an office that looked like it might contain birth records. However, at 1:45 in the afternoon, the building seemed to have been evacuated for lunch. On the second floor she heard voices and followed them to the end of a long corridor. The voices came from a room richly decorated in blue silk. Rows of chairs occupied by well-dressed men, women and children were drawn up in front of a simple table. Behind it, a portly man in a black suit stood talking to a bride and groom.

The ceremony ended with kisses, hugs, handshakes and camera flashes. Heidi startled the presiding official by interrupting to ask where she could get information on someone's birth. He gave her a quick look up and down, offered her a glass of champagne and asked her to wait a moment.

The rosy glow on his face clashed with the tangerine decor of his office which overlooked the lake and park. The official still carried a half-full bottle of champagne, which he placed on the desk after topping off both their glasses. He settled himself next to her on the settee.

"I am responsible for both marriage and births—after all, what is one without the other?" he said.

"I want to look up someone's birth certificate."

"And why, Mademoiselle?"

"I'm a writer. I'm doing a story."

"It must be someone famous. There are not many from Annecy." He looked like he was about to pat her knee. "Who is it, may I ask?"

"Marcel Bresson."

He almost bit through his champagne glass. *"Oui, oui. Il est vraiment très important."* He stood up and began to pace. "We do not have the records that go back that far."

"Where can I find them?" she persisted.

He sighed as if he did not want to tell her. "Well, it is not secret." He shrugged. "The departmental archive would have the records."

"Where's that?"

"On the way out of town." He vaguely pointed west, "Across from the hospital. But it is not open."

"Ever?"

"It closes Wednesday afternoon."

"What other records do you have here?" she asked.

"Marriages."

"Good. I would like to look up his parents."

"Our office is not open until three o'clock."

"I'll wait."

He thought about that for a moment. "No, perhaps it would be better if you looked in the registry now. Fewer people, you see." He tried to smile.

He led her down the hall and through a glass door marked BUREAU DES MARIAGES. One wall was covered with large brown leather books with dates on the bindings going back to 1900.

"Soon we will also move most of these to the departmental archive. What year do you want?"

"I don't know exactly. His mother was born in 1923, so she would have been seventeen in 1940. I'll start there."

Heidi opened the first book and found all the listings to be chronological. She would have to go through every name. The task was complicated because each entry included not only address and identity-card numbers, but the names and numbers of the parents, in-laws and the presiding magistrate—often taking up a third of a page. Fortunately, the names of the bride and groom were printed. The signatures were illegible.

An hour later she had reached 1943, the year of Marcel Bresson's birth, when the registrar returned from lunch and demanded to know what she was doing. The registrar refused to listen to Heidi's answer and insisted it was impossible for her to work in the marriage bureau offices. Another half hour of wrangling ensued before she could continue reading the records at a desk out in the hall.

The year 1943 had no listing of a marriage between Marcel Bresson's parents. Heidi wondered if his mother could have been married at age sixteen. Or perhaps, given her fatigue, she had simply missed the entry. She decided to run through 1944, because it was a smaller volume than the rest. In the last full year of the war, marriage was evidently not a popular pastime. Still she found no record of a Bresson marriage.

Perhaps they were not married in Annecy, she thought, but in one of the small nearby towns. She was wasting time. Before the day ended, she hoped to visit the library and Marcel Bresson's school. But she could not resist quickly scanning the register for 1945, the last book in her lap. Again she found nothing. At the back, however, she found a postwar innovation, an index. She quickly ran down the list of names and there they were, *Ferdinand BRESSON et Marie Louise FOUCARD,* page 310. She found the page and read the entry. Marcel Bresson's parents had been married in a civil ceremony on September 17, 1945—two years and three months after he was born.

The Annecy library formed part of the Centre Culturel. A large all-glass structure only a few hundred yards from the Hôtel de Ville, the center also housed theaters, restaurants and an exhibition hall displaying a variety of racing cars that had recently won an Alpine Rally sponsored by Les Éditions Bresson. Heidi thought it looked like a mall.

She was looking for old newspapers that might carry Marcel Bresson's birth announcement, or even an account of his parents' marriage. The woman at the periodicals desk was busy reading the magazine *Marie Claire.*

"Excuse me," Heidi said.

The woman did not respond.

"Excuse me, I'm looking for some old newspapers."

The woman turned a page without looking up. "How old?"

"Nineteen forty to 1945."

"Impossible!" The woman closed the magazine and walked away.

Standing there, Heidi felt her anger getting the best of her. "Madame!" she shouted after her, "I demand an explanation!" But the woman disappeared behind a door marked *Privé.* When Heidi tried to follow, she found it locked. Very deliberately, she started banging on the door. "Madame! Madame!" All eyes in the room fastened on her, but no one moved. Suddenly the door flew open.

"We have nothing so old," the woman said as if Heidi knew that, and was being deliberately rude or stupid. "Go to the newspaper," she added, and slammed the door again.

Aware that everyone was still watching her, Heidi searched the rack of newspapers. Apart from a weekly journal devoted to livestock, and a local Communist paper that seemed short on social news, the only paper that had been publishing long enough was *Le Dauphiné*. The masthead indicated that the offices were a block away on the rue Président-Favre.

The clerk at the information desk inside the entrance to the 1920s art deco building passed her to the circulation manager, who took her downstairs to the archivist. He was a tight-faced young man with thick glasses and an earring. From his manner, Heidi imagined that at night he turned into a cycle slut.

"We must know the reason you want access to our archives," he explained.

"I'm writing an article on that period."

"What is it about?" he said, polite but direct.

She had not been prepared for a grilling. "A person," she answered awkwardly.

"Who?" he insisted.

Heidi knew it was a mistake as soon as she opened her mouth, "Marcel Bresson."

But he did not flinch like the official at City Hall. "Please fill out a request giving all the particulars." He handed her a piece of cheap pulp with the newspaper's logo on it. "And leave your address and phone number. You're an American, aren't you?"

"Yes, I'm staying at the Hôtel de Savoie. How long should the request take?"

"Oh, not more than a few weeks," he said, smiling for the first time.

On her way out, Heidi noticed a bronze plaque that she had not seen on her way in. It said: "LE DAUPHINÉ. FONDÉ EN 1927" and below it another, newer sign read, "PUBLICATION DES ÉDITIONS BRESSON."

Not since Jayson Lyman had been a trainee stockbroker with a quota for developing new clients had he resorted to such subterfuge. Marcel Bresson had given him one day to find Raffy Nichols and buy his block of stock in News/Worldweek. Both Raffy's butler and his lawyer refused to divulge his whereabouts. So Lyman called his dealer and presented himself as an art collector.

Raffy was in Camden, New Jersey, installing an exhibit at the Campbell Soup Museum.

As he drove up to the headquarters of the Campbell Soup Company, a complex of red brick buildings that sprawled along the Delaware River across from Philadelphia, he tried to imagine what a museum devoted to soup would contain. Holograms of the original Manhandlers? Bronzed claws from Campbell's first chicken noodle? Cuneiform tablets of unleavened bread used in history's earliest alphabet soup?

Once inside, he found that the museum was devoted to soup tureens. A kindly receptionist offered him a cup of bouillon and a handful of Goldfish crackers, an item also produced by Campbell Soup. Scores of workmen were carefully packing away a temporary exhibition of soup bowls in the form of human skulls which had been made in celebration of Mexico's *Dia de los Muertos*.

Raffy, clad in a bright orange jumpsuit, was in the back installing an exhibit of papier-mâché food. It looked to Lyman like a three-dimensional still life out of Rembrandt, except that everything was giant size and painted in glowing acrylics. The shadows and highlights were drawn in pen and ink.

"Vegetables, meat, dairy products," Raffy said instead of hello. "They've been neglected in Western art since the eighteenth century, don't you think?" In his late twenties, the artist appeared to be slightly overweight and already losing his hair.

"I guess so," Lyman responded. "I liked your animals, the big imaginary ones and wanted to see your latest work."

"The animals are for children. This is adult work. I intend to restore food to a central place in art as it is in life. Aren't you sick of machine art? Sculptures that are machines? Paintings of machines. Lithography of people who look like machines. And nouvelle cuisine! Ugh! Prissy little bits of this and that masquerading as art. They're all pathetic flower arrangements at heart."

His monologue did not invite a response. Lyman despaired of working Raffy around to the subject of control blocks of stock.

"Now this is art!" He caressed a bunch of fat, two-and-a-half-foot-long carrots. "Aren't they almost pornographic? And these sluttish tomatoes! Look at these slabs of beef, obscene, aren't they? Would you call these heads of cauliflower menacing? And this cheese, decadent? And these renegade onions—" Raffy suddenly stopped and looked at Lyman closely. "Are you a collector?"

"I guess you could say I'm more of a dealer."

"I already have a dealer, and an agent, and a gallery."

"I represent someone," Lyman added. "I'm authorized to buy on his behalf."

"No doubt. You see I know who you are. Julian Alexander warned me not to see you."

"So why did you?" Lyman asked, surprised but relieved.

"Curiosity," he said carefully.

Lyman knew that meant Raffy had already figured out that his interests and those of Julian Alexander might not coincide. "My position is simple," Lyman said. "I have a client who wants to buy the company. Do you want to sell?"

"Artists make terrible negotiators. We make things and really don't care whether we sell them or not. Businessmen always pretend that nothing is for sale, when of course everything is."

"Would you negotiate to sell your block separately?" Lyman pressed.

"Alexander tells me that would bring the 'poison pill' into play."

"You're on the board. You can fight to revoke the pill."

Raffy stood there stroking his carrots. "What price?" he finally asked.

"We've already offered $42.50 a share."

"The board rejected it."

"They were on the verge of accepting $36 last week."

"But Richardson might come in with a higher offer."

"Maybe. But I predict it'll be some complicated deal that will be almost impossible to value."

"I really don't know anything about this sort of thing."

"Then get involved. Go to the board meetings. Talk to us. We'll negotiate. If you sit around like a vegetable"—Lyman patted a voluptuous eggplant—"you'll get eaten."

The stone pediment over the entrance to Lycée Berthollet, where Marcel Bresson went to high school, proclaimed that it had been built in 1888. Constructed of white stone and rose-colored stucco and surrounded by wrought-iron fences and shrubs, the school occupied an entire block of a declining residential area. The buildings were meticu-

lously maintained, Heidi noticed, except for a modern concrete addition that was covered with graffiti.

She sat on a wooden bench in the hallway outside the prefect's office.
The wall opposite bore the names of students who had died in the First
World War, the Second World War and Indochina. Hundreds of names
filled the lists, a blow to any community as small as Annecy, Heidi
thought. She also noted that no list existed for those, like Bresson, who
had served in Algeria.

A stiff young man in his early thirties came out and presented himself
as the prefect. When she explained that she wanted to see Bresson's
school records, he said that would be impossible. After ten minutes of
flirting, pleading and arguing, Heidi still could not determine whether
his refusal to be helpful was required by law, regulation, bureaucracy,
or was just a manifestation of French kindness.

"Well, are there any teachers here," she pleaded, "who knew Monsieur Bresson as a student?"

"I don't know," he said.

"Let me put it differently. Is there anyone, a teacher, athletic coach,
maintenance man, who is here now and who was also here in the early
nineteen fifties?"

"I cannot take the time to look up everyone's employment record,
Mademoiselle. My predecessor was here then, but not now."

"Where is he?"

"She, Mademoiselle. She lives in a condo by the lake."

"Can you give me her address?"

"I will call Madame Artaud and ask if she is willing to see you."

Mme Artaud reminded Heidi of a bundle of dried flowers.

"My children bought this apartment for me a few years ago," she
said, showing Heidi into a low-ceilinged modern room crammed with
furniture.

She glanced around at the dark overstuffed chairs and sofas with
white crocheted antimacassars, the sideboards and tables of mahogany,
the oriental rugs piled one upon the other, the heavy velvet drapes, and
somber red cloth wallcovering. Every horizontal surface seemed covered with bric-a-brac; porcelain dishes and ceramic figurines, old snuff
and pill boxes, tiny fading photographs in tortoise-shell frames, miniature clocks, and tiny apparatuses with no discernible function. The
effect was dark and claustrophobic, despite a wall of glass looking out
over the lake. It smelled a hundred years old.

"I remember him. The Bresson boy was very famous when he came back to Annecy."

"You mean after he had become wealthy?"

"No, no. As I said, when he was a boy."

They sat at the window. A young North African woman entered and served herbal tea. Mme Artaud seemed to be talking in riddles. Was it the woman's age or Heidi's jet lag?

"Came back as a boy? I guess I don't understand," Heidi said.

"It was such a turbulent time. We had gone through so much." She sat back and gazed over the lake. "I've lived in this town more than seventy years and every day I am intoxicated by the view. But don't be fooled. This is not some idle and silly summer resort. We have a history. We have basic industry. Aluminum mills. Manufacturers. And of course that means we have Communists. They were despised until the war and the Germans came. Then the Communists led the Resistance. They were heroes. Annecy was a center of the Resistance. While the Parisians slept with the Huns, we died fighting them."

"Marcel's father was in the Resistance, wasn't he?"

"And a Communist, and a hero. What are you writing and why?"

Heidi explained that Marcel Bresson was buying News/Worldweek. "People in America want to know about him."

"I talked to a woman some years ago who was writing a book about him. Poor woman died in an accident. I never saw the book."

"She disappeared off Bresson's boat."

"Yes, a tragedy. She seemed very competent. Asked very good questions."

"Like what?"

"I can't remember now."

"But you knew Marcel well?"

"I could not help it. His mother taught German at the Lycée."

"Where did she learn German?"

"She was middle class. I suppose, like many well-bred ladies, she was taught a foreign tongue."

"But Ferdinand Bresson was a worker. That must have caused problems in the family."

"They were in the Resistance together. The old barriers broke down."

"She was a Communist, too?"

"Of course."

"And you said Marcel came back as a boy. What do you mean?"

"He was reunited with his parents."

"Mme Artaud, I still don't understand."

"Somehow in the turmoil of the war, the boy disappeared, lost. I think they thought he was dead. Then, after the war, there was a refugee organization that put families back together. Sometime in the early fifties, they found Marcel. He had been living with a couple in Grenoble."

"For a dozen years?"

"Remarkable, no? He had a hard time adjusting to his real family. I think the other couple had more money. Ferdinand Bresson made him work. Every day he rode his bicycle to the Restaurant Tante Pise down the lake. Twenty kilometers round trip. I think that is one reason he volunteered for the army."

"What did his parents think of that?"

"It was during the Algerian war, and the Communists were against it. His mother was heartbroken. His father declared he would never see him again."

"Was the break permanent?"

"So far. They are still alive, you know."

"Do you think they would talk to me?"

Mme Artaud's eyes narrowed, and for the first time, Heidi saw the glint of steel she must have needed to run the Lycée Berthollet.

"Never," she said in a way that welcomed no questions. Then she sipped her tea as her faced softened again. "You see, the boy came back to his family when he was twelve or thirteen and left when he was seventeen. You could say that he was just passing through their lives."

Lyman broke his rule and drank a glass of champagne during working hours. The helicopter had dropped him at the East 34th Street pier and a few minutes later he was in his office where de Grazia was handing out bottles of Dom Perignon from a washtub full of magnums. His United Elastic deal had closed. A major supplier to the apparel industry, UE, as it would now be called, had acquired Seabrook Insurance to become a major player in the financial services industry. Jayson drank to congratulate de Grazia, the staff, and secretly, himself, for at last getting Marcel Bresson under control.

In Lyman's mind, talking to Raffy Nichols had started out as a diversion, a play for time. However, he soon realized that Raffy offered him a chance to dominate the controlling asset in the deal. As small as it was, Raffy's block of stock was still the largest, and if manipulated properly, it could determine the fate of the company. By managing Raffy, Lyman controlled the transaction and also Marcel Bresson.

He allowed de Grazia to refill his glass as he talked to Bresson on the secure phone.

"I've got Raffy in my pocket," Lyman bragged. "He'll do whatever I say. It's obvious to him that Julian Alexander's playing his own game. I poured a little more poison in his ear and told him to ask Alexander whether he planned to take on Richardson as a client after the deal."

"What does this do for me?" Bresson asked.

"We've got a Trojan horse inside the board. It expands our options. We could end up with a negotiated deal and not have to go through the trouble and expense of a hostile tender."

Lyman had begun to feel enthusiastic about the deal again. Sitting in his office high over New York Harbor, with the Dom Perignon going to work and the crisp, clear air hinting at October, it was hard to believe that he was involved in something sinister. He allowed himself to think about what the deal could mean to him, what it would feel like to run Gould Axewroth. The other houses on the Street sensed the firm's weakness and would give him no quarter. Lyman would face a whole new level of challenge. Would that fill the growing emptiness he felt in his work? Was he ready to grow beyond himself to assume responsibility for others, for building an organization? Was he willing to play a role in society and not simply prey upon it? And what if that required closing a deal for a murderer? Of one of his own staff? He had to reach a decision about Bresson fast or he was going to become schizophrenic.

"You were supposed to buy Raffy's stock," Bresson was complaining. "Will he sell or not?"

"Marcel, we've got to be flexible," Lyman responded.

"I cannot stress too strongly the importance of adhering to the Bürgenstock Plan." He made it sound like an international treaty.

"Look, we've got an opportunity here," Lyman explained. "Raffy's asked for a board meeting tomorrow. He's going to propose setting up a special subcommittee to negotiate with us. That'll start talks rolling and get the toads on the board out of the way."

"Will we have to raise our offer?" Bresson asked warily. "I'm not going to bid against myself. If we talk, I want a counter proposal from them."

"Let's not get ahead of ourselves, Marcel. We're just trying to get our foot in the door. This isn't the time to make demands."

"I'm not about to beg!" Bresson shouted.

The conversation was getting off the rails. "Nobody thinks that," Lyman said soothingly. "But what's wrong with a little finesse? Between you and Raffy, you control almost a third of the stock. We're making major progress here!" Lyman insisted. "Raffy's an enormous asset to the deal."

"Can he bring it off by himself?" Bresson demanded.

"No," Lyman conceded. "He needs our help. But—"

"Exactly. That is why we will announce a tender offer tomorrow," Bresson said flatly. "That was our plan. I see no reason to change."

"Wait," was all Lyman could think to say.

"I want no more delay."

Lyman felt angry at the accusation, even though it was true.

"I have researched this Raffy Nichols," Bresson continued. "He is an artist. Why would the board pay attention to him, when it rejects me?"

Uh oh, Lyman thought, so it's ego. He should have seen it coming.

"A tender will strengthen Raffy's position," Bresson said firmly, "if, indeed, he is in your pocket as you claim." He stressed the word "your" as if he had seen through Lyman's effort to control him through Nichols. "If he is not, we are moving ahead as planned."

"This is a mistake, Marcel." He decided to be blunt. "A tender throws down the gauntlet. You're just going to undermine him. Get everybody riled up." Lyman's frustration was growing.

"I am not asking your advice. I am giving you instructions."

"I don't know if we can get space in the *Journal* and *Times* for the announcement."

"We planned for today. Against my own judgment, I delayed that. If you are unable to launch the offer tomorrow, I will find another investment banker."

Lyman could barely keep from telling Bresson to fuck himself. His mind raced through the options. Could I switch horses, he wondered? Represent Raffy and kill Bresson from the other side? You must be smoking dope, he told himself. Maybe I should just walk away. Wash my hands of the whole thing. And turn your back on Rankin? he asked himself. On the firm? On Heidi, who was in Europe somewhere taking God knows what risks?

"All right, Marcel. Whatever you say," Lyman gave in. "It's your money."

The road to Talloires wound up and down the face of the steep mountains that formed the eastern shore of the lake. Heidi's rented Ford

Escort passed several Frenchmen struggling up the steep grades on their black bicycles. She thought of Marcel Bresson making the trip as a boy twice a day.

The afternoon sun had dipped below the mountains to the west. Sailboats were heading to the small anchorages dotted around the margin of the long, narrow lake. The road carried Heidi past new spacious villas and tiny villages undergoing gentrification. Her destination was Tante Pise, the famous restaurant on the lakefront. She was working on instinct, not knowing what to expect, probing every lead, while she waited for the departmental archive to open its doors the next day. Her luggage still had not arrived, and she had been tempted to go shopping at the many small boutiques near her hotel in the old center of Annecy. However, Tante Pise had said she would only be willing to talk about Marcel Bresson that afternoon and for only fifteen minutes before dinner began.

The town of Talloires spilled down the hillside to a small harbor. There Heidi found the restaurant situated in a private park, tables set under the trees, guests sipping their apéritifs and watching the boats rocking at anchor. Tante Pise proved to be a formidable fireplug of a woman in her early seventies, dressed in a Chanel suit and exuding the charm of a construction foreman.

"Several of my *garçons* did not show today, so it is even more difficult to talk," she declared amid the din of the kitchen. "At least Marcel was always on time."

They walked along the gravel path at the edge of the lake. The fragrance of late summer roses filled the air.

"He was an unremarkable boy," Tante Pise said. "I remember him primarily for his gluttony and his envy."

"That seems like a harsh thing to say about a boy who was only a teenager," Heidi found herself defending him.

"We are a service business. To succeed, you must understand character. He could never make a good waiter because he was fat and customers do not want to be reminded of what food can do to you. And second, he so envied the clientele he would have ended up treating them arrogantly, like most waiters do in this country."

"How did you know he was envious?"

"He would spend his entire break staring at the cars in the parking lot." Heidi had also noticed the Ferraris, Rolls-Royce Corniches, and BMW M-6s as she came in the gravel driveway. "Or he would stand like a statue on the shore gaping at the girls and boys who were water skiing or sailing on the lake."

"Did he ever say anything?" Heidi asked.

"Politics? No, never. Bizarre when you think of his father as such an important Communist."

"Important?"

"A union leader, hero of the Resistance. I was surprised when he came out to ask me to give his son a job."

"Why did he do it?"

"He said he wanted the boy away from the town and the trouble he could get into there," she said doubtfully.

"You believe there was another reason?" Heidi pressed.

"Yes. I believe he wanted to cultivate that envy, make it burn deep so that it would sustain the resentment required to be a good Communist in France."

"Were you surprised when he left to join the army?"

"Very surprised."

"Did he do it to spite his father?"

"Possibly. It was his father who wrote to the local Communist Party paper, denouncing him for fighting in Algeria. You know he never fought, though. He was a cook."

They had come to a stone landing where small fishing boats were unloading their catch. Heidi noticed they used gill nets.

"Did you see him after he joined the army?"

"Only once," Tante Pise replied. "He came back to tell me that he was entering the University of Grenoble and asked if he might work here on holidays."

"You turned him down?"

"No. But I told him he was a fool to go to University. He would never be happy. He was a working-class boy driven by envy, not ambition. Nothing would satisfy him. It would be better to accept who he was."

"But if he had intelligence and capability," Heidi protested.

"American nonsense. A formula for frustration and discontent. Do you think today he is happier than these fishermen?"

An old man was laughing as he and another fisherman in a black sweater untangled the catch from the net. A young woman blossoming with a seven-month pregnancy helped sort the fish into boxes. They all looked tanned and healthy. Heidi answered, "I don't know," but for a fleeting moment she envied the young woman.

Tante Pise insisted that Heidi stay and eat with her in a private dining room behind the reception area. She told Heidi to try the fish paté and lobster à l'armoricaine along with a crisp chardonnay, which she poured from a cut-glass decanter. But as soon as the meal began, a crisis erupted in the kitchen and Tante Pise disappeared. Heidi ate the meal alone, hardly tasting the food, running what she had learned about Marcel Bresson over and over in her mind. She felt disappointed. She had developed more questions and no damning answers.

When she finished and her host had not returned, Heidi went to the kitchen to express her appreciation. Tante Pise was surprised to see her, evidently having forgotten she was there. But Tante Pise remembered the check. Her gracious invitation cost Heidi more than one hundred dollars.

It was dark as her car climbed the switchbacks out of Talloires and headed toward Annecy. Heidi was ready for sleep. She focused so hard on the road ahead and on staying awake that she hardly noticed the car behind her.

The blue BMW 535i kept a respectful distance. But the car carefully followed every turn Heidi made as she entered Annecy, stopping at the curb in a red zone when Heidi pulled into the public parking area. As she crossed the street and entered the maze of old streets that led to her hotel, a man got out of the BMW and followed her. It was Edouard. The Vietnamese driver remained behind the wheel.

14

Lyman considered a tender offer the closest thing Wall Street had to a genuine military operation. Dealmakers loved violent metaphors—"kill zone," "preemptive strike," "scorched earth"—but in Lyman's experience, most merger negotiations were fraught with tedium rather than danger, endless hours of talk and waiting relieved only by unremitting tension. After a dozen years in the business, Lyman could see that most merger moves were ritualized, the confrontations static. Even in a hostile takeover, the negotiations had all the kinetic energy of Japanese Noh theater, where spectators went out for lunch and returned to find the actors in the same posture still repeating lines at one another.

But a tender offer was action. It provided release and at least the illusion of power. With a hostile tender offer, a fuse was lit. Complex financial forces, legal and public relations machinery were set in motion. And regardless of how well prepared the combatants, the result of the battle was always in doubt.

As soon as Jayson Lyman had hung up on Bresson, his office became command headquarters. He ordered out for Chinese and began poring over the tombstones, the black-bordered formal notices in the *Wall Street Journal* and *New York Times* that would announce that a subsidiary of Les Éditions Bresson, Bresson USA, was offering $42.50 a share to purchase any and all of the outstanding shares of News/Worldweek. Stockholders would have twenty business days to "tender" their shares, that is, sell to Bresson at the offered price.

Lyman's staff assured him that the wording of the announcement had been triple-checked in advance by lawyers at Skadden Fried. He called McFadden Dworkin. The public relations firm had been reserving newspaper space for several days, not knowing exactly when the tender might be launched. Because insider-trading scandals had involved Wall

Street's invisible people—the messengers, printers, secretaries, journalists, computer operators and even cab drivers—special procedures had been developed to try to prevent the release of information before tender offers were published.

When McFadden Dworkin received Jayson Lyman's go-ahead, they waited until the New York Stock Exchange closed before notifying the newspapers that a tombstone would be printed the next day. Bonded messengers with padlocked carrying cases transported the layout and text to special offices at each of the newspapers. Carefully screened photoengravers at each newspaper transformed the camera-ready layout on Velox paper into a metal sheet containing an entire page to appear in the next day's edition. The metal sheets would be handcarried to the press rooms while facsimiles of the tender offer were also transmitted by AT&T satellites to the ten *New York Times* printing plants in the United States, and via Intelsat to the *Wall Street Journal*'s presses in twenty-two locations around the world. By midnight, eastern standard time, the presses were rolling from Edison, N.J., to Singapore, and any hope Lyman had of controlling the outcome was gone.

In the classic tradition of most military maneuvers, Lyman had also prepared a deception operation by reserving space for the tender announcement in the *Washington News*. He had no intention of putting a tombstone in the *News,* but sought to lull News/Worldweek executives into thinking that the tender had not started so long as the space remained unused. As a further tactic to guarantee surprise, McFadden Dworkin had arranged for the tender notice not to appear in the first edition of the *Times,* which was always sent by air to Washington.

After signing off on the tombstone, Lyman turned to the press release. It was embargoed for 9:00 A.M. the next day, meaning that journalists could read but not report it until that time. While McFadden Dworkin was enforcing the strictest security measures, Lyman called his favorite reporters at the *Times* and *Journal* to tell them they could ignore the embargo and use the material on a background basis for the stories in the second editions of their paper.

By one in the morning, he was staring at the consolidated financial statements provided by Maurice the accountant. They were crucial to the 14D filing with the SEC and the responses to the twenty-two-page Hart-Scott-Rodino questionnaire which had to be submitted to the Justice Department and the Federal Trade Commission.

Everything looked fine. Les Éditions Bresson appeared healthy. The only problem was that the numbers did not track.

"Get him on the phone!" Lyman yelled.

A sleepy voice came on the line.

"Maurice, your balance sheet does not add up!"

"*Alors*, add it correctly then," he growled.

"We did, and the balance sheet doesn't balance."

"What do you suggest? I do not know the American accounting."

"Like every place else in the world, Maurice, the assets and liabilities have to match."

"We worked very hard to develop this information," he replied truculently.

Yeah, your ass must be very sore from pulling numbers out of it, Lyman thought. "If you don't have better data, you've got two choices. You can increase the goodwill or reduce your net worth."

"What is goodwill?"

"When you pay more for an asset than its book value, the excess is called goodwill."

"Is it a big discrepancy?"

"A few million."

"Leave goodwill alone. There may be records of what we paid and so forth. Change the net worth. It is only a plug number anyway, assets minus liabilities. It can change day to day."

"Maurice, do you mind if I ask you a question?"

"What is it?"

"Where did you go to school to learn accounting?"

"I did not go to school. I worked in a bank in Italy, in Venice."

"Didn't they invent double-entry bookkeeping?" Lyman said as if that should have made Maurice an expert.

"But they never made any money"—he managed a short laugh—"until they invented triple-entry bookkeeping." He hung up.

Lyman handed the draft Hart-Scott-Rodino filing to Karen Kobyashi. "Adjust the net worth. And make sure there's a disclaimer in every document that disassociates Gould Axewroth from any of Bresson's numbers."

At two o'clock in the morning, the collating machine on the copier broke down. The secretaries moved into the conference room, spreading little stacks of documents all over the table. They formed a line to the copier, passing the paper from hand to hand like a bucket brigade.

At 2:20, the copier stopped working. Lyman was not reassured by the Japanese accent on the answering machine when he dialed the twenty-four-hour service number. He hated going to an outside copying house, even if he could find one at that hour. But he had no alternative. He called Hysteric Press, Wall Street's premier emergency copiers.

"Yo! Hysteric here."

Lyman explained his problem.

"No sweat," Tyrone, the night man, assured him. "We all hot to go down here. We get it done; don't have no fear," he rapped. "Your job ain't no big surprise. We all crazy fast besides!"

Lyman handed the phone to Marlene to work out the details. Maybe she spoke Tyrone's language.

It was still dark when the half-dozen couriers left Gould Axewroth for La Guardia Airport. Five of them would travel on the Pan Am Shuttle to Washington and the sixth, the back-up, would take the Trump Shuttle a half hour later. They were all from "Cohen-Is-Goin." In ten years, it had grown from a bicycle messenger business run by Hasidic Jews to a world-wide personal courier service.

The first team arrived at National Airport at 7:30 A.M. Each took a separate cab to his assigned destinations. Four of them headed over the 14th Street Bridge toward downtown and the fifth took Key Bridge to Georgetown. One stopped at the Pennsylvania Avenue entrance of the Justice Department. He showed his identification to the guard and was directed to the Office of Operations in room 3214.

The courier carried a bulky envelope containing a filing required by the Hart-Scott-Rodino Act of 1976, which had been designed to give the government better information with which to decide whether proposed takeovers violated federal laws prohibiting monopolies. The Justice Department also used the filing to see if any other federal laws or regulations were being broken. The Department had fifteen working days to challenge the takeover. If it judged the information inadequate, it could take another ten days, disrupting the deadline for the tender. That was why the envelope was so fat.

The courier found the office open and busy. He handed over the package and explained it was a Hart-Scott-Rodino filing.

"That's all right, honey, we'll treat it nice anyway," the long-legged woman at the plywood desk assured him while she signed the receipt. Then she winked and offered him coffee and a sweet roll. He was surprised. It was the iron law of his profession that all receptionists hated all couriers.

The second messenger also carried a copy of the Hart-Scott-Rodino filing. His cab dropped him a few blocks further down Pennsylvania Avenue, at the corner of Sixth, home of the Federal Trade Commission. The FTC also had a say over whether proposed mergers violated anti-trust laws. In the past, Justice and the FTC had sometimes disagreed. More recently, the FTC followed the lead of the Justice Department on takeovers in the communications industry. Still, the FTC demanded the information. The guard at the door sent the courier to the Pre-Merger Office on the third floor. At 8:35 A.M. it was still closed. He sat on the stairs to wait.

The third messenger hand carried a Form 14D filing to the Securities and Exchange Commission on Fifth Street, stopping first at the Roy Rogers next door for breakfast. The SEC's responsibility was to protect shareholders, and to do so, it required Bresson to file a 14D report containing information about his financial condition, sources of funds, and his purpose and plans for News/Worldweek and its executives. Lyman considered his 14D-1 a masterpiece of obfuscation. He accompanied it with a letter, which Bresson and Beck had approved, that Lyman knew would provoke Richardson's lawyers.

After downing a Trail Boss Egg Platter with chicken-fried steak, the courier delivered ten copies of the 14D-1 filing to the SEC's first-floor Documents Control Room. He also handed over the separate letter to the secretary of the Commission that Lyman had prepared. It exercised Bresson's right to conceal from the public the fact that the Swiss Bank Corporation was providing his funding.

The fourth courier delivered a 14D filing to the corporate offices of News/Worldweek at 16th and K Street. The guard at the reception desk signed the manifest and tossed the envelope onto a pile, along with a hundred other pieces of express and priority mail.

The fifth courier had the trickiest assignment. He was under instructions personally to hand the 14D to Drew Richardson at 8:30 A.M. If Richardson left his home before that hour, the courier was to give it to him immediately. The messenger had been sitting on the front fender of a parked car in front of Richardson's Georgetown home for thirty-five minutes.

Meanwhile, Richardson was in his upstairs gym pedaling his Schwinn Airdyne while reading the morning's *Washington News,* and

New York Times and watching his cable TV news network. He had quickly scanned the papers for Bresson's threatened tender offer, and finding none, allowed himself to relax. He felt increasingly confident that he would beat Marcel Bresson in the battle to take over News/ Worldweek. Three days had passed since the board had rejected Bresson's bid and not a word had come from him or his investment bankers. His own revised bid was almost complete. And with another twenty-four hours to decide on the specifics, Richardson was thinking of squeezing in a round of golf.

As he came to the ten-mile mark, he stopped pedaling and switched off the TV. That was when he heard the police sirens coming from his front yard. At the same moment, his wife burst into the gym.

"Come quickly," she said breathlessly, still in her dressing gown. "I called the police. A black man's been loitering in front of the house."

The front door bell began to buzz and the butler called up through the intercom, "Some gentlemen from the police department are here to see you, sir."

In the entry hall, Richardson found himself in the company of a half-dozen black men: his butler, four policemen and the courier. It was a unique and uncomfortable feeling.

"We received a complaint—" one of the police said.

"This man has been staring at our home for almost an hour!" Mrs. Richardson interrupted.

"I'm just here to deliver a letter!" the messenger protested.

"Then why were you loafing about?" Mrs. Richardson demanded.

"I'll tell you why. Just waiting for my husband to leave so you could break in and rape me!"

The six black men, including the butler, looked at Mrs. Richardson and then at each other. If, at some point, all women must choose between their faces and their behinds, Mrs. Richardson had surrendered the latter. Any attack through the yards of material she used to hide her girth would have been a harrowing journey, even for a courier from "Cohen-Is-Goin."

"If he's got something for me," Drew Richardson said with authority, "let's see it."

The courier asked him to sign a receipt first. Richardson tore open the package. Inside he found the letter from Gould Axewroth that he had been dreading.

"Sir, if you've no objection," said one policeman, "we'll let the man go."

"Can't really charge him with rape," chuckled another.

"Maybe not," Richardson said, his anger growing as he read the tender offer, "but he ought to be booked as an accessory!"

Lyman had come to hate the green secure phone. Since Bresson refused to talk on any other instrument, it kept Lyman confined to his office like a ball and chain.

"Within the hour," he was explaining to Bresson, "two hundred Wall Street stock analysts, money managers and arbitrageurs will each get a package explaining why this is a good deal. We're trying to build momentum. Make your offer look like the irresistible winner. Richardson could come back with a bid very close to yours. We want you to have the psychological edge."

Bresson said he was more worried about the political reaction in Washington.

"I've just signed off on five hundred mailgrams to newspaper editors and TV stations all over the country telling our side of the story."

"What kind of story?" Bresson asked.

"Americans own newspapers in Europe and Asia. Other countries are involved in the media here. Hell, the Japanese are financing most of our movies now! And there's some schmaltz in the message about Franco-American relations, Yorktown, Lafayette, *Liberté,* the Rights of Man. McFadden Dworkin prepared it." Lyman had felt nauseous when he read it.

"I'm also putting out a release explaining that you've taken this step reluctantly because of the board's rejection of your friendly offer. And on background, I'm telling key journalists that the board's playing a double game. It came close to approving a much lower offer from Richardson. We've got to challenge their integrity to keep them honest."

"But a press campaign could invite political interference."

"Marcel, the United States government has no legal authority to stop this deal. We don't need its approval. There's no antitrust problem, because you're foreign. The only national security grounds are if the company was doing classified work or providing strategic materials. News/Worldweek doesn't do either one. You can't own a majority interest in the TV stations, but I've sent a letter to the Chairman of the FCC saying you'll comply with that rule as soon as the takeover's completed. This isn't Canada or Britain or France where the government can stop a foreign merger for any reason it likes. This is a free country!"

"But the government could harass me, slow things down," Bresson fretted.

"Don't let it worry you," Lyman insisted, silently praying that that was exactly what would happen.

She smelled the French coffee even before she was fully awake. It sat on a tray just outside her door, together with a pitcher of hot milk and a basket of brioche and croissants. Heidi opened the shutters and let in the morning light, then she put the tray on the table by the window so she could eat and watch the people in the square below.

Heidi felt rested but apprehensive. Investigations took time, and she didn't have much time. Maybe Sean was wrong. Maybe she should be focusing on Bresson's current activities. If nothing unusual turned up at the departmental archive, she would have to reevaluate her approach.

The archive was located in a mustard-colored building that sat on a hill overlooking both the town and the lake. One wing was attached to a round medieval tower, while flying buttresses held up the opposite wall. In between, it looked like any other nineteenth-century government building. Heidi circled it several times before deciding to park in a courtyard reserved for the municipal gallery of art. The blue BMW pulled into the parking lot of the hospital on the other side of the highway.

The gallery turned out to be in the same building as the archive, which was housed in the tower. Heidi was greeted by a middle-aged man who regarded her as an interruption.

"I would like to see a birth certificate."

"Yours?" he asked, smoothing down the few hairs remaining on his head. "If you want copies, you must fill out this form. It will take a while."

"No, not mine. A Marcel Bresson, born June 1943."

"Then fill out this form. I'll get to it as soon as I can, but you can see I'm busy."

As far as Heidi could tell, he was moving a stack of cards from one place on his desk to another. "Maybe I could just look in the files myself?"

"Absolutely not!"

She filled out the form, using her pseudonym, and put her false passport number in the blank that called for her identity number. The space marked "reason for request" she left blank.

The clerk took the form and put it in a pigeonhole on his desk. She sat on a hard wooden chair and waited. After a while, a group of young students came in wearing American baseball jackets. In typical French style, most were embroidered with names in English that sounded peculiar. "Busy Action Team," "Task Force Hellcats." But two others had team jackets with Russian words in Cyrillic. A sign of the times, Heidi thought.

She paid no attention to what they were saying to the clerk until she overheard the words *"vieux journaux."* Old newspapers! The clerk allowed the students past the desk and pointed up the winding staircase. "You can look for yourselves, but put everything back. And remember, I know your names."

Heidi asked if the old papers went back to the 1940s. He nodded. "Could I look through them?"

"You are a student?" he asked suspiciously.

"No, a writer."

Suddenly, his tone turned respectful. "You want the second floor. Our purpose is to serve the intellectual life. It is an honor to help. What have you written? Who is your favorite French author?"

Heidi vanished up the stairs before she could be drawn into a discussion of Proust.

The newspapers lay in flat green boxes stacked on shelves. A whole wall was devoted to the nineteenth century. She located the boxes for *Le Dauphiné* labeled 1940–1942 and 1943–1945. Removing them from the shelf, she noticed that they seemed unexpectedly light. When she opened them up, she found that the papers were only a few pages each and that many dates were missing. However, the volume and issue numbers were continuous. That suggested that the gaps resulted from the newspaper's being closed by German or Vichy authorities. She quickly leafed through the pile, looking for a June 1943 issue that might have noted Marcel Bresson's birthday. She found several copies. Unfortunately, they carried neither birth nor death notices. Wartime austerity, she decided disappointedly.

Next, she searched for an issue that might have carried Bresson's parents' wedding in 1945. It was there, volume XXV, number 17. But the small notice in fourteen-point type said nothing more than the public document at the city hall.

Heidi reviewed her notes. Bresson was reunited with his family in 1955. She began to comb through the issues for that year. It took her over an hour before she came across an issue with a young Marcel Bresson looking at her from the front page. His return received a banner headline. The article ran down the right-hand side of the paper and onto the back page. Despite the length of the story, it was, like most French journalism, long on language and short on information. It covered the reunion in extensive detail but said nothing about how he was lost. The article described how he had lived for a dozen years with a couple in Grenoble. Heidi wrote down their name. It also reviewed the parents' war record, concluding cryptically that Madame Bresson had suffered extensively as a result of her role in the Resistance. That was it.

With deepening frustration, Heidi put the box back. She searched the shelves hoping to find another newspaper of record, but the other publications of the period were either devoted to sports, automobiles, or farming.

Just as she was about to go back downstairs, she noticed a glass front cabinet with yellowing papers stacked unprotected inside. She opened the door and looked at one. It was called *"La Patrie: le Journal de la Famille et du Travail"*—in English, *Homeland: the Journal of Family and Work*. Over the masthead was an engraving of a bundle of wheat. The earliest issue of the paper was dated 1941. Heidi realized she was looking at the local fascist newspaper.

Out of curiosity rather than purpose, she began to leaf through them. They followed a standard formula. The front page always contained one picture and four articles: an announcement from the German-controlled government in Vichy, a report on some happy collaboration in science or the arts between France and Germany, a dispatch from French "volunteers" with the German army, and a local story about increased production at the aluminum mills or ball-bearing factories. Often a front-page box reported some terrible outrage committed by a Jew. The photograph invariably showed young girls handing flowers to Nazis or French Collaborationist officials.

But Heidi noticed a marked change in the issues starting in the middle of 1942. The quality of the newsprint declined, the paper was reduced to eight pages, and photographs appeared infrequently. The tone of the reporting, always self-congratulatory, became more insistent and defensive.

By early 1943, notices began to appear in front-page boxes announcing a reward for information leading to the arrest of certain "Jews and bandits." Heidi began to read more carefully and with quickening interest. Soon, she found lead stories reporting the arrest or capture of certain unnamed "Jews, Communists, and bandits." In the March 17 issue, Heidi found a black-bordered box offering a reward for Marcel Bresson's father. Then, in the April 21 *Homeland,* Heidi discovered the name of Marcel Bresson's mother. She appeared in a long list of persons arrested for collaborating with Communist bandit gangs. The article reported that the entire group had been transported to Grenoble for "interrogation."

Heidi quickly searched through the remaining copies of *Homeland* looking for further news of Bresson's parents. There was nothing. Disappointed, she returned to the April 21, 1943, issue and stared at it for a long time. The article hinted at what Mme Bresson suffered for her role in the Resistance. Yet there was something else about the report. Something disturbing that she could not put her finger on. Finally, disgusted with herself, she put the copies of *Homeland* back into the cabinet and went downstairs to find out how the clerk was doing on her request for Marcel's birth certificate.

"It is good you came, Mademoiselle, I was just about to close for lunch."

"Can I see it?" she asked.

"I'm afraid I have bad news. The document is unavailable."

"Why?" Heidi demanded.

"It has been destroyed."

"By whom?"

"An accident, Mademoiselle. A fire. When we were moving to this building. It destroyed many valuable documents including almost all the birth certificates for 1943."

"How do such people get their identity cards?" she asked, incredulous.

"If they lost them? Well, there are records. Everyone in Annecy knows everyone. Relatives would make an affidavit. Family friends could give an oath."

"Where are those files kept?"

"The Prefecture. But I warn you, Mademoiselle, they are government papers. You could not see them without ministerial approval."

Suddenly, Heidi did not care. She did not have to see affidavits testifying to Marcel Bresson's birth in Annecy on June 17, 1943. She realized that the fascist newspaper report on his mother made the point moot. She had been arrested and sent to Grenoble two months before Marcel was born.

"Tell me again why we should offer paper," Richardson said.

Blackie Muldoon groaned inwardly. They had been going over the same ground for three days. He had seen it before in other CEOs; Richardson was paralyzed by indecision. But they could not delay any longer. Bresson's tender forced their hand. Yet he wondered if he could squeeze a decision out of Richardson. He had become surprisingly emotional. When, at the insistence of the board, they had to move their meetings to the Madison Hotel, Richardson had flown off the handle. "I know it's just for appearances," he had thundered, "but News/Worldweek is my company, dammit!" Now it was nut-cutting time. If Richardson didn't make a decision fast, Muldoon had to make clear that he would never control more than the point seven percent he currently owned.

"What will paper do?" Richardson asked again.

"Make it look like we're offering more," Blackie responded.

"That could be fraud," the chief financial officer warned. "The analysts will see right through it!"

"The paper will not be worthless," Blackie patiently insisted, smoothing back his oil-slicked hair and running his hands down his suspenders. "We have reduced the cash in the offer and put in convertible debentures. The whole thing adds up to at least $45.50 a share. We can legitimately claim it's $47 to $48 a share. There's no market to prove us wrong. Some analysts will say it's $45.50, others maybe more. But even if most of the Street says that it isn't $48, we've got uncertainty going for us. We're giving the board elbow room. It's a question of trust. Who're they going to believe, Drew Richardson or some Frenchman?"

Richardson looked uncomfortable.

"Your only other choice is to actually pay more," Blackie added. "Then you'd have sell off pieces to pay for it."

"You know I've ruled that out!" Richardson snapped. Over the last several days, he had become convinced that Muldoon wanted to break up the company so he could earn more fees.

Richardson glanced uneasily around the table. His staff was no help. All of them looked terrified. They had never been involved in a deal anywhere near the magnitude of the News/Worldweek buyout. He hadn't either.

"Every day you wait," Blackie concluded, "you, and any offer you make, loses credibility. Bresson's got the jump on you. If you don't decide soon, on October fifteenth, News/Worldweek will be his."

Slowly, Richardson nodded. "Let's go for it." He had been a CEO long enough to keep his voice from betraying the anxiety he felt.

"And the crown jewels?" Blackie pressed. "Bresson can't pay $50 a share if he doesn't get the cable outlets."

"All right," Richardson conceded. "Can we put the deal on the table today?"

"Maybe," Blackie hedged. "The Zeebergs could want some technical fixes to their participation."

Richardson nodded as if he understood, but for the first time he began to wonder if he was in the driver's seat.

The blue BMW followed Heidi from the departmental archive to the post office. At the international desk she arranged to phone Jay Lyman's mother to leave the number of her hotel. Mrs. Lyman kept her on the line for fifteen minutes, relentlessly asking questions, including whether Heidi was married and had children.

She then moved to a stall which had a phone attached to a video monitor that received tele-text messages. Hundreds of thousands of the Minitel machines had been given away by the French Post, Telephone and Telegraph service as a marketing ploy to increase usage of the phone lines. And it had worked. The French used Minitel for everything from looking up new recipes and stock quotes, to pornography. Unlike America, where dial-a-porn specialized in heavy breathing, in France the corruption of children at least required that they learn to read.

The machine also served as a telephone directory. Heidi quickly found the address of Bresson's parents in a part of town called Old Annecy.

Except for an ancient *Café-tabac,* the neighborhood turned out to be quite new. The Bressons lived in a public apartment block designed in the latest French style. Like the Beaubourg museum in Paris, the things that should be inside—wiring, water pipes, gas, heating ducts, staircases—were all on the outside. It had the beauty and elegance of an enormous insect.

Heidi had hoped to interview the Bressons' neighbors before approaching them. But it seemed unlikely that in such a new building anyone would remember little Marcel. Interviewing Bresson's parents was a critical step in the investigation. Mme Artaud's judgment that they would never cooperate made Heidi hesitate. But she had no choice. She would have to find a way to talk to them. After checking for their names on the mailboxes, Heidi took the elevator straight to the third floor.

The corridor had the Middle Eastern smell of cumin. A North African woman with a baby passed her in the hall. Heidi knocked on the door of 308. No one answered for a long time.

When the door opened, Heidi found herself confronting a woman in her mid-seventies with bright blue eyes, an unsmiling mouth and hair drawn back in a chignon.

"Yes?" she said without welcome.

"Who's there?" shouted a man watching television. He seemed to be confined to the couch.

Heidi gave her false name. "I'm writing a story about your son—"

Mme Bresson slammed the door in her face.

"I'll talk to him myself," Richardson declared angrily. "Call Toronto."

"That's a good idea," Blackie Muldoon agreed.

Karl Zeeberg came on the line. "That fucking Frenchman's giving us a run for our money." He laughed.

Easy for you to take it calmly, Richardson thought, I'm just a page in your portfolio. "Muldoon tells me you want to change the deal," he said, too abruptly.

"No, you want to change it," Zeeberg replied smoothly. "I just want to adjust my position to take that into account."

"Maybe Blackie didn't convey your thinking clearly." He tried being more diplomatic. "I have the impression that if I locked up the cable and TV stations, you wanted an option on the cable."

"Right."

Right? Right? Richardson raged. He was buying the company, not Zeeberg! He put his hand over the mouthpiece.

"Do we need his goddamned money?" he asked Blackie.

"I don't know where else we'll come up with $500 million by the end of the day. If he drops out, that'll send a bad signal to the others in the deal."

Richardson stared at Muldoon's sleek countenance and thought, the sharks are circling. By the time I own News/Worldweek, there'll be nothing left but bones. He took his hand off the receiver.

"Right," he sighed. "But we'll have to talk price."

The *croque monsieur* tasted delicious and it would help Heidi avoid crashing from jet lag. As she ate at the little *Café-tabac* across from the Bressons' apartment house, she read through the notes in her Filofax. At Sean Gordon's insistence, she had come to Annecy as a prelude to what she imagined would be the focus of her investigation—the mystery of what Marcel Bresson had been doing that would merit special handling by the CIA. But instead of establishing a baseline of facts, she had found only more mystery. No birth records. Parents married after he was born. Mother arrested and removed from Annecy *before* he was born. Lost at some unknown age and reunited with his family as a teenager. Heidi's list of questions filled three pages, and how would she answer them without the cooperation of his parents?

She finished her beer and looked around impatiently for the waiter. He was an old man who seemed overwhelmed by having three customers at once. As she turned back to her sandwich she found the young man at the next table smiling at her.

"You are American?"

"Yes." He was the last thing she needed, quite apart from the fact that he appeared several years her junior.

"You are looking for the waiter. I will get him." He came back in a minute and sat at her table.

"You are a tourist?" he said, grinning.

"No."

"You are lost?" He waved his hand at the neighborhood as if that could be the only explanation for her presence.

"No. Business." She did not want to encourage him, but he was nice to look at. He was much better dressed than the other people on the street.

"Maybe I can help you?"

She wished he could, "No thanks. I was just doing some research."

"You are a scientist?"

"Historian."

"I don't know much about the history of this area," he admitted as the waiter finally arrived at the table. Heidi ordered a double espresso. "But André knows. You have been here a long time, no?" André nodded with a sour look on his face. "He can tell you everything about this neighborhood."

"I even remember when it was a neighborhood," André said bitterly. "Now look at it. A laboratory for social experiments."

"Do you happen to know"—Heidi made a stab—"Ferdinand Bresson who lives across the way?"

André looked uncertainly at the young man for a moment. *"Bien sûr,"* he replied, "everyone around here does. He is the big hero."

"You sound like that doesn't impress you," she said.

"We went to school together. We were in the Resistance together. But he was a Communist and Annecy was a Communist town. Don't be misled by the fancy houses on the lake."

"You're not a Communist?"

"My father owned this *Tabac!* The Communists and their Socialist friends almost tore it down. Did the big man, Bresson, help me? No! He got himself a grand apartment for being the great hero."

"He wasn't a hero?"

"The Communists needed a hero. They picked him. If you ask me, his wife was the real hero."

"Why was that?"

"The Vichy police captured her and turned her over to the Nazis."

"Was that before or after their boy was born?"

André again looked uncertainly at the young man. But he simply smiled up at him.

"Marcel? He was born in the jail in Grenoble. The Nazis took the boy away from her. A family took care of him. It was many years later before the boy was found."

"And it's sure that the boy is Ferdinand Bresson's son? They were not married until after the war."

The old man seemed a little surprised at Heidi's question. He wiped his hands on his white apron. "Ferdinand always claimed they were married by the Party. But who knows? It's a sin, not a crime," he shrugged. "And the Communists play by their own rules." He excused himself to get her coffee.

"You are writing a history of the Communists, or Ferdinand Bresson?" the young man asked.

"An article about his son. He is becoming famous in the United States."

"If you did an article on me, would I become famous?"

He did have that Gallic charm, she warned herself.

"If you would let me take you to dinner," he continued, "I could show you why I should become famous."

Heidi laughed, but resolved to get away as soon as possible. She was tired and hoping for a phone call from Lyman. Her coffee arrived and she asked for the bill. She put down a generous tip.

"That is too much. The service is included," the young man said.

"André was very helpful. And so were you."

"Then you will accept dinner?"

"No, I can't, thank you."

"But I insist."

"You insist?" She forced a smile onto her lips. "Well, don't think of this as adieu"—she stood up and looked deeply into his eyes—"just good-bye forever."

The grin stayed on his face. He said nothing else as he watched her get into her car. A moment later, a Vietnamese pulled a blue BMW around the corner and he got in. They followed Heidi back toward her hotel.

"Meet me at Nell's," the voice said over the phone and hung up. The call from Max the Saint snapped Lyman back from the deal world into reality.

Andy waited downstairs with the limo. He got to Nell's in fifteen minutes. Lyman pushed through the crowd on the street, but the doorman refused to let him in until he mentioned Max's name.

A disco, club, bar, celebrity hangout, just what Lyman wanted after working forty-eight hours with only a two-hour nap. Unlike the hot and huge New York nightspots which usually occupied former TV studios, movie theaters, warehouses or churches, Nell's was considered exclusive and intimate. That meant the doorman kept out the tube-and-tunnel crowd from Queens and New Jersey, and only permitted four or five hundred people to cram inside each evening.

Lyman worked his way through the first floor parlor area, furnished with a score of overstuffed sofas set at random angles. Like birds of prey, very thin people perched on the arms and backs of the couches but not on the cushions. Max was not in that group. Then he searched the restaurant area which was divided from the parlor by a small bandstand. Sometimes the music was jazz, sometimes rock, New Age or underground. That night, Nell's featured an all-woman band called the Pop Tarts.

Lyman could not find Max among the tables and red plastic booths. He made his way downstairs to the basement, where the thud of thousand-watt amplifiers was inflicting permanent hearing loss on the dancers and inducing structural fatigue in the building's foundation. The dance floor seemed to be occupied primarily by cross-dressers: those in low-cut ball gowns had Adam's apples, those in white tie and tails did not.

The back room turned out to be a bar and staging area for the dance floor. Max and his party were gathered along the wall to the left. Lyman noted several features that set them apart from the rest of the crowd. The men wore suits and ties. On average, they were fifteen to twenty years older than everyone else in the room and had twice as many women as men in their group. Lyman approached through a gap that had opened up between them and the black rap group sitting on the nearby tables dressed in sweat pants, undershirts and unlaced high-top tennis shoes.

Max introduced Lyman around. He recognized one as a prominent U.S. Senator. The women were only allowed first names.

"How are we going to talk?" Lyman asked.

"Let's go to the bar."

Lyman ordered a McCallum on the rocks. Max, he noticed, had Pellegrino water. They were crowded close together, but Max still had to raise his voice.

"I checked on your friend."

"So?"

"I mean I really checked." He pushed his nose over to one side indicating that he had contacted Mafia sources. Down the road that would cost Lyman extra.

"So?" he said again.

"And offshore. I talked offshore." That meant he had used his contacts in the Bahamas and other world money laundries. Lyman braced himself.

"So," Max said slowly, "he's clean."

"You're kidding! They're covering up!"

"I didn't say he's unknown. He's done some dealing with the zips." Max used the New York "wiseguy" term for the Sicilians. "In order to run printing plants in Italy, but it's strictly business." He meant legitimate business.

"And drugs?" Lyman insisted.

"The wiseguys say no. The Bahamas say no. There's always a lot of new money in that business, so you can never be sure."

"No, this goes back a long time. It would be an established relationship."

"No sign of it. That doesn't mean some of their banks aren't in his deals. Money's a commodity. The boys in Medellín buy some CDs.

The cash goes into a loan syndication in Europe. That happens to IBM."

"So where would his money come from?" Lyman felt stymied. "The PLO?"

"They got cash," Max agreed. "But I talked to the Gulf, too. The Kuwaitis approached Bresson a few years ago fronting for Arafat. He turned them down flat."

"I still can't believe it."

"Believe what you want." Max sucked up the last of his bubbly water. "But you still owe me."

The limousine bounced and heaved over the potholes as Andy raced to catch the string of green lights heading up Park Avenue South. In the back seat, Lyman checked his watch. It was one o'clock in the morning, 7:00 A.M. in Annecy. Fumbling through his pockets, he fished out the slip with the number Heidi had given his mother. From his Mobile One cellular phone to AT&T International, and then to the French PTT, the call went through in less than a minute. A man answered.

"Mademoiselle n'est pas ici, elle est partie."

"Gone? Checked out? Already?"

"Oui, checked out, *définitivement."*

Had she found what she wanted, Lyman wondered, or come up empty, as he had? *"Merci,"* he said, and hung up.

The whole thing was beginning to seem improbable. What was the basis of his suspicion? Some U.S. government files that no one had ever seen, and Rankin. If the government had derogatory information on Bresson, it would move to block the deal. That wasn't Lyman's problem. And what about Rankin? Maybe he did commit suicide. Once before, Lyman had witnessed tragic behavior under the pressure of a deal. At a closing, a client toasted everyone with champagne, then asked to be excused. But instead of going to the men's room, he hurled himself through a plate-glass window down thirty-seven floors onto the street.

Or maybe it was an accident, Lyman thought. Rankin found some anomaly in Bresson's accounts and when I didn't come down right away, he flew off the handle, started throwing things around. Tossed his computer over the cliff. Then he realized what he was doing, panicked and fell. Lyman admitted that it didn't make much sense, but it made more sense than accusing a major international businessman of murder. Besides, wasn't that a job for the Swiss police?

The limo pulled up to his ground-floor apartment on East 76th.

"Pick you up at seven thirty?" Andy asked.

"Oh, God, no, I need some sleep. Make it eight thirty."

"But we'll need an hour to get to Greenwich. The service begins at nine."

He had completely forgotten. He had been bad-mouthing Rankin when he should have been thinking about what he was going to say about him. Mrs. Rankin had asked him to deliver the eulogy at the funeral the next day.

15

The *autoroute* from Annecy to Grenoble took Heidi down the length of Graisivaudan valley between the Chaîne de Belledonne and the Chartreuse Massif. Great concrete viaducts leapt deep gorges with tiny villages nestled below. The hillsides were covered with trees hanging heavy with fruit. Here and there, Heidi saw what seemed to be orchards of glass glinting in the morning sun. The trees were festooned with bottles, pears ripening inside. They would be harvested and filled with brandy before being shipped all over the world as Williams pear brandy.

The drive would have been pleasant except for Heidi's deepening sense that she was losing time. The three newspapers piled in the right-hand seat reported that Marcel Bresson had launched a tender offer for News/Worldweek. The *International Herald Tribune* and the London *Financial Times* were a day old and merely reported that the bid was well received by Wall Street analysts and that Drew Richardson might have a hard time topping it.

Le Monde, the French newspaper, was more current. It reported the sharply divided reaction in Washington, plus the remarks of unnamed sources high in the French government who declared that the acquisition was a test of Franco-American relations. The front-page article concluded that if the U.S. government tried to prevent the Bresson acquisition of News/Worldweek, France should reconsider the steps it had been taking to reintegrate its military forces into NATO.

The deal was gathering momentum, Heidi thought, and I'm wandering around in the French Alps trying to track down Marcel Bresson's birth certificate. Was his story so improbable? A young man and woman, in love, and in the Resistance. She gets pregnant, then arrested. She has the child in prison. It's taken away from her. After the war, the man and woman marry, and later still they are reunited with their child. But the twig is bent, and a few years later, the boy leaves home never to return. A sad tale, if not a tragedy, but certainly not a plot threatening the security of the United States!

So why, she asked herself, are you going to Grenoble? Because Sean Gordon had taught her to follow any avenue of investigation to the end of the line.

The first sign of Grenoble was the smoke: old-fashioned blue, gray and brown smoke pouring from tall factory chimneys. It did not evaporate like steam, but climbed skyward until it flattened out under the solid roof of clouds that now filled the valley and cut off the tops of the mountains. A drizzle had started. The windshield wiper on her side chattered across the glass, making it difficult to see.

The chaos of the morning rush hour added to her confusion as she searched for the Grand Hotel where the concierge had made a reservation. She passed through the Place Grenette three times before realizing that the Grand was the tiny hotel just around the corner on the rue de la République. Winding through the streets in quest of a parking place, she dismissed the idea that she was being followed by a blue car that she thought she had seen on the *autoroute*.

The man at the desk in the Grand Hotel was from Martinique. Heidi understood his English better than his French. He showed her to a small third-floor room at the back of the hotel. She complained that it had no toilet.

"You want a toilet in your room?" he asked dubiously.

"That's what I reserved," she insisted.

Shaking his head, he took her to a room on the second floor. The instant he opened the door, she smelled the toilet.

She gave in. "I'll take the room on the third floor."

Stretching out on the bed, she opened her Michelin Red Guide to the map of the city. Heidi decided to skip the Hôtel de Ville, which was on the outskirts of town, and go directly to the departmental archive located in *La cité administrative* only a few blocks away.

As she walked through the streets, Heidi found Grenoble to have a rough and ready, almost frontier quality. The older buildings looked in poor repair, and where small neighborhoods struggled to cultivate some charm, the effort was usually destroyed by the intrusion of some modern pile of concrete. But no matter how miserable the streets, the town was made beautiful by the spectacular mountains rising on every side. The rain had stopped, and the clouds were breaking up so that Heidi could see the top of the ruins of the Fort de la Bastille on the mountain which loomed over the city on the other side of the Isère River.

The *cité administrative* appeared to be a converted military *caserne* surrounded by a wall, but with no guard at the gate. Inside, each building was from a different period, as if to serve as a monument to every French war since Napoleon. Heidi wandered into the Department of Labor, the Department of Hygiene and the Department of Agriculture before locating the archive in a modern white fourteen story skyscraper.

The young woman at the information desk was not particularly friendly but nonetheless efficient. She took the form Heidi had filled out requesting a copy of Marcel Bresson's birth certificate and disappeared into a room full of card drawers. Five minutes later, she returned.

"There is no record of his birth on that date, Mademoiselle," she reported.

"Can you check July or August 1943?"

"I checked the whole year, Mademoiselle. There is nothing."

"Could you check 1944 and '45?"

"That is a lot of work, Mademoiselle."

"Maybe the first three months of 1944?" Perhaps she had just become pregnant when she was arrested, Heidi reasoned.

The woman returned quickly. "No, Mademoiselle. We have no record of such a birth."

Heidi wondered whether she had been released and returned to Annecy to have the baby. But then how did she get separated from her child? And what about the story of her giving birth to Marcel in prison? "Do you have prison records here?" Heidi asked.

"Only very old ones, before 1900," she replied. "More recent records are held by the Prefecture."

"Where is that?"

"The old building with the flag across the way."

"And what about newspapers from the nineteen forties? Can I see them?"

"This is an official archive, Mademoiselle. We do not keep newspapers!" She seemed insulted.

"But they have them at the archive in Annecy," Heidi replied.

"Perhaps, in Annecy," she sniffed, "they have nothing better to collect."

The Prefecture proved a dingy contrast to the archive. It smelled of Gauloises and cheap wine. The little man at the information desk had a face full of broken-veins and a cigarette permanently affixed to his lower lip. He liked Heidi right away.

"Anything you want, Mademoiselle!"

She instinctively fingered the top of her blouse to be sure it was buttoned.

"I'm looking for the record of someone who was in jail here in Grenoble."

"I would have to get permission for you to see any files."

"I only have a few questions. If you could look at this file and tell me—"

"What kind of questions?"

"It's a woman. Marie Louise Foucard. I want to know what dates she was in jail, and if possible whether she had a baby."

He raised his eyebrows, "When was she arrested?"

"April fourteenth, 1943, in Annecy. She was transferred here a few days later."

"Take a seat. Would you like some coffee?"

He poured a thick black liquid from a thermos into a paper cup. It burnt her fingers, and tasted like it was eating the enamel off of her teeth. He was gone for a half hour while the waiting room filled with people seeking information. A dozen men occupying desks behind the counter continued to chat with one another, read *L'Équipe* and talk on the phone, making no effort to help.

When the information clerk returned, he turned up his palms and shrugged. "We have no record of this person, nor of any baby. I am sorry."

Heidi refused to believe him. "But I read about it in the paper. It said plainly that she was arrested and taken to Grenoble for interrogation in April of 1943." People behind her began to complain that she was taking too much time.

"What paper, Madame?" he asked ignoring to the others.

"La Patrie."

"Ah! The fascists! And who did the interrogation?"

"I don't know." She started to look through her notes. The complaints behind her grew more strident.

"Was it the Gestapo? We have no such records! We're legitimate police, not gangsters!"

"I didn't mean to be rude."

"Of course not." He smiled. His teeth were the color of tobacco. "Did you try the archive for the birth certificate?"

"Yes. There's nothing."

"Ah, *oui,* " he nodded, ashes drifting down his shirt. "You see, the baby was born while the woman was in the hands of the Nazis," he confided. "There might be no record at all."

As he mounted the lectern and turned to the assembled mourners, Jayson Lyman still did not know what he should say. He felt sick from the thick odor of the mass of flowers crowding the front of the chapel, and dispirited by the vacuous words of the minister and Marshall Cooke.

"A bright candle snuffed out," the minister had intoned mechanically, as if he had said it a thousand times.

"A real comer, who is now gone," Cooke had said, demonstrating only that he wrote his own remarks. Lyman wondered why Cooke had bothered to attend Charles Rankin's funeral, since he hardly knew him.

Lyman scanned the notes he had prepared in the car. They were totally inappropriate. How could he say Rankin had led a full life when he died before reaching twenty-nine years of age? And how could he suggest there was some abiding purpose in his death when, one way or another, what happened was all because of a deal?

He set the notes aside, and tried to speak his mind.

"At a time like this we search for meaning. We want there to be a point. A life cut short is a tragedy . . ." He paused, not knowing how to complete the thought.

He stared at Carol Rankin sitting in the middle of the front row. Carol had been a hot currency trader at Citibank when she met Rankin. A math whiz who had graduated in computer science from Emory University in Atlanta, she specialized in "mambo-combos," arbitraging three or four currency options at once. She had also partied hard in the downtown club scene until she and Rankin had collided one night at a slam-dancing session at CBGB. Lyman had never heard either one of them express any regrets. Carol wore a black knit suit, her bright red hair tucked uneasily under a small, round taffeta hat with a dark veil. Her two boys, three and five, sat quietly on either side of her.

Lyman wished he could explain why they would never see their father again. He settled for trying to justify why they had not seen much of him when he was alive.

"They say nobody's last words are, 'I wish I'd spent more time at the office,' " Lyman began. "But Charles Rankin loved what he did. Perhaps he worked too hard, but the hours he devoted to his profession were a source of personal satisfaction. He worked hard out of integrity, not merely ambition."

So why did he die? Lyman could see the question on everyone's face: the young investment bankers Rankin knew on the Street, his tennis partners from the Greenwich Racket Club, the neighbors who car-pooled to the train station together and cooked steaks for one another in the summer. They all wanted to know if his work had driven him to suicide and whether it could happen to them.

"I guess I was the last one here to be with him"—Lyman was choosing his worlds carefully now—"and he was a happy man. He missed Carol and the children, but he spoke often about how he was building a future for them."

Carol's shoulders began to shake, and Rankin's father reached across and took her hand. The elder Rankin had created an ecumenical atmo-sphere by insisting on wearing his yarmulke. Lyman knew that Ran-kin's parents had given Charles a hard time because Carol was Catholic. But they had reconciled, compromising on a Unitarian minister for the wedding and, as it turned out, for the funeral as well. Where was the evidence of guilt, depression or alienation, Lyman wondered, that would have led Charles Rankin to kill himself?

"He knew he made a difference in the life of our company. I hope he knew he made a difference in our personal lives. His warmth, his silly jokes, his earnest friendship touched us, and will stay with us in our hearts."

Suddenly the dead spot Lyman had carried around inside since seeing Rankin lying in a broken heap burst into a quiet fury that he directed at himself. How could he ever have considered that it was suicide?

"There are a lot of unanswered questions that make Charles Rankin's passing even more difficult to bear. But one thing is not in doubt." He did not take his own life, Lyman wanted to proclaim, but instead he struggled to say, "We all will miss him terribly."

Someone played the organ as they all filed past the open coffin and out the door. Lyman tried not to imagine what the undertakers had done to make his body lie straight. Carol stood at the door, bravely thanking each person for coming. When Lyman murmured his condo-lences, she asked him to wait.

Lyman stood outside the chapel and looked out over the rolling Connecticut countryside, which was beginning to turn orange and yel-low. On the horizon he could see the bright stripe of Long Island Sound. He pondered the alternatives. It was either an accident or murder. He ran the possibilities back and forth through his mind, while every forty-five seconds the peace of the graveyard was shattered by the sound of corporate jets taking off and landing at Westchester County Airport.

When everyone had left, Carol asked Lyman to step back into the chapel. The boys played outside among the gravestones.

"I wanted to show you this." She dug into her little black purse and took out an envelope. "Mr. Cooke gave it to me." It contained a check made out to Carol Rankin. It was in the sum of $100,000. It had been drawn to the account of *Les Éditions Bresson.*

Blood money, Lyman thought bitterly.

"What should I do with it?"

"Cash it quick," Lyman advised her. "And don't send a thank-you note."

Heidi had reached a dead end. She was sitting in the Café Snob on the Place Grenette trying to decide what to do next. The rain had come up again.

Rummaging through her bag, she brought out her Filofax and began rereading her notes for possible leads. The local newspaper would be no help; she had already checked and found that Bresson owned it. The university offered possibilities, but she dreaded trying to track down Bresson's old teachers and classmates. That could take days, even weeks. She ran across the name Yves Coudert in her notes and tried to remember who that was. Of course, Marcel Bresson's foster father!

The central PTT stood across the street from the Cathédral de Salvador Allende. A brass plaque explained that the church was named after the President of Chile, overthrown and murdered in 1973 with the help of the CIA.

The Minitel at the PTT had no record of Yves Coudert. Heidi asked the clerk at the information window for an old telephone book. Before the Minitel, they had been notoriously out of date, often containing names of people dead twenty or thirty years. The clerk refused. The older books, he said, were reserved for official use only, evidently now a national embarrassment.

Next Heidi tried the public library. As in Annecy, she found it housed in the Grenoble Cultural Center, a squat, aluminum-clad building that looked like a low-budget set from *Lost in Space.* The reference section only had the newest phone directories. Finally, back at the Grand Hotel, the clerk from Martinique had the old telephone books she was looking for. And one of them showed a listing for M. and Mme Yves Coudert.

When Heidi drove out to the northeast suburbs to locate the address, she found herself in the Olympic Village. Built for the Winter Games of 1968, the buildings were subsequently turned into low-cost housing and a public recreation area. As far as she could tell, M. and Mme Coudert's house was now the site of the speed-skating rink.

Driving back to the center of town in a harsh downpour, Heidi reviewed her options. She could accept the story that she had learned so far. She had discovered nothing to contradict it. That choice led to the railway station and the first train to Paris.

Alternately, she could keep trying to find Yves Coudert, perhaps the stumpy little man at the Prefecture could help. Despite a day of disappointment and futility, she decided to continue to pursue the second option. For as she glanced into her rear view mirror, she concluded that she was definitely on the right track, because she was definitely being followed by two men in a blue BMW.

Traffic backed up on the Bruckner like a clogged sewer. Lyman lay inert in the backseat of his limo as he listened on the car phone to word of Richardson's counterattack.

"They're claiming it's $47." de Grazia said, "but there's paper in the deal, a convertible debenture, and even less cash. We put the value at $45.50, max!"

"That's still more than ours," Lyman pointed out.

"But the paper belongs in the toilet! I can get McFadden Dworkin to print a letter to shareholders hitting them for undermining the credibility of securities markets. Give them an integrity shot."

"Okay." Lyman found it impossible to work up much interest.

"And we're being sued, of course," de Grazia continued, "attacking our financing. False and misleading 13D, 14D, the whole nine yards. They're asking for expedited discovery."

"Our countersuits?"

"Skadden Fried's going in this morning. Just have to plug in a few details, like the fact that Richardson's trying to lock up the cable and broadcast TV properties."

"Any reaction from the company?"

"The board meets this afternoon."

"Christ, I've got to get a hold of Raffy quick." Lyman sat up. "What about Bresson? Has he heard about Richardson's countertender?"

"Let's just say he's been trying to crawl through the green phone on your desk."

The face of Heidi's friend at the Prefecture had become color-coordinated. His eyes now matched his nose. But he was even more pleasant, if rather less focused.

"Yes, everyone must register here. You too, if you stay more than a week."

"Then could you look up a Monsieur or Madame Yves Coudert?" She smiled warmly.

"That is government information, Mademoiselle."

"Oh, please! I just want to know if they're alive. They're supposed to be relatives."

"Then you are French?"

"My mother was," she lied.

"For your mother, I will help."

He returned in a few minutes with an old file folder which appeared to contain only a single sheet of paper.

"There is no record of their deaths," he said.

"Is there an address?"

He nodded. It turned out to be the same nonexistent street number in the Olympic Village.

"Should they have notified you if they moved?" she asked.

"Not if they left Grenoble. They must register in the next town."

"Is there a way to find out . . ."

"A copy of every document is sent to Paris. Perhaps the National Archive."

"Thank you." Heidi turned away. Another dead end. It was definitely time to go shopping. Then she turned back with another thought. "Were they natives?" she asked, her French beginning to fail after a long day. He did not understand. "Were they born here?" she explained. "Did they grow up here?"

"They are your relatives, Mademoiselle!"

"That's one of the things the family doesn't know."

He peeked into the folder which he held against his chest.

"No. They came from Brittany. That explains your fair skin."

She smiled and tried to blush. "When?"

"Oh, I can't tell you that, Mademoiselle." He clutched his files tighter. It seemed to be his idea of flirting.

"Oh, please," Heidi begged.

"Let's see." He peeked again. "1954."

Bresson was behaving strangely. He did not seem to care about the price, the lock-ups, or that the News/Worldweek board was meeting even as they spoke. He only wanted to focus on the lawsuits.

"Marcel, I'm a defendant too!" Lyman said impatiently. "I explained before we got into this deal that you would be sued."

"But Skadden Freid says they are demanding to look at my files."

"Only on this deal. They can't go on a fishing expedition. Just make sure they are nice and tidy."

"Does not French law protect me?"

"Sure, but not if you want to go ahead with the deal. Actually, you won't have to show them anything unless you improve your offer."

"What is the board going to do?"

"You want the best or the worst?"

"The worst," Bresson said.

"Decide to recommend Richardson's bid to the shareholders and give him his lock-ups on the cable and broadcast TV businesses. If that happens, the price of poker really goes up."

"And the best?"

"I talked to Raffy Nichols. He knows the script. He'll propose that a board subcommittee be set up to evaluate the bids and negotiate with both sides. But we'll still need to sweeten our offer."

"I understand," Bresson said. "We meet tomorrow."

The thought of getting on another airplane made Lyman want to dive under his couch. "Where?" he asked.

"Monte Carlo. And bring the lawyers."

"Fine," Lyman said with a trace more enthusiasm. At least he would be on the same continent as Heidi Bruce.

Bresson's silence on the line indicated that he had another question. It finally came out.

"Do you think that this *Raffy*"—he pronounced the name with disdain—"can swing the board?"

"He's going to try."

"An artist standing up to an executive like Richardson?"

"Marcel, I don't claim his heart's in this fight," Lyman replied, "but I can assure you his ass is."

Heidi did not consider herself a brave person, but she felt no fear at being followed. The Place Grenette was full of shoppers, and she was celebrating having found a crack in Marcel Bresson's story by trying to buy some clothes before her two dresses disintegrated. Her concern focused less on the Vietnamese who seemed to be tailing her than on the fact that everything was hideously expensive and nothing fit.

At five six, 120 pounds, Heidi was average for an American. But, in French sizes, that seemed to translate into giant. And the proportions were wrong, all leg and no torso, all derrière and no bust. The shoes were totally impossible. Only a few were long enough, and those were too wide. Attempting to be helpful, one petite French salesgirl suggested that Heidi might find shoes that fit if she shopped in Scandinavia.

For pantyhose, she suggested that Heidi try a small lingerie shop on the street behind her hotel. The Vietnamese dutifully followed her from the Place. Not the most impressive tradecraft, she noted to herself. He didn't exactly blend into the crowd. Then Heidi had the sobering thought that maybe he wasn't trying to.

The shop was very exclusive. Its only pantyhose came from Dior. Heidi bought half a dozen pairs and tried on a bra displayed in the window. She had always been proud of her full bustline, and despite its negligible construction, this bra made her look eighteen again. Heidi bought four of them in beige, black, red and white, and decided to wear the white one out of the store. She found the Vietnamese waiting for her on the corner of the square.

It had grown dark. Heidi turned and walked in the opposite direction. She was determined to show no concern. But the lingerie store was the last shop on the street. The rest of the block seemed to be lined with dark, uninviting houses. Glancing up at the back of the Grand Hotel, she could see her room—the only one with a light burning—and she wished she were in it. As she got further away from the square, she sensed that the Vietnamese was gaining on her. Heidi's anxiety began to rise. She was afraid to turn and look. If she knocked on the door of one of the buildings, she wondered if anyone would let her inside.

Heidi passed several doorways, her steps quickening, uncertain what to do next. Ahead and across the street, another figure came toward her. Was it the other man in the blue BMW? When the man crossed to her side of the street, Heidi's fear became panic. The next building had a banner over the door that said Museum. A sign in the window said FERMÉ, but lights flickered behind the curtains. The two men were closing in on her.

She pressed the bell. Nothing happened. Heidi could hear the footsteps of the men coming closer. She pressed the button harder and began to bang on the door with her fists. The footsteps grew louder. Suddenly, the door opened, then jerked to a halt on the end of a chain.

"We are closed," a woman in a shawl hissed. "It is the sabbath."

"Help me! I'm being followed!"

The woman hesitated.

"Please!"

She closed the door. In terror, Heidi whirled to face the two men. Then behind her, she heard the chain slip.

"Quickly," the woman said, and pulled her inside.

Raffy Nichols had never been in the new boardroom of News/Worldweek. He was surprised that no portrait of his mother, father or grandfather hung on the walls. An appropriate place above the head of the table remained empty. Richardson was evidently reserving it for himself. He would walk out of the meeting as the new owner of the company, unless Raffy could stop him.

The room smelled of wood polish. Before each chair, a secretary had placed a three-by-five-inch pad of paper and a gold mechanical pencil with no eraser. The message was clear. Board members were supposed to keep their comments short and not try to figure things out for themselves.

As the first to arrive, Raffy took the chair to the right of the head of the table. Roland Medvoy came in next. President of Stickney College in Tubeville, Pennsylvania, he had rescued the small school from the brink of bankruptcy by changing the name from Holy Trinity to that of its new benefactor, Horace Stickney, foremost manufacturer of inert ingredients.

General Royal Linx, U.S. Army (Retired), showed up a moment later. A highly decorated and widely admired hero of the Libyan invasion, Roy Linx was a no-nonsense, straight-ahead military leader. Raffy had read someplace that General Linx had presided over the development of more weapons systems canceled by Congress than anyone in Pentagon history.

He was immediately followed by two large men wearing cheap suits and what appeared to be hearing aids. That meant former Secretary of

State Hanson Zwiki was about to arrive. Rumor had it that the body-guards, no longer paid for by the U.S. government, consumed three-quarters of the former Secretary's income as a consultant to corporations on international strategic developments. Secretary Zwiki priced his services according to the number of phone calls he would accept. One hundred thousand dollars a year bought four calls. He never spoke to anyone less important than the president of the corporation and never put any of his advice on paper. No memos, no reports. Less successful competitors referred to his firm as Plausible Denial Associates.

Julian Alexander, Raffy's longtime lawyer who usually held the family's proxy, accompanied the Secretary. When he saw Raffy, he turned to him in midanecdote.

"What brings you out of your studio?" Alexander's effort at affability somehow turned out vaguely insulting.

"Isn't this going to be an important meeting?" Raffy responded.

"But devilishly complicated."

"I'll look to you for advice." Raffy patted Alexander's arm.

The last of the outside directors to arrive was the legendary foreign correspondent Worthington Connaught. Known to friends and associates as "Wort," he had cut his teeth as an eighteen-year-old reporter for *Worldweek* during the Italian invasion of Ethiopia in 1935. He bragged about having been instrumental in Truman's firing of General Douglas MacArthur, had a weak spot for Oriental art and Latin dictators, and spent three months out of every year drying out at the Betty Ford clinic. The title vice chairman had been intended as entirely honorific, but now that the chairman was trying to buy the company, "Wort" had to take the chair.

With the arrival of all the outside directors, the inside directors appeared en masse. Drew Richardson strode into the boardroom followed by the president, the chief financial officer and a half-dozen staff, who spread out in the seats along the walls. They were accompanied by assorted investment bankers and lawyers who took places at the table. As Jayson Lyman had warned Raffy, it was a show of force.

Shaking hands all around, Richardson hovered briefly over the chairman's seat, then realized he would not be running the meeting. Irritation clouded his face when he found that his alternate chair was already occupied by Raffy Nichols.

"I heard that you were honoring us with your presence today," Drew said with no effort at charm, as he evicted the president from the seat opposite. He wanted to sit next to the vice chairman so he could help Wort through the program.

"Gentlemen, we're here to consider the new offer from Drew's group," Wort read verbatim from the annotated agenda that Richardson's staff had prepared. "It looks pretty good to me, but let's have it from the horse's mouth. Drew, tell us about it."

"Mr. Chairman," Raffy interrupted, "I have a procedural proposal for the board to consider. Since it affects how we handle Drew's offer, I suggest we deal with it first."

Unsure what to do, the vice chairman looked at Richardson. He nodded toward the president, who spoke up.

"I have to object. The by-laws make clear that matters involving change of control of the corporation take first priority."

Raffy was ready. "Point of order." Lyman had coached him to raise a point of order, which always took precedence over all other matters. "Didn't you just say the purpose of this meeting is to consider a new offer by Drew's group?"

"Yes." He nodded without checking with Richardson. That was a mistake.

"Then the by-laws also state that no member of the board is to participate in matters in which he has a personal interest. I ask that Drew and the rest of his people leave the room."

"That's preposterous!" Drew exploded. "I haven't even made my offer!"

"And I haven't made my procedural proposal!" Raffy shot back. He hadn't had so much fun since he told his father he was going to the Esalen Institute in Big Sur instead of Harvard Business School.

"What's your proposal?" General Linx asked. "I haven't seen any proposal."

"I haven't either," said the former Secretary of State, sensitive as ever about being left out.

"Really? I sent a copy to Mr. Richardson," Raffy said innocently.

"I thought we'd take it up later," Richardson growled.

"I've got more copies." Raffy started passing them around. "It proposes a special board subcommittee of outside directors to evaluate the different takeover bids—"

"There's only one bid," Richardson interrupted. "The board rejected the other."

"—and if necessary, negotiate on behalf of the board," Raffy concluded.

"I don't see the point," the chief financial officer said. "The outside directors already have an investment banker."

"And legal counsel," the president added.

Two nice young men at the bottom of the table sat up straighter and smiled.

"I didn't hire them," Raffy said simply.

No one knew quite what to do. The vice chairman said, "Does this mean we have to vote or something?" He seemed incredulous. In the fifteen years he had been on the board, all the decisions had been by consensus.

Raffy had a realistic assessment of his strength. The outside directors were supposed to represent the shareholders. He was the only one in the room who owned any sizeable number of shares; they should be responsive to him. At the same time, they all owed their $30,000 a year in directors' fees to Drew Richardson.

"I guess we start with the point of order," the vice chairman said, trying to remember his *Robert's Rules of Order*. "Raffy proposes that Drew and his group leave the room. Do they get to vote on this?"

"Yes," said one lawyer.

"No," said another.

Richardson had also been carefully assessing his voting strength. "I'd be happy to have our group abstain," he said magnanimously.

"All in favor?" Wort asked.

Raffy raised his hand. He looked around at the other outside directors. After a pause, only Julian Alexander lifted his gold pencil. It was a free vote that showed his loyalty to his client but did not go against Richardson.

"All against?"

The Secretary, the general and president of Stickney College raised their hands.

"Guess the chair doesn't have to vote." Wort gave a short laugh that nobody joined.

"And now it's on whether to take up Raffy's procedural proposal. All in favor?"

Raffy was surprised that this time he was joined not only by Alexander but also by the general. Peering at the paper, he explained that he was voting in favor of an orderly decision process. But the vote was still six to three against the motion. This time, the vice chairman joined in.

Raffy had lost. He did not mind. It was going exactly as he and Jay Lyman had planned.

16

As Heidi's panic subsided, she looked around at the dark house. The foyer had a desk with a small sign that said ADMISSION 5F. VISITING HOURS 2–6 SUNDAY THROUGH THURSDAY, 2–4 ON FRIDAY." To the left a parlor flickered with candlelight. As her eyes became accustomed to the gloom, she could see a menorah on top of an old wooden chest illuminating a Star of David hanging above it. One wall was lined with glass cases. She could not see inside them, but the walls above were covered with weapons, ranging from old-fashioned Thompson submachine guns to Luger pistols. The near wall displayed clothing—suits and dresses with yellow stars sewn on them—alternating with posters proclaiming BOCHE/RAUS and TIREZ LES JUIFS.

"What happened, dear?" the old woman asked. She had large, dark eyes set off by white hair pulled back and held in a clasp.

"A man . . . maybe two men, were following me." The anxiety welled up again. "The street was so empty . . ."

"Should we call the police?"

"No!" Heidi said too sharply.

The woman looked at her carefully. "If you will light the stove, I will make tea. I have chamomile and hibiscus."

She led Heidi down a hallway lit by a dim bulb. Framed photographs on the wall showed people standing in front of firing squads, bodies hanging from various large trees, lines of children climbing into boxcars.

The kitchen had a two-burner gas stove, an industrial-size sink, a small refrigerator and a large table. The woman handed Heidi a box of matches.

"It is the sabbath," she explained. "I can't."

"This is a museum?" Heidi asked as she ignited the burner. The woman handed her a kettle of water.

"It is also my home."

"What kind of museum?"

"For the Resistance and the Deportation. In America you call it the Holocaust, no?"

Heidi nodded. The photographs, the guns, the clothes, the posters suddenly made sense.

"We call it the Deportation," she continued, "because many non-Jews in France were also sent to camps in Germany."

"To their death, like the Jews?"

"Some. But most of them for work. That was not pleasant for them, either." She asked Heidi to take the boiling kettle off the stove and pour it into a china pitcher containing chamomile leaves.

"I'm sorry. I'm Heidi Bruce," she said, remembering her manners.

"Mademoiselle Wormser." She held out her hand.

The tea tasted awful but felt good.

Mlle Wormser explained that the house had been a family home. The Wormsers had come from Alsace in the last century. During the war, she had been hidden by a French family until just after the Normandy invasion, when she was caught by the Gestapo at a Resistance meeting. Interrogated for weeks, she was finally herded onto one of the last trains leaving France for the German death camps.

"The Red Cross worked out an arrangement with the Germans to stop the train in return for the release of a few Nazi officials captured in Paris," she explained. "But General de Gaulle refused."

"My God, why?"

"He said, 'Nations without myths are doomed to freeze to death.' He wanted martyrs to wash away the stain of defeat and collaboration. Come, I'll show you what happened to me."

Heidi followed her up a narrow, winding back staircase that led to several rooms on the second floor that served as a library.

"This is how I looked when the Americans liberated my camp." She did not seem ashamed to show herself naked, emaciated, head shaved, her young breasts hanging flat like a grandmother's.

"Is it true," Heidi summoned the courage to ask, "that women stopped having their periods?'

"The lucky ones, yes. But not me. I had nothing to stop it, and the guards would not let me wash. The odor was very bad. One day, out of frustration, hopelessness, perhaps even envy, the women in my compound beat me so that I could never have children. Here is the record of my arrest and deportation." She pulled a large ledger from a group on the wall.

The book was covered in green fabric with a black swastika embossed on the cover. Mlle Wormser turned to June 15, 1944, and pointed to an extensive entry next to her name.

"I'm sorry, I can't read German."

"It simply says that I was arrested with a criminal gang. The interrogation and subsequent investigation proved I was a Jew. I was deported to Paris on August sixteenth, bound for Germany."

"What other records are here?" Heidi asked, an idea forming in her mind.

"This museum has most of the local Nazi records. Gestapo arrest records, prisoner logs. They were meticulous record keepers. The departmental archive refused to keep them."

"Do you have the prisoner log for April 14, 1943? Or even a few days later?" She was growing excited.

"*Mais oui!*" She pulled down another large volume. "You are looking for someone specific?"

"Marie Louise Foucard."

Mlle Wormser looked at Heidi sharply.

"Did you know her?" Heidi asked.

"No, but she was well known, at least after the war, when they found her son." She was running her finger down the pages. "Yes, here she is. She was arrested for consorting with 'Bandit Gangs,' in Annecy, April 14, 1943, and transported to Grenoble on the sixteenth. Interrogated five times with negative results, she was then deported to Germany."

"Deported?" Heidi asked in surprise. "When?"

"A week later. April twenty-eighth."

"And there is nothing about her having a child?"

"In the jail?" Mlle Wormser sounded incredulous.

Heidi nodded.

"The only thing she would get in a Gestapo jail is a miscarriage! She was interrogated five times!"

"Then when was Marcel born?" Heidi wondered aloud.

"I always understood," Mlle Wormser said, "that her son was born in Annecy, before she was arrested."

Blackie Muldoon had not been interrupted, so Richardson felt that the presentation was going well. Raffy Nichols' loss in both votes appeared to chasten him. Richardson calculated that in a real showdown, Raffy had no votes but his own.

Blackie asked for questions.

"What's the total value per share that's being offered?" General Linx asked.

"We believe it to be $47.50 per share—$37.00 in cash and $10.50 in securities. Of course, the market will ultimately value the securities, so it could be higher or lower."

Richardson liked that answer. It would not protect them from lawsuits but should avoid any adverse judgments.

"The SEC has to approve the securities, too, but I don't see any problem there, so far," Blackie added.

"Is this a better deal than Bresson offered?" asked the vice chairman, prompted by his memo.

"Absolutely," Richardson responded.

"If there are no more questions . . ." The vice chairman moved toward ending the short discussion.

Raffy interrupted him. "Could we adjourn for a moment? I'd like to make a phone call."

The vice chairman hesitated, looking at Richardson.

"I'm the largest shareholder," Raffy said. "My family founded the company. Don't I deserve ten minutes, as a courtesy?"

Against his better judgment, Richardson nodded.

"All right," the vice chairman allowed.

While Raffy was out of the room, the former Secretary of State filled the time by remarking that international diplomacy called for much finer judgments. "And, of course, I faced matters of life and death. War and peace—"

"I just wish I knew who he was talking to," Drew tried to make it sound light.

"That's the disadvantage of business," the Secretary said. "If this were an international negotiation, we could tap his phone."

"I'm afraid I have a few questions," Raffy said when he reentered the boardroom. "First, why isn't your offer all cash like your first one and Bresson's?"

The question had been directed at Richardson. Blackie answered.

"We're trying to maximize shareholder value. The securities not only improve the value of our bid over Bresson's, but offer an upside gain in the market."

"Or a downside loss," Raffy amended.

Blackie responded with a shrug. It was all a charade anyway.

"And will you"—Raffy turned toward the far end of the table—"give a fairness opinion on this bid?" The young investment banker from

Shearson First Jersey who represented the outside directors leaned forward.

"Yes," he said.

"Why wasn't Mr. Bresson's offer fair? It had more cash."

The young man stood up. "It did fall within the envelope of values we developed for the company."

"So why wasn't that offer accepted?" Raffy demanded.

There was silence. Then Richardson in a loud hiss whispered to Wort Connaught, "Business judgment!"

"Yes, that was it," Wort said from the Chair. "Business judgment."

"The board's entitled to take into account a wide variety of other business considerations besides price," Julian Alexander said helpfully.

"Like what?"

"Continuity of the business," Richardson finally said. "Bresson would have to sell off the TV stations. The shareholders wouldn't get that value; he would."

"You could do the same thing."

Richardson thought of his conversation with Zeeberg and decided not to respond.

"Any more questions?" Wort asked. "If not, I guess the outside directors have to chew this over and decide."

Richardson and his group adjourned to his office. He sank into his favorite chair while Blackie nervously paced the room.

"Nichols is talking to Bresson," Muldoon said, "or to Lyman. I know it."

"Relax," Richardson responded, "we have the votes."

"I'm just concerned that it not look too wired. A few more questions would have looked better on the record. Nichols was obviously trying to build a case."

"The board belongs to us," Richardson said confidently.

The intercom rang. It was the vice chairman. Richardson put it on the intercom.

"Drew, the Board accepts your offer—"

Richardson shook Blackie's hand. The president gave a little jump in the air and then hugged the chief financial officer.

"—and we'd like to talk about one detail."

The celebration stopped.

"What?" Drew Richardson asked.

"It's about these what d'you call 'em, 'lock-ups.' "

Looking through the curtains on the second floor, Heidi saw no one standing in the street in either direction. She worried that the men might be concealed in a car, but as far as she could see, there was no blue BMW anywhere on the street. She shook hands with Mlle Wormser and thanked her by folding a hundred-franc note into the donations box.

Glancing quickly up and down the street, Heidi hurried to the corner and through the Place to her hotel. She saw no sign of the Vietnamese. The West Indian at the desk gave back her key, along with what she thought was a strange look. Or was she becoming paranoid? She carefully opened the door to her room. Nobody was inside. Bolting the door, she went to the phone and asked the operator for a number in Washington. After several long minutes, the staff director answered his own phone.

"Where the hell are you?" he demanded. "You go to the chairman behind my back, and then disappear," he said angrily.

"I'm sorry. But I'm really getting somewhere on this."

"Like where? Four-star hotels?"

Heidi looked at the surroundings. "Hardly. Listen, the subject's birth information doesn't check out." She felt uneasy talking on the phone. "I can't say more on the open line."

"But what good is that?"

"He must have lied on his visa application. We can keep him out of the country."

"You've been away too long. His PR firm's working overtime. The press is treating him like the greatest thing since Lafayette saved the American Revolution. You'll need a hell of a lot more than that."

"And I'll get it." She hung up before he could draw her into a longer conversation.

Bresson hadn't been born in Annecy. And he hadn't been born in Grenoble. So where did he come from? His parents wouldn't talk. And where was he until 1954? His foster parents might hold the key to both questions, but they had disappeared.

Heidi called Dick Rensselaer. The phone rang four times before his answering machine came on. Heidi left a long and complicated message which she hoped he would understand.

Still keyed up and needing to talk to someone, she thought of Jayson Lyman. Why hadn't he called her in Annecy? Maybe he felt it was her turn to make an effort. She phoned his mother to leave her phone number. They talked for ten minutes about Mrs. Lyman's ailments. When Heidi hung up, her mood had not improved. Finally, she tried to reach Sean Gordon at his office. He was still on TDY.

She felt very alone. Hunger had started to gnaw at her, but she was fearful of going outside to a restaurant. She decided to wash out her underclothes in the sink. The familiar routine calmed her. She tried on her new Dior pantyhose. They looked wonderful until she took a few steps. They settled in doughnuts around her ankles.

As she stood laughing at herself in the full-length mirror, she thought she heard someone in the hall. Then came a knock on the door.

She panicked. Who was it? She was half-naked.

The knock came again. Harder. "Mademoiselle!" The voice was authoritative. It did not sound West Indian. Quickly, she snatched up her Filofax full of notes, pushed open the window and put it on the ledge.

The pounding became even more insistent as she rushed to get dressed.

"Open this door, or we shall be forced to open it ourselves!"

Raffy was not worried about losing the vote on Richardson's bid. Lyman had predicted it, and that the showdown would come over the "lock-ups."

"Drew is insisting," Raffy was saying, "that he be given an irrevocable option to buy the broadcast and cable TV businesses of this company—"

"What's wrong with that?" the vice chairman interrupted. "He's going to buy the whole company anyway. We already agreed to that."

"The board agreed to recommend to the shareholders that they tender their stock to Drew and not Bresson. But Bresson's offer still stands. He could increase it, and stockholders could tender to him. Drew wants the right to lock up these TV properties no matter how that comes out."

"I think we realize that," the general said. "What's the problem?"

"We're all fiduciaries. Our job on this board is to look out for the interests of the shareholders. Not management, not the workers, but the owners of this company, the people and institutions holding the stock."

"Are you accusing us of not acting responsibly?" A rumble of offended pride came from the former Secretary of State. "Are you saying I have to vote with you, no matter what, because you're a stockholder?"

"Not at all," Raffy said. "I would even be willing to join you to make the board's acceptance of Drew's bid unanimous—if he's willing to drop the lock-ups."

"I don't understand," admitted the former Secretary, for perhaps the first time in his life.

"The lock-ups will deter a higher bid. They will make it harder for Bresson to increase his offer."

"But we don't want him—" The vice chairman stopped in midsentence.

"If we give the lock-ups, we fail our shareholders by keeping them from receiving a higher bid," Raffy concluded.

"But we don't know that there'll be a higher offer," Julian Alexander said.

"If we grant the lock-ups," Raffy pointed out, "we'll never find out!"

At that point Richardson and his entourage reentered the boardroom.

"Drew," the vice chairman said, "Raffy is arguing that giving you these, uh, lock-ups will prevent a better bid."

"I prefer to call them options," he responded with maximum dignity. "In fact, what they'll do is prevent further screwing around!" He delivered the last with venom, staring into the eyes of each of "his" outside directors. "Delay and uncertainty is bad for any business. Particularly one like ours. People leave, they're lured away, recruitment stops. The strength of this company declines every day its future is in doubt. That hurts the shareholder more than anything."

"Drew," Raffy challenged him directly, "you know there could be a higher price or you wouldn't want the lock-ups."

"I bought these businesses for News/Worldweek when it was a declining publishing dinosaur," Richardson countered. "I got this company ready for the twenty-first century. I deserve to be able to buy these properties if something goes wrong."

"You mean, if there's a better offer!" Raffy's eyes swept the table. "Fiduciaries must not prevent a better bid. We're not just changing the organization chart so that Drew Richardson can run a tighter ship. This company's for sale, right? Our job is to get the owners the best price!"

Richardson's voice rose. "You're just worried about your stock."

"Damn right. So is every other stockholder. And they look to us to protect them. If we don't, the board's going to be sued. As a shareholder, I can personally guarantee that." He grinned at the others.

"Can you individually pay the judgment that could come down in a deal worth more than seven billion?"

The former Secretary of State, the retired general and the college president looked noticeably paler.

"How much could it be?" one of them said.

"More than your director's insurance covers," Raffy replied.

Blackie Muldoon tried to regain the initiative. "The courts have held that the 'business judgment' rule allows granting lock-ups."

"But not always." Raffy looked down at the lawyers, who nodded reluctantly.

The vice chairman then made his second mistake. He proposed a compromise.

"Raffy says he'd join in recommending your offer, Drew, if you'd drop the lock-ups."

Richardson was caught off guard by Wort Connaught's initiative. He hurriedly conferred with Blackie Muldoon, who kept shaking his head. Raffy thought he could see his lips form the word "promised."

"Drew, is your offer contingent on the lock-ups?" Raffy asked. "Is it all or nothing?"

That led to more head-shaking between Richardson and Muldoon. Finally Blackie spoke. "We need to confer outside."

When Richardson's team left the room, Raffy immediately called Lyman from the phone at the far end of the table. The call was short. Excited, he returned to his seat and addressed the other outside directors.

"If the lock-ups are an integral part of Richardson's deal," he explained, "then we really haven't considered the whole offer. The board's vote to approve it was meaningless."

"Let's just wait and see," the vice chairman said.

Raffy would not be stilled. "If the lock-ups are tied into their financing, we could see further complications. Maybe Drew's promised to sell the crown jewels to somebody else. Now can you see why we need to set up a committee to go over his proposal carefully? You need to protect yourselves," Raffy warned.

"Who would be on it?" the former Secretary asked.

"You could be," Raffy replied.

"No, I don't want to be on it."

"Neither would I," said the college president.

Raffy looked at the vice chairman.

"It'd be a conflict for me to do both," Wort said.

"Then it would be me," said Raffy, "Julian and General Linx"—who nodded as if it were natural for him to volunteer for rough duty. "The board would still make all the decisions."

At that point, Blackie Muldoon came back into the room.

"I'm sorry, but we're going to need a little more time to sort this out."

"Are the lock-ups tied into your financing arrangements?" Raffy challenged him.

"We are not withdrawing our proposal." Blackie ignored him. "We just need time to elaborate some elements."

"How much time?" the vice chairman asked.

"Maybe tomorrow."

"Make it Monday," Raffy suggested.

The rest nodded.

"And my suggestion for a subcommittee?" Raffy's tone was insistent.

Julian Alexander's face was hard to read, but the other outside directors, including the vice chairman, looked worried. The vote in favor of Raffy's proposal was unanimous.

He was beginning to like the deal business.

Two large Frenchmen in black raincoats stood in Heidi's doorway. The West Indian clerk hovered in the background.

"What do you want? Who are you?" She tried to sound brave.

"You must come with us, Mademoiselle Bruce."

Her tough act dissolved. They used her real name! If she tried to run or struggle, she had no doubt that guns would come out of their coats. They hurried her downstairs and into a waiting car.

"Where are you taking me?" she asked, and got the response she expected. Silence. After a short ride toward the river, the car stopped at the *télécabine* station that climbed up to Mont Rochais and the Fort de la Bastille. It was dark and closed. Each of the two men gripped one of her arms and half carried her up the steps to the waiting cable car while the driver entered the control room and started the motor. In a second, they were airborne over the river Isère, climbing up toward the ruined fortress on the mountain.

The men stood guarding the doors while she huddled on the slatted bench that ran around the walls of the cabin. Would they drop her out while aloft? No, she thought, they would wait to push her off the cliff so that it looked like an accident. That was Bresson's trademark.

As they rose higher and higher, so did the sound of the wind. The cables clashed and the car swayed sickeningly. Below, the lights of Grenoble began to wink out as clouds enveloped the cabin. Soon, they were surrounded by blackness and her two guards turned on flashlights. It became cold. Heidi started to tremble and clutched her wool jacket closer to her body.

Suddenly, the cabin came to a halt, and Heidi went sprawling on the floor. The two men picked her up without apology and moved her outside where other men were waving flashlights in the fog. They put her into another car, this time with only one guard. The driver had to use his windshield wipers to clear away the blowing mist. In a few minutes the car passed through a gate protected by armed guards. Heidi could make out several low white buildings through the drifting fog. One of them had a large dish antenna on the roof.

In the warmth of the car, Heidi had stopped shaking, but she hovered between panic and anger at herself for having tried to take on Marcel Bresson all alone. The men following her had been a warning. She wished she'd taken it.

The car stopped in front of a single-story structure that looked like all the others. Her guard escorted her from the car to the door of the building. It opened, and a young woman, approximately Heidi's age and wearing a uniform, escorted her down a long hall. There were no pictures on the walls and all the doors were closed. At the end of the corridor, the woman stopped and pointed to the last door.

"Entrez, Mademoiselle," she ordered.

Heidi turned the knob and stepped inside. It was a spacious but unpretentious office. A large picture window looked into the black night. The shadow of a man loomed against the wall cast by the light of a burning fireplace. He turned toward her. It was the Comte d'Uberville.

Standing next to his secretary's desk, stuffing M & M's into his mouth and reading the Reuters report on the News/Worldweek board meeting, Lyman wondered if he had done the right thing. N/W DEFERS ACTION ON RICHARDSON GROUP BID, the headline read. Maybe he should have let Richardson walk away with the company. He was finally offering a decent price, even if the value of the paper was overstated.

It was debilitating. Lyman was accustomed to ambiguity and uncertainty in the deal business. However, he had always known what side he was on. Who was the enemy in this transaction? Richardson? Bresson? He was beginning to hate his life.

"Here's the 'Dear Shareholder' letter." De Grazia handed him a layout taped to a stiff piece of cardboard. Lyman and Raffy agreed to keep the pressure on the board by urging the shareholders to demand a careful examination of any "paper" bids. Much of the stock of News/Worldweek was in "street name," meaning it was held in brokerage accounts at investment banks for anonymous clients. A full page Dear Shareholder letter in the *Wall Street Journal* was the only way to reach them.

Lyman okayed the letter and checked his watch. He had booked the 5 P.M. Air France red-eye to Paris where he would connect to a UTA flight to Nice. In nine hours, he would be looking down at the Bay of Angels. He thought of calling Heidi Bruce at the number she had left with his mother, but he distrusted his office phone. Instead, he decided to call from the first-class lounge at Kennedy airport.

They had already called his flight by the time he got through to the Grand Hotel in Grenoble. The lilting West Indian voice switched from French to English.

"No, mon, the Mademoiselle she went out."

"Let me give you the number where I can be reached tomorrow. Ninety-three fifty eighty eighty, in Monte Carlo. Do you have any idea when she will be back?"

"No, mon, I can't really say."

Lyman hung up and checked his watch with a sense of growing concern. By his reckoning, it was ten forty-five at night in Grenoble.

An orderly rolled in a linen-clad table for two set with flowers and a large silver ice bucket containing a bottle of Roederer Cristal champagne. D'Uberville filled a glass for Heidi and then poured a dollop of champagne into his brandy.

"You see, Mademoiselle Bruce, the lengths to which I will go just to dine with you *tête-à-tête*." He pulled out the chair for her to sit down.

"So this is pleasure and not business?" She lifted the silver lid on the plate in front of her and found little pancakes with caviar and sour cream.

"Unfortunately, it must be both." He held his glass up for a toast. "To a beautiful woman in an ugly profession."

Heidi drank to her own toast. She was surprised and relieved that her host turned out to be d'Uberville, and not Bresson. But a sense of apprehension remained. Whatever he had in mind, she decided a little charm wouldn't hurt.

"You should not denigrate your profession," she chided him cheerfully. "You have become a legend."

"But being responsible for intelligence matters can produce such awkward situations. For example, when you find that someone you thought was a friend is discovered spying on your country."

Heidi took another sip of champagne to wash down the little clutch of fear that rose in her throat. "Is it considered spying when questions are asked openly about a private citizen?" she held her ground.

"Is it open," he asked, ringing on a small bell, "if one does so under an assumed name? Claiming to be a journalist? What is your publication, if I may ask?"

The orderly removed the hors d'oeuvres plates and delivered a *truite bleue* with tiny roasted potatoes. d'Uberville poured them each a glass of Chassagne-Montrachet '81.

"You've made your point," Heidi said, without rising to his questions. "Now if you'll permit me to make mine, Marcel Bresson is trying to become enormously influential in my country. And I cannot even document that he is French."

"He has a passport issued by the French government."

"I haven't seen it, but if he claims that he was born in Annecy on June 17, 1943, it's a lie."

D'Uberville worked on the bones in his trout. "One must do so many things in life that are disagreeable. I detest fish, for example, but I must eat it according to my doctor. It's force majeur."

This was a preamble, Heidi was sure.

"This transaction of Monsieur Bresson's has become a cause célèbre in Paris. That may be ridiculous, but it is a fact. Were it to be known that an investigator for the United States Senate was in this country under a false name seeking to assassinate his character . . ."

"I'm just here to find the truth," Heidi proclaimed.

"Oh, the truth." He gave a Gallic shrug. "That is never an adequate defense."

"How does it involve you?" she asked.

"Your activities here could precipitate a crisis in Franco-American relations. That could affect our cooperation with the United States, our basic security."

And the White House would blame the Senate, Heidi realized, and the Senate would blame her chairman, and her chairman would have a tough time getting reelected. Forget becoming staff director, she would be out of a job.

"So I should disappear?"

"This is not Guatemala. You should merely desist."

"I'll have to report what I've learned so far, and that will create even more questions."

He sighed and rang the bell again. "You are very good. I wish you worked for me."

Heidi's eyes opened a touch wider.

"Do not be alarmed. I am not trying to compromise you in any way."

Salad was served. Her dressing was made of walnut oil. He took straight lemon. The orderly refilled their glasses.

"You are right. You must know the whole story. I trust you will treat what I am about to say with the utmost confidentiality. I realize you shall have to share it with your committee chairman, but I hope it goes no further."

He started his salad.

"It is a complicated tale. Marcel Bresson's mother was in the Resistance. That you know. You have also learned that she was arrested. Hers was a brutal interrogation. Then they sent her to a death camp in Germany. Dachau. Somehow, she managed to survive. During that time she had a child. It was taken from her and in time ended up with a family here in Grenoble. I think you know the rest."

Heidi was disappointed in him. It was not even a new story. It was the "born in jail in Grenoble" story shifted to Dachau.

"Was she pregnant when she got to Dachau?"

D'Uberville looked uncomfortable.

"How did the fetus survive this 'brutal' interrogation?" she pressed.

With obvious reluctance, he said, "She became pregnant while in Dachau."

"From someone in the camp? They kept the male and female prisoners separate. Most women stopped ovulating anyway. And Nazi orphanages weren't full of babies from concentration camps." Heidi shook her head.

"She was made pregnant by one of the SS officers in the camp. He arranged to keep the child. He was killed at the end of the war. Marcel ended up in a refugee camp and was adopted by the family in Grenoble."

"You've still left something out, haven't you?" she said.

He looked at her, expressionless.

"She was no hero. She collaborated, didn't she? That's how she survived. That's how she ate well enough to conceive and carry a baby to term. Marie Louise was a . . ." Heidi stopped.

"A whore?" d'Uberville said. "Ask yourself what you would do in such circumstances."

He rang for the orderly. Heidi refused dessert.

"But long after the war, the child inconveniently reappears," Heidi continued. "So a whole story is invented to protect the myth of Marie Louise Foucard, heroine of the Resistance."

"Do you know how many Frenchmen welcomed the Nazis?" d'Uberville asked heatedly. "How many informed on their neighbors? Helped send personal enemies to the work camps? How many fought *against* the Resistance?" His face showed genuine anger. "After the war, we needed pride in ourselves again, Mademoiselle, not more stories of collaboration and moral corruption!"

Heidi thanked him for being so candid. He offered brandy, but she declined. She asked only one favor: not to go back down the mountain on the cable car.

17

A bright red Aérospatiale Écureuil helicopter picked them up at the Cannes airport and headed directly out to sea. Lyman sat on the left-hand side of the craft, with the lawyer from Skadden Fried on the right and the PR expert from McFadden Dworkin in the middle. They all put on headphones to muffle the beat of the blades overhead and to listen in on the conversation of the pilots. No one had explained where they were going. But wherever it was, Lyman knew his proposal was going to produce fireworks.

The chatter on the radio took place in French and English, but to Lyman, it could have been Albanian. All he learned was that the U.S. fleet was having an exercise in an exclusion area in the direction of 195 degrees while they were on a heading of 143 degrees. He also noted that they passed over two fishing trawlers bristling with antennas and flying the hammer and sickle.

A quarter of an hour into the flight, the pilot pointed to a speck on the horizon. A few minutes later, they circled a sleek, white yacht and settled on to a helipad amidships. Crew members in white pants and blue-striped shirts led them toward the stern, which Lyman judged to be about half a football field away.

Bresson was waiting on the fantail with a bucket of champagne, receiving his daily foot massage. Lyman introduced his traveling companions. To his surprise, Bresson was on his good behavior. He graciously dismissed the masseuse and greeted them all warmly.

"To a smoothly working campaign," he toasted, as two white jacketed waiters filled their glasses. "Now, Jayson, are you not glad I insisted you approach the Nichols family?"

Lyman forced a smile. His job was to let clients hog the credit. "It's a little soon for champagne, Marcel. We slowed the board down, but we're still faced with a higher bid."

Bresson waved the thought away, spilling his champagne in the process. "You talked with Raffy." He said the name with new respect. "Give me all the details. I want to taste them."

They all were invited to sit on the soft down sofas that ringed the rear deck while Lyman recounted the events at the News/Worldweek board meeting. The sky above was cloudless; the sea, moderate with only an occasional white cap. Still, the combination of the red-eye, the helicopter, champagne and now a gently rolling ship was taking a toll on Lyman's inner ear. Only the fresh breeze kept him from dashing for the side.

"Basically, we've repositioned the board," Lyman concluded. "Before, they were trying to protect Richardson. Now they're trying to protect themselves."

"It has a good feel, no?" Bresson was almost gleeful. Lyman wondered if that was what was making him sick. "With Raffy on our side," declared Bresson, "we cannot be stopped!"

"Raffy's an ally, Marcel, not an agent," Lyman warned.

Bresson suddenly became somber. "I'm glad you are here," he said, pointing at the lawyer. "A serious problem has developed." He picked up the phone on the glass coffee table and spoke rapidly in French. Hanging up, he returned to English. "The lawsuit. They demand my files! They demand to interrogate me!"

"Depose you," the lawyer corrected him. "Don't worry, we'll get you prepared. And they can't ransack your files. We'll insist that they confine discovery to the files of your acquisition subsidiary, the company that you set up to take over News/Worldweek."

"But that is only a paper shell."

"Exactly," the lawyer beamed. Obsessively well-organized and compulsively focused on merger law, he was one of the best, Lyman thought, but not somebody you wanted to sit next to on a transatlantic flight.

"I am not so worried about myself," Bresson was saying, "I'm worried about him." He gestured toward the smoked-glass sliding doors to the ship's interior, which opened to reveal Dr. Sperile Beck of the Swiss Bank Corporation.

The new round of introductions allowed Lyman to shift to a chair under the canopy. He could see the PR man from McFadden Dworkin already getting red from the sun.

"Herr Doktor Beck has also been asked to depose," Bresson explained.

"This I cannot do," Beck announced. "Swiss law concerning the confidentiality of banking—"

"Not if your client wishes to cooperate," the lawyer corrected him.

"But it is against bank policy!" Beck protested.

"Mr. Bresson," the lawyer said, "he has got to talk. The suit's about the adequacy of your financing. He's the financing. It was a big mistake to try to conceal it in the first place."

"Your laws allow it," Beck said defensively.

"But our politics don't," Lyman spoke up for the first time.

After a pause, Bresson said, "The bank could make an exception." It sounded more like an order than a question.

"We have made far too many exceptions for the sake of American law," Beck insisted. "It is destroying the confidentiality of the Swiss banking system."

"When do they want to conduct the deposition?" the lawyer asked.

"Monday," said both Bresson and Beck.

"In most U.S. legal proceedings," the lawyer explained, "delay's the name of the game. In this case it's not in our interest. If you want to complete this deal in less than four weeks, you should agree."

Bresson stared at Beck. "When do we prepare?" Bresson asked. Beck sighed and looked at the deck.

"Don't worry about it. Jayson and I have done this dozens of times. We'll put you through a mock deposition. Tell them Monday's fine and get them over here right away. If we need more time, then we delay."

"It's better to have 'em in Europe shopping than in New York dreaming up new lines of attack," Lyman added. The coast of France had appeared on the horizon and was a settling influence on Lyman's stomach.

"And you both should do it in the same place," the lawyer cautioned. "So you can coordinate your answers."

"The bank will want its lawyers there also," Beck said.

"*Bien.* We do it in Zurich on Monday," Bresson announced. "Now for some lunch!"

They filed down a staircase to another open deck more protected from the sun and the sea. The waiters served a seafood salad and more champagne. While the towering Alpes maritimes loomed closer, the PR man described how he was creating a wonderful image for Bresson—a frugal, hard-working poor boy who made good. Lyman wondered when the discussion would get back to the deal. He had some unpleasant news and he was looking forward to delivering it.

By the the time the fruit and coffee arrived, the principality of Monaco stood out white and glittering against the mountains, the office and apartment towers rising from the sea like a Mediterranean Hong Kong. Lyman decided he could not wait any longer.

"Marcel"—Lyman interrupted the aimless banter—"we do have to talk about a counteroffer."

"The board has not acted on Richardson's bid," Bresson responded diffidently. "I told you I would not compete with myself."

"Fine. Wait. But on Monday you may face a board endorsement of Richardson if he withdraws the lock-ups!"

"Do not get upset, Jayson." Bresson was toying with him. He enjoyed humiliating people in front of their colleagues. First it had been Beck; now Lyman sensed it was his turn. "How much do you recommend? I suppose you have a proposal?" Bresson added sarcastically.

Lyman nodded and opened his briefcase.

"Not more paper, Jayson!" he taunted. "Just your famous 'bottom line,' please."

Lyman steeled himself. "Forty-eight to $49. Even $50 if you can afford it."

Bresson and Beck looked shocked. And unhappy. "But you said Richardson's offer was only $45.50!" Bresson exclaimed.

"Richardson's reaching the end of his resources," Lyman responded. "He's trying to make his bid look better than it is. Still, some analysts claim it's a $47 offer, and that's what you've got to beat. Fifty dollars would break his back." Lyman hoped it would break Bresson too. For the first time in weeks he was having fun.

"Herr Doktor Beck and I will consult." Bresson tried to sound nonchalant, but his face was stiff with strain.

The yacht was passing under a cliff that towered five hundred feet above the sea. "That is the rock of Monaco," Bresson said, trying to change the subject. They all looked up at it. "It was the site of a Roman stronghold and a Saracen citadel before the Grimaldis from Genoa seized it by masquerading as monks and then massacring the guards. Now that was a hostile takeover, no?"

They all laughed obligingly. An uncomfortable silence followed.

"Do not worry about the price," Bresson finally said as heartily as he could. "I know I must pay more than Monsieur Richardson. The company is also worth more to me," he said, closing on a confident note. Beck, however, had not stopped frowning.

As the ship drew up to its berth on the Quai Antoine Premier,

Bresson set another meeting for ten the next morning. Cars were waiting to take them to their hotels. Lyman had learned that his companions planned to stay at Loews', so he chose the Hôtel de Paris.

He crawled into the back of the stretch Peugeot. As always after a transatlantic crossing, his body ached in a way that made him wonder if he had picked up the flu, and his fatigue had a hard edge that would make it difficult to sleep. As his car climbed the Avenue d'Ostende to the Place du Casino, Lyman was grateful that along with his room, he had had the foresight to reserve a massage from the hotel masseuse.

The Hôtel de Paris stood on the west side of the square, separated from the Casino by a narrow street. It seemed unchanged from his visit five years earlier. The front steps were guarded by several exotic automobiles, a vintage 1952 flame-red OSCA roadster, a somewhat dated Rolls-Royce Silver Spur, and a special-bodied Maserati Quattro four-door convertible. The three-story lobby had grandeur for every taste: marble columns, mahogany paneling, rococo plaster mouldings, cut-glass mirrors, scores of oriental carpets and potted palms. It was largely empty in that quiet hour between lunch and tea.

The clerk at the reception desk knew Lyman immediately. "It's good to have you with us again, Monsieur Lyman," he said as he handed over a stack of messages along with his key. "You have suite eight, the Churchill Suite. Madame awaits you in the room."

Lyman looked forward to her massage. As he rose in the tiny elevator he reflected how that was the hallmark of a true luxury hotel. Sending the masseuse to his room so as to save him the additional inconvenience of going down to the spa. Making his way along the silk-brocade-covered corridor, he also wondered what "madame" would look like. Probably a broad-shouldered Brunhilda with arms like Popeye. Anyway, he was too tired. And he should be thinking of Heidi. Where was she? How was she? What had she found out? He would try to reach her again as soon as he got into his room.

It turned out, he did not have to. She was sound asleep on top of his bed.

When Lyman woke up on the couch, Heidi was gone. He thought she might have been an hallucination until he found her note on the dresser in the bedroom.

Jay—

Sorry to crash in on you. No other room at the inn. I'm in the spa being remanufactured after a week in the French provinces. Give me some privacy in the suite after 5:30, and I'll meet you in the bar at 7:00. Might even buy you dinner. Much to talk about.

H.

Lyman smelled the note to see if it was perfumed, then felt silly. The paper came from the pad next to the phone. He checked his watch. Five fifteen! He had to move fast. Wait a minute, he thought, this is your suite. She's already taking over, telling you when to come and go! "Stop wasting time," he told himself out loud. "Get out of her way."

His luggage had been brought directly from the airport and the porter had already unpacked for him. Quickly, he rummaged through the closet and dresser drawers to find a fresh suit, shirt, tie, underwear and a bathing suit. With the suit over his shoulder and carrying a nylon bag with his shaving kit, he headed down to the spa.

Lyman emerged onto the California Terrace, a huge, oval, indoor pool filled with warm sea water. One wall opened to a wide sun deck overlooking the port and the old town. In the best authoritarian fashion of French health spas, he was instructed to swim and sauna before his massage. No madame awaited him in the massage booth, but Monsieur Charles's work proved swift, brutal and refreshing. By six fifteen, Lyman was re-dressed in a gray striped shirt with a white collar, mauve tie, dark blue double-breasted blazer, and gray slacks. He was ready, but had forty-five minutes to wait.

Excited and restless, he decided to take a walk. The weather was warm and humid. The Place du Casino was full of British tourists exploiting the first weekend of off-season rates. Pink and white, they all looked vaguely unshelled without their woolens. Lyman headed directly for the Casino gardens that overlooked the sea. Every species of flower thrived in Monaco's average two hundred and sixty days of sunshine. The approach of autumn had not dulled their brilliant colors. As he strolled down the carefully maintained paths, Lyman closed his eyes trying to identify the scents that wafted up to him with the sea breeze. He could smell rose, lilac, mimosa, marguerites, orange and lavender. Then he walked into a telescope.

He stubbed his toe, very painful in soft Italian loafers, and bashed a shin, almost tearing his pants. Cursing, he hobbled to a nearby bench to inspect his wound. No blood, just scraped skin. But his right big toe felt broken. He decided to rest until it stopped throbbing.

Lyman was sitting on a promontory to the rear of the Casino facing back toward the port. From there he looked down on Bresson's yacht, where a small launch was being lowered into the water. The boat maneuvered to the stern and picked up a passenger descending a ladder. The launch then had to wait for the opening of a line of floats that sealed the entrance to the harbor in order to keep out the trash, both human and man-made, that increasingly fouled the coastal waters of the Riviera.

The motorboat headed in Lyman's direction. Curious, he limped back to the telescope and put in a franc. As he brought the image into focus, he could see that the passenger was Marcel Bresson. He looked up from the telescope to judge the boat's direction. It seemed headed for the Sporting Club, a modern complex of casinos, restaurants and nightclubs built out onto the sea on landfill.

Lyman was about ready to head back to the hotel when he saw the boat suddenly swerve toward the narrow artificial beach along the Avenue Princess Grace. At that late-afternoon hour, it appeared deserted. Putting another franc into the telescope, he watched Bresson climb out of the boat and wade ashore. Another person emerged from a car stopped along the boulevard and started across the sand toward him. The distance made it hard for Lyman to make out much detail, and then the two walked out of his angle of view.

He looked around quickly and spotted another observation platform down the hill to his left. Oblivious of the pain in his toe, he dashed down several sets of stairs and raced along the path's multiple switchbacks. When he arrived at the observation spot, he found a crowd of British tourists in line for the telescope. He asked if they would mind if he went ahead of them.

"Sod you!" one replied.

"Bugger off."

"Queue up like the rest."

It cost him 150 francs to jump the line, and still a stalwart garden-club woman in sensible shoes refused to relinquish her turn.

By the time Lyman got to the telescope, Bresson and his companion were walking away from him. He could see, however, that it was a man in a dark suit, and probably elderly from the cane he used to help himself struggle through the sand. They then turned back toward him. Lyman could not make out the other man's face under his hat, except that he wore a beard. It seemed obvious they were arguing. The old man vigorously shook his head. Bresson waved his arms, bending at the waist and holding up his palms in the universal gesture of pleading. Then he shook his finger at the old man before throwing up his arms and turning away in evident frustration. Finally, the old man stopped, drew himself up, pointed his cane at Bresson and shook his head very slowly. A gust of wind picked up the old man's hat just as the telescope decided to go black. By the time Lyman had fed it another franc, Bresson was standing at the edge of the water holding the hat and staring at the old man as he walked to the waiting car and left. With fascination, Lyman watched Bresson wade back to his motorboat, carefully holding the hat high out of the water so it would not get wet.

She looked gorgeous. Heidi swept into the bar in a midnight blue silk dress that made her skin glow and her eyes gleam. A single strand of pearls rolled sensuously across her uplifted breasts and down to the valley in between.

Lyman had been sitting in the far corner, impatiently nursing a scotch and reading the weekend edition of the European *Wall Street Journal.* He was plowing through the lead article on how defaults by Poland and Hungary on World Bank loans would cost their guarantor, the USSR, more than $10 billion, when he heard the Italian at the next table exclaim, *"Che bella ragazza!"*

He looked up and Heidi stood framed in the doorway. Their eyes met, and as she moved toward him, he leapt to his feet, bumping the table and spilling both his scotch and a bowl of mixed nuts all over the floor. She smiled her blazing white smile as if she knew she looked good enough to eat.

"You always make me act like a jerk," he said.

She held her cheek out to be kissed. "It's a ploy to make me feel powerful. You know I can't resist that."

Busboys scrambled to clean up around them. Lyman placed her next to him on the banquette. He ordered another scotch and a kir royale for Heidi.

"It's so good to see you," he said simply.

"I'm very happy to be here." She became serious. "I hope you don't think I'm taking advantage of you."

"And I promise not to take advantage of you taking advantage of me." He wanted to answer her unstated concern.

The waiter brought their drinks and a silver bowl full of French hand-cooked potato chips. When he left, there was an awkward silence.

"How long will you be here?" he finally asked.

"I haven't decided what to do next. You?"

"Monday, I'm supposed to be in Zurich. I have a meeting with Bresson tomorrow morning."

"God! I don't want to think about him another minute!" she said loud enough to turn heads throughout the bar. "Let's just drink and eat and dance and forget him."

They clinked glasses.

But another restless silence followed.

"The bastard's sitting right here, like a ghost," Lyman finally said. "Why don't we get it over with? I'll tell you mine, if you'll tell me yours."

"All right, but you first."

"Mostly dead ends," he began. "No substantial drug or Mafia tie-in. Nothing new on Rankin except I've decided that suicide was impossible."

"You've stopped blaming yourself?"

"No, I've stopped blaming Rankin."

He sucked up half his scotch. "The most interesting thing is what I saw today through the telescope in the park. Bresson was down on the beach obviously arguing with an older man."

"What did he look like?"

"Balding, maybe a beard, used a cane. They were a long way off. I wouldn't have known it was Bresson except I watched him from the time he left his yacht in a speedboat until he waded ashore. Got soaked to his waist!"

"Did it look like a secret meeting?"

"It was out in public."

"That can be the best place."

"The strangest part was how they seemed to interact. Bresson looked like a supplicant. The old man appeared disdainful, even contemptuous. I'm talking body language. And Bresson just took it."

"Like the old man was his boss?" she suggested.

"Sort of," Lyman replied uncertainly, "but it was almost more like he was his father."

They sat there for a moment, quietly sipping their drinks, each lost in thought.

"I've been peeling an onion for the last week," Heidi said. "Each time I pull away a layer of facts about Marcel Bresson, I find nothing there."

For the next ten minutes she detailed each of the stories about Bresson's birth, and how they had dissolved on close inspection—except for d'Uberville's version, that Bresson was born in a German concentration camp. The only thing she left out, was that she had been followed.

"What's your bottom line?"

"This morning I drove more than five hours from Grenoble through the Alps," Heidi replied. "I guess it's some of the most spectacular scenery in Europe, but I really didn't see it. I kept going over all the questions I'd asked and all the answers I'd gotten. And they all had the same quality."

"What was that?"

"Plausible. Completely plausible, and almost no way to check them. The experts say that the perfect cover story is the one that can't be verified. When I did manage to get some information, of course, the stories collapsed."

"Including d'Uberville's version?"

"No. I believed it. At least until an hour ago when this was delivered to your room." She took a folded sheet of paper from her purse. It was a teletext message from Dick Rensselaer.

He started to read it:

From: Dick Rensselaer
To: Heidi Bruce c/o Jayson Lyman
       Hotel de Paris, Monte Carlo, Monaco.
Re: Ms. Bruce's request for poop on M. and Mme Coudert.

Lyman stopped. "Who are these Couderts?" he asked.

"Bresson's foster parents."

He began reading aloud.

"National Prefecture's files contain no current address. Last known location: 91 rue du Bot, Brest. Yves Coudert born February 4, 1917 Brest. Married, Brest June 15, 1938 to Danielle Kermandec (b Oct 28, 1920, Brest.) Both died May 8, 1943."

The postscript to Lyman made him blush. "Data damn difficult to come by. Hope she pays you properly. R.R."

Apologizing would only be more embarrassing, so Lyman asked a question instead. "Wasn't Bresson born in 1943?"

"Supposedly," she nodded.

"Then how could they be Bresson's foster—?"

"They couldn't."

"It makes my head hurt."

"Let's sleep on it," Heidi responded, then it was her turn to blush. "I mean let's not think about him for the next twelve hours."

"Deal!" They held up their glasses and finished their drinks.

But as soon as they ordered a second round, the deal came unstuck. When the waiter returned with their drinks, he also delivered a small hand-addressed envelope with an embossed anchor on the back flap. Lyman took out a card. It, too, was hand-lettered.

"Marcel Bresson invites Monsieur Jayson Lyman to dinner tonight aboard the Steam Yacht *Christina,* 8 P.M."

There was no RSVP. He was expected to be there. And across the bottom in a different hand was a personal message, "Please bring your lovely lady friend."

Edouard helped her on board. He smiled knowingly at her. In spite of her surprise, Heidi bravely smiled back. The evening held a lot of promise, she thought.

Lyman had been adamantly against her going. Heidi said she would not miss it for anything. "I've been chasing a phantom," she argued, "a shadow, and now I have an invaluable chance to get a measure of him. Besides, he already knows I'm here."

And what I'm up to, Heidi thought, as Edouard deposited her onto the deck.

The night was calm and guests were gathered around a huge swimming pool at the stern. Heidi found them an odd collection: political science professors, economists, politicians, government officials and corporate celebrities from Western Europe and the United States, along with academicians from the USSR. Heidi discovered that they all had been attending a session of the Bilderburg Conference, worthies who met once a year in the most exclusive and luxurious resorts to discuss world problems, like hunger, poverty, and disease. Bresson had also invited a sprinkling of off-season nobility: Counts, Countesses, Grafs, Gräfins, Fürsts and Fürstins who looked like they made the A list only after the weather began to turn. Heidi was relieved to find that the other Americans consisted of a senescent former Attorney General, a socialite Undersecretary of State, and a perennial candidate for President, none of whom knew her.

Bresson plowed toward them asking to be introduced to the beautiful young lady. Before Lyman could speak, Heidi held out her hand.

"Heidi Bruce."

He kissed it, leaving a wet mark on the back. "*Enchanté*. And what blessing brings you to Monaco?"

"You, Monsieur Bresson. I'm working on an article about you for the *Harvard Business Review.*"

"Hush!" Bresson shouted. "Do not say a word! Journalist present!" He laughed.

"That's how I met Jayson," she beamed. "He says the most terrible things about you."

Bresson laughed again, "And he knows so little! Come my dear, I will show you the private world of Marcel Bresson. Ascetic, self-sacrificing and lonely." He took her by the arm and steered her inside the ship, leaving Lyman standing there like he had roots.

Heidi was not happy to be suddenly alone with Marcel Bresson. It would not take much effort to pick her cover story apart. If he found out she was lying, how would he react? And if he already knew, what game was he playing?

"The *Christina* is not the biggest in Monaco," Bresson was saying. "You cannot win that game. An acquaintance of mine spent millions to build the largest yacht on the Riviera. Then, at the Monte Carlo Regatta, Prince Charles docks next to him in a cruiser! My friend could not even see the sun, and of course, he did not get invited to tea."

They had entered the formal dining room furnished in Louis XV antiques. "This ship is only sixteen hundred tons with a crew of fifty. Aristotle Onassis had it converted from a Canadian frigate. He gave it the name *Christina* after his daughter. I did not change it. That is bad luck. Later, it was owned by various Arabs and others. They ruined it. Made the ship into a harem. I restored everything exactly as Onassis built it," he said as they descended a wide sweeping staircase, "except I have installed an office and a gymnasium where he had another dining room and a playroom for his children."

The luxury of the ship dampened her feelings of apprehension. Each of nine guest suites was named after a different Aegean island. Every one had an adjoining marble bathroom with faucets of gold shaped like the mouths of fish. "Onassis had them copied from a nearby château where he lived while the ship was under conversion," Bresson explained. As they headed deeper into the vessel, Heidi wondered if the ship had a brig, and whether it also had gold fixtures. She did not want to find out.

Bresson's private suite consisted of three rooms. She relaxed a little when he said he would not show her the bedroom. His large, paneled study boasted a Van Dyke on the wall over his desk. The bath had a huge kidney-shaped pool set in a floor of Siena marble. "The mosaic tile on the wall is copied from the Palace of Minos at Knossos."

By adhering to Onassis's original design so carefully, Heidi realized, Bresson had done an amazing thing. He had managed to own a ship full of personal luxuries and idiosyncrasies that revealed absolutely nothing about himself.

They returned to the aft smoking room where a woman played Broadway show tunes on a Steinway grand piano. Bresson pointed out the fireplace made of lapis lazuli. Glowing with pride, he showed her the bar lined with rare nautical charts and models of legendary sailing ships. He knew the history of every one. She began to regard him as somewhat less of a monster than she had imagined. He was trying to be gracious in a crude sort of way. His energy and enthusiasm were contagious. Despite her reservations, he had behaved correctly throughout their tour of the ship. She stopped herself. Was she gaining perspective, she wondered, or merely succumbing to her weakness for power?

Heidi slipped onto the white-upholstered bar stool, which Bresson explained was covered with whale skin. "As Onassis used to say to the young ladies who sat there, 'You are now perched upon the world's largest penis!' " He laughed self-consciously like a naughty boy.

Heidi felt relieved when dinner was announced. The respite proved short; she was placed to Bresson's right where he continued to scrutinize her. Lyman wound up seated at the far end.

Heidi found it difficult to stay out of the conversations that enveloped the table. Continuing the Bilderburg Conference discussion of "stable economic growth," Georgi Arbatov of the USA Institute in Moscow proclaimed that Western Europe should recognize that its economic future lay in Eastern Europe and the Soviet Union. Heidi thought Arbatov had the face of an overweight ferret. She knew he had somehow survived five different Soviet leaders, and wondered if he spoke with his mouth barely open in order to hide the fact that his tongue was forked.

"To trade with America and the Third World, Western Europe must compete with Japan and the United States. But Russia is an untapped market. And we will give preferences to Western Europe."

"That's just your old tactic of trying to divide Europe from America," a British Permanent Secretary countered.

"America is turning toward the Pacific anyway," a German industrialist said. "Why shouldn't we turn to our frontier which lies in the East?"

Heidi wanted to say that West German businessmen lend billions so the Soviets could afford both refrigerators and rockets. And while the USA pays to counter the rockets, West Germany sells them the refrigerators. But she bit her tongue and remained silent, like the rest of the ladies at the table.

The State Department representative was saying, "We all want the same thing. An international system that encourages stable economic growth and—"

"All your talk about growth," Bresson intruded from his end of the table, "you gentlemen forget the most important thing—scoundrels. What room in your theories do you allow for scoundrels? They are the engines of progress. Krupp, Farben and Thyssen in Germany, Astor, Vanderbilt, Rockefeller, Ford in America. The Rothschilds in France and England.

"Look at Monte Carlo. It was the first full-scale resort development in the world. The Société des Bains de Mer created everything, not just the Casino and hotels. It built the roads, the sewers, the water and electricity services, schools and even the churches. And not just Catholic, but Protestant, Orthodox, Russian, Armenian! In a century it has gone from a barren plateau to the financial center of the Mediterranean, with more than forty international banks! And who built Monte Carlo? Scoundrels!

"François Blanc took over a pathetic gambling concession and half-finished hotel in 1861 and turned it into the most fashionable place on the Riviera. Who was Blanc? A convicted embezzler. And after him came Sir Basil Zaharoff, the Merchant of Death, who sold arms to both sides in the First World War. An embezzler, whoremonger and blackmailer, he bought the Société to get his hands on the security files of the Casino so he could expand his opportunities for extortion." Bresson was warming to the subject.

"And after the second war, when Monte Carlo lay in ruinous condition? Aristotle Onassis rescued it. Some of you may have known him or his family, so I won't commit slander, but it is well-known that he made his fortune selling oil to the Axis and was pursued vigorously by the American FBI." He stopped to suck on his cigar. No one interrupted him.

"These villains all had one other thing in common. They were true internationalists! They put themselves above country. François Blanc was a Frenchman who lived most of his life in Germany and even contributed to the German side in the Franco-Prussian War. Zaharoff was born Greek, lived in France and got his title from the British. Onassis claimed citizenship in Turkey, Greece, Argentina and Monaco. These are the kind of men you should have at the next Bilderburg. They will tell you how to provide stable economic growth!"

Laughing at his own joke, he leaned over to the marchese on his left, pointed at a full wine glass and asked if it were hers. Heidi heard the marchese say yes, and then watched as Bresson put his cigar in her glass to drown it.

Loud explosions signaled the start of the fireworks display and saved the guests from having to respond to Bresson's monologue. Heidi wondered whether Bresson's remarks were aimed at her. They all returned to the rear deck where the swimming pool had magically been replaced by a vast dance floor. As the exploding skyrockets illuminated the mountains and the sea, an eight-piece orchestra began to play from the upper deck. When the climactic barrage died away, Heidi felt grateful to find that Jay Lyman had worked his way to her side.

"He's been keeping me out of position all night," Jayson complained. "He put me between a woman who talked about nothing but her Lhasa Apso, and a polo twit. Let's get out of here."

"No." Heidi whispered back, surprising herself. "I'm going to ask him straight out. If I don't, he'll think something's strange. Besides, I can't miss this chance."

Her opportunity came immediately, as Bresson cut in between them and maneuvered her out onto the dance floor.

"You have to help me with my article," she said.

"What do you want to know?"

"Where were you born?"

"As far as I know, Annecy." He did not miss a beat. His steps had the mechanical precision of someone who has spent long hours with a dance instructor. "But I only remember growing up with my foster parents in Grenoble. Then I went to Annecy as a teenager."

"There are no birth records."

"I know."

"And did you know that your mother was at Dachau?"

"Yes, but my parents never talked about it." He was definitely a better liar than a dancer.

They had moved to the starboard side of the dance floor, where she asked to sit down on a couch next to the rail. Lyman approached and Heidi waved him off.

"And could you help me talk with your parents?" she was saying.

"I wish I could. But we are estranged."

"How about your foster family?"

"The Couderts? I am afraid they died many years ago."

"In 1943? That's what the National Archive says."

"You must have the wrong Couderts," he said calmly.

She had not considered that frustrating possibility. He clipped and lit another cigar.

In the safety of the crowd, and on the open deck with Jay Lyman nearby, she decided to be more direct. "So why have you had me followed?"

"You mean Edouard?"

"And the Vietnamese."

"I am worried about you, Mademoiselle." He dropped his voice and added, "Worried about your safety."

"Why?" she said more sharply than she intended.

"I have enemies, like anyone. But I have no family. No business partners. So my enemies strike those near to me. To hurt me or embarrass me."

Sitting back, he knocked the tip of ash off of his cigar and onto the teak deck. "Another woman was once writing a story about me, a book in fact. And on this yacht she fell overboard and drowned. I cared deeply for her. I never thought it was an accident.

"And then there was the unfortunate Mr. Rankin," he continued. "I did not believe that was an accident or suicide. It was a brutal attempt to disrupt our transaction."

"Who would do this?"

"All of this is off the record, of course. A man in my position cannot make accusations without proof. And there is no proof." He paused. "But I thought I should warn you."

"Warn me?"

"I am an instinctual person. That is how I built my business. Now I have a bad feeling about your article. Not that you will say bad things about me. I am sure you will be fair. If you send me written questions, I will be happy to respond."

He then leaned closer and put his hand over hers. "No, my worry is more serious. That if you stay in Europe and continue your research, something terrible might happen to you."

Heidi could feel herself getting angry and scared at the same time. "And that's just intuition?"

He squeezed her hand until she thought it might be crushed.

"That," he smiled, "and the fact that you have two American passports in two different names."

Lyman was furious. Who the hell did Heidi think she was? She spent the whole evening with Marcel Bresson while he was stuck trying to hold a conversation with living Quaaludes. And when he finally got into a good discussion of forward interest-rate swaps, she demands to go back to the hotel! He looked at her sitting in the corner of the limo saying nothing and staring out the window as if he didn't exist.

"Do you want to go dancing at Jimmy'z?" He vowed this would be his last try. "It's a fabulous place, great music, pools, fountains, Oriental gardens, gazebos."

"No, I'm really tired," she mumbled.

Great, he thought, an evening on the couch!

When they reached the suite, she went directly into the bedroom. Lyman had to satisfy himself with the TV and a bottle of Kronenbourg from the mini-bar. Flipping angrily through the thirty-six channels, he stopped at the National League playoff game between the Giants and the Mets. Life might not be a complete bummer. The score was three all in the eighth, with Jefferies on first. Dave Dravecky tried to pick him off three times before finally pitching a fast ball to Hernandez, who chased it low and outside for strike three. With only one away, Darryl Strawberry came to the plate in a chorus of boos from the fans at Candlestick. He took three balls high and inside. The hit and run was on. Strawberry fouled a fastball down the left-field line. Then, just as he grounded a change-up into double-play territory, Heidi appeared at the bedroom door in her nightgown.

"Jayson," she said, "would you please stay with me?"

Lyman undressed in front of the television. When he entered the bedroom, Heidi was already under the covers and turned away from him. He slipped into bed and lay still. Should he say anything? What did she expect? He knew what he wanted.

Very tentatively, Lyman reached out and put his arm around her. He could feel her trembling. His hand touched her cheek. It was damp with tears. Christ, Lyman said to himself, is she thinking of her old boyfriend? As if to reassure him, she reached up and pulled his hand away from her face and down onto her breast.

He felt like he had entered into a dream. As Heidi moved his hands across her hardened nipples, he bit into her shoulder. She turned toward him, her lips sweeping across his chest and up his neck, urgently seeking his face, her mouth anxious for his. Tumbling, twisting, she kissed and bit him, her hands locked in his hair. Gripping him between her thighs, she sat up and pulled her nightgown over her head. She offered her breasts and he eagerly buried his face in their softness. As the salty taste of her skin filled his mouth, she arched back, reaching down between his legs, and began to stroke him. Gasping at her touch, he fell away from her, against the pillow. On her face he saw a look of delirium, in her eyes, desperation. He put his hands on her waist, lifted her up and over onto her back. For an instant, he felt the hot, wet spot she had left on his stomach turn cool. She lay open and waiting. Her hand reached up to guide him. As he lowered himself toward her, the phone rang.

"It is an emergency," Bresson said. "You must come immediately."

"I'm busy!" Lyman was in no mood for puns.

"We are at the Radio Monte Carlo offices."

"It's two in the morning and I'm in bed."

"A car will pick you up," he said as if he were deaf. And rich. And the client.

The streets on the way up the mountain toward Radio Monte Carlo crisscrossed one other, winding around the new office and condominium towers like a tangle of fresh pasta. Radio Monte Carlo comprised a series of turn-of-the-century townhouses, all painted a dull orange with blanked-out windows staring vacantly back at the street.

Lyman's driver turned out to be the same Vietnamese who had chauffeured him around Paris. He dropped Lyman in front of a pair of glass doors that had been built into the entrance to give the conglomeration of buildings a more modern and businesslike facade. There was nothing gracious about the lobby. The guard at the desk pulled down a metal shutter and locked the door behind him. He took Lyman up three floors and through a labyrinth of narrow corridors lit by single bulbs and filled with files, cardboard boxes, bookcases and shelves stuffed with audio and video tape cassettes. All the offices were dark, except for an empty studio where two reels of tape revolved slowly on a wall of electronic equipment. When Lyman felt completely lost, the guard stopped, opened one side of a double door and ushered him through.

Lyman entered a darkened suite illuminated only by a partially open door with the light on inside. He pushed it open and found Sperile Beck and Maurice the accountant sitting silently at a conference table which extended out from a massive desk occupied by Marcel Bresson. He watched Lyman come into the room without rising or acknowledging his arrival.

"What's the emergency?" Lyman decided to be equally ungracious. The others looked at Sperile Beck. He cleared his throat.

"We face some problems on the financing of the new offer," he said.

"Like what?"

"My commitments committee does not believe it is appropriate to increase the bank's contribution to the purchase."

"You're working a little late for a Saturday night," Lyman observed. "Wait till I tell the boys at Citibank."

"This is not a time for jokes," Bresson snapped.

"Relax. So we get some mezzanine financing. GE Credit. Electra House in London. The Bass brothers."

"I do not want anyone else in the deal," Bresson declared. He had pushed his chair back against a heavy curtain that covered the wall. Lyman then noticed that all the walls were covered with heavy drapes, and wondered if it were some kind of security measure.

"All right." Lyman took a seat. "Just kick in more of your own cash."

Maurice the accountant spoke up. "That would not be realistic in view of the other commitments of Les Éditions Bresson."

It was an emergency all right, Lyman thought. They didn't have any more money.

"Richardson offers paper, why can't we?" Bresson asked.

"Depends on the paper," Lyman replied. "It changes the whole deal. Cash is simple. You pay, you take. Securities have to go through the SEC. News/Worldweek's board has to value them. We'd have to decide what kind. Notes? Debentures? Convertibles? Junk bonds? And can you meet the premiums and also pay off the Herr Doktor's loans? I take it his commitments committee is already worried about coverage."

"There are no advantages?" Bresson said.

Lyman had learned that when he asked questions like that, he usually knew the answer.

"Yes, flexibility. We can make a two-stage offer. Fifty dollars for the first fifty-one percent of the stock and pay the rest in paper. That would put a lot of pressure on Richardson. Stockholders would rush to tender to us."

"What happens if more than fifty-one percent of the stock is tendered?" Maurice asked suspiciously.

"All the stock goes in a pool. We buy an equal percentage share of everybody's stock. What's left over gets paid for in paper at, say, $45 a share."

"You can do that to stockholders in America? Give one group $50 and others $45?" Maurice acted as if he had at last heard something about America that he admired.

"Well, they can always refuse to tender."

"What happens then?"

"If you get control of seventy-five percent, you can freeze 'em out, swap your paper for their stock. But there are problems, Marcel. The poison pill would come into effect unless the board revoked it. And you'd have to act fast or you'd delay the tender and give Richardson a chance to get in ahead of you."

For the next several hours they examined the complexities, advantages and disadvantages of a front-loaded two-step deal, a one-step cash/paper deal and alternative financial instruments. At that time of night, it was the kind of discussion that normally put Lyman to sleep. But he was kept awake by one happy thought. Whoever had been bankrolling Bresson all these years, finally had yanked his chain.

Pulling off her sunglasses, Heidi looked out to sea. She briefly considered crossing the few yards of sand for a swim or going up onto the terrace of the Monte Carlo Beach Hotel for a midmorning daiquiri. But it was easier to lie there and let the sun's rays burn out the restlessness.

She slathered on more Bain de Soleil 25. Admit it, she said to herself, last night was a disaster. Bresson proved more than she bargained for. Whatever he was hiding, she didn't know how to get at it. And the cocky bastard had the gall to send her a gift! You're frightened, baffled, anxious and unsure of yourself, she thought, and that's before you even begin to consider the fiasco with Jay. She felt plain humiliated.

Lyman was still off consorting with the enemy. She sensed an ambivalence in him about Bresson that she could not fathom. One moment he seemed to despise him, and suspect him of murder or worse, and then he would dutifully go off and do whatever he was told. Was it the money? Or perhaps he just didn't understand. She wondered if she did. Maybe she was relieving Lyman's guilt by going after Bresson, while he closed a deal that would pay him $20 million!

Heidi began to feel angry and exploited. When that happened she had come to learn that something else was bothering her. The usual answer was to look out for herself.

She felt a shadow fall across her body.

"Hello." It was Jay's voice.

She squinted up at him. He looked terrible. "Your meeting's finally over?"

He nodded. "I'm sorry."

"You said that last night. If you want to swim, I brought you a bathing suit. It's in the cabana."

Obediently, he went inside to change. Heidi sat up and looked around. Rows of pink canvas cabanas lined the small man-made beach. Each one was shaded by a palm tree and had at least two lounge chairs. At that midmorning hour, the sunbathers were mostly women and a scattering of children. Two boys on jet skis showed off by plowing lazy figure eights in the sea. Heidi made up her mind. Last night she needed him. This morning she wanted him.

The cabana had two rooms. In front was a sitting area with chairs, a low table and a small refrigerator.

Lyman stood in the darkened changing room in the back. He was naked except for his socks. Heidi came up quietly behind him, reaching around to run her hands over his chest. He let out a sigh. She pulled down the top of her bikini and rubbed her breasts across his back while she ran her hands down the inside of his thighs.

"Heidi, I don't know," he groaned. But his growing hardness spoke for itself.

Lyman turned to face her. She stepped away, appraising him coolly. He looked ridiculous. Socks, erection, day's growth of beard. She could smell his excitement. Untying her bikini bottom, she stepped toward him again, kissing him, seeking his tongue, lifting her leg and reaching down. She wanted him inside her. Then she felt him lift her off the ground. She wrapped her legs around his hips and pushed herself onto him. She could not hold back a moan. He began to move inside her. She began to shake convulsively. Her head fell back as she felt his mouth devouring her breasts. Then she heard him groan as she began grinding her hips against him. He pulled out, then slammed back in. She was wide open and vulnerable. He crushed her against him harder.

Suddenly, she could feel him contracting, pulsating, exploding, filling her up.

"No! No!" she cried.

Clinging to him tightly she began to vibrate. She wanted more. A great void expanded inside. With her hand she desperately tried to push him deeper even as he became smaller. He staggered backwards and fell onto the cot, slipping out of her.

Heidi pushed him onto his back, kneeled down and took him into her mouth. She could taste the both of them.

"Oh, I can't. God, Heidi—"

Moving up and down, gently caressing him with her hands, lips, and tongue, she could feel him respond. He began to swell, then to get hard again. She climbed on top of him. He reached up to hold her breasts. His eyes were wild, unfocused. Heidi could feel the tension building deep within her. She would lift herself slowly until only the tip of him was inside and then drop down to impale herself. Rising and falling, she moved more and more slowly until she felt herself beginning to tremble. He was merging into her. She was losing control. He gripped her breasts so hard they hurt. The pain shot straight down into her womb, finally detonating all her stored-up fear and anger and need. She went rigid. She could feel him throbbing, about to come. A cry escaped her clinched teeth. He was coming. She was coming, clinging, shaking, crying, at last oblivious.

Lyman awoke on the floor of the warm, dark cabana. He felt luxuriously exhausted. "Heidi," he murmured. She was not there.

Stepping outside, he squinted into the bright sunlight. She was not in the lounge chair nor on the beach. He climbed the few stairs to the deck surrounding the seawater swimming pool. She was not there either. The position of the sun suggested that it was midafternoon. Adding six hours to his watch, which he kept on New York time, confirmed that it was about 2:30. With growing concern, he again surveyed the beach, the sea and the pool area. No Heidi. He looked out to the terrace of the hotel restaurant, which sat perched on a rock promontory. When he saw her sitting next to the balustrade, Lyman was flooded with a happiness that surprised him.

"I thought I was seduced and abandoned," he said, putting his arms around her and kissing her hair.

"It was a close call," she said in a brittle voice, "but I thought I should stay so we could talk."

Oh God, Lyman thought, why can't women enjoy a good screw without a lot of metaphysics. He sat down in the chair opposite her. What would it be? That she was still loyal to her boyfriend? Or that she was thinking of moving to New York. Or just that she wanted to know how he felt? Well, he felt just fine.

"I'm thinking of dropping the Bresson investigation," she said.

"Why?" he said, surprised.

"Nobody cares about it."

"I do."

"Really? Disappearing in the middle of the night? Admit it. You're making the deal happen."

"I thought we had an understanding," he protested. "I would drag it out while you would dig up the dirt."

"That was a bad bargain. What's your downside, Jayson? If the deal doesn't go through."

"I get a five-million-dollar fee. But my firm's still under water."

"You know what my downside is?"

He wasn't going to walk into the trap. He waited.

"My downside is that I get dead."

"Come on—" He wondered if this was some kind of postcoital depression.

"Jayson, listen to me. His people have been following me! Last night Bresson as much as threatened to kill me if I didn't stop investigating him!"

"But he told me you were wonderful." Lyman did not want to hear this. Images of Rankin's contorted body hanging on the end of a crane flashed through his mind. "He said he sent you a present."

"He did. It arrived this morning with a note apologizing for taking you away last night. You want to see it?"

She took a small Bulgari box out of her purse and gave it to him. He lifted off the lid. A teardrop-shaped emerald gleamed in the sun. From the weight in his hand, Lyman judged it to be at least sixty carats. Jayson felt a stab of jealousy. He immediately thought of saying he would buy her a diamond. Instead he made the error of asking what she wanted him to do.

"Make up your mind," she replied. "You're ambivalent. You want the deal. You want to beat Richardson. You want to get Bresson, too, but you also want his fee. You can't do all of these things."

"Do you know what $20 million could mean?" He almost added, to us, but stopped short. "That's a million and a half a year, tax-free. You could buy a new Rolls-Royce every month, throw the old one away, and still have almost a thousand dollars a day spending money and fifteen million in the bank! You could buy a horse ranch in Kentucky, a house in the Hamptons, a château in the Loire and a flat in London and still be rich! You could endow a college, start a foundation. You could get yourself elected to the Senate! Send a thousand ghetto kids to college every year! Don't act as though twenty million is a pile of crap."

"Jayson, you've got to decide whose side you're on."

"But I'm a go-between! An intermediary! That's all I've ever been." He felt disgusting. "I hate irreversible choices."

"Indecision's also a choice. Being an intermediary doesn't mean you're independent. You just get used by both sides. And it only gives the illusion that you're not responsible for what happens."

"Let's be practical." He had to get her down to his level. "What can I do that I'm not doing? I'm dragging the deal out, giving you time for your investigation and helping the News/Worldweek stockholders get the best price. Bresson may crater anyway. He's reaching the limit of his resources. What else can I do?"

"You can find out who's behind him."

"And how do I do that?" he said defiantly, as if he did not know. But he did. And he knew Heidi did too.

"Just like Deep Throat told Bob Woodward during Watergate, 'follow the money.' "

"And what'll you be doing?" Lyman responded angrily, feeling trapped. He picked up the emerald and held it to the light. "Retire with your winnings?"

She snatched it back.

"Is it very expensive?" she asked.

"Very."

"Good."

She stood up and tossed it into the sea.

18

As the Falcon 900 took off from Nice, Lyman looked down on the golden hills of Vence. Years earlier when Lyman had first visited the Riviera, he had realized that Southern California, where he grew up, possessed the same climate and even better beaches. But Orange County had been ruined by developers, and he had been dispirited to think that it would never look like the Riviera. Now, as the aircraft turned sharply over the condo-cluttered Côte d'Azur, he had to admit that it finally did.

There were exceptions, oases like St-Paul-de-Vence and the Colombe d'Or where he and Heidi had spent Sunday night. He already missed her. They had continued their argument, eaten wonderful meals, made love, and argued some more. Dining on the terrace under fig trees with fruit so ripe it hung in their faces, the two of them tried to develop a plan. Lyman promised to try to discover who backed Bresson, if Heidi would return to Washington. He insisted she would find more by digging at the CIA than by rummaging through the musty archives of Europe. And she would be safer. When he said that, she gave him a look that forced him to abandon his lobster ravioli and take her directly upstairs to bed.

But Heidi resisted going back to the U.S. She had thought of a new lead that she wanted to follow up. Her stubbornness was reinforced by an exchange of phone calls with Dick Rensselaer in Paris who, at her urging, had spent the weekend trying to locate the boyfriend of the woman who had written the biography of Bresson. Late on Sunday Rensselaer called with the information. The man's name was Pierre Coutier and now lived in Geneva. The international operator provided a phone number and street address, but the phone did not answer. Despite Lyman's objections, Heidi decided to go to Geneva.

They said good-bye at the airport in Nice. Bresson, the lawyer from Skadden Fried and the rest of the entourage were also there.

Heidi stood in the Pan Am line pretending to be bound for New York. Bresson kissed her hand and said he hoped he would see her again.

Bresson's Falcon 900 had room for fourteen passengers. Lyman took one of the four tables for two. Dr. Beck sat opposite him. During the flight, Bresson intermittently talked on the phone in several languages to several different countries, while reading three newspapers at once— *Nice Matin* and the *Svenska Dagblat,* which he owned, and the *International Herald Tribune.* So far, there had been no sign that Bresson questioned Lyman's loyalty or commitment to the deal. But given his relationship to Heidi, how could Bresson not be suspicious?

So why wasn't he fired? Lyman wondered. Probably because it would hurt the deal. Changing investment bankers in the middle of a hostile takeover was the ultimate no-no. When Bendix's Bill Agee called in Bruce Wasserstein to replace Salomon Brothers in the midst of his attack on Martin Marietta, it was the beginning of the end for both Agee and Bendix.

And there was Machiavelli's maxim: Keep your enemies close, so you can keep an eye on them. At the moment, that seemed to Lyman a more pertinent explanation. Lyman had all the documents Bresson had submitted to the U.S. government spread out in front of him, ostensibly preparing for the deposition, but in fact searching for a way to break the ring of secrecy surrounding his finances. Dr. Beck, facing Lyman, watched everything he did.

As the aircraft climbed high over the Alps, Lyman concentrated on a copy of the Richardson complaint. It would form the basis for the depositions by Bresson and Herr Doktor Beck. Most of it appeared to be boilerplate until he got to the allegation that Bresson did not have adequate financing to complete the transaction. In paragraph thirty-six, it pointed out that Bresson's 14D listed only the Swiss Bank Corporation as the source of the funds. Paragraph thirty-seven pointed out that this was highly unusual, particularly in a transaction so large. The normal procedure would be to syndicate the loan, have other banks participate by lending a part of the money. However, the complaint found no indication in any of Bresson's documents that a syndicate existed, let alone who was in it. Richardson's lawyers noted a further anomaly in the phrasing of the statement in Bresson's 14D, Item 4, Source of Funds: "The Swiss Bank Corporation guarantees that adequate credit in the sum of $6.2 billion will be available to complete the transaction." According to the complaint, that raised the question of whether the Swiss Bank Corporation planned only to be a guarantor of other "unstated and unknown" sources of capital.

Finally, the complaint referred to the letter from the Swiss Bank Corporation accompanying Bresson's offer, which stated that they were "confident" that they could furnish the financing. The day of the offer, Muldoon had called to point out that "highly confident" had long been the standard for tender offers, and the complaint now exploited that point to allege that Bresson's financing was not in place, and that his offer was fraudulent.

Lyman checked Bresson's original documents, and the complaint was factually correct. They had a powerful case. Bresson would have to respond. Sitting back in his seat, he stared thoughtfully out the window at the rain clouds that rose to meet them as they dropped down toward the Zurich airport. The lawsuit was a godsend. He could use it to probe for information on Bresson's financial backers. And the person he would focus on most would be Herr Doktor Beck.

As the Falcon 900 rolled to a stop at the private aviation terminal, Lyman was feeling secure and in control of the situation. The door opened and the stairs let down. Two Mercedes 560 SELs awaited them. Bresson and Beck got into the first one. Edouard directed Lyman and the lawyer into the second. Then Lyman heard Edouard tell the pilot something that shattered his composure.

"Refuel the aircraft," he ordered. "We're departing immediately for Geneva."

Climbing the steep cobblestone street from the central shopping area along the Rhone, Heidi carefully looked back every few minutes to see if she was being followed. She thought that if Bresson was still keeping tabs on her, his people were being far more discreet than in the past. The others on the Grande Rue, as the narrow street was called, appeared to be shoppers, students and tourists.

Heidi knew the old town of Geneva well. While in college, she had spent a semester at the University of Geneva. She had not liked the city. It was cold, damp, and of her two roommates, one had turned out to be a lesbian, the other a kleptomaniac.

At the corner of the rue du Puits-St-Pierre, she turned right, looking for the rue des Granges. The address for Pierre Coutier was number 18 Bis. She tried phoning him from both the airport and the hotel, but with no response. Rather than wait indefinitely for the number to answer, she decided to make sure that he still lived there.

Pierre Coutier could prove a crucial source. While it might be too much to hope that he had a copy of his deceased girlfriend's manuscript, he might have read it, talked about it. He might remember facts and sources that could provide leads. When Lyman had asked Heidi how she planned to make Coutier talk, she said money. When he pointed out she had none, she pointed out that he did. As a result, she now carried $10,000 in cash, which Lyman had obtained at American Express in Nice on his platinum card.

Number 18 rue des Granges proved to be an old, four-story, flat-faced, gray building. The *Bis* in Coutier's address meant that he lived in the back. A buzzer opened one of the large double doors facing the street. Heidi passed through a courtyard and into a shabby foyer with a once-grand staircase. Plaques on the wall announced that Monsieur P. Coutier lived on the fourth floor, above the Banca Fata Morgana and the Banco de los Exilios which occupied the second- and third-floor apartments. Private banks, Heidi noted, were obviously the local cottage industry in Geneva.

Despite the general decrepitude of the stairwell, each of the doorways gleamed with beautifully polished wood and bright brass hardware. The peeling paint and cracked plaster was apparently just for show. Small windows along the stairs looked out the back of the building and suggested that the apartments had a magnificent view of the Alps over the ancient ramparts of the city.

Pierre Coutier had the only apartment on the top floor. She pushed the bell hesitantly.

There was no answer. She could not even hear whether it had rung.

She knocked on the door, surprised to find that it was metal painted to look like wood.

Still no answer.

Opening her Filofax, she tore out a piece of note paper. In her best French she left the number at the Noga Hilton and asked him to call. Then she slipped the note under the door. Descending the stairs, she worried that he wouldn't call. Europeans could be very careful with strangers. But how could she "incentivize him," as Jayson would say. She was so lost in thought she almost fell over the stout woman standing guard at the bottom of the steps.

"Can I help you, Mademoiselle?" It was the concierge.

"I was looking for Monsieur Coutier."

"So it seems is every other young girl in Geneva."

"Is he away?"

"On weekends he stays on his boat. In the winter, he skis. During the week he has parties with his friends. He has too many friends for a young man. I tell him he should work."

The concierge clearly disapproved of Pierre Coutier and just as obviously liked him. Her talk of his friends gave Heidi an idea how to encourage him to call. She dashed back up the stairs, and using a comb, fished her note out from under the door. She added a P.S.: "I have a present for you from a friend."

Back on the street, Heidi wandered slowly through the old town, heading down the hill in the direction of the lake. Below the garden of St. Peter's Cathedral, she stopped in a small square where a carousel played. She watched boys and girls climb aboard the horses, giraffes, rocking boats, toy motorcycles and cars. The children were very orderly and did not argue over who would get what ride. The young mothers and nannies spread handkerchiefs on the seats to protect the little girls. After watching for several minutes, Heidi concluded that she was still not being followed.

Plunging into the crowd on the Rue de Rive, she saw a sign that offered to satisfy a desire too long denied. The Big Mac and fries with a vanilla milk shake tasted just like home. Later she strolled through the shopping arcades, relieved that she had been reunited with her luggage at the Geneva airport, but disappointed that she could no longer rationalize $500 for a new fall suit. She crossed a bridge where the lake turned into the Rhône River and walked along the Quai to the Noga Hilton, watching the famous *jet d'eau* send a plume of water three hundred feet into the sky. The concierge handed Heidi her key and two messages.

The first was from Jay Lyman in Zurich. She tried to call him from a phone in the lobby, but the secretary who answered the phone said he was in a meeting and could not be disturbed.

The second message came from Pierre Coutier. He wanted to meet her at 5:30 on his boat, *La Revanche,* slip number 188, on the Quai Gustave Ador in front of the Iran Air sign. Heidi checked her watch. That gave her enough time to check out an idea that came to her on the Pont Mont Blanc. Assuming d'Uberville had told the truth, there had to be some record of Marcel Bresson as a refugee. And Geneva was the headquarters of the United Nations High Commission for Refugees.

Zurich was a lovely city, even in the rain. Not too large, it had nicely proportioned buildings and a park lining the lakefront. Gentle hills surrounded the center of town and steep mountains rose in the distance, giving both a sense of scale and space. But Lyman hated Zurich. To him it was the loneliest place in the world. He not only missed Heidi, he was worried about her.

As he stood on the balcony surrounding the top floor of the head-quarters of the Swiss Bank Corporation, which looked out over the Parade Platz and the Munsterhof Cathedral, Lyman reflected that this was the first time Zurich had been his destination. Before, he had always been on his way somewhere else, waiting a few hours at the airport, or the train station, often staying overnight at the Hotel Baur au Lac in order to catch a morning flight back to the United States. He had acute memories of spending evenings alone in the hotel's polished mahogany bar, nursing several of their famous dry martinis, along with other single businessmen, and of breakfasting in the sunny, round room in the park by the lake, where the solitary patrons at each table buried themselves behind newspapers so as to avoid staring at one another. Those who sought the isolation of Nepal or the Sahara or Antarctica in order to find themselves, Lyman decided, should try spending a few days at the Baur au Lac in Zurich.

Bresson's mock deposition was over, and he had departed for the Hotel Dolder Grand for a rest. He had cleverly finessed all the routine questions about his birth by providing a copy of his French identity card. No matter how hostile the question, Bresson proved imperturb-able. He "couldn't recall," or he would "have his staff look into it," or "Herr Doktor Beck can answer that question better than I." But now it was Beck's turn.

The lawyer for Skadden Fried signaled that they were about to begin. Lyman came in from the terrace just as rain again started to fall. The room was perfect for a deposition. Paneled in blond wood, it had nothing on its walls except a clock. The table matched the walls, as did the hard wooden chairs. The Swiss Bank Corporation clearly favored short meetings.

The Skadden Fried lawyer took Beck through the preliminaries.

"Just let the questions wash over you. Don't get upset. This is not a university exam. The worse the answer—and I mean vague, tangen-tial, incomplete—the better from our point of view. But you've got to be careful with outright falsehoods. And don't volunteer anything. You can demand clarification or challenge a question. If they ask, 'Have you stopped beating your wife,' you don't have to say yes or no. You can say, 'I never beat my wife.' "

Lyman thought he saw a brief look cross the Herr Doktor's face that suggested he probably had.

The lawyer then took Beck through a series of preliminary questions relating to his identity, role in the transaction and the authenticity of various documents. The only thing Lyman noted was Beck's comment that he was senior vice president of the bank's Middle European Division.

With the standard questions completed, it was Lyman's turn. He decided to get tough.

"Item 4 of the 14D submission, Source of Funds, states 'The Swiss Bank Corporation guarantees that adequate credit in the sum of $6.2 billion will be made available to complete the transaction.' What does that mean?"

"I do not understand," Beck replied.

"You don't understand your own words?"

"I do not understand the question."

"It is 'guarantee,' but not a 'source of funds.' Why?"

"We are arranging the financing. We have a syndicate."

Beck looked around the room for his lawyer. He nodded.

"Yes, we have a syndicate," Beck repeated.

"Isn't that normal in a loan this size?"

"Yes," he said, relaxing a little.

"Then isn't it misleading for you to state that you're the source of the funds?

"No," Beck protested. "We arranged it."

"But you admit you tried to conceal it."

"We did not!"

"Then provide us a list of the members of the syndicate."

Beck stopped. "One minute, please." He conferred with his lawyer. "That is proprietary and confidential information," he finally said, "which under Swiss banking law I am not required to divulge."

"Okay, let's break right there," Lyman said, dropping his hostile tone. "That's not the right answer." He sensed he was nearing pay dirt, and was not going to let Beck escape behind legalisms.

"But that is our legal right," Beck insisted.

"This will happen over and over during the deposition. They'll press for more information. We're better off giving it, unless there's a real problem." Lyman turned to the lawyer for Skadden Fried.

"Richardson would get an injunction halting our tender until you produced the list," he explained. "Delay is what they're after."

"What would be the grounds?" the Swiss lawyer asked.

"They'd argue we're hiding something. And we aren't, are we?" Lyman stared Beck in the eye.

"Of course not. Here is the syndication list," he slid a folder over to Lyman. "But I will need my superior's approval to release it."

Trying not to look too eager, Lyman opened the file. Instead of paper clips or staples, the documents inside were tied to the folder with dark green ribbon. He quickly read down the list, expecting to see banks from the Cayman Islands, Beirut, Luxembourg, Macao, the Bahamas and the Netherlands Antilles. But instead of a rogues' gallery of money laundries, the syndicate read like a who's who of European banking— Banque Nationale de Paris, Deutsche Bank, Crédit Agricole, Société Générale, Barclays.

He was deeply disappointed. There was no smoking gun nor even a hint of impropriety in that list. Lyman continued aimlessly asking questions for several minutes, but his heart had gone out of the game.

Then he stumbled onto the right path.

"And what portion of the overall loan is each bank taking?" he asked.

"It is on the list," Beck pointed out.

He pretended to study it carefully. As he did so, the automatic calculator that whirled in his mind alerted him to the fact that something was odd. The syndicate added up to one hundred percent. He handed the folder over to the lawyer from Skadden Fried, who began looking back and forth between the various pages.

"How much of the loan is the Swiss Bank Corporation taking?" Lyman asked casually.

Beck hesitated. "We have syndicated all of it," he admitted.

"So there is no Swiss Bank Corporation money in this deal at all?" Lyman's tone was incredulous, accusatory. "And the statement in the 14D is not just misleading, it is false! You are not the source of any funds whatsoever!"

"The language was meant to say we are providing the guarantee," Beck struggled to explain.

"What guarantee?"

"We guarantee to the syndicate that the acquisition company, Bresson USA, will pay back the principal and interest."

"You're going have to do something about these documents," the lawyer interrupted. "You've got people on the commitment fee list who aren't in the syndicate."

Lyman compared the two pages. "Herr Doktor, you have a record of a fee paid to the Sommer Bank of Vienna but they are not part of the loan syndicate."

"That's a finder's fee."

"For the syndicate?" Lyman had returned to using the voice that suggested he was lying. "You're trying to tell us that the Swiss Bank Corporation can't put together a loan syndicate of the most prestigious banks in Europe without the help of a finder?"

"Not for the loan." Beck was almost pleading for Lyman to stop.

"For what?"

Beck did not want to answer.

"Fee for what?" Lyman pressed harder. "For a kickback? For a bribe?"

"My God, no!" Beck protested. "For the guarantee!"

Now Lyman was baffled. "You gave them a finder's fee for your own guarantee? That doesn't make sense."

"There is another guarantee. We have a guarantee from someone else, like reinsurance, to protect ourselves—"

"Wait a minute. You guarantee the syndicate if Marcel can't repay the loan?"

He nodded.

"And if that happens, you have a guarantee that pays you. So you have no risk at all!"

"It is good business!"

"And who's providing this other guarantee?" Lyman asked, "The Sommer Bank?"

"No."

"Herr Doktor Beck, who is the ultimate credit in this deal?"

"The guarantee comes from a company called Liechtinvest."

"Liechtinvest? I never heard of it," Lyman said scornfully. "They have the resources to guarantee a $7 billion loan?"

"They have substantial resources and collateral," Beck said defensively.

"You're starting to volunteer information," the Skadden Fried lawyer broke in. "Just say 'yes' or 'no' or 'we're satisfied.' "

"Right," Lyman said. "But I want to know what collateral."

Beck looked extremely unhappy. "The stock."

"What stock?"

"The stock in Bresson USA, the subsidiary we are using to take over News/Worldweek," he said, finally getting angry.

Lyman paused. Not only was Liechtinvest the credit, but it would in effect become the owner of News/Worldweek, just like the bank owned his car and the mortgage on his apartment. It was the perfect financial bubble, and completely legal. Bresson was buying News/Worldweek with loans guaranteed by the stock of the company buying News/Worldweek.

"Will I really have to go into all of this?" the Herr Doktor complained.

"You'd better hope not," Lyman replied, praying they would.

The Palace of Nations dominates a hillside in the suburban Ariana Park overlooking Lake Geneva. Built in 1936 to house the ill-fated League of Nations, it had become one of the regional headquarters for the United Nations. A guard explained to Heidi that the UN High Commission for Refugees was located in the wing of the building farthest from the main entrance.

The building looked like a Hollywood set designer's fantasy. Broad ramps rose to vast porches with pediments held aloft by massive square columns. Inside, the Palace boasted foyers four stories high, sweeping staircases, and seemingly endless hallways wide enough for a parade. It was a treasure house of art deco appointments, from the magnificent brass *torchères* and sconces which lit the corridors to ashtrays and rounded, overstuffed chairs and couches that furnished the lounge areas. Heidi had read a great deal about the failure of the League to stop fascism. Walking through the Palace, she realized that the first defeat had come at the hands of the fascist architects. The building was a trip into the past, and she feared, a plunge into a bottomless international bureaucracy.

The UN High Commission for Refugees gave her short shrift. She was directed to a stocky little Englishman with a florid face and eighty-proof breath. He did not beat around the bush. They had nothing to do with refugee programs or refugees themselves, he explained, they only dealt with policy.

"For anything else, dear," he said, "you'll have to go to the Registry. That's where all the documents are kept."

The Registry was in the opposite corner of the Palace. A quarter of an hour later, Heidi found herself at a broad teak counter manned by a single Indian. Row after row of shelves piled with documents stretched behind him. They also reached upward through the ceiling as far as she could see. No one could help her, he explained. They were all on their afternoon break. He could not help her because he had to man the counter. What did "man the counter" mean if he could not help her?

"Yes, that is it exactly," he agreed mysteriously and returned to reading a Hindi girlie magazine.

Forty minutes later, a few other clerks of various nationalities drifted in, declining to assist her because they were already busy. After almost an hour of being rebuffed by one clerk after another, she rapped on the counter and announced at the top of her voice, "I'll pay a thousand dollars if someone can help me!"

All of the clerks remained unmoved except a Chinese man who asked in halting English what she wanted. But when she started to explain, Heidi could see that he had no idea what she was saying. He disappeared. But a few minutes later he came back with a sullen blond girl.

"You are wanting something?" she said in singsong Scandinavian English.

Heidi went through it again as the girl began to shake her head.

"All of the records of UNRRA, the United Nations Relief and Rehabilitation Administration, have been turned over to the French National Archive in Paris," she said. "The International Refugee Organization has its files in New York."

"There's nothing in this whole place about refugees?"

"Very little. Some records from the Evian Convention in 1938. Perhaps some papers from the war years."

"Could I see those?"

"Oh, we do not have them. You must go to the archivist of the League of Nations."

"Well, where am I?"

"This is the Registry for the United Nations." She then gave Heidi a room number, M-1214. It was back across the Palace, in the direction she had just come.

"You said you would pay to be helped?" The statement ended with a question mark, as had all her other sentences.

"I give at the office," Heidi responded.

On her way to M-1214, she encountered a crowd of delegates from the International Advisory Group on Standards for Dried Fruit. They had spilled out of their conference room, making it hard for the experts from the Working Group on the Peaceful Uses of Outer Space to caucus in the hallway. Heidi spotted the American representatives instantly: pants too short, suit jackets hanging open, longer in front than in the back. In contrast, the Third World delegates looked like they spent half their countries' GNP on their wardrobe. Heidi moved through the crowd quickly, hoping to avoid a chance encounter with someone she might know from Washington.

Her route took her past the main assembly hall of the League of Nations. The room itself had the depressing feeling of deferred maintenance. The domed skylight needed cleaning. Watermarks stained the ceiling, and in places the teak veneer was curling off the walls. But the Salle des Pas Perdue, a green marble entrance hall with a wall of glass overlooking the garden and the lake and Mont Blanc towering in the background, was as glorious as it was in the 1930s. She thought it must have made the onrush of World War II seem unreal.

Heidi found room M-1412 around the corner in a nearby corridor. The door opened with the tinkle of a shopkeeper's bell. She found herself in a small room with walls completely covered by stacks of documents stuffed into bookshelves. No one sat at the small desk, which was also obscured by piles of paper. A voice called out from an adjoining room. From where she was standing, it seemed similarly crammed full of documents. A large, heavyset man with a red beard and a Germanic accent appeared in the doorway.

He introduced himself as "the archivist of the League of Nations, and other dead organizations." He invited her to take a seat, offered tea, but was not able to help her either. The UNRRA records were in Paris, IRO in New York. The Evian Conference consisted mainly of speeches.

With a sigh, Heidi decided to accept the tea. As he puttered with the kettle, she tried to identify the smell in the room. It was a musty and stale odor that penetrated the whole building. Finally she recognized it: paper, old paper. The palace had to be an asthmatic's nightmare.

"Exactly what are you looking for?" the bearded man asked as he handed her the tea and settled behind the desk. He had the earnest manner of someone who had not talked to another soul in weeks.

"I'm trying to track down a young boy who was a refugee during the Second World War."

"Oh, you want a person! An actual person. I don't think UNRRA would help. They provided food and so forth. Their records would be grocery lists," he chuckled. "And IRO would be similar. Documents to describe the refugee assistance programs, records of meetings, budgets, resolutions. No, I think I know what you need."

He got up and went to the wall, unerringly extracting a thin sheaf of papers from the undifferentiated mass. Flipping over several pages, he began to nod.

"Yes, in English it is called the International Tracing Center. General Eisenhower set it up after the war. They took over a small concentration camp in Arolsen—that's in Westphalia—where they brought refugee children from all over Europe until they could be reunited with their families. Or accepted by other institutions."

"That won't help much now."

"You are looking for the records of a particular child? You might find them there."

"It still exists?"

"Yes, as a memorial. And as an archive. You may have to search through much microfilm. Hundreds of thousands of children passed through it."

"Thank you very much," said Heidi gratefully. "I'd never heard of it."

"It is not well known," he agreed, a distant look passing over his face. "Except, of course, to those of us who went through it."

Heidi could have skipped down the wall of steps of the Palace of Nations. Instinctively, she felt that finding the International Tracing Center was a breakthrough. Now she looked forward to the challenge of trying to get information out of Pierre Coutier. As she sank into the back of a taxi, only one thing bothered her. The Vietnamese was following her again.

Drew Richardson had spent the entire weekend trying to get the Zeebergs to retract their demand for an option on the cable television division of News/Worldweek in return for their part of the mezzanine financing. Unless they did, Richardson could not drop his demand for a lock-up from the board. Karl Zeeberg first said he would think about it. Then no, then maybe, then no, then yes, but with impossible conditions. It was now 8:00 A.M. Monday and Richardson, together with Blackie Muldoon, sat in his garden drinking tea and waiting for another call from the Zeebergs.

The board had imposed a 10:00 A.M. deadline for clarification of his bid. The chairman of News/Worldweek knew he was at a complete disadvantage in dealing with the Zeebergs, and not merely because he needed their money. Karl Zeeberg had the leverage because he had dozens of deals going. If this one did not meet his requirements, he could move on to another. Richardson had his whole life wrapped up in only one.

The phone rang. Richardson answered. It was Zeeberg. After a moment, Richardson covered the mouthpiece.

"He'll forget the option and take a bigger piece of the financing if he can be subordinated only to the banks," Richardson explained to Muldoon.

"We'd have to renegotiate every other piece of the mezzanine financing and I don't think it would work. GE Credit get in line behind the Zeebergs? Won't happen. And we've only got two hours."

Richardson made it simple. He said that there was not enough time.

After several more minutes of listening to Karl Zeeberg, Richardson put his hand over the phone again.

"Is there any way we can do the deal without this cocksucker?" he asked.

Muldoon hesitated, then shrugged. "Maybe."

Turning back to the phone, Richardson interrupted Zeeberg. "Sorry, Karl," he said, "I guess we can't do business this time," and hung up. That would prove to be his happiest moment of the entire deal.

Richardson and Blackie Muldoon sat staring at one another. Unless they could come up with a new structure in two hours, the deal was dead. Bresson would walk away with it. The airplanes taking off from National Airport roared over their heads every thirty seconds.

Blackie spoke first. "Here's the deal concept. Instead of a one-step transaction with cash and paper, make it an old-fashioned two-stepper. We keep all our commitments in place, maybe downsizing the participation, but use the cash for the front end. Then we go with our own junk on the back."

"Bresson was ahead of us," Richardson pointed out. "They'll tender to him first."

"That's the beauty here. You really front load at $55 a share for fifty-one percent. The back end can be forty bucks. The stockholders will be killing each other to get in the front-end proration pool."

"What if Bresson comes back with the same kind of thing?"

"He won't. I guarantee. Under Delaware law, it could take him three years to get control of the board. You've already got it."

"Can we put this together in two hours?"

"You go in and tell 'em your dropping the lock-ups, but want some golden parachutes. That'll keep 'em busy arguing for a few hours. I'll get on the phone."

Richardson looked uncertain. "Can we afford $55, plus junk bonds? The company's got to generate enough cash to cover the interest!"

"I'll look at the numbers. But remember you've got great assets. Even if you took some of these divisions out and shot 'em, you're still looking at a liquidation value of $8 billion."

"But I'd have to break the company up." There was almost a whine of defeat in his voice.

"No, no. It would be a restructuring," Blackie reassured him. "Break-up is bad. Restructuring is good."

"Golden parachutes are a disgrace!" Raffy Nichols was saying. "Why should the company reward Drew and his team for losing their bid to take it over?"

"Speaking for myself," the president of News/Worldweek said, "the issue looks different. I want to stay with the company, and I hope Drew and the rest of us can buy it. But we might lose. I've already had a half-dozen phone calls from executive recruiters offering me enormous bonuses to jump ship. I've got to decide whether to do that or hang in here and maybe wind up with nothing."

"It's a management raid on the shareholder's equity," Raffy protested.

"If we can't keep our top management," Richardson countered, "we're jeopardizing the company and dissipating our stockholder's equity."

"I don't know about the rest of the outside directors, but I've gotten calls too," the former Secretary of State said. "They're suggesting I resign from this board and serve on others."

"You are particularly vulnerable," Richardson said sympathetically, his hand sweeping to encompass the outside directors on the other side of the table. "That's why you deserve parachutes, too. You'll all get sued. No matter what happens there'll be some disgruntled shareholders out there." He looked at Raffy. "You'll have a continuing liability but no further compensation. You'll have to give depositions, maybe even go to trial. You should be paid for that."

By this time, all the outside directors were nodding their heads vigorously, except Raffy Nichols. He judged it was time to retreat so he could later mount a counterattack.

"I move we adopt the proposed golden parachutes," he said to his surprised colleagues.

"Second," said the former Secretary of State. Richardson had won his parachute. If he lost the bidding contest with Bresson, he would get a $10 million settlement from the company.

"Now what about your bid, Drew?" Raffy demanded. "We're past the deadline."

He looked at his watch. Where the hell was Blackie Muldoon?

"Let me start by giving you the background of the offer," Richardson responded, playing for time.

The actual depositions had been a bust as far as Lyman was concerned. Richardson's lawyers were using them as a fishing expedition instead of attacking the source of financing. Bresson and Beck were only too happy to let them get away with it. As a result, Richardson's lawyers had not discovered the role of Liechtinvest and Sommer Bank, let alone whether someone else was behind them. Life was full of ironies, Lyman's father used to say, by which Jayson understood him to mean that it was mostly the shits.

While the lawyers relentlessly pursued ever more meaningless minutiae, Lyman stepped out to take a phone call from New York. Cooke was on the line, reporting that the crisis at Gould Axewroth had eased. They had decided to appoint a five-man committee to explore ways to solve their liquidity problems. Lyman wondered why he had bothered to call until Cooke explained that de Grazia would be on the committee "because you're tied up full time on the News/Worldweek deal." Lyman was not a bureaucrat who wrangled over turf, but he did not like it. Before he could object, Raffy Nichols came in on another line. He had to cut Cooke off.

Lyman was pleased with Raffy's report on the results of the board meeting. He was certain Bresson and Beck would not be. He asked for a recess in the deposition so they could talk.

"Good news and bad news, Marcel." Lyman was pleased to see that even with the meaningless questions, Bresson was sweating from the strain of two and a half hours of interrogation. "The good news is that Richardson has made a two-tier offer. Fifty-five dollars cash on the front for fifty-one percent of the stock and $45 in paper. No lock-ups. But massive golden parachutes probably worth $25 million all together."

"What is good about that?" gasped Herr Doktor Beck.

"It makes a two-tier offer by you legitimate," Lyman explained.

"But the cost!" Bresson exclaimed.

"The average cost is only slightly more than $50 per share," Lyman said neutrally. "The cash is less, only four and a half billion dollars."

That caused the Herr Doktor to look relieved for a moment until despair overwhelmed him again. "But the interest burden and the risk!"

Bresson appeared uncertain. The deal hung in the balance. Lyman hoped it would go away. He would fly to Geneva, pick up Heidi and head for the Pensione Verbano on Isola Pescatori in Lake Maggiore. They would stay in bed for a week.

Herr Doktor Beck burst his bubble. "I have an idea," he said.

Since this was unheard of from a Swiss banker, both Lyman and Bresson paid attention.

"The bank does not want to look foolish compared to the American banks. We might be able to match Richardson's offer, but without having seen News/Worldweek's books, we cannot exceed it."

"Yes, yes," Bresson said impatiently. "Get to the point."

"The point is that the syndicate might calculate the risks differently if we could see the books."

New life stirred in Bresson's eyes. "I can immediately announce that I am matching the offer of $55 cash, $45 paper, and that I will exceed it or any other offer by Richardson if I have access to News/Worldweek's books!"

Lyman had to admit it was a smart ploy. All books revealed problems, giving Bresson a hundred ways out of his promise. "The good thing," Lyman started off positive, "is that you would have maximum financial flexibility. And you're going to need it."

Bresson's self-congratulatory smile began to fade.

"Because the bad news," Lyman continued, "is that the board refused to revoke the poison pill. It's now in effect against both you and Richardson."

Don't be afraid, Heidi told herself, the plan will work. Her problem was how to get to Pierre Coutier's boat without being followed. She was standing at the window of her hotel room timing the ferries that crossed to the other side of the lake from a dock in front of the Hilton.

At 5:15, Heidi put ten $1,000 bills into her bra, pulled on her raincoat and headed for the elevator. She paused in the pink lacquered hall to check her purse for her real passport. It was there; the phony remained with the concierge at the front desk. She took a deep breath to calm herself.

The elevator arrived. She rode down in the company of two South American couples. She maneuvered them out the door first so she could check the lobby to see whether the Vietnamese was waiting for her. The way was clear.

Heidi avoided the main entrance. Walking to her left down a corridor lined with jewelry displays, she made her way to a shopping terrace overlooking the lake. From there she took another elevator down to a pedestrian passageway that crossed under the street running along the lakefront. Heidi emerged only 150 feet from the ferry ticket booth. There was a line! She stood nervously for several minutes, trying not to look over her shoulder, until at last she was able to slide her one franc fifty through the window to the cashier. As she picked up her ticket, she saw a boat about to depart. Running would call attention to herself. If she didn't, she would be late. Worse, she might be seen while waiting for the next boat. Heidi dashed down the pier, and leaped on board just as the captain cast off.

As he expertly moved the boat out into the lake, she took a seat along the side of the low-ceilinged cabin while anxiously scanning the shore for any sign of the Vietnamese. There was none. The other passengers on the small ferry appeared to be businessmen heading home, burdened with heavy coats and briefcases. The air in the cabin smelled of damp wool and infrequent dry cleaning. Heidi told herself to relax.

As she watched the lakefront glide by, she suddenly realized that she had made a terrible mistake. The ferry was not crossing the lake. It was headed along the bank. She was on the wrong boat. Over the captain's chair, she saw a large map painted on the bulkhead. Instead of directly crossing the lake, the ferry would make five other stops before arriving at the boat basin where *La Revanche* was berthed. She checked her watch. She was supposed to meet Coutier in seven minutes.

The first stop was in front of the Mausoleum of Charles II at the narrow end of the lake where the river Rhône began. Heidi saw no sign of taxis, and stayed on board. The ferry then crossed the lake to the Quai Général Guisan. She left the boat and hurriedly climbed the stairs to the street. The clock on the Rolex building showed she was already late. Frantically, she tried to hail a cab, but they proved infrequent and full. In desperation, she boarded a tram. As it moved silkily through the stubborn traffic, Heidi tried to compose herself. She had to be calm. So what if she was late? He expected something from her. She had to project the aura of having the upper hand. Just as she was getting control of herself, the tram turned left and headed back across the Pont du Mont Blanc toward the Noga Hilton. Heidi let out a scream and yanked the emergency cord. The tram ground to a halt. The doors popped open, and Heidi took off running.

She paused in the English Garden to catch her breath and check the time again. She was now fifteen minutes late. How long would he wait? She started walking again as quickly as she could without gasping, and tried to comfort herself with the thought that anyone trying to follow her would certainly be lost. The Iran Air sign lay ahead. She took the stairs from the street down to the quai. Kids on skateboards sailed by, darting in and out among the boats pulled up on the dock. She tried to avoid getting knocked down.

Approaching the harbor police station, Heidi noticed several men scrambling down a ladder to a waiting rescue craft. An officer on an observation deck shouted through a bullhorn at three police boats maneuvering around one another in the basin. Heidi's French was good, but not good enough to understand what he was saying. She continued to hurry along the quai until she found the correct pier, then started to look for Coutier's slip. From the numbers, it appeared that his boat would be out at the end, exactly where the police boats were churning up the water and a small crowd had gathered.

An ambulance, its two-tone siren blaring, screeched to a stop on the quai behind her. An emergency medical team rushed by. Apprehensive, Heidi had slowed down. Where the pier divided, she took the dock running parallel to the one where *La Revanche* was berthed. When she got to the end, she had a clear view of Coutier's boat.

It was a huge forty-foot, low-slung Italian speedboat. Paramedics and police had climbed aboard and were crowded around a large opening in the deck in front of the cockpit. Heidi stepped up onto a locker to get a better view.

The hole appeared to be a Jacuzzi. The medics were pulling something out of the turbulent water. It was a man. He was naked. A syringe sticking out of his thigh fell onto the deck and shattered. They put the limp body on a stretcher and covered it with a sheet.

Heidi dashed for the street. She ran three blocks before flagging down an empty taxi. She asked for the airport. Going back to the hotel was impossible. The police would soon find the note she had left for Coutier with her number on it.

Inside the terminal, she found a Lufthansa flight leaving shortly for Cologne. She was the first on board and sat anxiously gripping the arms of the seat until the door closed and the plane started rolling down the runway.

"Don't worry, Fraulein," said the elderly German sitting next to her, "flying is very safe these days."

But the fear did not subside until she felt the plane rotate and the wheels leave the ground. Heidi had been very lucky when she took the wrong ferry boat. She was supposed to have been on board the *La Revanche,* with a dead man full of drugs, when the police arrived. She might have been able to explain her note. She would never have been able to explain the $10,000 in her bra.

The huge corner room once had been the favorite of the Khedive of Egypt, but it gave Lyman no comfort. He could not sleep. He had missed Heidi's return call, and when he again phoned the Noga Hilton in Geneva, they insisted on knowing his name and where he was calling from before saying whether she was there. He hung up on them. Something was wrong. But what could he do?

Lying on his bed in the Hotel Baur au Lac, staring up at the paneled ceiling, with his only company the occasional sound of a late-night tram gliding along the lakefront, Lyman realized it was up to him. No Heidi. No client. No help from his firm. None from Richardson's lawyers, and none from Skadden Fried. Under the circumstances, Lyman did what any investment banker would do. He called his secretary. She was still in the office working on the filings for Bresson's amended offer.

"Go to a telephone in another office and call me at the Baur au Lac. I don't trust ours."

It took her a half hour to get back to him.

"I want you to open an account in my name at the Sommer Bank in Vienna," he explained. "Make the initial deposit one million dollars. You'll have to liquidate some stock. Sell the pork-and-beans, the steel, the drugs, movies and oil. And I want good execution."

Marlene pointed out that all the U.S. exchanges had closed.

"Sell in Tokyo. I need the account opened first thing in the morning, European time. And yes, you'll get overtime."

Lyman put the receiver down and pulled a Tele-Art card out of his wallet. He needed a package sent and a favor from someone with special skills whom he could trust completely. Pushing RECALL, then R, he watched the LED display as it cycled through the entries. The number he wanted came up. The phone rang for several minutes before Carol Rankin answered.

19

The rain had not let up since the evening before when Heidi landed in Cologne. It pounded the windows of the tiny *Gasthaus* where she spent the night, and now buffeted her rented Ford Escort as she pushed it past the 100 km/hr mark. The blowing drizzle had turned the A1 *autobahn* into a nightmare. A parade of monster trucks sealed off the right lane like an endless railroad train. The huge tires kicked up clouds of oily spray that smeared her windshield and made it impossible to see. Kamikaze BMWs and Mercedes Benzes hurtled down the left lane, lights flashing, horns blaring, forcing smaller cars to hew compulsively to the middle lane. Periodically, one truck would try to pass another, a tiny coupe would pull out to pass the truck, and a sedan with halogen headlamps would refuse to yield, leading to an explosion of brake lights, vehicles sliding sideways and a two-mile traffic jam. Even if Heidi could have broken her concentration without killing herself, there was nothing to see on the side of the highway but the hulking shapes of steel mills, petrochemical plants, refineries, and factories.

Switching onto the A44 outside of Dortmund heading toward Kassel, the traffic eased slightly, but the rain, if anything, intensified. Soon the blight of West Germany's industrial heartland was behind her, and she was driving through the gently rolling hills of Westphalia. At Diemelstadt she turned off the *autobahn* and followed the sign indicating that Arolsen was fourteen kilometers away.

The town came as a surprise. She did not know what a concentration camp town would look like, but she did not expect what she found—a seventeenth-century baroque village with quaint gabled houses lining a wide main street that ended in a miniature version of the Palace of Versailles. The camp, with the offices of the International Tracing Center, turned out to be on the outskirts of town. It did not look like Versailles.

To Heidi, the Holocaust had always been an abstraction, something

266

that existed in books, like the Black Plague or the burning of witches. Even the American Civil War seemed more real to her than World War II, for she had visited the battlefields of Manassas, Gettysburg, Vicksburg and Richmond. She had found an old shell casing in the dirt at Lookout Mountain. The gaunt and dead young men who stared vacant-eyed out of Matthew Brady's tintypes seemed more real than all the news film of bombs falling from airplanes, tanks crashing through forests, or anonymous soldiers collapsing on the beaches at Normandy. All her life, the Russians had been the enemy; the Germans, at least those in the West, were our friends. She had traveled widely in Europe but, two generations after the war, she had never seen a trace of the most devastating war in its history.

Until she saw the barbed-wire fence at Arolsen. Only a hundred yards of it had been preserved, along with a few cement-block buildings that had housed the prisoners. The remaining broken concrete fence posts and the brick foundations that bore witness to the rest of the camp disappeared into the surrounding wheat fields. Heidi saw no crematorium, no gas chamber, but standing on the muddy ground staring up at the fence, she could imagine herself on the wrong side of it.

But what side was that? Victim? Or murderer? For an icy moment she could picture a world so in chaos that those were the principal choices. And with that leap, she began to envision the people running the camp, ordering it built, conceiving of mass extermination as a government policy to accomplish . . . what? Her imagination failed at that point. The crumbling stretch of fence, the plain blockhouses glistening in the rain showed how matter-of-fact the horror. Was it so easy for everyone to forget because it was so hard to understand, Heidi wondered, or because it was so simple?

The International Tracing Center occupied a series of unadorned stucco buildings with square casement windows, the kind of prefab structures built hurriedly after the war that were now decaying all over Germany. She entered the building marked INFORMATION and walked down a long asphalt tile corridor to a middle-aged German woman with a thick blond braid wrapped around the back of her head.

"I'm looking for the records of a particular individual," Heidi explained.

"Have you written us a letter?"

"No. I'm a journalist with an urgent assignment."

"Normally, we require written inquiries." The thought that someone might just walk in the door with questions seemed to be an affront.

"Could you make an exception?" Heidi decided that humiliating herself was the only strategy. Maybe it was the influence of the barbed wire outside.

The woman hoisted up her brassiere and patted her braid. "What nationality?"

"French. Did many French come through here?"

"Two and a half million French were brought into Germany during the war. Take one of the rooms down the hall. I will bring you the microfilm. What is the name?"

"Marcel Bresson." Heidi wrote it out in capital letters on a piece of paper and handed it to the woman. "Will it take long?"

"We have more than twenty miles of shelves," she informed her.

Bresson's sudden departure without saying a word stirred Lyman's anxieties. Beck's deposition ended by 10:00 A.M. He was forced to describe the participants in the loan syndicate, but again, Richardson's people missed the guarantee from Liechtinvest.

Bresson slipped out of the room and disappeared before it was over. Lyman had wanted to give him some good news: his offer to best Richardson's bid if he could see the books was receiving favorable press comment. McFadden Dworkin planned to keep the heat on with a series of Dear Shareholder letters urging calls to the News/Worldweek board to support the proposal.

As they left the Swiss Bank Corporation building, he asked Beck where he could reach Bresson.

The banker looked at him like he was yesterday's stock tip. "Should he wish to, Marcel will get in touch with you," he said coldly, as he climbed into the limousine and drove off. Face facts, Lyman told himself, you're not paranoid; you have enemies.

He crossed the street to Jelmoli, the largest department store in Switzerland. In the electronics section, he found what he needed, a Zenith Turbo Sport 386 laptop computer with built in modem. Returning to the Baur au Lac, he stopped at the concierge desk. Heidi had called again, but left no message or return number. He felt frustrated, but he breathed a little easier. Lyman asked the concierge to make a reservation, arrange for a rental car, and check on an address. In fifteen minutes, he had packed, checked out, and was headed out of town on the N-3 toward the Walensee, Bad Ragaz, and Vaduz, capital of Liechtenstein.

Lacking an airport or even a railroad, the Fürstentum of Liechtenstein could only be reached by road. Once an isolated outpost of the Roman, then Austrian, empire, the 60.7-square-mile country was now a continuous suburban sprawl along the right bank of the Rhine as it passed through the Vorarlberg mountains. To Lyman, Vaduz had all the charm of a ski village in mud season. The buildings were largely stucco, ochre, yellow, pink and beige with tile roofs and painted-on moldings. The dark Castle of Prince Hans Adam brooded over the town on a rocky spur, connected to the hillside by a covered wooden bridge.

Lyman parked his Audi 200 in the large public parking lot that graced the center of town. The concierge at the Baur au Lac had researched the address of Liechtinvest, and Lyman quickly located it in a small two-story building on the main street. A real estate office that took up the ground floor displayed photographs of newly built alpine cabins taped in the windows. The door that led upstairs was lined on both sides with signs indicating that in addition to having three notaries, the second floor served as the world headquarters for thirty-six different international corporations. On the left hand side, right after KAMAG ANSTALT and LIECHTAKTEN GESELLSCHAFT, Lyman found the plaque for LIECHTINVEST GmbH.

A woman at a small desk guarded three blank doors at the top of the stairs. She spoke four languages and proved adept at saying nothing in each of them.

"If you leave your name, address and telephone number, you will be contacted as appropriate," she said, refusing to tell Lyman anything about Liechtinvest.

"But it's urgent! How can a company do business that can't be reached?" he countered in frustration.

"If the company wished to do business with you," she replied calmly, "you would know how to contact them."

Lyman's next step was the Bureau of Commercial Documentation at the Hall of Records. For five Swiss francs, the clerk there was more than happy to provide the registration documents for Liechtinvest. Unfortunately that turned out to be one three-by-five card. The purpose of the company was given as "Commerce and Finance." The place of business was "Foreign," the ownership, *"Privat."* It had been signed by the notary whose name was on the wall at the Liechtinvest "office," and the local address was the same.

That left Lyman with the plan he had set in motion the night before.

Checking his watch, he found that he had about an hour and a half to wait. His alternatives were to spend it at the postage stamp museum or at lunch at the Hotel Real which served a special salad famous throughout Europe. After days of saucy French and heavy German meals, the salad won.

The dining room of the modest hotel was decorated in alpine kitsch with windows looking out onto the street. The salad proved to be a mixture of different greens more complex than any he had seen in California; raddichio, leaf lettuce, endive, escarole, rapunzel and others he could not recognize. The dressing was a delicious vinaigrette with a mysterious aroma and aftertaste. The waitress explained that it was a mixture of olive oil, wild mustard, vinegar, soy sauce, a touch of sugar and *areomat.* When Lyman asked the waitress the exact properties of *areomat,* he found that, like everything else he wanted to know about, it was a secret.

Working through a half carafe of crisp, white Dôle, Lyman began to feel depressed. What was he doing? He was no private eye. Even the U.S. government had a hell of a time prying corporate information out of European banks and governments. His plan was amateurish. And the one thing he had learned on Wall Street was that amateurs always got killed going up against the big boys.

Finishing lunch, he returned to his car. He moved it to a space at the south end of the parking lot where he could keep an eye on the Liechtinvest building. Then he tried not to fall asleep.

Sitting in the tiny darkened room waiting for the woman with the braid, Heidi had time to think. She repressed the memory of the pale wet body being lifted out of the turbulent hot tub. But that helped explain why the terror of Arolsen seemed so real. She too, was being persecuted by forces beyond her control. And her only ally was Jayson Lyman, whose sense of public responsibility was, to put it charitably, fetal. He had good instincts, seemed to know right from wrong, but he lacked a sharp sense of injustice, dulled perhaps by too much money too young. He was a risk taker, she admitted, but disliked risks he couldn't measure in dollars and cents.

Hold on, she admonished herself. Think about that $10,000 in your purse. You're being awfully hard on someone who has every reason not to help but has gone out of his way to do so anyway. Are you angry because he hasn't been sitting by the phone when you called? Or are you shifting the blame to him for your own likely failure? If so, she knew that meant she was falling for him.

The woman rapped on the door frame.

"Look in this roll of microfilm. The records are alphabetical by the date they arrived here."

Heidi's only surprise was to find that Marcel Bresson arrived at Arolsen only a few weeks before he was transferred to his parents on July 6, 1955. His file contained only three documents. An affidavit from M. and Mme Coudert stated that Marcel was born in Dachau, on June 17, 1943, to Marie Louise Foucard. Nothing explained how he came into their hands nor how they knew his birth date, location, and mother's name. This was attached to a document signed by Marie Foucard Bresson acknowledging that Marcel was her son. The third item was a letter dated May 12, 1955, from the Couderts to the International Tracing Center reporting that they had a boy living with them who had been a displaced person and asking how he might be reunited with his parents.

Heidi felt let down. There were no new leads.

Returning to the information desk, she requested copies of the documents in the Marcel Bresson file. While waiting, she asked the woman with the braid if someone could tell her how the Tracing Center operated. The woman rearranged her brassiere once again and said she could answer any questions.

"How did you verify the identity of the children?"

"That was not our responsibility. The parents or relatives did so. Sometimes the children could help. Only in rare cases, when documents existed, did the center call people and say we have your child, you must come and take them. Usually the parents were anxious to prove that a boy or girl was someone they had lost. Personally, I believe many mistakes were made. Children wanted parents. Parents wanted children. Does it matter so much?"

"How could this child's foster family—they were in France—know so much about how he was born?"

"I do not know. Is there nothing in the file? Perhaps there were conversations at the time. I was not here then." A clerk handed photocopies of the documents to the woman. She looked through them. "Yes, I understand your question," she admitted. "But there were so many tangled stories. Some things will never be explained."

Heidi was getting nowhere. "Is there anything else unusual about the file?" she was pleading again.

"No, only that the boy came so late, 1955. But we had some cases into the nineteen sixties." She looked at the papers again. "It is somewhat unusual that the case seems to start with the foster parents notifying us. Normally, it is the parents."

"How did they locate Miss Foucard?"

"Probably her own file."

That took a moment to register. "What file could she have?" Heidi asked.

"Marie Louise Foucard was in Dachau," the woman said patiently, as if Heidi were retarded. "A displaced person. She would have a file also."

If the brakes on the truck had not squealed, Lyman might have slept right through the critical moment. He came awake just as the Federal Express driver reached the door of the building. The package looked perfect. It was at least six feet long and four feet square. From twenty-five yards away, Lyman could see the Extremely Fragile stickers all over the wrapping. He had instructed Carol Rankin to insure it for $250,000. That should get their attention. Now all he could do was wait and keep his fingers crossed.

Five minutes went by, then ten. That was a good sign. Lyman wished he had a phone tap on the building. They had to be talking to whomever really ran Liechtinvest.

He moved out of his car and stood on the sidewalk where he could see the door to the second floor of the building. A light rain had started again. Suddenly the door opened and the Federal Express man emerged. The plan worked! He was carrying the package!

Lyman started running toward the truck. Had he misjudged the distance? Putting on a burst of speed, he slipped in a puddle and went down. The courier paused and turned. Rolling to his feet, Lyman took several more strides and slammed into him, sending the package floating out of his hands and onto the wet pavement. Another step and Lyman snatched it up. The driver yelled at him to stop. Lyman smashed the package against the side of the truck. It disintegrated into a shapeless bag of paper with wooden sticks poking out.

The Federal Express man looked like he might have a heart attack. He stood paralyzed, while Lyman read the new forwarding address: Sommer Bank, Wien 6821, Österreich. Dropping the mess in the gutter, Lyman then walked calmly to his car. While the courier fearfully picked up the dripping remains of his quarter-million-dollar package, Lyman drove off. Carol Rankin's suggestion had been ideal. She had sent, care of the managing director of Liechtinvest, her son's Chinese box kite.

"This Marcel Bresson, he is now a famous man, isn't he," the woman at the Tracing Center said as she handed Heidi another roll of microfilm. Heidi nodded perfunctorily. "There was a big controversy when he bought magazines in Germany. Now, no one cares."

Marie Louise Foucard's file was surprisingly personal. No government agency in the U.S. could reveal such data without permission. It contained a French translation of the results of a Nazi medical exam that revealed among other things, that she had two broken ribs and a broken bone in her left hand when she arrived at Dachau. There was an order directing her to serve as a governess for the children of the camp's *Sturmbahnführer*. Nothing else indicated that she might have received favorable treatment, nor was there any record of collaboration with the Nazis.

Heidi also could find no document suggesting that she had ever had a child. In a transcript of an interview with a U.S. Army Medical Corpsmen conducted when Dachau was liberated, she described her arrest in Annecy, imprisonment in Grenoble and transfer to Dachau. But she had said nothing about a child. Other paperwork relating to her repatriation to France identified her parents and brothers and sisters, but again Heidi found no mention of a son.

Finally the last document on the film identified Marcel Bresson as her son and stated that he had been born in Dachau in 1943. It was a letter from Marie Bresson requesting that the International Tracing Center help find him. It completed the whole picture. Except for one jarring note: the letter was dated May 19, 1955, a week after Marcel's foster parents informed the Tracing Center that they were looking for his mother.

Heidi handed back the microfilm and requested hard copies. "May I also ask you a personal question?" she said to the woman with the braid. "Do you have children?"

She began to hoist her bosom around again. "Three children. Two boys and one girl. All grown now."

"If you had lost one of them, would you wait ten years before trying to find them?"

"That is the same question the other woman asked."

"What other woman?" Heidi was surprised.

"When his name seemed familiar, I began to remember. A few years ago, a woman came to look at his file, too. She was writing a book. I wondered what happened to it."

"She died before it was finished." Heidi was afraid to ask the next question. "Do you remember anything about her, about your conversation?"

"Oh yes. We talked about Marie Louise Foucard's time at Dachau. I had her speak with Frau Gissle, who used to work here. She was in Dachau, also."

"Did Frau Gissle know Marie Louise Foucard?"

"I do not know."

"Where is Frau Gissle now?"

"I am not sure that she is still alive."

"Then where did she live?" Heidi said more impatiently than she intended.

She looked slightly offended. "Frau Gissle was a half-Jew and a socialist. How she survived Dachau no one knows. Probably because she was, how you say, so against!"

"Contrary?"

"Just so. Very Viennese. Only that explains why she would return to that city! You must understand, merely because someone survived the camps, that did not make them a good person. Also, you have no obligation to like them."

To de Grazia, Marshall Cooke's office had always looked like the bridge of a space ship. The president of Gould Axewroth sat with his back to the spectacular corner view of the East River, Governors Island, and New York Harbor. A desk of black composite studded with a half-dozen video monitors swept an eight-foot arc in front of him. At his fingertips, Cooke had an eighty-line telephone system with direct connections to every office of Gould Axewroth in the U.S., Europe and the Far East, as well as dedicated lines to the floor of every major exchange in the world. In a glance, Cooke could take in the bond prices at the latest Treasury auction, see where the dollar was trading in London, Tokyo and Singapore, and tell how gold was faring in Capetown, silver in San Francisco and pork bellies in Chicago. A wall-to-wall stock ticker set near the ceiling paraded the prices on the New York and

American Stock exchanges. It was a marvel of communications technology and de Grazia wondered whether Cooke ever used any of it.

The only concession to comfort was a large leather bench opposite the desk. De Grazia sat down and waited for Cooke to finish his call. He could hardly see him over the tops of the video monitors. He shuddered involuntarily, not because he was in awe of the firm's president, but because the office thermostat was always turned down to sixty-five degrees Fahrenheit.

"Bresson called me a little while ago," Cooke said, putting the receiver back into a raised control panel. He rose from his chair to sit on the edge of the desk so he could see de Grazia. "He's not happy."

"Why not? The deal's going good. The News/Worldweek board meets today to decide if we can see their books. We've got an op-ed piece in the *Journal of Commerce* supporting our demand. I think we'll win this round. I've got a team of analysts ready to swoop down on 'em."

"That's not his problem."

"So what is? The poison pill? He shouldn't take it seriously."

"Not the pill," Cooke interrupted him. "It's Jay." He got up and walked to the window. "Bresson says he's not focusing on the deal. He had some bimbo that he was fucking in Monte Carlo. Have you heard from him?"

"Yes," de Grazia paused. His dealmaker's antenna sensed an opportunity. "He called to say he'll be in Europe another day."

"Did he say why? Or where?"

"No," de Grazia replied as neutrally as possible. "But he said he'd call in."

Cooke stood at the window apparently absorbed in the construction of the new Williamsburg Bridge. Finally he spoke, but without turning around. "You're on the Liquidity Task Force. You know how important this deal is to the firm." He turned to de Grazia again. "Don't get me wrong. You're doing a helluva job. I've got full confidence in you."

He paused and chewed on the end of his glasses. Since he quit smoking three months earlier, he had devoured four pairs.

"My problem," Cooke continued, "is that you're doing all the work and Jay's taking down half the fee. That twenty million dollars would help ease our liquidity crunch. And give us all a bigger bonus pool at the end of the year."

De Grazia knew he had to proceed cautiously. The best response was to be oblique. "I've got a way to short-circuit the deal that would increase the chance that it will happen," he said.

"Does Lyman have to be involved?"

"No."

"Let's hear it."

The staff director of the Select Committee on Intelligence hated the bean soup, but that's all the Chairman ever ordered when they ate together in the Senate Dining Room. "It's a classic," he would say, ordering them both another bowl. "People from all over the country try to get in here just to taste it."

One taste is enough, the staff director always wanted to say, but never did.

Since the restoration of the Capitol, the Senate Dining Room had become the most elegant in Washington, besting the Hay-Adams Hotel by virtue of its tall windows that looked out over the park and the Supreme Court Building. At one time, senior staff could reserve tables, but with the explosion of committees and employees, the practice of democracy in the dining room stopped. Now the staff director ate there only when the Chairman invited him. And it was always business, usually bad business.

"Have you talked to her?" the Chairman asked.

"Yes," the staff director responded. "She claimed she was on to something, but wouldn't say what."

"Where is she?"

"She wouldn't say on an open line."

The Chairman's eyebrows climbed his forehead.

"That's standard procedure. We have to assume that anybody with a satellite dish can tap overseas calls to the committee. My problem is that the Swiss police have asked the State Department to locate her. They've got her phony passport."

"What the hell's that about?"

"A possible murder in Geneva."

"Jesus Christ, I don't need a goddamned scandal," the Chairman whispered intensely. Then he abruptly stood up and with a broad smile, shook hands with Anne Wexler and Tom Karamasinas, two of Washington's most powerful lobbyists.

"Next time you get her on the phone," he said when he sat down, "I want to know everything. Taps or no taps. Otherwise order her home."

"What if she hasn't yet got the story on Bresson?"

"Dammit, what's taking her so long? I'm supposed to have a big role in the Commerce Committee's hearings on this News/Worldweek take-over. But I've got to have something strong."

"I don't see why we don't use our own committee," said the staff director.

"Because to get this damn job," the Chairman said, "I had to promise the majority leader and the President that we'd never hold public hearings. After the circus the last chairman put on, we're lucky that the Select Committee wasn't abolished! We can hold a closed hearing, but anything we want public will have to go through the Commerce Com-mittee. Hell, it'll be a lot better for me! I won't have to preside, and I can swing a lot harder at that Frenchman. But she's really got to have some dirt."

"What if Heidi fails?"

"I'll be embarrassed as shit with my colleagues"—the Chairman pushed away his beans—"and she'll be through."

20

The Transalpine Express hurtled through the night toward Vienna. As Jayson Lyman sat swaying in his compartment trying to brush the mud from his trousers, he felt he was being swept along, not by outside forces, but by his own motives, which he no longer understood.

Public service had always been way down his list of priorities. He would go to a fundraiser here and there. He had turned down a few blue-ribbon commissions because he could not stand the stuffed shirts. Lyman considered himself a conservative. Politics were for those who were too incompetent to make money.

Now Heidi had recruited him into the netherworld of international politics, where he felt clumsy and stupid and had difficulty telling right from wrong. She had gotten him to spy on his client, just as she was spying on the CIA. Wasn't that the bottom line? The CIA knew something about Bresson that she wanted to know, too. Put that way, it didn't sound like something they should be risking their necks for.

And if he found out who was behind Bresson—no small assumption—then what? If they turned out to be villains of some kind, what then? Would he hand the information over to Heidi and go on about his business? He doubted that's what she had in mind. Where was she anyway? What was she doing? As his questions became increasingly obsessive and unanswerable, he realized that he was showing the first signs of telephone deprivation. Lyman decided to force himself to sleep.

When the train jerked to a halt at Vienna's Südbahnhof the next morning, Lyman quickly disembarked and dragged his bags to the terminal telephone office. He wanted to call de Grazia and Raffy and the lawyers and the PR people, and maybe even Cooke. But first he would call his mother, hoping that Heidi had left a number. The woman at the desk directed him to cabin number two, helpfully reminding him that it was 2:30 A.M. in New York.

He settled for calling his office. Surely one of the raccoons would be there. But there was no answer. They were screwing off while he was away! His office was collapsing, his firm collapsing, his deal collapsing while he was running around central Europe chasing financial will-o'-the-wisps. Bresson's secret backers would probably turn out to be nothing more evil than a venerable brotherhood of international tax evaders!

A man knocked at the door of the phone booth. Lyman realized he was sitting with the receiver in his lap. He excused himself and let him take the seat. With his computer over one shoulder and his suitbag over the other, he made his way out of the gloomy railway station into an equally depressing rain-slicked square where he caught a taxi downtown.

The doorman at the Hotel Bristol greeted him as Herr Doktor. While Lyman unloaded his luggage, a brown Fiat that had followed him from the train station stopped across the street in front of the Opera to let out a passenger. A man dashed to the middle of the Ringstrasse to seek the cover of a glassed-in tram stop. After checking in, Lyman stood at the window of his room looking down at the man, as tram after tram passed him by. But no alarm bells went off. Jayson was too preoccupied with the message confirming that Herr Doktor Theo Sommer, managing director of Sommer Bank, would be delighted to meet him that morning at 11:00.

Forty minutes after Lyman's train arrived, Heidi Bruce climbed down from the Mozart Special at Vienna's Westbahnhof. She went directly to the taxi stand and asked to go to 6 Kleine Mohrengasse, the last known address of Frau Birgid Gissle. Heidi had tried to reach her by phone from Arolsen, but the Vienna operator said that there was no listing for that name and no telephone installed at that street number.

The taxi took her to a five-floor tenement in the old Jewish quarter of Vienna near the Danube Canal. Young boys wearing yarmulkes on their shaved heads, with long curls spiraling down in front of each ear, played in the damp street. On the sidewalks, men in long black coats and round fur hats bargained over barrels of shoes, trays of cosmetic jewelry and racks of clothes covered with plastic. The cabdriver insisted that she pay twenty schillings in advance for him to wait.

Heidi climbed up four flights of stairs, stepping over a dark red stain on the second-floor landing. The hallways were unheated and full of the smell of cooking cabbage. She knocked on number 410. A stout woman in a bad wig opened the door and, with a broad smile, invited her in.

She sat Heidi on a threadbare velvet couch and offered her cakes and a glass of hot tea but no information. She spoke only Russian. An old gray-faced man emerged from another room. His Yiddish and Heidi's tourist German also failed to connect. Finally, one of the children she had seen in the street came through the door. They could understand one another.

"Do you know a Frau Gissle?"

The boy asked the woman and the old man. "We don't know anyone by that name," he answered.

"Did you know the woman who lived here before you?"

Again the boy consulted the others. "The apartment was empty when we came."

"When was that?"

"Two years ago."

"And you don't know what happened to the woman who was here before you? Whether she's alive or dead?" Heidi was determined not to let the trail end there.

But all three just looked at her blankly. Then the old man spoke. The boy translated.

"The committee found us this apartment. Maybe they know something."

"What committee?"

They conferred, then debated, then argued.

"My grandfather says it's the Committee on Soviet Jewry, but my mother says it was the government."

"What do you think?"

"My grandfather is right."

"Why?"

"Because," the boy said, "that is where I take the rent."

When Heidi returned to the street, the taxi was gone. She walked down Schmelzgasse to Taborstrasse where she was able to hail another cab. As she asked the driver to take her to the Intercontinental Hotel, a man who had been strolling along behind her in a long coat and fur hat waved his hand. A green Volkswagen pulled alongside and he jumped in, tossing his hat in the back seat. As the car took off after the taxi, his coat was still sticking out the door.

The Sommer Bank was not headquartered in a high-rent area. It occupied a six-story building next to a construction site on Lerchenfelderstrasse at the edge of the Seventh District. The featureless dun-colored facade bore a small brass sign announcing SOMMER PRIVATBANK. Closed and yellowing venetian blinds blocked the windows on the ground floor.

Lyman pushed the buzzer beside the door and it clicked open. Inside, there were no tellers' windows or cashiers' desks. A lone uniformed guard stood at a podium. Only the small center hallway with a staircase and elevator gave away the building's former identity as an apartment house.

Directed to the third floor, Lyman was greeted at the elevator door by a well-dressed middle-aged woman in pearls. She escorted him down a short unadorned hall to a modest reception area. He was welcomed by a short bald man in a dark three piece suit whose vest failed to cover a lifetime of Viennese *schlagobers*.

"Dr. Lyman, I am Theo Sommer, welcome to our bank." He had a friendly smile on his face, and his English was impeccable. He led Lyman into a large but unpretentious office. No founder's portrait hung over the large uncluttered desk. On the left, a tall arched window, which overlooked the construction next door, let in the morning light. A vault with an ornate antique door occupied the center of the opposite wall.

"My mother wanted me to be a doctor," Lyman said, "but it's just plain 'Mister.' "

They sat themselves on separate sofas in the corner by the window, as the secretary with the pearls served thick, dark coffee and a variety of pastries.

"It was an unexpected pleasure yesterday to receive your deposit," Sommer began. "Your fortuitous presence in Vienna makes it possible to resolve expeditiously certain questions regarding the opening of your account." Sommer's polite tone made Lyman uneasy.

"I thought that might be the case," Lyman responded, "and I'm glad your schedule made this meeting possible."

"My pleasure. But I cannot help wondering what brings you to Sommer Bank. We are hardly what you would call a full-service institution."

"But you have an excellent reputation," Lyman countered, "among a select clientele. Perhaps you could tell me more."

Herr Doktor Director Sommer's smile looked forced for the first time. "Of course." He got up and began to pace. "My father started the bank after the war when currencies were no good. It was really a barter trade business, steel for grain, lumber for oil. Ten telephones calling all over the world. Slowly we accepted certain deposits. Sold guarantees of delivery, letters of credit, other trade-related instruments. When I came back from school in London, we began foreign exchange arbitrage and added some traditional banking services. That is where we are today, a bank that specializes in international trade in all its aspects. But we do not trade stocks and bonds. We have no trust accounts. We do no mortgage finance. Our only real estate activity is to construct our new building next door. And of course we do not accept retail deposits."

"But you accept foreign accounts."

"Yes, but only from certain clients. For example, we have no South American accounts except for governments in the oil trading business. What could we do for you?"

"This million dollars is only an initial token deposit, of course," Lyman said easily. "We're looking at a capital pool of several hundred million." He watched carefully to see if Sommer's expression would change. It did not. "My co-investors wish to remain anonymous, but I can assure you that the funds are derived from legitimate business enterprises. We are attracted by the, uh"—he paused—"tax advantages your bank might offer."

A genuine smile of understanding appeared on Theo Sommer's face.

"We would want to participate in some of the financial instruments that the bank handles, commercial paper, banker acceptances and the like. We also might go in for some longer term commitments, guarantees and so forth. And as for stocks and bonds, we manage our own portfolio, but I assume the bank would have no difficulty acting as nominee for our shares?"

"Not at all." But he still did not look convinced that he should accept Lyman's "pool of capital."

Lyman played a final card. "In the main, however, we would leave the deposits in cash."

Sommer looked intrigued for the first time.

"We're looking for special situations in the European Community," Lyman explained, "and want to be able to move quickly." They both knew that was a convenient lie to explain parking a hoard of cash where the IRS could not find it.

"We could not pay interest, and there would be fees for various transactions . . ."

"My colleagues and I are more interested in security and confidentiality."

"On that you need not worry." Sommer went to his desk and withdrew a file from a drawer. "We will assign your account a confidential number."

"I'll need to be able to make electronic transfers at any time of the day or night."

"That can be done." He put the file on the coffee table and made a note. "Here is the telephone number for access to our computer, and the password. You must also give me a password for your account."

"And who else will have access to my account number and the passwords?" Lyman tried to sound casually paranoid.

"The bank officers will know the number but not the identities behind it. That is only for me. My secretaries will know your password. They will give you a letter of instructions."

"And the hard copies of my financial records?"

Theo Sommer pointed to the vault door. "It looks old, but that is a facade. Inside is one of the most modern vaults in all Europe."

Lyman made himself look satisfied. "My password will be 'Freud.' "

Sommer was surprised. "That is not a popular name in Vienna."

"That's why I picked it. Are there documents for me to sign?"

"Just these." He passed several sheets from the folder, and Lyman quickly signed them.

"Thank you, you've been very helpful." Lyman was sincere. He had gotten what he came for.

"It is our pleasure," Sommer said, as he put the file away in his desk. "Oh, and I almost forgot. We have a common acquaintance. Herr Doktor Beck sends his regards. I spoke to him this morning."

The room at the Intercontinental Hotel was tiny. It had a single bed set into the wall on the right, and a desk built in on the left. One round chair at the window provided the only amenity. The telephone rested on a shelf above the headboard. The cord did not reach to the desk, and Heidi had to sit on the bed to use it.

Calling Jayson's office was out. She reached his mother's convalescent home, but the receptionist would not disturb Mrs. Lyman until 8:00 A.M. Heidi left her number. She also left a message on the machine at Sean Gordon's office.

The phone book confirmed that there was no number for Birgid Gissle, but it had a dozen other listings for Gissle. After the first call to an Anton Gissle produced an incomprehensible conversation with a drunken Viennese, Heidi decided it might be easier to try the Committee on Soviet Jewry. She was quickly given over to Rachel, an American volunteer from Beverly Hills who must have been the only person in Vienna using first names.

"Well, Heidi, I just don't know. Let me look and see if we have a record on Birgid Gissle. Two *s*'s right?"

She was gone a long time. "No, can't find a thing on Birgid. No record she's ever been a refugee that we've handled. Name doesn't even sound Russian."

"You didn't understand what I was saying," Heidi strained to be kind. "She wasn't a refugee. At least not from Russia. She lived in an apartment that one of your Russian families was put into."

"What's their name?"

"I don't have it." Heidi cursed herself for being stupid. "But I've got the address."

"That won't help much. We'd need the names of the people there now. Maybe . . . Can you wait a minute?"

Heidi could hear but not understand a conversation in the background.

"Birgid Gissle was in the apartment before? Did she own it?"

"I think the whole building belonged to her family before the war."

"I'll look in our donor's file. Hold on."

Heidi wanted to pace the floor but the short telephone cord kept her tethered to the bed. She closed her eyes and prayed.

"Yes, we have a file," Rachael came back to the phone. "She gave us an apartment on Kleine Mohrengasse."

"That's right!" Heidi said excitedly. "Do you have her current address?"

"We have some correspondence with her about the donation while she was at the Allgemeines Hospital. But that was two and a half years ago."

"Is there any suggestion in the file," Heidi asked fearfully, "that she died?"

Lyman knew he had to work fast. If Sommer and Beck hadn't already figured out what he was up to, they soon would. His only hope was that they were overconfident about their security procedures.

He arrived back at the Bristol, still oblivious to the brown Fiat that had tailed him throughout the morning. The doorman greeted him as

"Herr Baron" because of the fifty-dollar tip Lyman had given him for making a small purchase while he was at the bank. A new telephone extension cord was waiting for him on top of the coffee table in the sitting room of his suite. Lyman used it to replace the existing line on the bedroom phone so he could bring the cord into the living area. He then plugged it into the back of his Zenith Turbo Sport, which he had set up on the writing desk in the bay window, next to the other phone.

The flat electroluminescent screen glowed with life. The date, time and other housekeeping symbols appeared in the upper-left-hand corner followed by a $C>$. Satisfied, Lyman picked up the other phone and dialed direct to the United States. A sleepy Carol Rankin answered.

"Sorry to wake you, but it's showtime."

"S'okay," she mumbled, "just let me get to my computer." After a minute she came back on the line. "Now let me hang up the other phone." Another minute. "All ready. You've got your computer on?"

"Yes, at the C prompt."

"Let me explain what we're going to do, then we'll try it, okay?" She did not wait for an answer. "First we'll get into your modem. You're sure you've got a communications package on your hard disk?"

"The salesman said I did."

"Fine. Then we'll call the bank. You've got the number?"

"Yes, and a password to the computer and personal account numbers and a special password for the account."

"That's trickier than I thought," she said. "Did you find out what kind of computer?"

"I couldn't figure out how to ask."

"Too bad. What does your account number look like?"

"It's four digits and the letter N."

"All right, this is how we'll approach it. You'll use the modem to call the bank's computer. Then you type the password. At that point, we'll use a sample iterative routine to search every combination from 0001-A to 9999-Z. Then we will pray that one of my back-door passwords will get us through the second door."

"Back-door passwords? What are they?"

"When the techies install a computer, they have their own master passwords so they can hack around inside the machine to test and service it. On the older machines, they were even buried in the operating system. Not even the owners knew about them. The computer companies stopped doing that several years ago for security reasons, but a lot of the machines sent to Europe still have these imbedded passwords. That's our hope."

Lyman wasn't sure he understood it all, but said, "Fine. How will we know when we get the Liechtinvest account?"

"We look for the name. We look for Les Éditions Bresson, or News/ Worldweek as labels. How much is the guarantee for?"

"At this point, $4.6 billion."

"We look for that number. Then we pull the whole file and hope it tells us what we want to know."

"What if they use code names for everything?"

"We could be out of luck."

Lyman sighed. "Okay, let's get started."

"We should make a practice run on your account. Just to get you familiar with the procedures."

"Okay. I want to get my money out of there anyway."

"Do you know the name of your communications program?"

"No, but I can look it up."

"Never mind, first type in *TREE.* That should give you a list of all the files on your hard disk."

He did what he was told.

"Jesus Christ!" he exclaimed. "We're screwed!"

"What's the matter?" Carol Rankin asked.

"Totally screwed!"

"What happened?"

Lyman was rummaging around in the carrying case. He came out with the computer manual. "What a fucking idiot I am!"

"Mr. Lyman, computers do this to people," Carol said soothingly, "tell me what is going on and maybe I can help."

"It's my computer—"

"Is it broken?"

"It might as well be. It only speaks German."

The Committee on Soviet Jewry had no record of whether Frau Gissle was alive or dead. Rachel suggested Heidi try the hospital where they had sent their last letter.

The Allgemeines Krankenhaus responded with a recorded voice that said *"bitte warten,"* which Heidi took to mean "please wait." Finally, she was given another extension and *"bitte warten,"* then a third *"bitte warten."* Twenty minutes and a dozen extensions later, she was routed back to the Records Department for the third time.

"I'm trying to locate a former patient of yours," she said like a broken record, repeating Frau Gissle's name.

"Bitte warten," the disembodied voice said on the other line. Heidi felt like jumping out the window, except she feared that if she didn't die, she might end up at the same hospital. Then the voice came back on the line.

"I cannot give out medical information on the telephone."

"Is she alive?"

"I can only say she did not die in our hospital," the voice responded with precision.

"And do you have an address?"

There was a pause as if the voice was weighing a great moral dilemma, a petty bureaucratic rule, or both. "Biedermeier Convalescent Residence. 127 Löwengasse, in the Third District."

Carol Rankin had a solution. "You just let me do it from here."

This is not a question of your manhood, Lyman told himself. It's only information. "What do I do?" he asked.

"Just tell me the phone number, the account number and the password."

He gave them to her and waited.

"Way to go," he heard her say. "I'm inside and I've got your account. All the program instructions are in four languages, even Russian. Where do you want your money to go?"

"Back to Citibank. Leave a dollar balance." He gave her his New York account number and password.

"All confirmed."

"You're sure you didn't put it in your own account, now?" He allowed himself to make a joke.

She laughed, "Now that I've got your passwords, I can get a loan from you anytime I want. Ready for the real test?"

"Let's do it," he said helplessly, gripping the phone.

"I'm out of your account now and starting at triple zero one A and, uh oh!" There was a sudden clacking of keys on the line.

"What's happening?" Lyman said anxiously.

"It won't accept the back-door password. I've got some others we can try."

Lyman tried to relax.

"No, that won't work either. Let's try another," she said to herself and to the computer, only incidentally to Lyman.

He felt himself dying a little.

"No, we'll have to go again." Carol Rankin's voice remained calm.

"How many back-door passwords are there?" Lyman asked, as he could hear her keys clicking.

"My friends at the lab gave me . . ." There was a pause. "Oh my." Her voice betrayed concern for the first time. "The bank's computer just sent me a message."

"What? What!"

"It says, 'Entry denied. Improper passwords employed. Authorities being notified of possible security violation.' Then I was disconnected."

"Can you try it again?"

"Sure." She sounded unsure.

Almost a minute dragged by in silence. "We're connected," she finally said.

"Great!" Lyman exhaled.

"Oh, that's what I was afraid of."

"Now what?" he wanted to climb through the phone.

"It requests my telephone number for the log. But I'm sure it also uses the number as part of its security routine."

"I don't understand."

"It cut me off again. The computer isn't accepting any more calls from this number."

"Can't you lie?"

"No. It verifies the number."

"How about switching your two lines?" Lyman refused to give up.

"I've got about fifty possible passwords here. I'd need a dozen different lines."

"You could go to the office. Use one of the trading desks. They've got about eighty." Lyman was searching his mind for every possibility.

"But I've got to connect my computer to each one," she explained.

"Shit! Damn! Hell!" Lyman shouted.

"Jay, there's another problem. This computer seems really well protected. I doubt they failed to erase the back-door passwords. And even if I can find a way to keep trying, I'd bet that after a few more disconnects, the whole computer shuts down."

"Christ! We were so close!"

"Actually," Carol said, "we didn't get to first base."

The telephone book showed a listing for the Biedermeier Convalescent Residence. Heidi called and reached a receptionist.

"Frau Gissle can't come to the phone. She will be in therapy for another twenty minutes."

"When are your visiting hours?" Heidi asked, trying not to sound exasperated.

"You can come then, or after lunch."

"Where is the Biedermeier Residence?"

"In the Third District, across from the Hundertwasser Haus. You can't miss it. Look for a monstrosity surrounded by tourist buses."

"And how is Frau Gissle?" Heidi did not know exactly how to ask the question. "I need to discuss something with her."

"The only problem," the receptionist replied with a Viennese yawn, "will be to get her to stop talking."

"I don't know what else to suggest," Carol Rankin said.

"I'll think of something," Lyman responded. "Stay near the phone." As soon as he hung up, the red message light started blinking.

"I have a telephone message from Frau Lyman," the operator said. "It came in about forty-five minutes ago. Shall I send it up?"

"Read it."

" 'Miss Bruce is at the Intercontinental Hotel in Vienna, 1-75-05. Shall I connect you?"

"Absolutely!"

The moments crawled by.

"The Intercontinental operator says that Frauline Bruce's line is busy. Do you want to wait?"

She was in Vienna! "Yes, I'll wait . . . No." Maybe he should go right over there. No, he could miss her. "Yes, I'll wait."

"I've disconnected. I'll try again."

Lyman suffered through another long pause.

"Her line is still busy. *Bitte warten,*" and she left the line.

Lyman paced to the window and back carrying the phone receiver cradled in his shoulder. Where the hell was the operator? Had he been disconnected again? He hated being put on hold. For all he knew, the operators had all gone off for coffee! He imagined Heidi on the phone to the porter, asking for her luggage to be picked up. He could see her getting into an elevator and going downstairs. A cab was waiting to take her to the airport. Lyman could not stand it any longer; he slammed down the receiver, grabbed his raincoat and headed for the door.

A grand imperial city, Vienna formed the crucible for much of the triumph and tragedy of the twentieth century: Josef Hoffman and Otto Wagner in modern architecture, Ludwig Wittgenstein in philosophy, Ernst Mach in physics, Arthur Schnitzler in the theater, Arnold Schoenberg and Gustav Mahler in music, Sigmund Freud in psychology, Theodor Herzl, Zionism, and Adolf Hitler, genocide. The city still had the greatest art collection and finest music in the world. But in the area of Heidi's most urgent concern, it was like any other town. It was raining and she could not get a cab.

The doorman haphazardly held an umbrella over her while futilely blowing his whistle. The wind blustered from the northeast, carrying the first icy undercurrent of winter. Each time the doorman stepped off the curb to wave at a taxi, Heidi was hit by a blast of wind and water. A bus full of tourists pulled up and stopped, halting traffic altogether. Apologizing in an incomprehensible dialect, the doorman busied himself with their luggage and left her soaking in the rain.

He could have walked the six blocks between the Bristol and the Intercontinental faster than the cab could get through the traffic. Now as the rain intensified, the street became a parking lot.

"How far to the Intercontinental?" Lyman asked the driver.

"Two streets."

"I'll walk." He gave him thirty schillings and climbed out. It was raining so hard that Lyman did not notice a man get out of the brown Fiat behind him and follow him up the Johannesgasse.

At the corner of the Kantgasse, Lyman could see a woman standing in the rain waving for a taxi. Could it be? He started running and could feel the wet seeping through his raincoat. As he drew closer, he was certain it was Heidi. The traffic had started to move again. His now empty cab passed him. Lyman started waving his hands and shouting.

"Heidi! Wait. It's me!"

She stepped into the street and stopped a cab. It was the one he had just abandoned!

"No! It's me!" he cried out, but the door shut and the driver moved back into the traffic. Drenched and breathing heavily, he sprinted to reach the taxi but was almost run over by a brown Fiat and then a green Volkswagen. The traffic moved forward, then halted, started up again, then stopped, but the cab carrying Heidi always remained just out of Lyman's reach.

Stumbling through puddles and gasping for breath, he finally had to stop at the Heu Market. He stood bent over, trying to suck air into his lungs for several seconds before realizing that he was next to a taxi stand with an empty cab. The driver sat drinking a coffee and eating an afternoon strudel. He refused Lyman's offer of fifty schillings to interrupt his break. He accepted five hundred schillings.

As they wound through the streets of the Landstrasse District, Lyman seemed to find himself in some sort of caravan: a green car behind a brown car behind Heidi's taxi, with Lyman pursuing the three of them. At the next intersection, the brown car pulled into another lane and then settled in behind Lyman. When Heidi's taxi darted up several narrow streets they all fell in line again, and Lyman could no longer deny the conclusion that they were being tailed. And openly! When Heidi told him that she had been under surveillance in France, he had not allowed himself to believe her. Now it was obvious that they were both being followed. In an instant, Lyman went from wet and exhausted to enraged.

At the intersection of Rasumofskygasse and Marxergasse, he ordered his driver to pull up next to the green Volkswagen. He looked inside. Immediately, his anger was doused by fear. He could not see the other driver, but the Vietnamese who worked for Bresson stared back impassively.

He checked the car behind him. Its darkened windows prevented him from seeing clearly, but there appeared to be no one in the car but the driver. Lyman's odds were better than Heidi's.

The procession turned up Löwengasse. Ahead, Lyman could see a collection of tour buses in front of a building that looked like a misplaced piece of Disneyland. Painted white and blue and yellow and lavender, it had a wide balcony, towers and oddly slanted roofs. The facade was plaster and brick, with mosaic insets and walls of glass. Strange arches, and irregular shaped windows appeared at random. Topped with onion domes and cartoon chimney pots, the building seemed to laugh at its dour middle-class surroundings.

Heidi's cab came to a halt in the midst of a throng of tourists. By the time Lyman's taxi worked its way through the crowd, she had disappeared. Lyman saw the green car pull to the curb. It took only an instant for him to decide what to do.

"I think I'm being followed."

"*Ja,*" the driver agreed.

"Can you lose him?"

The driver did not respond.

"For another five hundred schillings?"

The sudden acceleration tossed Lyman backwards against the seat. The car hurtled around the corner and up the Custozzagasse while the Fiat behind them hesitated to avoid the tourists. Lyman told the driver to turn at the next street and hit the brakes. The cab slid to a halt on the slippery cobblestone. Lyman threw open the door and dove into the nearest doorway as the cab took off again down the street. A moment later the Fiat flashed by in pursuit.

Frau Gissle looked almost like a doll sitting in the enormous stiff-backed chair. Heidi had asked about Dachau, but Birgid Gissle wanted to complain about her room.

"Then why did you give up your apartment?"

"This may sound cruel, but there were too many immigrants in the neighborhood."

Heidi did not know what to say.

"I know what you are thinking. That I am a Jew. That I was in a concentration camp. All true. But I am also Viennese. A European. These people from Russia call themselves Jews. They are fanatics. They are against the State of Israel. They are primitives. They wail and sing. Their wives have to cut off all their hair and wear wigs. Women have no rights. This is not Jewish culture as it has evolved over four thousand years!"

Heidi judged her to be in her midseventies. She had broken her hip and needed a walker to get around, but her tongue had lost none of its sharpness.

"Could we talk about Marie Louise Foucard?"

"Many people would like to pass judgment on her for what she did in the camp," said Frau Gissle. "I do not."

"Judgment for what?"

"She survived the best way she could. The Nazis could do whatever they wanted with our bodies anyway. So she was pretty and pretended to like it. At least she did not hurt others to save herself as many did."

"So she slept with camp guards?"

"It was forbidden for them to have sex with the Jews. Race defilement. So they concentrated on the others. But that did not protect me.

'Half-Jew,' they would say. 'Show your behind.' I have trouble in the WC to this day."

"Was it a guard that made Marie Foucard pregnant?"

"Pregnant? Who told you she got pregnant?"

"Didn't she have a baby?"

"Yes, she got pregnant. I helped her abort it."

"But she also gave birth," Heidi insisted.

"In Dachau? Don't be foolish. If they knew she was pregnant she would die, but not until they had had their fun with her and with the fetus."

The images that rushed through Heidi's mind made her ill. She forced herself to concentrate on her questions.

"You are saying she never gave birth. That there was no baby born to her Dachau?"

"No baby."

"How do you know for sure?"

"We lived in the same barracks. I was there before she came. And I worked in the nursery where they kept all the babies while they experimented on them in the laboratory. In Dachau, no baby ever lived more than a few weeks. The experiments . . ."

Heidi tuned out. She had unwrapped all the boxes within boxes and the last one was empty. She had failed to track down Marcel Bresson's birth. And there could only be one explanation. He didn't exist.

Working his way back down Löwengasse, Lyman tried to stay out of the rain and out of sight of the green Volkswagen. He stopped on the corner opposite Hundertwasser Haus. One tourist bus was boarding as another arrived. He could not see the green VW, and decided to use the crowd to cross the street and take shelter under the building's first-floor balcony. From behind a shiny metal pillar, he could see the Vietnamese talking to the driver of the taxi. Heidi had obviously asked him to wait. The Vietnamese handed him something and the taxi quickly drove off. The Vietnamese returned to a doorway on the other side of the street.

They waited. What the hell was Heidi doing there, he wondered, sightseeing? And was the Vietnamese tailing her, or stalking her? The tourist bus departed and the street was momentarily empty. Far down the block, Lyman thought he could make out the green Volkswagen parked at the curb, but he could not get a better view without revealing himself. Another bus arrived and disgorged a mass of camera-wielding tourists. Lyman kept watch on the doorway that concealed the Vietnamese.

Lyman was so absorbed in watching him that he failed to see Heidi emerge from a different building across the street. Only when the Vietnamese came out of hiding, speaking urgently into a hand-held radio, did Lyman look around and see her coming down the block searching for her taxi. He stepped out and called to her, but was immediately blocked by the departing bus. As it moved past he could see the green Volkswagen racing down the street. It headed right toward her! Heidi looked up, saw him. She broke into a smile.

"Jayson! Jayson!" She started to cross the street.

"No! Lyman screamed, and began running toward her.

The whine of the car's engine filled his ears. She looked back paralyzed. He dove, pushing her aside. The car careened by, the side mirror hooking him under the shoulder blade, tossing him into the air and onto the sidewalk. Heidi rushed to him.

"Are you . . . ?"

"I don't know . . ." He shook his head as she helped him to his feet. His back felt numb.

Down the street the green VW was turning around.

"Oh, God!" Heidi cried. "He's coming back!"

They started running across the street.

"The bus!" Lyman pointed toward another tourist bus coming toward them on their side of the street. If they could reach it, the car would have to veer off. But the bus was slowing down.

"Under there!" Lyman pointed at the entrance beneath the balcony of Hundertwasser Haus. He glanced back at the Volkswagen bearing down on them. Could they make it? He heard the car hit the curb. Looking back, he saw it climb the sidewalk, following them under the balcony. It was almost upon them. He gripped Heidi's hand, waiting for the impact. The car scraped against a wall.

Suddenly he was jerked off his feet and into a doorway. He landed on top of Heidi as the car ground by, pieces of trim and glass flying in every direction.

"It's Edouard," Heidi gasped. "He's driving the car!"

It caromed off a pillar and fishtailed wildly back onto the slippery street, barely missing the bus. The tourists rushed around yelling at one another in some excitable language. Lyman pulled Heidi to her feet and they dashed for the safety of the crowd. Down the street the green Volkswagen was turning around again. Lyman could see the Vietnamese coming toward them with a gun. They were trapped.

He pushed Heidi to the ground in front of the open door of the bus. "Get sick," Lyman ordered. He climbed on board gesturing and pleading in English for the driver to help her. Reacting slowly, the driver struggled out from under the steering wheel and went to the door. He bent over to look at Heidi who lay moaning in the street. Lyman put his foot on his rear end and pushed. He went flying into the crowd of tourists.

Reaching down, Lyman pulled Heidi on board. Two seconds later, he had the bus moving jerkily forward in the wrong gear.

"Look out," Heidi shouted.

The Vietnamese stood in the middle of the street, holding his pistol with both hands. Lyman stepped on the gas and ducked as huge holes exploded in the glass. Then he felt a nauseatingly soft impact. He looked up to see what used to be the face of the Vietnamese embedded in the windscreen.

He slammed on the brakes and the body flew off into the street. Instantly, the bus was rocked by a collision at the rear. Heidi picked herself off the floor and looked out the door.

"It's Edouard's car!" she shouted.

Lyman finally found first gear. "We'll exchange insurance cards later," he said, and the bus surged down the street.

The stretch Mercedes 560 turned off Madison Avenue onto 77th Street and stopped in front of the Carlyle Hotel. Marshall Cooke was waiting at the curb. Marcel Bresson got out.

"How was your flight?" Cooke asked.

"Unproductive. Have I received messages?"

"No." Cooke thought Bresson looked tense. He wanted him to relax. "This is just exploratory. But the fact that he's willing to meet suggests you've got the upper hand."

They entered the elevator. "Penthouse," Cooke said to the uniformed operator.

They rode in silence to the top. The elevator opened onto a small hallway decorated with an antique English breakfront full of china from the Tang Dynasty. They waited at the door. Bresson said, "When could we close?"

"If this works, you'll still have to go through with the tender offer.

That's thirteen more business days. But it's a formality. We could wind things up sometime next week."

"Good."

The door to the east penthouse opened to reveal a two story foyer with a spiral staircase coming down from the balcony. A butler directed them to the left through large double doors into a library. De Grazia occupied the couch with Blackie Muldoon. And in a leather wing chair, drinking coffee, sat Drew Richardson.

"This is crazy," Heidi declared. "We should get the hell out of this country, not ride around dressed up like mimes!"

"You just keep an eye out for Edouard," Lyman ordered, "and for a brown Fiat that's been following me."

After ditching the bus, they had taken a subway and then a taxi to a Eurocar office on the Schottenring where Lyman rented the biggest Mercedes on the lot. Then they split up; Lyman went to a hardware store near the Naschmarkt, and Heidi shopped for clothes in the Graben. They met back at the Café Central where for several hours they sat eating pastry and trying to calm their nerves with the music of Johann Strauss from a string quartet. At 10:00 P.M. they each changed clothes in the toilets, switching into black bicycling tights, which they covered up with raincoats. They kept the ski masks in their pockets.

Lyman had put the car in the underground parking area near the Opera. Bolt cutters, a short sledgehammer, a crowbar, rope and other purchases from the hardware store were locked in the trunk. As he pulled out of the garage, he suddenly realized that he had forgotten something. His passport was still in the computer carrying case in his hotel room.

Heidi argued adamantly against going back for it. Fifty people on the bus could identify them. The police could be waiting in the lobby. She claimed that they could bluff their way across the German border. She would use her passport while he hid in the trunk.

Lyman had rejected the argument. "If there's one thing I know about Europe," he insisted, "it's that your papers better be in order."

The doorman again greeted him as Herr Doktor Baron and said he could leave the car at the curb. In the lobby the concierge cheerfully gave him the key. No one was waiting in his room. Lyman emerged in minutes with his passport and only one new worry. He had taken the time to check with his office, and he had not received one phone call that day.

They circled the block where the Sommer Bank was located. "I'm going to go around one more time," Lyman said. "You make sure we're not being followed."

"Jayson, it's dark. I can't tell if the lights behind us belong to one car or another! This is ridiculous," Heidi continued to complain. "We've got everything we need on Bresson!"

"All you learned is that he's a phony." He stopped the car on the quiet side street next to the construction site beside the bank. "I could've told you that from day one." He popped the trunk and took out a box of tools.

"And that he's a murderer."

"Shhh! I told you that too!" he whispered.

"But you didn't believe it yourself," she hissed.

"Wrap the blanket around the head of the bolt cutters to muffle the sound," he ordered. "You still don't know who Bresson is. Who he's fronting for." The chain-link fence snapped easily. "The answer's in the bank."

"And how the hell are you going to get to it?"

A car passed by in the street. Lyman held a finger to his lips.

He was no expert on robbing banks, but he understood bankers. They were obsessed with money and numbers. They placed the highest priority on keeping both secure in their vaults. Most people also thought bankers were boring, and they were right. But that did not account for their ability to spend a lifetime in the dreary business of designing revolving credit arrangements. No, the secret reason bankers could put up with the endless ennui of banking was that they were lazy. Lyman was counting on Theo Sommer to be lazy enough to keep frequently used information at his fingertips.

"We're not cracking the vault," he whispered as he cut the last link to make an opening in the fence. "We're stealing a desk."

He crawled through, pulling her after him. The overcast night was extremely dark. Headlights from the traffic on Lerchenfelderstrasse frequently flashed through the shell of the new six-story structure. With a small flashlight, Lyman picked his way across the first floor, avoiding the gaping holes that fell out of sight and the twisting hoses that threatened to send them sprawling. Finally he found what he was looking for—a makeshift wooden ramp that climbed a stairwell to the upper floors.

Lyman figured the third floor was on the same level as Sommer's office. He was wrong. The bottom of the window was near the ceiling. More worrisome, there was a five-foot gap between the two buildings.

They returned to the ramp and climbed to the fourth floor. Removing a couple of planks that covered a hole, they pushed the boards out, tilting them down to rest on the sill of Sommer's office window. Lyman had to crawl down the incline to examine it. He expected to find alarm tape fastened to the panes. He did not anticipate that the leaded glass would turn out to be welded iron. No sledgehammer would get him through.

Lyman crawled back up the planks. "We're fucked! It's like a steel cage. We'll never get in."

Heidi thought for a moment. "What's the sill made of?"

"Wood."

"I saw something on the third floor." She dragged him back to the ramp and down to the next level. "See." She pointed the flashlight at a large wheelbarrow. "There's a pile of sand on the ground below."

Lyman maneuvered the barrow down the ramp. In the dark, he could only find one shovel. Heidi used her hands. In a few minutes it was full of sand and they both were struggling to push it back up the ramp.

"We're making too much noise," he gasped on the second landing. "I've got to rest."

As they sat there breathing heavily, Lyman noticed lights going on and off in the windows of the bank. The watchman was making his rounds on the first floor.

"Do we wait?" Heidi asked.

"No. Maybe he comes over here next. Let's go."

When they got to the third landing, Lyman whispered, "I don't think it's heavy enough."

"You're crazy." Heidi was on the point of collapse.

"See if there's a faucet on the next floor and look for a hose." He turned the barrow around and started dragging it up the last section of the ramp. The lights began blinking on and off on the second floor.

"Hurry," he said, as loudly as he dared.

"There's a faucet on the fifth floor," she appeared next to him. "But no hose."

"Look below."

Lyman pulled the barrow onto the fourth floor and maneuvered it toward the edge by the window. He would need Heidi's help to wrestle it onto the planks. She emerged from the dark, hose in hand with water splashing out of it. "Should I fill it up?"

"No. Help me get this up on the planks first."

It made a lot of noise. Lights appeared on the third floor near the front of the bank building.

"Okay. Make it as wet as you can, but not soupy. Doesn't the water come any faster?"

"No pressure."

The lighted windows, coming on and off, moved inexorably toward them.

"We can't wait any longer. No, just a minute." He looked wildly around and finally came up with a short two-by-four.

"Okay. As soon as I'm inside, get back to the car and have the engine running."

He climbed up on the planks and lifted the handles of the wheelbarrow. The planks sagged and creaked under the weight. The barrow wanted to run away from him down the incline. He leaned forward and gave it a shove. The wheelbarrow full of wet sand smashed into the window, caving it inward like a basket, sending glass flying in all directions. The planks bounced upward, tossing Lyman into the air. One of them dropped into the gap between the buildings. The other fell back onto the sill and Lyman landed on top, clinging for his life.

He looked up to see that the wooden frame had given way and the window, wheelbarrow and sand had fallen into the room. An alarm was ringing wildly. "We did it!" Heidi cried. She handed him the board and his tool bag, which he tossed through the opening. He then inched along the plank until he could reach what was left of the sill and haul himself inside.

Sliding down the mound of wet sand, he grabbed the board, moved quickly to the door and jammed it under the knob. Lyman could hear footsteps pounding down the hall. He dragged his tool bag to the desk and zipped it open. Taking out the crowbar, he stuck the blade into the top of the file drawer and yanked upward. The desk top splintered, but the file drawer held.

A guard started shouting and banging on the door, futilely twisting the knob. Lyman's heart was beating so fast he wondered if it might explode. He forced himself to examine the drawer. It was steel, set in a steel frame. In a rage, he pulled out the sledge hammer and began smashing the desk top. At the same time the guard started using a fireax on the door.

Suddenly the desk split open, and Lyman could see down into the drawer. The top was not steel. Swinging the sledge upward, he tried to knock the desk top loose from the base. On the fourth blow it came apart. He now could go through the files as if he had opened the drawer. The point of the guard's ax was now penetrating the wooden office door.

Quickly he searched for a file entitled Liechtinvest. He could not find it. The guard was cursing and grunting as he continued to pound with his ax. The alarm felt like it was drilling holes in Lyman's head. He forced himself to go through the files slowly. Nothing! Could he have been so wrong?

Wood was now flying off the inside of the door. Lyman dumped the tools out of his bag and started stuffing it with file folders. The ax head came crashing through a door panel. Jamming in the last file, Lyman climbed up the pile of sand, pausing only long enough to snag a Rolodex. A hand pushed through the hole in the door, groping for the knob. As Lyman got to the window sill, the door burst open. He took one step on the plank, and sprang onto the next building.

The guard started shooting. Bullets whined overhead as Lyman stumbled over the hose. The shots ricocheted wildly in the dark as he dashed down the ramp to the car. The front door stood open. Clutching his bag full of files, he dove inside as the car squealed away into the night.

Lyman tried to take deeper, slower breaths. After a few blocks, he managed to say, "I think we're screwed. I couldn't find a Liechtinvest file at all!" Heidi kept her eyes on the road.

"So I took everything, and I also found this." He held up the Rolodex. "Let's see if it's in there." Turning on the map light he spun the knob to L. He found the card. But it only contained the name of the lawyer in Liechtenstein and the phone number. Lyman held it close to the light. Nothing else was typed on the card. But in the lower right-hand corner he found something, a single word in delicate feminine handwriting. Probably a note by Sommer's secretary. It said "Kreditorg."

"Kreditorg," Lyman repeated. "That rings a bell . . ." He started rummaging through the files in the tool kit. Finally he brought out a stack of Ks.

"Kreditanstalt, Kreditkonsum, Kreditmobil, Kreditmotorschaft. Yes! Kreditorg. Christ! It's all in Russian! Heidi, have you heard of this?"

"I think Miss Bruce is very familiar with the organization." Edouard's voice came from the back seat. But Lyman did not turn around, because he could feel the barrel of the gun pressing against the back of his neck. "Tell him about Kreditorg."

For the first time Lyman noticed that tears were streaming down her cheeks.

"Tell him!" Edouard ordered, jamming the gun into Lyman's head for emphasis.

"It's supposed to be an arm of the Soviet Ministry of Foreign Trade. It finances imports, exports and barter deals. But it also makes investments in the West. Kreditorg was implicated in a KGB effort to take over some banks in California in 1986."

"The fucking Russians," Lyman heard himself say in awe, "trying to buy News/Worldweek!"

"Turn here."

"Where are we going?" Lyman asked.

"You'll see."

The car soon approached a bridge crossing the Danube.

"Stop and get out. Don't try to run. I'm going to give you a chance." He motioned for them to stand against the railing. "You are lovers, no? So you have a suicide pact. The Danube is fast, with many currents. You go first," he pointed to Lyman. Heidi bolted.

Edouard reached out and grabbed her hair, yanking her backward. He pulled her close. "We want this to look like an accident, but it doesn't have to."

"Cocksucker," she said. "You really like your work."

Lyman stood transfixed as he saw her hand move between Edouard's legs.

"Climb the railing," he ordered.

Heidi's hand gripped his crotch and gave a vicious twist. He screamed, let go of her and dropped his gun. As he doubled over, Lyman's fist came up, catching him on the upper lip. His nose seemed to disappear.

They took off running. Lyman glanced back to see Edouard crawling around on the sidewalk searching for his gun. He turned around again saw another car heading toward them. Even under the orange light of the sodium-vapor bridge lamps, Lyman recognized it. It was the brown Fiat.

"Heidi!" He grabbed her shoulder. "That's the other car." They stopped and turned back toward the Mercedes, but Edouard had his gun on them, blood running off his face. He started firing. Lyman wrapped Heidi in his arms in a useless gesture of protection. The car bearing down on them flashed past. It plowed into the Mercedes, wedging it into the railing.

Trapped behind the car, Edouard was firing into the Fiat. The door flew open and someone rolled onto the street. Edouard ducked down to reload. When he stood up, the man behind the Fiat emptied a clip from a submachine gun. Lyman saw Edouard's intestines explode through his back. The top half of his body jerked over the railing and fell into the river. The bottom toppled onto the pavement.

Lyman stood frozen in horror. He hardly felt Heidi pull away from him. She was moving toward the gunman. What was she doing? The man dropped his machine gun and turned to her. She collapsed in his arms.

Dazed, sick and confused, Lyman stumbled toward them. Heidi was crying and clinging to him. As Lyman got closer, she raised her head from his chest. Through her sobs she managed to say, "Jay . . . this is . . . this is . . . Sean Gordon."

PART III
COLD COMFORT

MOSCOW, USSR,
FRIDAY, SEPTEMBER 26.

The headquarters for Soviet Air Defense Forces, PVO Strany Central, began tracking the Falcon 900 at 12 degrees 37 minutes longitude over the Baltic. Twenty-three minutes later, the air controllers at Tallin in the Estonian S.S.R. reported that the aircraft had notified the airport at Turku, Finland, that it was proceeding to a private airstrip at the Papelatorpa paper mill north of Riihimaki. The plane descended, then disappeared from Finnish and Soviet ground-control radars.

A Soviet MAINSTAY airborne warning and control aircraft, orbiting over Lake Ladoga near Leningrad, reported to PVO Strany Central that the Falcon 900 had descended to three hundred feet and executed a turn to 110 degrees east southeast. It projected that the plane would cross into Soviet airspace in seventeen minutes in the region of Narva. The PVO Strany Central duty officer notified Leningrad to scramble two MiG 31 FOXHOUNDS and make positive identification of the aircraft.

Once across the Soviet border, the plane climbed back to fifteen thousand feet. The lead MiG 31 reported on an encrypted voice circuit that the aircraft was a Falcon 900 with tail number MB 2718. At Staraya Russa, the escorting FOXHOUNDS turned back and were replaced by Su-27 FLANKER interceptors from Naro-Fominsk. When the aircraft was twenty minutes from Moscow, PVO Strany ordered the air controllers at Sheremyetrova airport to keep all civil aircraft at the gates and to hold all landings.

Maintaining radio silence, MB 2718 skimmed low over the barren farmland, its powerful landing beams illuminating the stands of fir and leafless birch in the darkening twilight. The aircraft bounced twice before settling onto the runway. Instead of turning toward the terminal, it taxied to the military side of the airport where a black Zil limousine waited.

The door of the aircraft came down, and a stocky man in a military uniform stepped out. On his shoulder he wore a general's star, and on his sleeve, a patch bearing the sword, red star and golden shield, insignia of the Committee on State Security—KGB. The orderly at the bottom of the stairs saluted, said, "Welcome, General," and escorted him to the car. The old man waiting in the back seat of the Zil addressed the general with a name more familiar to him.

"Hello, Marcel."

"Yuli, why have I been called back?" he demanded before the door closed. Bresson was covering his fear with bluster in the classic Russian manner. Sitting back in the seat, he pulled down the front of his uniform. It made him feel constricted. Zurich, two trips on the Concorde and New York had caused him to gain weight again.

"I warned you in Monte Carlo that this project was getting out of hand," the old man said as the car began rolling. "I told you that things were changing in Moscow. New attitudes. A new generation. I can't continue to protect you."

Bresson saw genuine concern on Yuli Byrakoff's face. "Do not worry, *Papi.*" Bresson reverted to the name he had used when Yuli was his foster father in Grenoble under the name Yves Coudert. "I can take care of myself. What upsets them? Vienna?"

"Of course! We've not left bodies in the street since the 1950s! And your targets got away. There's worry that the project will be exposed and the General Secretary will be hurt by the blowback. He's planning to meet with the American President in December."

"We should have liquidated Frau Gissle long ago," Bresson said bitterly, "together with everyone else who knew about my so-called 'birth.'"

"You mean finish what the Nazis started in Dachau? Anyway, that's not your only problem."

"What else? The money? I'm restructuring the offer with the help of our capitalist friends."

"You'll find out." He said no more.

By the time the limo turned off the ring road toward the suburban complex of concrete and glass that served as the KGB headquarters, a deep silence had grown between the two men. Bresson felt a new sensation. It had started during their confrontation on the beach at Monte Carlo, and now the feeling had developed into a firm conviction. The News/Worldweek project was his declaration of independence from *Papi.* The old spymaster had been more than an instructor and a control officer. Yuli was the only father he had ever known, the only family. But Bresson was over fifty years old. He had built an empire. Thousands of people worked for him. He was a billionaire and a general in the KGB. Still, they treated him like a child. It was time they all understood that he had grown up.

As Bresson's car approached the gate with its single uniformed guard, he marveled at how little security he encountered inside the Soviet Union. The KGB put all its effort into sealing off the borders. And, he thought, the Committee for State Security was coasting on its reputation.

The car descended into a garage where two escorts took them to a waiting elevator.

"Will I see the General Secretary on this trip?" Bresson asked.

"You will be lucky to see our Chairman," Yuli warned.

They stopped on an unnumbered floor, and were led down a blank corridor to a windowless room. From the enameled green walls and rude chairs and table, Bresson realized it was not a conference room. It was an interrogation room.

Three men in civilian clothes came through a door in the opposite wall. Bresson noticed that two wore fashionable pin-striped Western suits, the third a black double-breasted Soviet bureaucrat's special. They all sat on the other side of the table. Ominously, his *Papi* joined them.

"I don't think you know the new head of Directorate S," Yuli said, "Vladimir Bogdanov." He gestured toward the pinstripe with gray hair. They did not shake hands.

"And these gentlemen are from Department Eight"—the bald man in the Stalinist suit nodded—"and Service R." A young blond man in the other pinstripe adjusted his glasses.

"Where is Altznov?" Bresson asked.

"The chief of the First Directorate is occupied. He instructed us to make the preliminary debriefing." Bogdanov then nodded toward the officer from Department Eight.

Bresson knew what was coming. Department Eight, once known and feared as Department V, was the part of the KGB responsible for terrorism, sabotage and assassination. But a defection in 1971 had led to a brutal reorganization. They would be unhappy with Bresson's conduct of "wet affairs" on his own.

"Where did you receive authority to attempt the liquidation of the U.S. government agent Heidi Bruce?"

"She's an employee of the United States Senate, not an agent."

"But she was conducting an investigation. The committee is part of the American intelligence community."

"Not really, but I won't quibble," Bresson was not going to fight over definitions.

"And Gospodin Jayson Lyman—"the Department Eight officer pressed.

"For more than thirty-five years," Bresson interrupted him, "my prime directive, the prime directive of all illegals in Directorate S, has been to protect our identity. At all costs!"

"The directives have been changed, General," Bogdanov said. "It is your responsibility to stay informed on such matters."

"So you had no specific authorization," concluded the officer in the black double-breasted suit. "What permission did you have to employ the two men who were killed, Tran Van Huong and Edouard Lucier?"

"They were my driver and bodyguard. In the West you must provide your own security. I'm an important man. The possible target of criminals."

"Why didn't you seek the proper assistance through Line-N?"

"I wanted to insulate the KGB! Tran and Lucier are fictitious names. They won't be connected to me or to the Committee."

"And your authority to execute the young man in Geneva?" He was relentless.

"When the liquidation of his girlfriend was authorized to protect my identity," Bresson explained with forced patience, "the Committee was very clear about him. He would be paid and allowed to live only so long as he remained quiet. In my judgment, he was about to violate that condition. None of you were here when that decision was made." Contempt had seeped into Bresson's demeanor. "Check the files."

"And Mr. Charles Rankin?"

"That was an accident," Bresson replied simply. He could tell they did not believe him, but he knew that, as usual, the truth was not the issue.

"The Committee for State Security cannot afford such accidents," Bogdanov said, "particularly when it risks the exposure of a project of such magnitude."

"I was trying to protect the operation," Bresson insisted. "He had discovered that we operate at a deficit. These bankers are not fools. That would have led to dangerous questions."

"But Mr. Lyman pursued the matter anyway," Bogdanov pointed out.

"He has learned nothing. I talked to Sommer. He assured me that all the financial records are secure in the vault."

"Did he also tell you that they took files from his desk that show a connection between Liechtinvest and Kreditorg?" Bogdanov asked.

"They can do nothing with that, believe me. Money's a commodity. Everyone buys and sells and lends and guarantees and trades securities of all kinds. International banking relationships are so complex you could prove that the Rockefellers are underwriting *perestroika!*"

"Yet you tried to kill Jayson Lyman."

"And failed," the thug from Department Eight added.

Before Bresson could respond, Bogdanov gestured to the young man from Section R, who had remained silent.

"I would like to pursue the question of why your companies operate at a deficit," he said.

Bresson raised his eyebrows. He had not encountered Section R before. He only knew vaguely that it had to do with operational evaluation.

"You have a significant share in each of your markets. You have economies of scale and niche businesses that should be cash cows," the young man noted. "Why a deficit?"

"I pay more for labor. You don't expect me to exploit our comrades in the CGT? And what they get, I must pay elsewhere in Europe. You say I have market share. Do you think that comes free? I have promotions. Discounts. And to build this enterprise, I often have to pay the highest price. I must amortize that and meet interest payments."

"But what do we get in return?" the young man asked.

Bresson felt himself turning red. "You question the most successful 'active measures' program in the history of the KGB? Almost single-handed, my newspapers forced the Americans to negotiate on the Euromissiles, and we've blocked any possibility of modernizing the short range ones! All over Europe, NATO defense budgets are dropping. The General Secretary is more popular than any of his predecessors. Increasing numbers of Europeans believe America is the greatest threat to their security. We have enormous influence over politicians in West Germany, France, Italy. Do I really have to go on?" Bresson was outraged.

"Our analysis suggests something different," said the young man without flinching. "The reputation enjoyed by the General Secretary is due to his policies and his own efforts. The Americans pressed for Euromissile negotiations, our side walked out. American blunders created its image problems which, I must add, it's now correcting. The influence you wield is directly proportional to the conservatism of your publications—"

"Stop right there! Of course I must pretend to be conservative. I have to protect our identity and credibility . . ." Bresson sputtered.

"Our content analysis shows that your publications are fifteen percent more conservative than the average papers we do *not* control."

"This is preposterous! Are you saying I have failed to serve the Party and the State?"

"To some extent of course," the young man conceded, "but are you worth a subsidy of $300 million a year? Perhaps that money can be spent more cost-effectively elsewhere."

"Where do you get such numbers?" Bresson's voice was rising.

"Do you challenge them?"

"Who is this young whelp? Where does he come from?" Bresson angrily demanded.

Bogdanov answered, "Harvard Business School."

When Bresson spoke again, his voice was full of rage. "I am one of the most powerful men in Western Europe. Presidents and Prime Ministers beg to have lunch with me. I run a business empire of two hundred and fifty thousand employees in ten countries. My assets are over six billion dollars. When I buy News/Worldweek, the combined assets will be almost fourteen billion. You are treating me and my organization like a shoe collective that has missed its quota. This is the biggest intelligence operation ever undertaken in human history!"

Bogdanov nodded gravely. "Perhaps too big," was all he said.

The long black Zil moved rapidly through the dark toward Bresson's midnight meeting at the Lubyanka fortress with the Chairman of the KGB. Sitting in the back seat, Bresson felt waves of anger, humiliation, outrage, fear and hunger. He tried to collect his thoughts. He was in trouble. But how deep? Perhaps he would never emerge from Lubyanka. It had happened to others.

As they cruised at over a hundred kilometers per hour down the center of the street in the VIP lane, Bresson found himself staring out the window at the traffic. It was surprisingly heavy for that late hour in Moscow and seemed to consist mostly of young people slowly cruising along in beat-up Togliatfis with fenders missing and open exhaust pipes. The boys had long hair and jewelry, the girls, bleached blond crew cuts with red, green and blue face paint. He could hear the rock music blasting from their tape decks. What was happening to the Soviet Union?

He turned to Yuli Byrakoff and suddenly asked, "*Papi,* who am I?" The old man had been watching him intently. "What do you mean?"

"Where do I come from?"

"I don't know exactly. I was told that you were found wandering in the rubble when the Nazis retreated from Moscow. You were a baby."

"Yes, I remember tanks and shooting. But I have memories of a big home and crowds of people in strange clothes. And a woman, a beautiful woman, and pearls, and being hungry."

"The mind plays tricks."

"Every day that I worked at Tante Pise, beautiful women would come into the restaurant. I would watch them. And sometimes I would think I saw her. Dark hair, delicate mouth and chin. I would watch her from behind, her long neck bent over the table. But when the woman turned, the memory vanished. The eyes would be wrong and everything changed. She would be just a loud Italian girl or a rich spoiled French tart."

"Would you like a woman?" *Papi* asked, "We can arrange it."

"Who? Some pathetic creature from Gosfilm? I can buy my own whores! I can buy everything in life, but a life! I have no wife, no daughter, no son. I have no real friends, no home, no country—"

"Don't talk like that."

"All I have is my business, and you. Both are frauds!"

"You are a hero of the Soviet Union," the old man said patiently.

"According to the new order, I am a fraud too!"

"Misha." Yuli used the name Bresson bore when he first taught him French at Komsomol 708. "Are you pushing the News/Worldweek project because you want to be unmasked? Do you want the world to know how clever you are? I have seen that in others," the old spymaster warned. Bresson did not reply.

The limousine turned from Dzerzhinski Square into Lubyanka, the massive stone prison that housed the offices of the Chairman of the KGB. Border guards in mustard-colored greatcoats and bearing AK-74 assault rifles escorted them up three flights of marble stairs. They entered a large conference room with twenty red velvet chairs drawn up at a long narrow table. Two large crystal chandeliers filled the cream and gold walls with light. There was no hint of the cruelty that inhabited the dungeons below. As the door opened, Yuli hissed, "Pull yourself together!"

Bresson had not seen the Chairman since he had visited Moscow as a member of a delegation of Western publishers. At that time, the chief of the secret police had been charming and easygoing, a raconteur of Russian folk tales, trying hard to prove there was a new KGB to go with the era of *glasnost*. Now he had reverted to a short, pig-eyed, bullet-headed cop. Like Bresson, he began the meeting without a greeting.

"You had an excellent record in Komsomol school."

"That was a long time ago, Comrade Chairman. I've done a few things since."

"You must remember terms like 'opportunist,' 'self-aggrandizer,' 'deviationist,' 'capitalist roader.' You were charged with some of them."

"Yes." Bresson flushed.

"They are out of fashion now," the Chairman continued. "I know members of the Central Committee who have in all seriousness said that you should be brought back home, given a new identity and directed to run the Ministry of Light Industry."

"I'm very flattered."

"Don't be. They haven't seen your books. You know, of course, I have recommendations to dismantle your operation."

"That would be a terrible mistake."

"Yes, you're bankrupt. After the debts were paid, we would lose a fortune. Can you give me one reason why I should not cancel the News/Worldweek project? You've had a massive security break, and there are already four dead. We had fewer casualties when we invaded Czechoslovakia!"

"I'm convinced the security break can be contained," Bresson began. He could sense that the Chairman was negotiating. This was a deal, and he was a businessman. "Walking away from the transaction will raise more questions than completing it."

"But can you?"

"Without question."

"What makes you so confident?"

"I have the management and the board on my side." He then proceeded to describe his meeting with Drew Richardson. "There are steps yet to take, but the deal is arranged."

The Chairman sat quietly for several minutes, staring at Bresson. Finally he said, "It was the unanimous recommendation of the staff that you be severely disciplined for exceeding your authority."

Bresson stared back. "Only you know my true value to the KGB. Would you jeopardize such a source?"

The KGB Chairman grimaced. Bresson knew he had found the right pressure point.

"All right, you may proceed to take over News/Worldweek and merge it with Les Éditions Bresson. But on two conditions."

Bresson braced himself. "What are they?" he asked.

"First, that you succeed. Failure will result in the traditional sanction."

"And the second condition?"

"From now on, you must make a profit."

21

The Assistant Secretary of the Treasury for International Affairs wondered why the CIA wanted to come to the meeting. The National Security Council staff had called to ask that CIA be invited to the Committee on Foreign Investment when it addressed the News/Worldweek takeover. As chairman of CFIUS, the Assistant Secretary had no objection, but it was the first time in his memory that CIA had asked to be included. The committee, which also consisted of Commerce, State, and Defense officials, often included CIA when it dealt with national security issues such as whether Fujitsu would be allowed to buy National Semiconductor. In that case, CIA participated by providing an assessment of Japanese microchip technology and the consequences of illegal diversion to the USSR. But a publishing and broadcast conglomerate? What interest would CIA have in that?

The Assistant Secretary called the meeting to order at 3:00 P.M. in Room 213A of the Treasury Department. Apart from the White House next door, the Treasury was the oldest building in the executive branch, and among the most beautiful. It had a classic facade of marble columns reminiscent of the Parthenon and a sunken front plaza that gave the structure the look of having been unearthed by archaeologists. Inside, the rooms ranged from the grand to the grungy, reflecting the ambivalence of a government agency devoted both to spending and husbanding the national wealth. Room 213A, where the fate of the $8.6 billion News/Worldweek deal would be considered, was particularly dismal. The maroon drapes had turned brown from years of neglect; the hems had unraveled and were dragging on the floor. A rust-colored stain ran down the wallpaper from a huge air conditioner that stuck through the grimy windows overlooking the bleak center courtyard. Instead of graceful chandeliers, the light came from brown metal fixtures with fluorescent tubes. The Assistant Secretary hated the room and hoped to keep the meeting short. He planned to get a head start on the traffic to his weekend home in Virginia.

"The Senate Commerce Committee and the House Subcommittee on Telecommunications are holding hearings on the proposed takeover of News/Worldweek by . . ." the Assistant Secretary checked his notes, "Les Éditions Bresson. I thought we should get together and hammer out an executive branch position."

He looked around at his colleagues. No one seemed eager to speak. Finally a lieutenant colonel from the Defense Department lifted his index finger off the table in a gesture that meant he had volunteered to get shot at by the others.

"I don't know how to put this, except it kind of makes me uneasy to see so much of our TV, newspapers, books and all, in the hands of a foreigner. What if we have a war? Will he be patriotic and support it? Or if one of his papers discovers a military secret, would he cooperate with the government and not print it?"

The rest of them looked at the military officer as if he had stepped out of a time capsule. After an embarrassed silence, the woman officer from the State Department said what was on everyone's mind.

"Do we know any *American* media that would help the government like that anymore?"

"We have to adhere to our principles," the Commerce Department representative declared.

"For example?" the lieutenant colonel asked.

"America believes in free trade, and unrestricted movement of capital," the man from Commerce intoned. "We've vast investments abroad. How can we object when foreigners want to invest here?"

"Invest, sure," the military man responded, "but buying us out is something else. And aren't most media in foreign countries owned by the government?"

"The largest international newspapers are American," the Commerce Assistant Secretary pointed out. "The *Wall Street Journal* and the *International Herald Tribune*."

"The UPI wire service used to be owned by a Mexican," the woman from State added. "Now it'll be owned by a Frenchman. So what? State believes that the purchase will strengthen Franco-American relations."

"I would remind the committee," the chairman said, "that we have no statutory authority to block this transaction. We're only advisory. To raise a national security objection to the President, we need something specific." He glanced at the CIA representative.

The CIA man said nothing.

The Chair looked to the lieutenant colonel representing Defense.

"If everything's for sale to anybody," he said, "I guess I just wonder whatever happened to our national sovereignty."

"Sorry," the chairman said, "that's not in our charter."

He looked around one last time. "No objection? So be it." The committee adjourned.

As he headed for the parking garage, the chairman of CFIUS felt the meeting had gone smoothly. He continued to be troubled by only one question. Why did the CIA want to attend the meeting?

Heidi Bruce and Jayson Lyman sat across the aisle from one another in the economy class of Lufthansa's flight 400 from Frankfurt to New York. Heidi was thinking about Bresson and Jayson. Lyman was thinking about Heidi and Sean Gordon.

With the plane full, it was difficult to talk. But Heidi felt that Jay had been unusually quiet since Sean Gordon had put them on the aircraft at Munich. And he hadn't said much in the car before that. His only comment while they waited to change planes in Frankfurt was to complain that first class was sold out and that the men's room was flooded with water. A dozen Arabs were trying to wash their feet in the sinks.

She looked over at him. He had his eyes closed, but she knew he wasn't asleep. He was pouting because of Sean Gordon. Men and their fragile egos!

Sean had read through the Russian-language files Jay had stolen from Sommer Bank. They clearly indicated that Liechtinvest was an arm of Kreditorg. It even looked as though a big Kreditorg trading account in the Sommer Bank was pledged to back up the secret guarantee for the News/Worldweek loan. She had the makings of a dynamite hearing, particularly if Jayson would testify.

Heidi was proud of him. He'd shown enormous courage in the last twenty-four hours. Heidi wanted to run her hands up the hard muscles in his back and bite the hair on his chest. She thought briefly of the privacy of the lavatory but thought he would be shocked. Besides, he was in a sulk over Sean.

And where was Sean? Disappeared again, "To take care of the mess in Vienna," he said. Not a word about her and Lyman. She didn't know which she found more irritating, Sean's understanding or Jayson's jealousy.

Lyman did not think that he was jealous. He had abandoned his cardinal rule, looking out for himself, and was now paying for his foolishness. He had been suckered into risking his life and his career to chase down Bresson. For what? For a girl! And in the last act, her father figure returned and carried her off!

Lyman opened his eyes a crack and saw her across the aisle, reading. He would never forget the expression on her face when she was clinging to Sean Gordon. When *he* had saved her from Edouard and the Vietnamese, Heidi hadn't fallen into his arms like that. What was the return on his investment? A busted deal. A wrecked romance. And a permanent place on the KGB's Ten Most Wanted list.

He was an investment banker. Not a second story man. Not a spy. He did deals, and he was going back to doing deals if his firm hadn't self-destructed while he was gone.

The Fasten Seat Belts sign flashed on, and Heidi could feel the pressure start to build on her eardrums. She glanced at Jayson. They only had fifteen minutes to decide what they were going to do next. Did he want her to spend the night in New York, or what? Jayson didn't look like he was going to say a word. She would be damned if she was going to beg him for anything. Had she done something wrong?

The wheels scraped the ground and the aircraft rolled across the runway to the gate. Lyman could feel the tension between them as they walked, apart but near one another, through the labyrinth of halls, stairways and escalators at JFK's International Arrivals Building. Neither had luggage, so they proceeded directly to Customs, Heidi going through first and then pausing to pretend to look in her purse so Lyman could catch up. They passed through the double doors and into a vast hall thronged with people waiting for arriving passengers. Someone asked Lyman if he had come from Puerto Rico. He shook his head. When they had finally worked their way out of the crowd, they both stopped.

"Well, good-bye," he said.

"Good-bye," she replied and turned toward the exit.

"Are you just going to walk away like that?" Lyman demanded.

"Why are you behaving this way?" she turned back. "Is this how you handle jealousy? Punishing me because of Sean Gordon?"

"Why should I be jealous of a Peeping Tom who's been following us all over Europe just waiting to see if we'd be killed!"

"He saved us, Jayson."

"He saved *you*! If I were alone, do you think he would have saved me?"

Heidi paused. "I don't know," she admitted. "But he's not the issue. I want to know if you're going to help me. I need you as a witness against Bresson."

"Sean Gordon. Marcel Bresson. What about Jayson Lyman? Do you care at all about me? I did all this crazy stuff for you!"

"Because of me?" She was not flattered. "That's just another form of selfishness. Don't you care about your country? Don't you care about stopping him?"

"I think taking twenty million dollars of his money is the best possible revenge."

"This is just a game to you," she said, disappointed. "Money's just a way of keeping score."

"Heidi, in case you hadn't noticed, I'm not political. I do what most Americans do, worry about making money. I earn it, and I spend it. That's my contribution to the American way of life."

"Doesn't it bother you at all"—she was shouting now—"that the Russians might own and operate most of what we read, see and hear?"

"Heidi, I killed somebody!" he whispered fiercely.

"It was self-defense."

"That doesn't help. I'll leave the more difficult stuff to you. And Sean."

"Don't make me choose between the two of you." She was on the verge of pleading. "We could all work so well together."

"As a team?" he said bitterly. "Would I be Mr. Inside or Mr. Outside? Or would we get to switch off?"

"Jayson," she said angrily, "grow up!"

The doors opened, and a plane load of Puerto Ricans flooded into the hall, carrying them apart.

"Heidi!" he called back, "Get a life!"

"If ya don't mind my sayin' so, Mr. Lyman, you look like hell." Andy whipped the long stretch Cadillac through the narrow, cluttered lanes of JFK. "You sure you don't want to go home first?"

"No. The office."

"What happened to you?" Andy asked.

"A little trouble. You almost lost a customer."

"Rough stuff? Hey, you need help, I know guys that do strokes."

"Strokes?" Lyman asked.

"You know." He slammed his fist into his palm.

That gave him an idea. "Do they do bodyguard?" He tried and failed to pick up Andy's locution.

"Sure. For you?"

"Yes." Who knew what Bresson or the Russians might try next? "And," he sighed, "someone in Washington."

"Miss Bruce? Just give me her address."

"But it's got to be discreet."

"Leave the whole thing to me."

When Lyman walked into his office, everyone seemed to avoid him.

"Do I look that bad?" he asked his secretary.

"You could use a press, a shave an' a bath," Marlene said. "Otherwise yer fine."

He looked down at himself. Small bits of cement from the Sommer Bank construction site still stuck to his shoes. When Lyman first came to Wall Street, he'd noticed that investment bankers were particularly obsessive about keeping their shoes shined. The Lady Macbeth syndrome, he decided. They spent their days trudging through crap.

"Get me a shoeshine guy."

"Can't. You got to wait till they show up. Part of Cooke's economy program. He took away their beepers."

"Then give me my phone messages," he said curtly.

They were the usual. Five from his mother. Two from Mr. Malcom. Three from Mrs. Pierce and four from the chairman of RATCO. "Nothing from Bresson?" he marveled. "Or Sperile Beck? Or Maurice the accountant?"

Marlene shook her head.

"Nothing from Richardson's people? Blackie Muldoon? The News/Worldweek people? Our lawyers? The PR guys?" He was becoming incredulous.

"De Grazia's taking the calls on the deal," Marlene explained.

"Where is he?"

"In a meeting. Uptown."

"On what?"

She shook her head again.

"What's everybody working on?" he asked suspiciously.

Marlene shrugged evasively.

He marched into the Raccoon's Den, where the analysts were glued to their computers.

"Karen, what are you working on?"

"Something for Mr. de Grazia."

"What?" he insisted, bending to look at the screen.

"Uh." Karen Kobyashi hesitated, then hit the save button. "He said it was confidential."

"Goddammit, I want to know what you're doing," Lyman said angrily.

"Jayson, ease off." Marlene was standing behind him at the door. "Things have changed around here in the past few days."

"What the hell do you mean by that?"

"If you want to know anything about the News/Worldweek deal, you gotta talk to Cooke."

The president of Gould Axewroth stood at what he called the bridge, a twenty-by-six-foot desk, equipped with banks of telephones and ranks of video monitors that commanded the trading-room floor. Lyman and everyone else in the firm knew Cooke had not the faintest grasp of trading, but it had been built by Billy Gould, and Cooke used it to display his authority and impress clients. Besides, John Gutfreund at Salomon and Ace Greenberg at Bear Stearns had desks just like it.

The good thing, Lyman realized as he strode through the trading floor in a rage, was that the bridge left Cooke vulnerable. No heavy doors to hide behind. No battery of secretaries. Lyman worked his way through rows of traders shouting into the telephones and screaming at each other. The market was down twenty-seven points in the last hour and had only fifteen minutes till the closing bell. In the chaos, Cooke did not see him coming.

"Jayson!" he said surprised. His name boomed out of loudspeakers on the trading floors on four continents. Cooke had just picked up the "hoot and holler," which let him simultaneously address the firm's trading rooms in New York, London, San Francisco, Los Angeles, Tokyo, Hong Kong and Sydney. He carefully put the receiver back in its cradle.

"You're back. You look like shit." He turned his attention to his desk as if he was busy with some papers. "You ought to get yourself some clothes. You see this?" Without looking up, he fingered the lapel of his dark blue chalk-striped suit. "Huntsman. Savile Row. Three thousand in pounds." Lyman could see he was vamping, trying to figure out what to say. "When it gets old and baggy, you send it back. They take out the lining and float the suit in a Scottish stream." He kept his head down, shuffling his papers. "When they put it back together, the suit's like new. Lasts forever."

"You know how they make the cloth?" Lyman asked. Cooke finally looked up at him. "They soak the yarn in sheep urine. What's the story on News/Worldweek?"

"You're out of it." Cooke looked back at his desk. "You fucked up. The client hates you."

Lyman was surprised that he felt no surprise.

"De Grazia's in charge," Cooke added. "And he put the deal together while you were getting your rocks off in Europe."

"What do you really know about Bresson?" Lyman challenged him.

"I know we've got a golden goose here, and we're not going to let you kill it."

"And what if I told you he's underwritten by the Russians?"

"I'd say you forgot to take your lithium."

"If I had proof?" Lyman countered calmly.

Cooke looked him in the eye, but he began to fidget with the papers again. "What do you mean 'underwritten'?"

"A Russian agency put up the guarantee for the loans to buy News/Worldweek."

"Shit." Cooke visibly relaxed. "So what? The world's one big financial market, or hadn't you noticed?"

"The fucking Kremlin's going to control News/Worldweek through Bresson!" Lyman insisted.

"Are you smoking dope?" Cooke became scornful. "Look, we're not doing anything illegal. There's nothing illegal that I can see in what Bresson's doing. Even if the Russians put up some money as guarantees or whatever, that's not illegal either! So what's your problem?"

Lyman paused. Cooke wasn't just being an asshole. He really didn't see it.

"What do you think the management committee will say?" Lyman finally asked.

It was Cooke's turn to pause. The shouting among the traders was reaching a crescendo. When Cooke spoke, Lyman had to strain to hear him. "I know you've been scheming to get my job. You go to the committee with a 'twilight zone' story like that, and you'll be lucky to stay a partner. You've missed your window of opportunity to run this firm. I've solved our liquidity problem."

"How?"

"You'll find out along with everybody else. But the twenty million we don't pay you is a start."

"If I were you, I wouldn't begin counting the News/Worldweek fee."

"The deal's set," Cooke declared.

"Yeh?" Lyman managed a weary smile. "But we both know it's not 'set' set."

The thing Lyman liked about his ground-floor maisonette apartment on East 76th Street was that it was dark. That had enabled him to sleep most of Saturday, except for a brief period when he got up to go to the bathroom and to eat. He ordered Ethiopian take-out, and while waiting for it to arrive, he had sorted through his mail. Among the bills, advertisements and tickets to $1,000-a-plate dinners, he found a genuine social invitation. Philip Thornton, Lyman's personal lawyer, and his wife, Bunky, were having an out-of-season house party in East Hampton that weekend. He called, and Bunky assured him it would be fine for him to come out on Sunday. Lyman then ate the Ethiopian stew, drank most of a bottle of wine and went to bed for another twelve hours, interrupted only by throwing up in his sleep and almost strangling.

He woke up early Sunday more purged than refreshed. In the deal business, Lyman was used to quick changes of fortune, but the shocks of the last several days had left him drained. He knew that if he was going to get back in the News/Worldweek deal—block the transaction, or turn the situation somehow to his advantage—he should not be going to the Hamptons. He should be on the phone. But he couldn't face it.

The pulsating water from the shower massage beat down on the spreading yellow and black bruise where the car had hit him. Lyman examined his body. He used to be proud of it, and the way it could take abuse. Now he was a wreck. He could grab hold of the 'love handles' over his hips, and the muscles on his abdomen, though flat, had lost their definition.

Give it a rest, he thought. Put Heidi Bruce and the whole transaction behind you. There's a million women and deals out there. If she needs her daddy, let her have him. And forget News/Worldweek. So you won't make $20 million. With the special bonus pool for M&A and being head of the department, Lyman calculated that if the deal happened, he would still make almost $5 million.

Lyman suddenly had to grab the handle on the shower to steady himself. He couldn't catch his breath. Something was wrong. Turning off the water, he stumbled out of the stall and opened the bathroom door to let in fresh air. Still shaken, he sat on the bed. That was the first time in his life he had ever felt indifferent to $15 million. He needed time off.

When he emerged from the maisonette, Andy was waiting with a partner who had thick hair growing on the backs of his hands. They drove him to the Marine Air Terminal at LaGuardia. Lyman was flying Shelter Airlines. The man at the desk, who sold the tickets and loaded the luggage, also turned out be the pilot. Shelter Airlines had previously been Hampton Air, Long Island Air and Montauk Air. The company's business cycle seemed to consist of flying in the summer and going bankrupt in the winter.

Once the nineteen-passenger Bandeirante aircraft was airborne, the chaos and decay of Queens and Brooklyn resolved itself into a pattern of orderly streets and green parks. Lyman told himself that a little time away from everything would give him some perspective. And Phil Thornton always gave sound advice.

Soon he could see the whole breadth of the island, from the glistening Atlantic shore of Fire Island to the brownish green of the Sound. He quickly picked out the expressway that Andy and his partner would take to East Hampton. On a Sunday morning, the drive would take them only two and a half hours. Friday evening, the same trip could consume five hours. Lyman had sworn he would never buy a house in the Hamptons until he could afford to fly out and back at will. If he had made the $20 million on the News/Worldweek deal, he would have almost been rich enough.

Bunky had warned him that she would send one of the unattached ladies to pick him up. As the aircraft coasted up to the shack that served as the terminal of the Hamptons airport, Lyman spotted her. She was blond and wore the *de rigueur* Hamptons Sunday uniform, a white tennis dress. Though she was young, Lyman judged her old enough to have put away at least one husband, a major love affair or both. She introduced herself as Samantha, and as they pulled out of the parking lot in her Mercedes 450 SEL convertible, he could not resist noticing the fine blond hairs on her smooth, tanned thighs.

Just past the ponds and the stone clock tower that marked the entrance to East Hampton, they turned off Route 29 onto Orchard Lane. At the end of the street, a large frame Victorian stood on a grassy knoll. The deep green lawn ran down to a fresh-water pond. High dunes rose on the other side. Lyman could smell the sea and hear the surf crashing against the sand, but could not see the ocean.

Bunky greeted him with a one-cheek kiss, which told him that he was not fully in favor for having arrived on Sunday. House parties in the Hamptons had an industrial character. Scheduling was everything. The logistics of picking people up and delivering them back to planes, trains and the Hampton Jitney was the easy part. Guests also had to be transported to the beach, to shopping, to lunches and picnics, to tennis, to softball games, to cocktails and to dinner. Lyman's late arrival was like dropping a loose gear into a transmission.

He had to do as he was told. That meant getting out of the way while lunch was prepared. Sammy wanted him to play tennis. She beat him, 6–4, 6–2, on the grass courts of the Maidstone Tennis Club.

When they returned to the house, Lyman was reassured to see Andy and his friend parked outside the driveway. The other guests were gathered on the veranda that surrounded three sides of the house. Lunch was informal. The men were allowed colored shirts with their jackets and ties and bare feet inside loafers and deck shoes. The bright October day with a crisp edge of autumn had the women dressed in expensive fall tweeds and woolens from Ralph Lauren. The country weekend atmosphere did not eliminate jewelry or keep the women from being immaculately groomed and coiffed. In the past, East Hampton was jeans and tennis shoes and Southampton the place where one dressed up. Now, as the newly rich bought up the surrounding potato fields, East Hampton was turning into Park Avenue without stockings.

The guests, Lyman found, were mostly natives. The European aristocrats who increasingly preferred the Hamptons over the traffic and trailer parks of the Riviera, had long since returned to their apartments on the Ile St-Louis, their flats in Kensington and their houses by the Alster in Hamburg. The autumn people were New Yorkers, this crowd primarily Wall Street with the required leavening from the arts.

Lyman was amazed at how quickly weekend house guests adopted certain standard roles which often conflicted with their basic personalities. One dynamo executive, whose day job was to run a major brokerage, arrived at cocktails with an armful of French bread and immediately departed for ice. He had become the "errand boy," the one who constantly went out to the store because he did not know what to say to people.

His female counterpart was the "invalid." She sat in a stiff chair in a corner of the porch, her feet on a stool for her bad back, an inhaler at her side to combat hay fever, sipping straight Russian vodka—the only drink to which she was not allergic. Lyman discovered that in real life the invalid ran a modeling agency where her beautiful young women and men had an average professional lifespan of eighteen months before she tossed them onto the trash heap of fashion.

Lyman talked briefly with a thirty-seven-year-old partner in a money management firm who cast himself as adventurer. At 127 pounds, he bragged of not gaining an ounce since high school. Then, he was considered a scrawny wimp. Now, he ran marathons, and his weekend revenge consisted of luring his out-of-shape colleagues into activities such as windsurfing that put them in the hospital.

The gathering also had its weekend therapist. A plain, pleasant-looking woman, she did nothing but elicit other people's troubles because she was afraid that in a real conversation she might blurt out her own. Finally, Lyman encountered the artistic twosome practiced in the craft of Éponge—sponging. He was a pianist and she was an opera singer. They spent every unemployed weekend, which were unfortunately many, visiting friends in the Hamptons. With gross incomes barely above the poverty line, they were expected to reciprocate by entertaining after Saturday dinner.

As Lyman moved among the guests, he felt strangely dissociated, as if he were playing the role of a ghost. Snatches of conversation came to him.

Real estate developer: "So this major pile of shit walks into my office . . ."

Huntress to huntress: "I really wanted to get to know him better, but I was having my period . . ."

Child bride explaining her attraction to an old bond trader: "We experience a form of communication beyond the porpoises . . ."

The old bond trader explaining why he dumped his long-suffering wife for the child bride: "Look, there was thirty years between the bid and the ask!"

Lyman was grateful when the little bell signaled lunch.

They all trooped down to a long table set under a tent on the lawn. Lyman found that Bunky was still mad at him. She seated him at the far end with her father, a cantankerous old Wall Street lawyer whose name lent dignity to an otherwise rapacious firm. Lyman had spotted him earlier as the weekend "sage" who handed down judgments to anyone within earshot.

"I've seen 'em come and go, and they do that faster and faster these days," the old lawyer proclaimed to no one in particular. "Financiers once were men of affairs. They took money from Europe and built America's railroads and steel mills. They put together the biggest corporations in the world, U.S. Steel, Standard Oil, General Motors. Investment bankers advised Presidents and became statesmen, like Bernard Baruch and Averell Harriman, Douglas Dillon and Robert Lehman."

He was aiming his remarks directly at Lyman now. "Becoming a partner meant something more than getting a fatter slice of the bonus pie. You were admitted to a profession renowned for its probity and integrity. A partnership was a badge of respectability. You assumed leadership not only on Wall Street but for our entire nation. My generation of investment bankers were the architects of America's rise to greatness. They were figures on the world stage."

He paused in his address to wipe his lips, and then almost to himself, he muttered, "I admired these men. That's why I built a law firm devoted to serving them. Now," his voice rose, "we spend most of our time making sure that when they're convicted, they don't have to work in the prison laundry!"

Lyman excused himself from the table and walked down to the edge of the pond. He stood there for several minutes watching a flight of ducks practice their amphibious takeoffs and landings. Then he felt the presence of someone behind him. He whirled quickly and put up his hands.

"Easy!" Phil Thornton said. "It's just me."

"Sorry," Lyman blushed. They had been classmates in college. Thornton once had a boyish face full of possibilities. Now it only reflected the possible.

"Are you in some kind of trouble?" he asked. "I saw those characters at the top of the drive. I almost called the police until they said they were with you."

"Let's take a walk. And keep an open mind until I tell you the whole story."

As Lyman began to talk, they set off on a path that skirted the pond and then plunged into a thicket of reeds and cattails. Soon they emerged onto a wooden footbridge which carried them across the marsh to the sand dunes. Trudging over a narrow trail through the fragile dune grass, they arrived at a broad beach at low tide. Lyman took off his shoes and let surf wash over his pant cuffs as they walked along the shore.

When Lyman finished his story, Philip Thornton stopped and looked out to sea. A pale moon was already rising on the afternoon horizon.

"I hate to tell you this," he said at last, "but Marshall Cooke is right. There's no law against this guy Bresson buying News/Worldweek. Every newspaper, cable TV station, movie company, magazine and book publisher in the country could be owned by the Russians."

"Bresson's concealing their role!" Lyman protested.

"The Russians are creditors. Even if there were a case for equitable subordination, in effect, if they own the company, there'd be no problem. People can buy stock on behalf of anyone they like. Gould Axewroth does it for customers all the time. It's only a problem if that breaks some law. I don't see any laws being broken here, by him or Gould Axewroth." He stopped and they turned around.

"But with all this deception going on," Lyman shook his head trying not to hear what he was being told, "there's got to be some illegalities."

"From what you say, he's lied about his identity and misrepresented certain facts about his financial condition. But whether that can be proved and whether that's material to a violation of law has to be established. You'd need the resources of the federal government to do it."

They walked a while in silence. Seagulls screeched at one another over something dead that had washed in with the tide.

"What if I went to the Feds?" Lyman finally asked.

"Assuming they'd believe you? That's a big if, but okay. Let me give you some facts of legal life. The SEC basically deals with civil law and securities. So far Bresson's offering cash. The SEC can conduct an investigation, but unless and until he's filed a fraudulent proxy, there's nothing actionable in the securities code. And the SEC can't look beyond that."

"What about the U.S. attorney?"

"I was getting there. That's an even sadder story. In theory, he has jurisdiction over everything. But look at what you've got in the U.S. Attorney's Office for the Southern District of New York. Everybody there is either running for office or trying to ingratiate themselves with future clients and employers. They have no sense of haste. It took ten years to deliver an indictment against the Hunts. There's incredible turnover. You could have five consecutive assistant U.S. attorneys handling your case, and each would start from scratch. That could take years, and during that time Bresson could be suing you! Word would go out on the Street: you're a troublemaker. You can't be trusted.

You're in the Feds' pocket. The years go by. Meanwhile, Bresson owns News/Worldweek. He's collecting political chits. We get a new President. A new Congress. The investigation's dropped. Your ass is hanging out there. Not to mention the cost of a bodyguard for the rest of your life."

Lyman laughed. "You don't have to sugarcoat things for me like that, you know."

"My advice, as your lawyer, is to forget it. Steer clear. Let this Heidi Bruce and her pal Gordon carry the ball."

"And your advice as a friend?"

"The same. Plus take out some more insurance."

"I don't have any beneficiary except my mother, and she's already set."

"That's another thing. It's time you had some beneficiaries. Forget that woman."

"How?"

"With another."

"Like Sammy?"

"Yes. But Bunky wanted me to tell you to be careful with her. She looks like strength and health, but Sammy's very fragile emotionally. Less than a year ago her husband was shot and killed by a client."

"Drugs?"

"No. Her husband was a stockbroker. He churned his client's account down to zero."

They had arrived back at the lawn and were climbing up toward the house.

"I'll be as kind as I know how," Lyman assured his host, "I'll try to stay away from her."

Heidi was so excited she almost danced along the balcony toward the hearing room. The CIA had sent its deputy director of Central Intelligence to testify on Bresson. She had hit a raw nerve.

When she pushed open the glass doors, she found the DDCI, an assistant and two bodyguards crowded into the small waiting area. Photographs of former Senate Intelligence Committee chairmen stared down at them from the walls. Stopping at the guard desk to show her badge, Heidi gave them a polite nod which they only grudgingly returned. She then stepped over the copper-lined threshold and into the SCIF—Secure Classified Information Facility—a small hearing and conference room complex built for the Senate Intelligence Committee and designed especially to prevent penetration by hostile electronic intelligence. Essentially a room within a room, the SCIF was low-ceilinged and had a raised floor.

The other staff members were already seated on the high bench that ran behind the green horseshoe-shaped table that was reserved for the Senators. The hearing chamber had mauve-colored seats for an audience of thirty-six, plus space for four more at a small white and black witness table. The walls were gray with mustard yellow and blue accents on the columns, arches, moldings and light sconces. Heidi described the room as art deco tarted up to look postmodern.

Since the staff director was out of town on a job interview, Heidi took his place behind the Chairman's seat. As usual, no Senator had showed up on time for the hearing. Heidi did not feel like joining in the small talk among the staff. Her briefing of the minority staff director had been the normal unpleasant experience. As she expected, he denounced her for conducting an investigation "behind everyone's back," but she became offended when he accused her of trying to make a "big something out of the little nothing" that she had uncovered.

Twenty minutes after the hearing was scheduled to begin, no Senators had appeared. Heidi called the Chairman's office. He had been in the Senate gymnasium having a steam bath and was supposed to be on his way. She invited the deputy director of the CIA inside and offered some coffee. He agreed to come in, but refused the coffee.

They continued to wait. Heidi tried to remain focused on the questions she wanted the CIA to answer. For the past seventy-two hours she had been in a work frenzy, generated largely by the anger and disappointment she felt toward Jayson Lyman. Over the weekend she had prepared a full report on her investigation, a briefing memo for the Chairman and an extensive set of interrogatories for the CIA. She had also cleaned her refrigerator, removed the dead plants, vacuumed her apartment and shopped for clothes to replace those she had lost. Her only really bad moment came when the salesgirl at Ann Taylor talked her into trying on a cocktail dress. Standing in front of the mirror, she had momentarily wondered if Jay Lyman would like it, then burst into tears.

When neither the Chairman nor any other Senator had shown up at thirty-five minutes past ten, the DDCI announced that he had a meeting at the White House in less than an hour. He suggested the hearing be rescheduled for some time the following week. Heidi objected and began wrangling with the minority staff director. They finally compromised by having the DDCI begin by reading his prepared statement to the assembled staff.

He read slowly, lugubriously, in a style Heidi had come to know as a deliberate attempt to make the subject as boring and uninteresting as possible—not only to put Senators and staff to sleep but to prompt as few questions as possible. The deputy director described in excruciating detail the record of recent exchanges of correspondence and telephone calls with members of the committee and staff on the subject of Marcel Bresson. He elaborated at length on the various offices at the Agency that had looked into the request for information and how they had gone about it. Ten minutes into his presentation, the deputy director of the CIA had still not told them anything about Bresson.

Then the Chairman appeared at the door. "What's going on here?" he demanded, slamming his cane across the table for emphasis. "A hearing conducted by staff? Why don't we abolish Senators altogether!" he thundered. "Start your testimony all over again!"

The DDCI objected that he had a White House meeting.

"Take the oath and submit your statement for the record. Just tell me in plain English what you know about this Frenchman or whatever he is."

The DDCI did not look happy at the prospect of giving sworn testimony but had no grounds to object.

"The information I am about to give you comes from an extremely sensitive source. I'm going to have to request that all the staff leave the room."

"First you don't want to talk to the Senators," the Chairman responded. "Now you don't want to talk to the staff. Do I get the impression you don't want to talk at all?" He cleared the room of everyone except Heidi and the minority staff director.

"Our information," the deputy director read from a note card, "is that Marcel Bresson was born in a concentration camp in Germany and not reunited with his family until he was a teenager. His parents were French Communists, heroes of the Resistance, but he broke with them over the war in Algeria, in which he served honorably. After university, he worked as a journalist before buying his first newspaper. His business interests now include every type of media and publishing and span the entire continent of Europe. Politically his publications are generally conservative, though not particularly pro-U.S.—"

"Why don't you stop right there," the Chairman said. Heidi had pushed a note in front of him. He read it slowly, elaborately, then held it up. "And what if I told you that we know the source of that information and that it's a crock!"

"This comes from very sensitive liaison arrangements with a friendly and reliable intelligence service—"

"Well, we didn't depend on anybody. We did our own little investigation. This Monsieur Bresson wasn't born in any concentration camp. His mother and father aren't Resistance heroes."

"Where did he come from?" the DDCI asked.

"That's what we want you to tell us!" He looked exasperated. "Did you-all know that his takeover of News/Worldweek is guaranteed by a Russian bank account?"

Heidi noticed a swift glance pass between the deputy director and his assistant.

"We haven't been collecting against that kind of target," the DDCI said.

"Why not?" the Chairman demanded.

"That isn't one of our intelligence priorities."

"Sounds like we need Miss Bruce's Economic Intelligence Bill after all," the Chairman said.

"Give us the information you've developed, and we'll follow up on it," the deputy CIA director said stoically.

"Damn right you will! I'm gonna give you everything. And in return, I want everything, and I mean everything you've got squirreled away out at Langley on this mystery man. If there's even the slightest suggestion that you're holding out, I'll get the Committee authority to subpoena your underwear."

"It could take some time, Mr. Chairman."

"I just came from having a good steam with the chairman of the Commerce Committee. We agreed to hold a public hearing with Marcel Bresson as the principal witness at eleven A.M. next Monday. I want you here no later than ten A.M. with your report."

De Grazia was worried. Deals had a rhythm, a pace. He could feel the momentum going out of this one. Bresson and Richardson weren't getting closure. Part of the problem was that Bresson kept disappearing. But for some reason, Drew Richardson was hesitating, too.

He had decided to have an "unauthorized" meeting with Blackie Muldoon, and found that he couldn't even get agreement on where to have a drink without a half-day of negotiation. First Blackie said Palio's, then "21." Next he suggested the Promenade Room, the bar next to the Rainbow Room on top of Rockefeller Center. Finally, he agreed to the China Grill at "Black Rock," the CBS Headquarters building. Now he was fifteen minutes late. While waiting, de Grazia ordered four raw kumimoto oysters in black bean vinaigrette to go with his Edna Valley Chardonnay. He would charge it to Bresson as an out-of-pocket expense.

He surveyed the restaurant again to make sure he hadn't missed Muldoon among the crowd of young professionals that thronged the bar. The room was huge, with three-story glass windows looking out on 53rd and a pocket park. He watched a man in the park fold up a card table and chair, put a mobile phone in his briefcase, place everything on a cart and roll it away. The man was rumored to have once worked for E. F. Hutton in the building next door until the merger with Shearson Lehman American Express. Then he was fired along with hundreds of others. Now, he was known as the homeless investment banker.

The bartender served the oysters. The restaurant, a spin-off from Stars in San Francisco, was fully booked at lunch by media executives who believed that nouvelle California Chinese food would help cut down their cholesterol. In the evening, the long bar dominating the center of the room provided R&R for the shock troops from the financial services boutiques and conglomerates that were turning Sixth Avenue in the mid-fifties into a new Wall Street. On any given day, Bruce Wasserstein could be seen lunching at Le Bernandin. His partner, Joe Perella, would be at Bellini. Henry Kravis seemed to like Palio's, and Michel David Weill of Lazard Frères remained loyal to "21." De Grazia had to admit that even the mere "gonna-bees" who flocked to the China Grill were far more attractive and put-together than their counterparts downtown. As de Grazia day-dreamed of how closing the News/Worldweek deal would lead to an offer from an uptown firm, he spotted Blackie Muldoon snaking through the crowd.

Blackie had no dreams that afternoon, only anxieties. Richardson was keeping him on an intolerably short leash. Bresson's generous offer had only confirmed Richardson's irrational belief that he was somehow in a strong position. Instead of seizing it, he was displaying the classic syndrome that affected CEOs who suddenly saw billions of dollars changing hands—greed.

"Sorry, I got caught in traffic," Blackie said as he pushed up to the bar.

"You told me that wouldn't happen if I moved uptown."

"Fuck you, de Grazia, I was just being polite." He ordered a lime Calistoga water.

"I'll be polite, too. What the hell's happening to our deal?"

"SOS."

"Same old shit?" He slurped down an oyster. "Money?"

Muldoon nodded.

"I was afraid of that. There's no way, shape or form that we can give you a better price."

"Price wouldn't help. Richardson finally woke up to the fact that his partners will own everything anyway."

"So what does he want?"

"Think of some new permutations and combinations."

"Cut the crap. What do we have to do to close the deal?"

Blackie downed the little bottle of soda water in one swallow. Then he belched. "I think you have to find a way to put some money in his pocket."

The harsh desert winds blowing across Interstate 10 rocked the Lincoln Town Car as Andy worked to keep it moving smoothly in a straight line. In the back seat, Lyman was lost in thought.

On Monday, he had tried to occupy himself with the details of life that he had long ignored. He paid bills, answered phone calls and letters, and even took his mother to lunch.

The lunch proved to be an ordeal, a relief and an inspiration. An ordeal, because all his mother wanted to talk about was Heidi Bruce. Who was she? Were they serious? She seemed like such a nice girl on the phone. Why hadn't they met? It was a relief because all of her illnesses seemed to have disappeared.

The lunch was an inspiration when she responded to his complaints about Bresson and Cooke by pointing out that he should discuss it with Billy Gould. As a result, Lyman and Andy had taken the morning United flight from JFK to Los Angeles and were now climbing over San Gorgonio Pass on their way to Palm Springs. Gould had been staying at the Eisenhower Medical Center getting ready for a quadruple bypass.

Everyone Lyman talked to in New York agreed that Bresson's take-over of News/Worldweek was not illegal. The word ethics never crossed anyone's lips. His mother's comment stimulated him to formulate the issue in terms of corporate image. Let Heidi worry about the law and politics. He understood business, and having a client like Marcel Bresson was bad business.

The morning *Wall Street Journal* reported that the Senate Commerce Committee would be holding hearings in less than a week. No secret lasted forever, and too many people already knew about Bresson. When the story came out, it would reflect badly on Gould Axewroth. The firm was already shaky; the partners' capital would be placed in jeopardy. Cooke was blinded by Bresson's fee and the need to hold onto his position. But Billy Gould's name and posterity were at stake. He would understand.

"Pardon me, Mr. Lyman," Andy interrupted, "but what's that?" He pointed off to the north. Miles and miles of barren desert were covered by thousands and thousands of tall towers topped with long awkward propellers. "Looks like an army of Martians," he said uneasily.

"It's just a deal," Lyman reassured him. "A deal gone sour. That's a 'wind farm.' Under Jimmy Carter, the Feds gave tax credits for alternative energy projects. The government decided that wind farms were better for the environment than coal or oil."

"It's ugly as hell, if you'll pardon the expression." Coming from Andy, who lived in Passaic, New Jersey, that was a harsh judgment.

"It's worse than ugly," Lyman replied. "First, energy prices dropped. Then the tax credits dried up. Finally, just so the investors would be totally screwed, the IRS came out here and saw that a third of these windmills don't work. They cut the tax credits retroactively. Investors had to give back thirty percent."

"You can't trust the Feds," Andy said.

"That's for sure." Lyman thought of Heidi and her misplaced faith in government. Bresson posed a business threat. He had to be dealt with by business methods.

The Eisenhower Medical Center was located in Rancho Mirage, a suburb of Palm Springs—if a suburb can have a suburb. They turned off I-10 onto Bob Hope Drive and proceeded for a few miles until they came to Doris Day Drive. The landscape was a bizarre checkerboard of empty, bone-white tracts of desert, walled-in housing developments surrounding lush green golf courses, and abandoned groves of date palms which served as breeding grounds for clouds of flies. Golf appeared to be the organizing principle of existence. A billboard boasted that the valley had seventy-two golf courses. Jayson Lyman shuddered that corporate titans like Walter Annenberg would choose such desolation for the last chapter of their lives.

At the Eisenhower Center, the receptionist startled Lyman by announcing that Mr. Gould expected to see him in the operating room. A male nurse escorted him to a small lounge where the doctors changed into their surgical gowns. Lyman undressed, placed his clothes in a locker, and put on green cotton pants and shirt, together with a paper hat and booties. The TV set was on, and Lyman noticed that the doctors were tuned into the Financial News Network.

The nurse escorted him down the hall and through a double set of doors into an operating room. The person on the table was covered by sheets so that Lyman could not tell which end was which, but the patient's middle was open, and heavy work was going on inside. Billy Gould sat perched on a high stool, alternately peering into the cavity and watching a color video monitor. He breathed through a mask connected by a tube to an oxygen tank. His greeting to Lyman was an indifferent handshake.

"What's going on here?" Lyman whispered.

"Bypass," Gould answered. "And you don't have to be quiet. The patient can't hear you. That's the heart-lung machine." He pointed to a pile of machinery tended by a man reading a copy of *USA Today.*

A plastic hose full of dark red blood emerged from under the sheets and ran into a round apparatus. A circular cam pressed against the hose, moving the blood along the way children squeeze Coke from a straw. That was the heart. The line then fed into the top of a two-foot-tall transparent cylinder that sat on the floor. The blood was sprayed downward from the top and then bubbled through a set of plates where it was frothed with air. A series of traps and filters kept the bubbles from entering the bloodstream.

"Look at the monitors," Gould ordered. "You get a close-up. See that thing flopping around that looks like a fish? That's his lungs. You should've been here at the beginning when they used an electric hand-saw to open up his chest."

Lyman felt slightly green. "Why are you watching this?"

"I'm scheduled for one of these. I like to know what I'm getting into."

Lyman picked up the thought. "That's why I asked to see you so urgently. The firm's getting into something we'll all regret."

"How so?" Gould sucked harder on the oxygen.

"Marcel Bresson and News/Worldweek. It's a big fee, but Bresson's the target of a Senate Intelligence Committee investigation. There'll be a big hearing next week. I know for a fact that he's been involved in criminal activity in Europe, maybe even murder, and he's getting his money from very unsavory places." Lyman stopped short of naming the Russians, because no one ever believed him.

"I see what you mean," Gould said, but his attention was focused on the doctor's needle and thread work.

"Will you help me to get the firm to drop him as a client?"

"I can't do that."

"Why not?"

"I've optioned all my shares in the firm."

"Sold all of them?" Lyman could not believe it. "Including the Axewroth family shares?"

"Jayson, there isn't any Axewroth family. Never was an Axewroth. In the old days you had to have a WASP running the syndication department, or the white-shoe firms wouldn't answer your phone calls." He took a long pull on the oxygen. "So I went 'em one better. I found an Anglo-Saxon to be my partner. Actually, he was my butler. His name was Jones. That sounded too cheapside, so I made up Axewroth."

"But the stock was yours?"

He nodded.

"And who did you sell to?"

"The man who's buying the firm," he said evasively. "It'll all be announced when the News/Worldweek tender closes."

"Buying the firm?" Lyman had a sinking feeling. He really did not want to press the question, but he did.

"Who's that?"

Gould took a deep breath before answering. "Marcel Bresson."

"I don't give a goddamn what some simpering senior vice president says," Leonard Kleinman thundered, "I'm the managing editor of this newspaper, and I decide what we print!"

"The order came down from Richardson himself," the assistant editor of the *Washington News* said nervously. "It covered all News/Worldweek companies without exception."

They were standing at the doorway of Kleinman's glass-walled office on the edge of the city room.

"Richardson could be out on his ass in less than ten days. We all could be on the street if this Frenchman takes over. I want the senior editorial staff in my office in ten minutes."

As they filed into his room, carrying their own folding chairs, Kleinman kept his head buried in the morning edition of the *Washington News.* After everyone had arrived, he continued reading for another five minutes. Then he neatly folded the paper and leaned back with his hands behind his head.

"You all did a great job while I was away in China," he began quietly. "I've only got one question."

The assembled editors knew enough to stay quiet.

He leaned toward the editor of the Sports section, "Billy, what's the most important on-going story in Washington today?"

The last to arrive, Billy had no idea what the meeting was about. He looked around and grinned. "That we might, maybe, possibly, finally, get a major league baseball team again?"

Kleinman clapped his hands. "Now there's a man who's focused! He knows his beat. What if I asked you that question?" He pointed at the Business section editor. "Or you, or you." He turned to the Feature section, and the Metropolitan section. "Or you!" He ended with the national editor.

"Okay Len," the national editor responded. "We'd all say the News/Worldweek takeover, but—"

"Then why is it buried on page five of the Business section? This is the biggest story in town, maybe in the country. The Congress is holding hearings in both House and Senate, and we're printing press releases, for Christ's sake!"

They all talked at once to defend themselves.

He cut them off. "Don't tell me about any gag order from Drew Richardson. If that was serious, I would have expected every one of you either to resign or be fired."

Len Kleinman stood up. That meant assignments were coming.

"I want the Business section to run a continuing series dissecting every aspect of Marcel Bresson's empire. Feature, I want you to get the most vicious reporter on your staff to bore into every corner of Bresson's personal life. Ditto Richardson. Metropolitan, I want stories on how this takeover fight is affecting this company. I want reaction of everybody from the executives down to the paper boys. Foreign, get our correspondents digging into Bresson's impact on other countries, how he uses his political clout. Get me quotes from foreign politicians, intellectuals, journalists, anybody!"

He paused and looked at the national editor. "I want this story on the front page every day."

"What are we going to write? Take today for example. Nothing's happening."

"How about starting with the fact that the board of News/Worldweek tried to keep us from covering this story!"

There was an uneasy silence. Then the sports editor raised his hand. "Len, what do I do on this one?"

"Billy, I'm glad you asked," Kleinman said. "You get an interview with Marcel Bresson on what he's going to do about bringing major league baseball back to Washington."

Lyman and Andy filed off the Pan Am Shuttle at the North Terminal of Washington's National Airport. Two of Andy's friends met them at the curb with a rented Cadillac Fleetwood equipped with bulletproof windows. "It didn't cost much more than a regular Caddy," Andy explained, "so why take the chance?"

Lyman had an 11:30 appointment with Raffy Nichols. He didn't know where else to turn. Bresson had outmaneuvered him. He was out of the deal and soon he would be out of Gould Axewroth. During the long flight back from the coast, Lyman concluded that Bresson did not have the money to buy his firm unless the News/Worldweek deal went through. The $60 million fee would be Gould Axewroth's principal cash asset. Bresson would borrow against it, then buy his firm using its own money as a down payment. He would end up getting junk bonds for his partnership shares. Lyman had to stop the News/Worldweek transaction. Raffy was the only one in the entire deal that he could still talk to. Thank God he cared about something other than money.

As the limo crossed the 14th Street Bridge, Lyman imagined Heidi arguing that he was only acting out of self-interest. The hell with her. Maybe he was the sort of person who needed material incentives. Being near her in Washington brought back memories of how she smelled in the dark after making love.

Lyman knocked on the window to the driver's seat, "Hey, who's guarding Miss Bruce?"

"We got into a little problem," Andy answered for them. "The boys got arrested last night by the Capitol Police."

"What happened?"

"Apparently Miss Bruce took exception to bein' followed around. We explained we was protectin' her for you. But she wasn't very gregacious about it."

"What did she say?"

"I don't think I should repeat it. She's got a pretty tough mouth."

Lyman could only remember how soft it was. Could he possibly come to Washington without trying to reach her? He tried to think of Sammy, but she did not fill the hollow place in his chest.

The long black car pulled up to a large shed in an alley just off of Columbia Road in Washington's Latin barrio. The walls were spray-painted with "U.S. Hands off Guatemala" and *"Yanqui fuera del Centro America."*

"This is Mr. Nichols's studio," Andy assured him.

Inside, Lyman found a huge room divided by a transparent plastic curtain. One side had been separated into a half-dozen work stations where young men and women were busy at computers. The other half was filled with a pile of enormous objects that were difficult to discern through the plastic sheet. When Lyman stepped through the curtain, he could see that they were giant pieces of jewelry, gold rings four feet across and monster bracelets and twenty-foot diamond necklaces and huge pearl earrings and towering jeweled tiaras—all looking remarkably real, but so out of scale Lyman felt like an ant. Raffy stood on a tall ladder spraying something noxious on an emerald scepter. He waved and climbed down.

"Good to see you, Jay," he said, pulling off his respirator. "Let me get out of this." He unzipped his overalls, and to Lyman's surprise emerged in a button-down shirt and tie. "Let's talk in the office, it smells better in there."

"What happened to the vegetables?" Lyman asked.

"Too perishable. Now I'm into things of enduring value. You taught me that."

Raffy's office looked like the library of a French château. Through the windows he could see beautiful formal gardens.

"It's a stage set. I bought the scenery from the National Theater," Raffy explained as he put on a suit jacket. "See"—he poked the walls—"it's made of canvas."

"Very ingenious," Lyman allowed. "I hope you can be as creative about a little problem with the News/Worldweek deal."

"Anything you want. Thanks to you, we're going to get top dollar for our shares. What's up?"

Lyman went through the story carefully, leaving out only the parts he considered tangential to the transaction—like the fact that he had robbed a bank, almost been murdered and run over someone with a bus. Raffy listened attentively.

"Pretty wild," he said when Lyman had finished. "But I don't think I can help you."

"Why not?" Lyman could not keep the sound of failure out of his voice.

"You saw all those people out there at the computers. You know what they're doing? Financial analysis. We're going to clear a billion and a half dollars on our News/Worldweek stock. I've got to figure out what to do with it."

"A high-grade problem," Lyman agreed.

"Really challenging. I'm so busy, I'm having a tough time finishing my new sculpture in time for a show next week at the Corcoran! The deal flow's unbelievable! The phone's ringing off the hook with proposals from your buddies on Wall Street. They want me to get into hostile takeovers. We ought to talk about that. Maybe you could help me. But I can't stop this deal. I've got fiduciary responsibilities. My sister. Other members of my family. Not to mention some new partners. If you had an alternative . . ."

"Not at the moment," Lyman admitted.

"Sorry, Jay," Raffy said, pulling on his artist's overalls again, "but business is business."

Sean Gordon's assistant was waiting for him on the tarmac as the C-141 "Starlifter" whined to a halt in front of the Special Air Mission terminal at Andrews Air Force Base. They found each other among a crowd of happy families welcoming their boys home from Europe.

"I've got a car and driver." Gordon's assistant pointed toward the street. "The deputy director said he wanted to see you as soon as you landed."

"Why?"

"They're pretty strung-out about the blow-up in Vienna."

"What line are they taking?" Gordon asked as he got into the car.

"The front office acts mystified." His assistant joined him in the back seat. "The DDO says you're off on your own again, and demands you be reined in. CI's defending you, saying it's part of our effort to track down the security break, but privately they're real pissed that you haven't kept them informed."

"What've you been saying?"

"I've tried to appear as though I know something but can't tell them. It was either that or just look stupid."

"I think it's time we all got educated. Keep operations out of it. Work with Counterintelligence. Dig up everything you can on current Soviet agent of influence operations. Go through all the old KGB defectors reports."

"Sean, Jesus! Most of that defector stuff isn't even on computer. Nosenko was interrogated nonstop for a year!"

"I want you to check all of it," Gordon said flatly.

"Excuse me," the driver interrupted, "but do you want to take the Beltway?"

"If that's the fastest way to Langley," Sean Gordon replied.

When the doorbell rang, Jayson Lyman realized that he had overslept. He wrapped a tattered bathrobe around himself and went to the door. Carol Rankin was waiting, all bright and smiling.

"Am I early?"

"No, no. I'm a little slow off the mark this morning. You've been able to arrange everything?"

"The children are at their grandparents. I've got the whole weekend free."

Lyman ushered her into a small room with doors to a tiny garden. A desk and computer took up most of the space.

"The computer's a Compaq 386 with a forty-meg hard disk and another megabyte of RAM above the main board."

"If it runs DOS and OS2, we'll be fine," she said.

"You fire it up," Lyman said, "and I'll put on some clothes."

Lyman could no longer work out of his office. De Grazia and Cooke had cut him off from the firm's computer. He believed his office phone was tapped. He wasn't even sure he could trust Marlene, his secretary for six years. Fortunately, he had found his News/Worldweek files still stuffed in a briefcase that he had left in his closet upon returning from Bürgenstock. He had managed to sneak his all-important Rolodex out of the office in the middle of the night, wrapped in dirty laundry.

Lyman had set up shop in his apartment. The computer, printer and fax were rented. A new telephone line and number cost him almost a thousand dollars to avoid a three-week waiting period. Andy made the payoffs and supervised the installation, to be sure it came bug-free. Carol Rankin was happy to work part-time as an assistant and analyst.

Lyman was about to jeopardize his professional reputation by searching for someone other than Marcel Bresson to buy News/Worldweek. Selling a target company out from under your firm's client violated one of the few remaining rules in the merger business. But it wouldn't be his firm for long unless he did exactly that.

"I want you to focus on possible corporate buyers," Lyman explained to Carol. He had pulled on jeans and a sweatshirt, and was making coffee. "Most media companies can't swallow the whole deal without antitrust problems. So we're basically looking for firms in related businesses that might take a big piece. Get a readout on their acquisition policy, and go through their financials to see if they've got the cash or borrowing power to be serious players. I'm hooked into Compuserve. They should have all the necessary data."

As she started her search for corporate buyers, Lyman began to call the financial players who could react fast and who cared less about the company's business than its balance sheet. Since a single buyer was unlikely, Lyman's strategy was to sell News/Worldweek as a bust-up. He planned to stitch together a consortium: the corporate buyers would take pieces; the financial players would cash out as the company was liquidated. Pricing the parts in the short time before Bresson's tender offer expired would be impossible. Instead, Lyman proposed to put a global value on the company, get the interested parties to take shares and then later swap stock for assets in a tax-free transaction. He knew it was a real long shot.

His list of financial entrepreneurs included Jay Pritzker, who owned half of Chicago as well as General Dynamics; Victor Palmieri, who had saved the Penn Central Company and Baldwin United; Sid Bass, who had redoubled his uncle's oil fortune by opportunistic investments in everything from Disney to Texaco; and Richard Rainwater, who had once worked for Bass but now commanded an investment fund of almost a billion dollars. Lyman once did a $500 million deal with Rainwater in fifteen minutes at a Fort Worth ice cream store during a birthday party for Rainwater's seven-year-old daughter. Lyman even put in a call to T. Boone Pickens.

He also tried to reach entrepreneurial media tycoons like Malcolm Forbes, J. J. Curley of Gannett, and Ted Turner. Several people on his list said they would not even consider his proposal unless Lyman could assure them that Donald Trump would not be in the deal.

By Friday evening, several of Lyman's calls had generated interest in seeing his material on News/Worldweek. To the question of what was happening with Bresson, and how he fit into the deal, Lyman tantalized them with "If you're still interested when you've read the sales memo, then I'll explain."

Lyman and Carol Rankin worked all night on the sales memo, much of it cribbed from his presentation to Bresson at Bürgenstock. She finished typing at three in the morning, and he began proofing while she slept on the couch. At four, he started sending it out on his fax machine. He did so with a powerful premonition that he was going to get his ass sued off.

Saturday morning, after a few hours' sleep, Lyman began his corporate calls. Few CEOs were in their offices, and he refused to talk with presidents or chief financial officers. He had to stimulate the imagination of the top decisionmaker. Such an unorthodox concept would be nibbled to death by bureaucratic goslings. Lyman expected to catch a lot of chief executives playing golf or on the tennis courts, but he was surprised to find many of them out buying antiques. It was a leading indicator that inflation was coming back.

By midafternoon, the responses were flowing in. Rupert Murdoch was strongly tempted, but he wanted only those parts of the business that would give him a rematch with Senator Edward M. Kennedy, who had passed a special law forcing Murdoch to sell the *New York Post*. Only later had the law been struck down as unconstitutional.

Almost everyone wanted to buy the TV stations and the *Washington News*. Nobody wanted the TV production company or the wire service. Carl Icahn and Irwin Jacobs both would take the film studio for its Los Angeles real estate, but neither wanted the film library. Several companies wanted the cable TV properties, but were already quibbling about price.

By Sunday, Lyman had a hodgepodge of interested parties, all expressing conditions and reservations and proposing complicated schemes of participation in the transaction. It all added up to a definite maybe.

Exhausted, Lyman let Carol Rankin go home, and then did something that he knew was stupid. He called Heidi Bruce.

She had been sitting on her bed eating ice cream, watching TV and thinking about him. Her conclusion was that she should have nothing to do with either Lyman or Sean Gordon once the Bresson thing was finished. At lunch with her girlfriend over the weekend, she had already announced that she was giving up men altogether.

She had to be cold and rational. There was no way to be just friends with Sean. Underneath his aloof and mysterious professional demeanor, she knew he was very needy. And very sexy. That did not bode well for platonic camping trips in the Shenandoah. Besides, by the time their first child was out of college, he'd be in his sixties! And he already had a son. Of course, who was thinking about getting married anyway?

Jayson Lyman, she decided, was too much like her—only on an alien wavelength. Government existed on another planet as far as he was concerned. She had to admit that she felt the same way about the deal business. But why did she have to choose between Washington and Wall Street? What about the rest of the universe? They could explore it together if Lyman weren't so stubborn, narrow-minded and totally lacking in moral principle. No, she would have nothing more to do with him.

But she took his call.

"I know you're having the Bresson hearing tomorrow," he explained, "and I thought I might wish you luck."

"What's happening with him?" she asked neutrally.

"I don't really know. I've been kicked off the deal."

"I'm sorry," she said sincerely.

"I'm trying to find another buyer for News/Worldweek. That's the only way I can see to stop him."

"And I suppose you'll still get tens of millions of dollars in commission?"

"Jesus Christ, Heidi! I only know how to do what I know how to do! If you and your friend Sean can slow Bresson down a little, put a dent in his credibility, I'll have a better chance to put together an alternative buyout group!"

Heidi bristled. How like Jayson to think Sean was doing it all. "It's my hearing. I'm doing just fine all by myself. When I get done with Bresson tomorrow, he'll be afraid to shake his head."

"Well," Lyman said wearily, "I'm glad everything's going so well for you."

There was a pause on the line. By the time Heidi managed to say she was glad he called, he had hung up.

24

They looked like a flying wedge coming down the second floor hallway toward the Senate's Central Hearing Facility. Heidi had difficulty keeping up and briefing the Chairman at the same time, particularly since the staff director asserted his prerogatives by sticking firmly to the Chairman's side. Every time they passed someone in the hall, Heidi had to fall to the rear.

"So it comes down to two alternative lines of questioning," she was saying. "You can assert the facts as we've developed them and force a denial, or you can set him up by asking simple questions like where he was born and then trap him. Your notebook is structured for either approach."

"What about the CIA?" the Chairman asked.

"They insist they've nothing more on him."

"What about the material you gave them on Bresson?"

"They claim they haven't had time to check it out."

"Who do they think they're messin' with?" the Chairman said angrily. "I'm gonna cut them a new . . ." he did not complete the sentence. He never said "asshole" in front of a lady.

They turned into a narrow corridor that led to the rear of the hearing room. Heidi had to drop back into third place.

"That's why it's important to get Bresson on the record as much as possible," she shouted.

"Don't worry, darlin'," the Chairman called back, "I always believe in lettin' a man hang himself."

The Central Hearing Facility was designed to bring the U.S. Senate into the television age. A room the size of three basketball courts, it had wood-paneled walls that opened up on both sides for cameras, and windows high in the back and on the right for the news anchors. Heidi was pleased to see that all the networks plus CNN and C-Span were covering the hearing. She had been on the phone all week trying to persuade them to come, but had had no success until the *Washington News* started running stories about Bresson on the front page.

The Senators took their seats in front of a huge marble slab which had been selected to provide an impressive backdrop for the tube. Heidi slid into a seat behind her Chairman. He would not run the hearing. That would be done by the chairman of the Commerce Committee, which officially sponsored the session. The chairmen of several other committees had also been invited to participate. Senators were so deferential in their speech that Heidi anticipated a bewildering display of chairmen addressing one another as "Mr. Chairman."

As the clock approached 10:00 A.M., the hearing room was packed and a line of people waiting to get inside had formed down the hall. The press galleries were full. Both CNN and C-Span had lights on in their anchor booths indicating that they were carrying it live. An excited sense of anticipation flowed from the staff through the Senators to the press corps, all primed by a systematic series of phone calls from Heidi suggesting that the hearing would produce fireworks.

By ten o'clock, the time for the hearing to start, Marcel Bresson had not appeared. Neither had his lawyers nor any other representative. At ten past the hour, the Senators began to fidget. "Where the hell is this guy?" Heidi's chairman growled. She looked baffled. Soon, the audience and press corps began to grow restless. The Commerce Committee chairman looked up and down the row of Senators and staff as if someone should have an explanation of why the star witness was late. He started polling his colleagues about whether to start the hearing without Bresson.

Finally, at twenty-two minutes after ten, a young man in a three-piece suit came through the large center doors at the rear of the hearing room and marched up to the witness table.

"Who are you?" the Chair demanded.

He tapped the microphone to see if it were live. It was.

"I'm from Skadden Fried. We represent Mr. Bresson."

"Where is he?"

"He's had a medical emergency. He won't be able to testify today."

"I extend the committee's condolences," the Chair said without a trace of sympathy. "What kind of emergency?"

"Dental surgery for the removal of a tooth," the young lawyer responded.

"The old dentist ploy!" the Chairman of the Intelligence Committee roared. "Mr. Chairman, I urge the committee to demand proof that this emergency is real. If Monsieur Bresson is ducking this inquiry, I recommend he be subpoenaed!"

"We would be happy to provide the committee with the name of the oral surgeon in New York who performed the procedure," the lawyer said. "I can assure you, our client is not attempting to avoid an appearance before the committee."

"Fine. Then we will reschedule his testimony for Wednesday, October eighth. Assuming he has no complications."

"Thank you for your consideration, Mr. Chairman," the lawyer said.

"And to guard against any complications," the Chair added, "we'll prepare a subpoena as well."

He hammered for order and continued. "Mr. Bresson's not the only witness scheduled today. We're examining the vital question of how much foreign ownership of American business is consistent with our national sovereignty and well-being." He began reading from a prepared text. "This raises fundamental choices about our commitment to free trade and free capital markets, as well as crucial issues involving our basic freedoms set forth in the Constitution and Bill of Rights. We will now hear from Professor . . ."

But by that time, the cameramen were packing and most of the press was headed for the doors. Half the Senators and staff also had disappeared out the back. Heidi and her Chairman were among the first.

Lyman switched off the TV set. He could not wait until Wednesday. Time had become the most important factor. Lyman needed time to put his buyout team together, work out differences, secure financing. But the passage of time also slowed the momentum he had gained from the novelty of his idea. Potential players would start to have more and more doubts about whether he could pull it off. From bitter experience, Lyman knew that deals were not the product of rational calculation of cost and benefit. They were emotional roller coasters, in which reason took a backseat to the glory of winning and the fear of being a loser.

Without some new element, he was dead in the water. No, that was optimistic. Doing deals, you were either moving forward or sliding backward. He could not sit around and wait for Heidi's hearings to derail Bresson's juggernaut. Lyman had to act. But what could he do that he had not done already? All of his buyers were waiting for someone else to make an irrevocable commitment. He needed a partner who was determined to do the deal. Lyman could think of only one alternative.

He placed the call. The secretary put him through immediately.

"This is Jayson Lyman."

"Yes, Jayson, what can I do for you?"

"I have a concept that will materially increase your chances of success."

"You do? Well, I hope you won't mind my putting you on the speaker phone, so we can all hear what you have to say."

Lyman could not miss the snide tone in his voice. Working with Drew Richardson would not only test his skill as a dealmaker, he knew it would also be an exercise in humiliation.

De Grazia paced the lobby of the Stanhope Hotel. This was the showdown, and Marcel Bresson was late. He had urged a premeeting strategy session, but Bresson said he had another engagement. What else could be more important?

Drew Richardson had arrived exactly on time and was already in the suite. With egos as big as these two, it was a bad omen for one to jerk the other around by making him wait. De Grazia went out to the curb to look up the street.

The sidewalk café was already filling with customers from the Metropolitan Museum across the street. Straining to see every limousine as it came down Fifth Avenue, de Grazia missed Bresson getting out of a plain blue Ford a block away. When he saw him crossing at the corner, de Grazia was stunned by the swelling on the side of Bresson's face.

"How do you feel?" he asked.

"Terrible," Bresson responded. "We will finish this negotiation today. I am not giving up another tooth to escape the committee."

"Richardson may try to stall to see how the hearing comes out tomorrow," de Grazia warned.

"If that's his plan," Bresson responded as they entered the elevator, "he makes a big mistake."

From the window of the fifth-floor suite, Richardson watched Bresson get out of the car up the street. "Cheap bastard," he said to Blackie Muldoon. "No wonder he's embarrassed to come to the hotel entrance, look what he drives around in." He expected intense pressure from Bresson and was pumping himself up to meet it. He was determined to string him along, then, after the hearing, he could move toward either Bresson or Lyman. Or perhaps he wouldn't need either one of them. The door opened and Bresson entered the suite. Richardson offered a pro forma handshake. They each took a seat facing one another on the separate couches that flanked the fireplace. Coffee, tea and Perrier were available on the coffee table between them. De Grazia spoke first.

"Maybe I should summarize where we stand."

Richardson nodded his agreement. He did not want to have to begin by reacting to Bresson's offer at their last meeting.

"We propose to sell you the News/Worldweek TV stations, the movie studio with the film library and certain cable franchises for $1.2 billion. Those are essentially the crown jewels that you sought from the board. We believe that $1.2 billion is a bargain price for those properties. In exchange, you drop your buyout effort and support our offer," de Grazia concluded. "We stand by our tender offer for fifty-one percent of the stock at $55 cash, but having seen the books, we're prepared to up the back end to $47 in debentures."

"Since Mr. Bresson can't legally own the TV stations," Blackie Muldoon responded, "we believe we're doing you a favor by taking them off your hands. And as I mentioned to Mr. de Grazia, price is not the only consideration."

"I did not come here to listen to our advisors haggle." Bresson addressed Richardson directly. "I have talked with Karl Zeeberg. He will pay $1.3 billion for the package I have offered you."

That son of a bitch, Richardson thought, turning red.

"He's Canadian," Blackie said. "He can't own the TV stations either."

"The stations would go in the name of his brother who lives in L.A.," de Grazia explained.

"I can do the deal with him," Bresson continued. "But I prefer you. It would be smoother, make less difficulties for the company."

Richardson knew he was talking about the board. He could feel his leverage increasing the more Bresson talked.

"So I am prepared to undertake the following. You would step down as CEO, thus triggering your golden parachute, but you would become a consultant at an annual compensation of $200,000 per year plus expenses. In addition, you would receive, before the acquisition is completed, 100,000 shares of News/Worldweek stock at an option price of $12, which you could tender at $47 a share. That would amount to $3.2 million for your options."

Without hesitating, Richardson said, "Two hundred and fifty thousand shares."

Bresson paused, looked at de Grazia and said, "Done."

Richardson sighed. "Well that's a very interesting proposition. I'll have to give it some consideration." He was wondering how much more he could squeeze out of Bresson.

"I understand that the proposal is complex and that it is a difficult decision for you," Bresson said easily. "And I assume you would like to talk with your advisors, perhaps even consult with Jayson Lyman."

Richardson was startled by the mention of Lyman.

"That is why," Bresson continued in the same calm voice, "You will answer, yes or no, right now."

"It's the Director of the CIA," Heidi's secretary said. "He wants to talk to the staff director."

"Put him through to me," she ordered.

"Just a moment," she pushed a button on the telephone console, "pick up on 07."

"This is Heidi Bruce. . . . No, the staff director is not here, he'll be out of town for a few days. . . . A meeting with the Chairman? Before the hearing? . . . I'd have to check his schedule, but I would think he could squeeze you in. I'll call if there's any problem. Otherwise, plan on the Senator's office at nine fifteen." Heidi put down the phone, "Yowee! The DCI wants to personally brief the Chairman on Bresson tomorrow," Heidi exulted. "We've got 'em!"

"Gee, that's great," her assistant said. "Because I think this is bad news." She handed Heidi a bulletin from the Reuters ticker.

New York October 6 (Reuters) Representatives of Les Éditions Bresson and the buyout group led by News/Worldweek executive Drew Richardson announced today that they had agreed to join forces to acquire the giant media conglomerate. Under terms yet to be disclosed, it is understood that Richardson will purchase the broadcast TV stations and other properties. In exchange, Richardson will withdraw his bid and recommend that the News/Worldweek board approve Bresson's most recent tender offer. This virtually assures that the French media magnate will acquire the company, barring a last-minute hitch, which some observers believe might arise at tomorrow's Senate hearings. (More to come.)

Heidi immediately thought of Jayson. He must be crushed. She tried his office. He was not in. She punched up his home number. On the third ring, a woman answered. Heidi hesitated, then put down the phone.

In New York, Carol Rankin looked at Lyman's phone and shook her head. "Whoever it was, they hung up," she said.

"They probably heard the news," Lyman said, turning off *Wall Street Round-Up*. He had just seen the report of the Bresson/Richardson deal. "They know we're dead."

He thought briefly of calling Heidi, but what would he say? He had nothing to offer her now.

Heidi watched from the second-floor balcony as the Director of Central Intelligence made his way across the marble-clad atrium of the Hart Senate Office Building. He was accompanied by a retinue of three bodyguards and two assistants. As he passed under the giant black stabile, "Mountains and Clouds," Alexander Calder's last work, Heidi could see that the DCI's aides were not the usual bag-carriers and congressional-liaison types. One was the CIA's general counsel and the other the head of the Clandestine Service. Whatever they planned to say, it must be serious.

At CIA insistence, the meeting had been shifted from the Senator's office to the Secure Classified Information Facility. The agency usually preferred to massage Senators in the comfort of their private offices. The CIA Director's insistence on meeting in the SCIF further under-scored the sensitivity of the information he planned to provide.

Heidi used the telephone at the guard desk to advise the Chairman that the DCI was on his way. When the CIA chief arrived, Heidi showed him and his two assistants into the hearing room. The body-guards waited outside.

The Director of Central Intelligence was a large, avuncular and slightly disheveled-looking man who had once been a Congressman and thus enjoyed sympathetic relations with Capitol Hill. He was the soul of courtesy and friendliness, precisely why the President had picked him. However, no one had ever accused him of being on top of his job. He was only wheeled out in a crisis.

The Chairman arrived and shook hands all around. Before he could begin the proceedings, the CIA director surprised him by taking the initiative.

"Mr. Chairman, we need to talk in private."

Heidi glanced over at her boss. She knew that those were the words that every chairman of the Senate Intelligence Committee dreaded. Not only did it usually mean bad news, but it made him an accessory to the secret being shared. It deprived him of anonymity should he have to resort to the Senate's ultimate weapon against CIA foolishness—the leak.

"You've got us outnumbered already," the Chairman pointed out. "Your people can sit outside if they want. Anything you tell me, you can tell Miss Bruce."

"We're appearing here under the special procedures of the Intelligence Oversight Act," announced the CIA general counsel.

They're really upping the ante, Heidi thought. When the Senate passed the Bill establishing oversight of the U.S. intelligence community, they created a special restricted arrangement for sharing the most sensitive operational information. That procedure not only excluded the staff, but also all the other Senators on the committee except the vice chairman. Heidi knew she was out of the meeting.

"That's fine by me, Mr. Chairman," Heidi said to preempt further useless argument. The last thing she wanted was for the Chairman to refuse to hear what the CIA director had to say. "Let me just show you what's in your folder."

As he took his chair, she bent over him and whispered, "The key point is that his identity for the first fifteen years of his life is false. There's layer upon layer of phony stories about who he is, and how he was born, that cannot be substantiated. This is characteristic of a 'legend,' the false identity of an intelligence agent. We've no proof that he's an agent except that his current effort to take over News/Worldweek is secretly guaranteed by an agency of the Soviet government. See if they know these facts, and if they do, demand to know why they've withheld the information from the committee."

"I'll try my best to live up to your expectations," the Chairman said dryly.

Heidi and the CIA general counsel sat in the tiny reception area by the guard desk. The general counsel looked the perfect combination of corporate lawyer and spy. Medium build, medium height, medium brown hair, middle-aged, gray suit, nondescript tie, he seemed to disappear in front of her eyes. She made several efforts to get him to talk about what was going on inside. Nothing worked.

Checking the clock over the guard desk, she worried that the Agency was giving the Chairman a snow job. She had to have faith. He was tough, and wasn't exactly a summer intern. But she watched with growing concern as the clock approached 10:00, the time the Bresson hearing began. The Central Conference Facility was next door and she could hear the audience lining up outside in the hall.

At a quarter past ten, Heidi considered sending in a note to remind the Chairman that he was fifteen minutes late. What could they be talking about? She was sure that CIA was making the matter as complex as possible, if only to diffuse their own responsibility for failing to tell the committee about Bresson.

Finally, at 10:30 the Chairman emerged, looking grim. Heidi knew better than to ask any questions until they were well away from the CIA officials. As they worked their way up the narrow corridor behind the walls of the Central Hearing Facility, she said, "Is there something I should know?" She tried not to sound eager.

The Chairman shook his head and said nothing.

The hearing was well under way. Bresson sat alone at the table in front of the Senators listening to a question about the loyalty of the press.

"To whom does it owe allegiance?" the Chair was asking. "To the country in which it operates, or to the owner of the newspaper or cable channel?"

"I believe the press owes its allegiance to the truth," Bresson said. "Now you may ask, what is the truth? Some say that the facts are the truth. Others say that facts are merely stones on a pile waiting to be assembled according to ideas, concepts and values. To my way of thinking, a free press owes its allegiance first to the facts, and beyond that, to the democratic values that make a free press possible."

Heidi wanted to throw up. It wasn't just Bresson's treacly and well-rehearsed answers. Her chairman's uncommunicative attitude made the butterflies in her stomach feel like bats. He was scribbling furiously on a sheet of paper in his briefing folder. From over his shoulder, she could see it was not a document she had prepared. He then wrote a note which he sent down the line of Senators to the Chair. Usually, he would have had Heidi carry it.

"Is there anything I can do?" she whispered anxiously.

As he saw the Chair nod in his direction, he said, "No, we're in good shape now."

As he concluded his questions, the Chair announced that he would skip over the regular committee members to give the floor to some of the Senators from other committees who had been invited to participate. He would start with the Chairman of the Intelligence Committee. Heidi edged forward in her chair.

"Mr. Bresson, you probably wonder why the Chairman of the Intelligence Committee would be interested in your business affairs."

Heidi began to relax. He was following her script. That was the question she had been using to tease the press.

Bresson smiled. A battery of photo flashes exploded on the right.

"I'm here," the Chairman continued, "because the Intelligence Committee is deeply concerned about 'disinformation'—Soviet propaganda disguised as real news and designed to discredit the United States and advance Soviet interests."

That was not exactly how Heidi proposed to proceed, but she had to admit it was not a bad tack to take.

"In the media you now own, Mr. Bresson, how do you deal with such covert propaganda efforts, and what safeguards do you plan for the media in this country?"

Where the hell did that question come from? she wondered. Is that what the CIA was being so hush-hush about? She considered "disinformation" an obsession of the lunatic fringe. No matter how technically sophisticated, most Soviet disinformation, forged letters from U.S. ambassadors, bogus White House memos and the like, almost always turned out to be politically crude and far less damaging than what politicians in most democracies routinely said about their governments.

". . . check sources carefully," Bresson was responding. "We follow the American custom of insisting on at least three sources for every story, which as you know, is not a common practice in Europe."

With that out of the way, Heidi thought impatiently, maybe we can get to the meat.

"Thank you, Mr. Bresson," her chairman said. "It's rare for top American media executives to come and share their philosophy with the Congress. That you have done so, is to be commended."

Don't go overboard, Heidi said to herself.

"I'm sure we'll all benefit from this testimony. If only the American press were as responsive and forthcoming, it might enjoy a more positive public reputation."

Come on! Stick it to him, Heidi silently urged.

"I have no more questions for the witness," the Chairman of the Intelligence Committee concluded.

Heidi thought that she hadn't heard correctly. Or maybe he had made a mistake. Where were all the questions? As the Chair called on the chairman of the Judiciary Committee, she leaned forward and tugged on the Chairman's sleeve. He pulled away and stood up. She hurried after him into the tiny lounge area behind the marble slab.

"What happened?" she demanded.

"I just dodged a bullet"—he picked up a phone and punched four numbers—"and Mr. Bresson is free to pursue his legitimate business interests."

"But what about his identity?" She was trying not to shout. "The Russian money?"

He put his hand over the receiver. "You, my dear, don't know what you're talking about."

Heidi felt devastated. Bewildered. What had the CIA told her Chairman? He refused to say. She needed to take out her anger and frustration on someone. When she saw Sean Gordon in the audience, he became the natural choice.

"You got me into this," she said pouring her third beer, "saying Bresson was 'hot'!"

They were sitting in the back room of the Dubliner Pub near the railway station. At 11:30 A.M., the place was not full.

"Could I remind you that Jay Lyman first asked you about him."

"What's in this for you, Sean?" The Harp Lager was having its effect on her. "Is this some convoluted game where you're using me and Jay in some Agency scheme. Are you trying to discredit the committee, or my Chairman, or me?"

"The truth's troubling enough. You don't need to add any paranoia."

"Well, what's your role in this? You show up in Europe. You show up at the hearing this morning. You feed me little tidbits. You try to get in my pants. Did you watch me making love to Jay Lyman on the beach in Monte Carlo?"

"Don't be crude, Heidi. It doesn't look good on you."

"No, seriously. Tell me, whose side are you on? You act like you're against your own Agency. Maybe I'm going after the wrong person. Maybe I should be investigating you!"

She saw him struggling to control his temper.

"I'm on the side of all the men and women in the Clandestine Service, who screw up their lives and families by serving their country in godforsaken places. I work for those whose job it is to make friends in order to turn them into traitors, people who get so that they don't know what friendship is, don't know what loyalty is, people whose only certainty is their commitment to one another and to their country, a country that periodically turns around and screws them!"

Heidi could see that the midmorning beer was also having its effect on Sean.

"And I'm not on the side of the bureaucrats and politicians who dream up stupid and vicious things for us to do, and then hide behind the veil of national security when it turns to shit in public." He poured himself the last of the Harp and ordered another pitcher.

"What's going on?" Heidi muttered, baffled and blitzed. "Your boss obviously told my boss to lay off Bresson. Nothing can stop him now."

"Since I got back from Europe," Gordon said reluctantly. "I've been trying to get permission to open an official inquiry on Bresson. Yesterday, the deputy director literally slammed the door in my face."

"I bet you and me and Jayson are all going to be fired." Heidi felt herself rapidly sliding into the stage of self-pity.

"It's a cover-up, Heidi!" She had not seen such intensity in him for a long time. "I don't know what's being concealed, but Bresson's identity is the key."

"I don't know what else to do." She was fading fast.

"I have an idea, but I need your help."

"God! What now?"

"I want Jay Lyman to work with me."

25

"He'll probably consider it unethical to tell us anything," Sean Gordon advised Lyman, as the elevator rocketed up toward the twenty-sixth floor. "So avoid attacking his professional integrity."

"You just keep peeking in people's windows," Lyman said as they got off the elevator. "I'll handle the sales work."

The dentist's office occupied a suite at the end of the hall. A bell tinkled as they entered.

"I'm Jayson Lyman, I've an appointment with the doctor," he announced to the nurse behind the counter.

"You haven't been here before," she noted. "Do you have dental coverage with your medical plan? If not, that will be $75 in advance, plus additional charges depending on the procedure. We accept Mastercard and Visa."

"It's just a consultation," Lyman said, giving her a credit card.

He and Sean took seats on opposite sides of the room. Lyman found Gordon unfathomable. In Vienna, he blows a guy apart without flinching. But in New York, he won't even ask a dentist a few questions, because the CIA is not supposed to operate in the United States.

He had to admit that Gordon's idea of trying to learn something about Bresson's identity from his dental work was creative. Also probably futile.

"Dr. Witte will see you now."

Lyman disappeared through a door, and Sean Gordon remained in the waiting room. Gordon warned himself not to imagine what was going on in the dentist's office. He had developed a rule when running agents: never picture what they are doing. It tainted the agent's debriefing with preconceptions. The rule also saved emotional wear and tear when something different than you imagined happened to your agent—something almost always bad.

But envisioning Jay Lyman with the dentist was preferable to picturing Lyman with Heidi. What did she see in him? Yes, he was rich. That wasn't her style. He was still a kid. Of course, I can't exactly consider Heidi a matron, he thought. Did it just come down to age? As if time were trivial.

Time had filled Sean Gordon's life with friends he had lost, mistakes he had made, successes he had to hide, craziness he had to deny, fear he had to control, hate he needed to overcome, and love he wanted to forget. Instead of questioning Heidi's feelings, perhaps he ought to take a long look at his own. If he cared for her, maybe he should consider what was best for her.

The nurse interrupted his thoughts. "The doctor asked if you would join them."

Gordon found Dr. Witte to be in his early thirties, short, with more hair on his upper lip than on his head. He was bent over a magnifying glass and talking a mile a minute.

"Unusual. But I had seen it before. Just out of school, I did my first work at a clinic near Coney Island, actually Brighton Beach. You saw dental work from everywhere, Latin America, Africa even. And of course Europe. The refugees. Prewar, postwar. Styles, methods told you when and where it was done. I'd look in some of these oldtimers' mouths and say, 'you came over in '38.' So I'd be a few years off. The Germans, I hate to admit, did the best work, meticulous. The English, forget it, but they made nice crowns. France was elegant but sort of idiosyncratic. They have their own system."

"And Bresson?" Gordon wanted to get to the point.

"Bad teeth. Must have eaten a lot of sweets as a boy. The work is mostly what I call French provincial."

"Mostly?"

"Except the tooth I took out. It was such a classic, I saved it. Here, look." Dr. Witte pointed to the magnifying glass set up over a small stand.

"I've seen this a hundred times out at Brighton Beach. It's typical emigré."

"He means Russian," Lyman added.

"How can you be sure it's from Russia?" Gordon asked.

"Experience. But it's more than that. Look."

Sean Gordon stared through the magnifier at the tooth.

"This was his first molar. Came in probably when he was eleven or twelve. Immediately attacked by decay. He let it go. Then he got a helluva toothache. They drill it out and fill it in. But the filling's soft. It's not silver amalgam. It's crap. That's the white stuff you see there.

We use it for temporaries. It looks good cosmetically, but breaks down and the decay continues underneath. I call it Potemkin dentistry."

"But why are you certain Bresson got this filling in Russia?" Gordon pressed.

"Because I don't know any other place where people get their teeth filled with cement."

"How'd you convince him to talk?" Sean Gordon had to admit that Jay Lyman had done a skillful job. They were waiting for the elevator. Bresson's tooth, wrapped in a little box, was in Gordon's pocket.

"I gave him a line. Said I was a reporter."

"He believed that?"

"No, then I said I was a private eye. Finally, I said I was from the CIA."

Gordon groaned.

"It worked. Or, I should say that and a consulting fee of $5,000. The tooth cost an extra $500."

Sean shook his head.

"Everything in New York has a price," he explained.

The elevator opened and they got inside.

"What are you going to do with it?" Lyman asked.

"Go back to Langley. Use it to raise hell. See if it will tell our technical people anything more about Bresson. You?"

"I'm going to see Bresson and try to stop the deal."

"That could be dangerous," Gordon warned.

The elevator paused at the eighth floor and a Hasidic diamond dealer and a bicycle messenger got on board. They all rode the rest of the way down in silence.

Out on the street, Sean Gordon raised a question that was on both of their minds.

"What are your plans as far as Heidi's concerned?"

"That's really none of your business," Lyman answered. He was not about to admit that he had no plans, at least none in which he could imagine reconciling their separate agendas.

Gordon hailed down a taxi. "Well, let me give you a piece of advice. You'd do a lot better if you stop thinking of her as a deal."

Marcel Bresson kept de Grazia shuttling back and forth to the phone while he sat on the 12th floor terrace of Washington's J. W. Marriott

Hotel soaking up the warm October sunshine and reading about himself in the newspapers. De Grazia was in contact with Blackie Muldoon, who was providing continuous reports on the News/Worldweek board's deliberations about whether to endorse Bresson's tender offer.

The phone rang. Through the hum of the traffic on Pennsylvania Avenue, Bresson could hear de Grazia's tone of voice, but not his words. He sounded contemptuous. And for the first time in fifteen phone calls, de Grazia did not appear at the terrace to relay any news.

"Who was that?" Bresson called out.

De Grazia dutifully came to the door. "Jay Lyman. He wants to see you."

Marcel Bresson just grunted. The phone rang again and de Grazia disappeared inside. Bresson returned to reading the *Washington News.*

The story on the Senate hearing could not have been better. It was front page, but only a single column below the fold. TAKEOVER HEARINGS END, the headline said. The subhead was NO SURPRISES. The story read, "French media czar Marcel Bresson's testimony before the Senate Commerce Committee went smoothly yesterday, clearing away any political obstacles to his controversial takeover of the News/Worldweek Corporation. Questions by the Chairman of the Senate Intelligence Committee, whose participation had provoked widespread speculation, concerned ways to prevent Soviet exploitation of Western media. The hearings concluded with all the Senators praising Mr. Bresson's candor and responsiveness. Later in the day, the House Subcommittee on Telecommunications shelved plans to call the French publisher to hearings it had scheduled for next week."

The story then skipped to an inside page.

"Let me give you a status report." De Grazia had reemerged on the terrace. Bresson put down the paper. "They're willing to endorse the tender, but say no to the last three items. No lock-ups, no representations and warranties, no cold comfort letter."

"Tell them I do not accept no for an answer."

"But Marcel, we've got a deadline. If the board is going to lift the poison pill and go along with the deal, it's got to file a 14D-9 today. Otherwise, the pill will still be in place when your tender offer expires."

"Why are they being obstinate?"

From the look on de Grazia's face, Bresson could tell he had not asked that question. The young man had become impatient to complete the deal, a bad quality in a negotiator.

"I'll find out," he said with a sigh.

Bresson turned back to the newspaper. He discovered another story on himself in the Living section, a profile written from Paris. This one did not make him happy. Words like "eccentric," "furtive," and "recluse" popped out at him. The article asserted that traumas in his wartime upbringing had produced a peculiar psychological makeup. The reporter quoted a prominent French psychologist as saying that the separation from his family had made it impossible for Bresson to form close relationships. The analyst concluded, "His business empire is his family. He must always make it bigger. If it were lost, he would probably become suicidal. It is typical in such cases that when he grows older and closer to death, he will realize he has no one to whom he can pass it on. At that stage, many such men enter a profound depression from which they never recover. The American Howard Hughes was an example."

Bresson tore the page out of the paper and crumpled it up.

"Excuse me," de Grazia said, "but the board says that since this is not a negotiated merger, they do not feel obliged to grant items that are normally part of such a process, such as the warranties and representations."

"And the lock-ups?"

"As a practical matter, Marcel, I don't see anybody else coming in at the last minute to take the company away from you. I hear Lyman's effort has collapsed. That's probably why he's calling."

"All right. But I want the comfort letter. What is so difficult for their accountants to say they have seen no material adverse change in the business? Besides, Sperile Beck says he needs it."

"Yes sir," de Grazia said without enthusiasm.

Bresson went to the edge of the terrace. To the right he could see the south lawn of the White House. Straight ahead of him, the Washington Monument towered above the roof of the Commerce Department. To his left, at the far end of Pennsylvania Avenue, the Capitol rose upon the bluff that overlooked the Mall. It was all coming together. He could feel it. This was the moment he loved.

"The board is still balking at the comfort letter," de Grazia reported. "Raffy said . . ." He stopped. He had made the mistake of saying too much.

"He said what?"

De Grazia hesitated. "He said owning the company should be cold comfort enough."

Bresson laughed. "The hell with them. Cut the deal. I'll take care of Beck."

As de Grazia went back inside to make the call, Bresson felt a rush of freedom like he had never experienced before. He had done it! He was going to be the most powerful press lord in the world!

"And get us a magnum of Roederer Cristal," he shouted after de Grazia. Then he sat down on the chaise lounge, unwrapped the balled-up article in the *Washington News* and read it for a second time.

When de Grazia again came out on the terrace, a waiter was right behind him. "They are releasing the following statement right now." He was flushed and smiling with success. " 'The Board of Directors of News/Worldweek voted today to recommend to its stockholders that they tender their shares to Bresson USA. The decision of the board was unanimous. Chairman and Chief Executive Officer Drew Richardson said that the decision was in the best interest of the company and its shareholders.' "

The waiter popped the cork. Champagne foamed out of the linen-wrapped bottle and into the glasses he carried on a silver tray. Bresson took one and held it up.

"To audacity!" He drank it down in one swallow. Then he stopped. "But you have made a serious error," he said menacingly, catching de Grazia in midgulp.

"What?" he sputtered.

"This is not Roederer Cristal, it's Dom Perignon." He laughed and poured himself another glass. "For this inexcusable error you must do two things."

"No problem," de Grazia said happily.

"Find me a beautiful woman for the night."

De Grazia's smile faded.

"No, make that two, and very young."

"And what else?" He prepared himself.

"Call Jayson Lyman. Tell him I will have lunch with him here tomorrow. And inform him he can leave his bodyguards behind."

It could have been the Marriott Rabat, or the Marriott Benin, or the Marriott Antofagasta. They all looked basically alike to Lyman. And their purpose was the same, to obliterate national and cultural differences and create an always familiar and reassuring world for the traveling executive—the world of business.

Although the J. W. Marriott was the company's flagship hotel and was convenient to News/Worldweek, Lyman was surprised that Bresson had not picked someplace more exclusive. The elevator door opened on the twelfth floor, ushering Lyman into a wide, block-long corridor with a deep maroon carpet and gray walls. Lyman knocked at the Presidential Suite. A waiter opened the door.

"Mr. Lyman? Monsieur Bresson is waiting for you on the terrace."

He heard his heels click on the marble of the foyer and change timbre as he crossed onto the parquet floors. The living area was the size and shape of a tennis court, decorated in sixties-style furniture with huge Chinese screens and chests for accents. A slight breeze wafted in from the balcony. His mind was clear and alert to every sensation. Lyman felt like a hunter at last closing in on his prey. He had no plan. He was operating on instinct.

"Jayson, it's been so long!" Bresson boomed as he welcomed him onto the terrace. "Where have you been? Come have champagne, we have much to celebrate. Our deal is in hand! And you deserve most of the credit!"

"Is that why you fired me?" Lyman knew he could not yield an inch to Bresson's bonhomie.

"Fire you? *Au contraire.*" He poured Lyman a glass of champagne. "Mr. Cooke told me that you were angry with me for some reason and no longer wished to work on the account. I had hoped that you wanted to see me so that we could clear up any misunderstanding between us. *À votre santé.*" He hoisted his glass and drank it down.

As Lyman sipped his champagne, he wondered for a moment if Bresson's version of events could be true. Then he remembered Edouard trying to kill him.

"You know, I think he did not want to pay you your rightful commission," Bresson continued. "I will take care of that when Gould Axewroth is mine."

He refilled his glass and topped off Lyman's.

"But you still look unhappy, Jayson. Come sit down and tell me what is troubling you."

This was not going as Lyman had expected. He felt the initiative slipping away as he sank into the soft cushions of the outdoor sofa. The day suddenly felt muggy. Sweat gathered in his armpits. He decided subtlety was not an option.

"What troubles me, Marcel, is that you work for the Russians."

"Because they have provided me a guarantee?" He was unfazed.

"A *secret* guarantee," Lyman emphasized.

"Of course it's secret. How else could they participate? But would you feel the same hostility if it were a Kuwaiti bank? Or the Bank of China? It represents the Chinese Communists!"

"You know that's not all of it." Lyman tried to counter. "You're not Marcel Bresson. You're not even French. I happen to know where you *do* come from."

A flicker of interest flashed through Bresson's eyes. "Where?" he asked.

"Russia, of course. Not many eleven-year-old French kids had their first molar filled in Russia in what, 1952?"

A look of admiration passed quickly over Bresson's face, followed by disappointment. "Is that all you know? Too bad. Yes, I was raised in an orphanage in Russia. And I recall the dentist. Very painful despite my first bottle of vodka. But I do not remember much before that. I had hoped you might tell me more. Come, let us have lunch, and I will explain everything you want to know."

Disoriented by Bresson's candor, Lyman obediently moved to the table. It was covered with white, yellow and gold chrysanthemums. The waiter served vichyssoise. Lyman had no appetite.

"At the orphanage, they told me that I had been found as a child wandering around the battlefield near Moscow after the Nazi retreat. I accepted the story at the time, but I don't believe it now."

Lyman noticed a tone of resentment had crept into his voice.

"I remember a big home. Many people, probably servants. Only a high party leader would have had such a house, and the son of a high party leader does not become an orphan in the Soviet Union. And I have other images from that time, even the words to a nursery rhyme, *"Tian shang lao ying fei,'* 'The hawk is circling in the sky.' It sounds Chinese. And I have this." He took a gleaming object out of his pocket. It was a large pearl. "My good luck charm."

The waiter cleared the first course. Lyman felt mesmerized, suspended between fascination and disbelief. All this had to be another of Bresson's lies.

The next course was crab cakes. The waiter poured them a white French Graves.

"I hope you like the wine. It comes from my own vineyard." He took a sip and told the waiter to keep it on the ice. "Actually the orphanage was more of a camp school. A very special one where they planned to send me abroad and trained me in French. When I met my new family, the Bressons, I hated them. Narrow-minded Marxists. They considered themselves materialists, but took no pleasure in life. They could have been Cistercians, who take vows of poverty. My so-called father railed endlessly against the exploitation of labor by wealth, but I believe he reveled in being poor. So I left them for the army. It was all planned in any event, to give me credibility. And slowly, with time, I built my business, until now it will be the greatest media empire in the world!"

"With a little help from your friends in Moscow." Lyman finally found his voice.

"Yes."

"You're really just a spy."

"No. Technically, I am an agent of influence."

Suddenly, Lyman felt panicky. The sound of yodeling and a picture of Rankin's broken body came back to him. "Why are you telling me this?"

Bresson put down his fork and pushed himself away from the table.

"I am proud of what I have accomplished, even if I am indebted to my 'friends in Moscow,' as you call them. But now I am on the brink of a new stage. A worldwide media combine, like chemicals, or automobiles, or oil. Why should not publishing and media be a global enterprise? The technology exists. The capital exists. Markets exist. Only political barriers remain!

"I realize you think that I am in the service of the Soviet Union," he got up and began to pace the terrace. "With this deal, our sales will be what?"

"About $14 billion annually."

"That's more than the budget for all KGB overseas operations! Don't you see, Jayson? Governments are obsolete! Ideologies are obsolete. Intellectuals who once talked like this were dismissed as naive liberals, 'one-worlders.' Now conservative businessmen like you and me have brought us to the brink of one world, through free trade and free movement of capital. We do not even need free movement of labor. We move the factories!

"Politicians object. They hang on to their little pieces of sovereignty. They demand loyalty and parade the flag around and conduct meaningless little wars to reassure themselves of their continued relevance. But the truth is obvious. They belong to the past."

Bresson paused at the railing of the terrace and surveyed the monuments of Washington.

"Nations still have a certain administrative value in their own localities, like provinces and towns. But for the most part, they are dangerously overarmed anachronisms. The earth will be ruled by global corporate organizations. And the key to global economic and political power is the media. Already, I can make and break governments in a half-dozen countries. I can decide what politicians will rise and which will fall into obscurity. I can choose which issues are important and which are not. We can set the agenda for the whole world!"

"We?" Lyman tried to make it sound ironic.

Bresson pulled over his chair and sat close.

"You know I am surrounded by bootlickers and incompetents. To be independent of 'my friends in Moscow,' I must put my business on a sound financial base. You can do that."

"Why me?" Lyman felt like he had fallen through a looking glass.

"You already know everything about me. That you discovered most of it yourself is a great recommendation. To find someone new and to explain everything would present great difficulties, even if he were capable and could be trusted. Cooke is unreliable, de Grazia not ready. You have passed many tests. I need someone who will stand up to me. Make a real team. Formulate strategy. Debate. Someone who can share my vision of the vast opportunity before us. Someone who can command a global empire when I am gone. You can be that person, Jayson. I know it, and what is most important, you know it." He reached out and placed his hand on Lyman's arm.

Lyman felt a wave of indecision.

"If you prefer, you can start by running Gould Axewroth. Perhaps you would take your $20 million commission as shares in the new holding company. That would make you a major partner. You could add your name—Gould Axewroth Lyman."

"What if I wanted cash?" Lyman said almost involuntarily.

"That would be up to you." He withdrew his hand. "You know we must restructure Les Éditions Bresson. I assume you could generate the cash in that process."

Lyman could not believe he was being drawn into negotiating the terms of his employment with this man.

"But I would prefer that you work more closely with me. You could be president of the new combined entity, with $14 billion in assets. We will build an international corporate headquarters in Monaco or New York. You could make that decision."

"And what happens to the others who know about you? Heidi Bruce, for example."

"The Senate hearing proved that she is neutralized. But I assume the two of you will marry. That should ensure her cooperation."

How many children does he expect us to have, Lyman wondered, his anger finally beginning to surface.

"As for Sean Gordon, I believe I can dispose of that problem. I assume you would not object."

"Like you tried to dispose of Heidi? And me? You tried to kill us, Marcel. You murdered Rankin." Lyman was struggling against Bresson's web of seduction.

"Rankin was an accident. I apologize to you and Miss Bruce. Edouard overreacted. He could be hard to control sometimes. Even governments have trouble handling their agents." He smiled with a hint of pride.

"I do not deny that I have done some terrible things. Who has not? I once visited Dallas, Texas, and dined at the Inn on Turtle Creek. I sat there looking at all the wealthy people with their gold and jewels, and my host said to me, 'There's not a soul in this room that didn't do something immoral, unethical or illegal to get rich.' " Bresson tried to imitate a Texas twang.

"Look at yourself." He pointed an accusing finger at Lyman. "In the short time I have known you, you have robbed a bank and crushed someone to death."

"That was self-defense!"

"No doubt. But you felt good killing that poor Vietnamese, n'est-ce pas?"

"I could go to the authorities right now," Lyman said angrily.

"Who would you talk to? American Intelligence? Certainly not the Congress. No one would listen to you."

"What makes you so sure?"

"No one wants the truth. Everyone hates the truth. And you know why?" Bresson did not wait for Lyman to ask. "Because everyone already knows what the truth is."

"The truth," Lyman shouted, "is that you work for the KGB!"

Bresson was silent for a moment. The wind had picked up, threatening an afternoon thunderstorm.

"The truth, Jayson, is that I also work for the CIA."

"Maybe it's just more of his horseshit," Lyman said.

"But it sure explains a lot," Heidi Bruce responded.

"More than you can possibly imagine." Sean Gordon added.

The three of them sat around a bridge table in the solarium of the Chevy Chase Country Club while a heavy rain pounded the windows and bright autumn leaves blew horizontally across the golf course.

After Jay Lyman left Bresson's hotel, he went directly to National Airport. But instead of boarding the Pan Am Shuttle, he ran down the connecting concourse to the main terminal, and exited the building. Skipping the taxi line, he crossed to the center traffic island where he grabbed a cab that had just unloaded its passengers. He told the driver to make a circuit of the airport. On the third pass, he directed him to the Metro stop, where a train was pulling into the station. Dashing up the stairs and across the platform, he managed to slip inside the car just as the doors closed.

Following Sean Gordon's instructions, he took the train to Metro Center, waiting until the last second to get off. He checked to see if he were being followed, then boarded the Connecticut Avenue line. At Woodley Park he emerged from the subway to find it was pouring down rain. After fifteen minutes of waiting for a cab without an umbrella, he finally took a bus. It let him off across the street from the country club.

As he walked into the solarium, leaving behind a little trail of water, Lyman could feel his socks squishing in his shoes. He noted that Heidi seemed totally oblivious to the fact that he had drowned.

"For one thing," she was saying, "it explains why my Chairman took a dive at the hearing."

"It also raises the question," Lyman added, "of whether Mr. Gordon here has been playing us for suckers."

Heidi looked sharply at Sean.

"How was it that you managed to keep track of us all over Europe," Lyman pressed. "A little help from Bresson?"

"Think about what you're saying, Jayson," Gordon responded. "It doesn't make sense."

"Then what were you doing in Europe?"

"I can't tell you." Gordon said flatly. He turned to Heidi. "Explain to this young man that there are compartments within compartments. I didn't know about Bresson and the Agency, but I'm going to find out."

"The question," Heidi said, "is what are we going to do?"

Lyman could see that she would not take sides. He realized that he had secretly hoped that by helping Gordon and confronting Bresson, he might reignite the spark between them. But she was all business. And that infuriated him.

"What are we going to do?" Lyman repeated. "Why do anything? Bresson's on our side."

"I'm not convinced of that," Heidi snapped. "Even if what he claims is true, we don't want the CIA running our TV and newspapers!"

Where, Lyman wondered, did she get her endless capacity for outrage? Fighting Bresson, the KGB and the CIA was obviously easier for her, he thought bitterly, than deciding which man she wants in her life.

"I'll buy stock in News/Worldweek and lay it all out at the shareholders meeting," she declared.

"That'll be more than a month from now," Lyman pointed out, "Bresson will already control the company. He'll call the meeting to order, vote his fifty-one percent of the stock for the merger and adjourn. You'd be lucky to get in the door; forget trying to speak."

"Then I'm going to the press."

Sean Gordon shook his head. "Your credibility may not be too high at the moment."

"I'll take my chances," she said stiffly.

"If this blows up in the press, a lot of innocent people on our side could get hurt," Gordon warned.

"That's always the knee-jerk Agency reaction," she shot back. "Whenever something rotten is uncovered, you scream, 'You're going to expose our agents!' It's bull!"

"Four people are dead already! Let me find out more," Gordon urged.

"He's got to be stopped somehow," she said defiantly. "If you can do it, fine. If not, I'm going to raise as much hell as I can."

Lyman looked at them at loggerheads with one another. He was an irrelevancy.

"What are you going to do?" Heidi asked, as if she had just realized Lyman had been left out.

"Me?" He wrung out his handkerchief into an ashtray, then wiped away the rivulets of water running down his neck. "I'm going to think seriously about going back to work for Bresson."

When Sean Gordon arrived at the DCI's office, the deputy director for Operations was with him. The DDO, as he was known in the Agency, was a cool Minnesotan whose idea of a Saturday off was to wear a sportshirt and a blazer to work. The director of Central Intelligence was dressed for tennis.

"You must understand, Sean," the DDO said, taking off his glasses and examining them, "Marcel Bresson has provided invaluable support to the Clandestine Service over the years."

The CIA director was perched on the edge of his desk, making clear he wanted to leave soon. The DDO sat on the couch in front of the window. From his chair in the middle of the room, Gordon could not see his face against the glare from outside. It was an old trick to put him at a disadvantage.

"He's provided cover for literally hundreds of our agents. They work as correspondents and staff people for his publications," the DDO continued. "And not only in Europe, but throughout the world. When the Congress stopped us from using the American press for cover, we had to go somewhere. You're on the wrong track, Sean. I handled Bresson myself for years."

"Maybe that's why you can't face the fact that he's betraying us," Gordon said.

"I know all about his arrangements with the Russians," he continued diffidently, "the money and so on. It's actually come in handy on occasion. He prints U.S. propaganda, and the Soviets pay for it."

"We pay for it," Gordon declared angrily. "In blood! We've had a security hemorrhage in our European and Middle Eastern operations. Twelve programs shattered in the last four years. We've turned this building upside down looking for a mole. Our liaison with foreign intelligence services is suffering. The Chinese have put our most important joint operation on hold. But the problem isn't inside, it's outside. It's Marcel Bresson!"

"It's all very easy to make allegations, but what's your proof?" the DDO challenged him.

"I haven't had time to review all the files again," Sean Gordon directed his answer to the CIA director. "But from memory, I can tell you that four blown operations had key agents under cover with organizations controlled by Bresson: the Gdansk operation, Red Wing in Armenia, the Stockholm Conference, and the New Faces program in Germany. I'll bet your retirement," he pointed at the DDO, "that all of the others will tie back to Bresson."

"We use him so frequently that those operations could easily have some link to him by pure chance. What you've said proves nothing," the DDO insisted, "except that we may be a bit too dependent on him."

"You don't want to get it, do you?" Sean let his exasperation show. "He's not *our* double agent, he's *their* double agent. And he's got to be stopped!"

Gordon turned to the director of Central Intelligence. The DCI was obviously struggling with the one thing he hated most, a serious decision on something he knew nothing about.

"You may have a point, Sean," he said, "but we can't be hasty in such an important matter." He was looking for a way out.

"We need a careful study." the DDO suggested.

"Just so," the CIA chief agreed quickly.

"The whole thing could be a Soviet provocation," the DDO offered.

"Yes, a systematic investigation is in order." The head of the CIA was already headed out the door. "You two see to it."

"That's much the best solution, Sean," the DDO said, as the director disappeared. "We'll meet on it, early next week."

"You put the study group together. I'll be busy."

"Don't do anything rash. You've created quite enough trouble already."

"In a little more than four days, Bresson will control News/Worldweek and become the most powerful media figure in Washington. You think Bresson's working for us. I'm going to make sure we don't end up working for him."

Lyman woke up exhausted. His dreams were not terrible, so much as tumultuous. He remembered having to sing "God Bless America" in a crowd that was pushing and shoving. He was amazed that he could remember the words in his sleep.

The Sunday *New York Times* seemed to weigh a hundred pounds as he dragged it inside the door. The front page, the Business section and

Week in Review all had pieces on the Bresson and the News/World-week deal. As Lyman skimmed them, he saw that the tone of the coverage had changed from neutral to negative. The front page story told of senior executives planning to quit News/Worldweek if Bresson took over. The Business page compared Bresson unfavorably with other foreign owners of U.S. media. The Week in Review recapped the Senate hearings, calling them "spineless," and the lead editorial condemned the deal. The *Times* restated its commitment to unhindered foreign investment, then labeled the Bresson takeover "an abuse." The paper called for new antitrust safeguards against the concentration of too much press power in foreign hands. Lyman was not surprised to see the media become aroused only after the transaction had become inevitable.

He tossed the paper aside and decided he needed fresh air, exercise. The jogging path around the Reservoir in Central Park was crowded as usual on Sunday morning. Lyman kept nodding to colleagues and acquaintances but did not stop to talk. They would want to discuss the News/Worldweek deal. He was becoming antisocial. He had dropped Samantha off at her building at 10:30 the night before. She hadn't been boring. He had been boring. She talked brightly about all the latest plays, gallery openings and movies. Lyman found her too well informed about things that didn't seem very important to him.

He paused to catch his breath and watch the runners in the Manny Hanny 10K pass by. That's what I should do, he told himself. Find a sport. Get a hobby. Sculling's fashionable, and you meet other guys. Forget about women, take comfort in the company of men.

As he walked back across Fifth Avenue toward his apartment, he thought about Bresson. The man was riding a tiger that he couldn't dismount and inviting Lyman on board. They had spent most of Saturday on the phone discussing options for restructuring Les Éditions Bresson and News/Worldweek. Lyman wondered how he could allow himself to talk to Bresson; he must have some massive personality defect, like the urge to run a $14 billion company.

Lyman made no commitments. He had pointed out that he would have to see the company's "real numbers" to give him sound advice. Bresson promised the data as soon as he completed the News/Worldweek merger. He had invited Lyman to a dinner party next Wednesday evening to celebrate the tender offer closing and also to the board meeting and press conference the next day. Lyman said he would think it over. He might show up at the dinner just to see Cooke's face.

As Lyman came down 76th Street, he saw a woman and two children standing in front of his maisonette. Carol Rankin was waiting for him. Her two boys were dashing up and down the sidewalk and swinging around the scrawny little trees that were struggling to survive on the curb.

"I found something you might want, and I didn't want to leave it with the doorman."

"You should've called," he said apologetically.

"We were coming into town for the Big Apple Circus anyway." She seemed very tense.

"I would have been here." He invited her inside.

"I didn't want to bother you."

"What is it?" he asked, sitting her on the sofa as the kids ran through to the garden.

"I finally got the courage to clean out Charley's office at home, and I found something in his computer." She took out two 750K diskettes. "He often sent copies of things home so he could work there too. This came from Bürgenstock. It's his consolidated analysis of Éditions Bresson. The papers that were missing when . . ." Her tears had started coming. "I thought it might be useful somehow," she sobbed.

Lyman took her in his arms. It felt good to hold her, but he did not know who was comforting whom. "Thanks for bringing it to me."

"Will it help?"

"I think it's too late."

Bresson's Falcon 900 broke through the overcast at 1200 feet and made a smooth landing at Nantucket airport. A jeep rented in the name of the pilot was waiting in the parking lot. Bresson climbed in and set off for Wauwinet at the far eastern end of the island.

The heather was glowing in fall colors as Bresson's jeep negotiated the hills along the south shore of Nantucket harbor. Wauwinet consisted of an old shingle-sided hotel dating from the turn of the century and a series of cottages scattered among the dunes that lay between the harbor and the sea. *Papi* was waiting at the entrance as Bresson drove up the unpaved driveway.

"We go further out," Yuli ordered as Bresson helped him into the jeep. They continued on the increasingly rutted road until it disappeared into the sand. They had reached the "haul-over," a narrow stretch of dunes where nineteenth-century whaling ships were dragged from the Atlantic Ocean into the Nantucket harbor. Bresson and his control officer got out and began to walk on the broad beach. It was empty as far the eye could see.

"Does this remind you of some other place?" Yuli asked.

"There are no mountains and I don't have to carry stones," Bresson said.

"You've come a long way."

Bresson nodded, acknowledging the compliment. "Everything is set," he said confidently.

"What about Lyman?"

"I believe he can be coopted."

"And the girl?"

"If he doesn't get her under control," Bresson said, "I will be seeking authority to eliminate her. The CIA has promised me they would deal with Sean Gordon."

"Good," Yuli said. He stopped walking and leaned on his cane. It sank into the sand. "I have your first assignment. To promote the summit meeting. The General Secretary will give your publications an exclusive interview."

"Isn't that a little obvious?" said Bresson.

"They want to 'amortize their investment more quickly.' That's what Bogdanov said. He also wants to place several illegals into your organization."

"To spy on me or the Americans?"

Yuli just laughed.

"And what about my subsidy?" Bresson asked.

"You heard the Chairman. You must be self-supporting."

"Then I will have to charge him. The advertising campaign for the General Secretary will cost him $15 million, and each illegal, $5 million a year plus expenses."

Lyman was actually enjoying himself. He was laughing. And stuffing himself with popcorn. And drinking beer in the afternoon. He had not been to the circus in years.

Carol Rankin's three-year-old boy sat in his lap so he could see the clowns better, but now the aerialists had begun, and every time the performers let go of the trapeze, the boy buried his head in Lyman's chest. At the same time, Carol would involuntarily grab his arm. It all felt wonderful until he asked himself a question. What the hell he was doing?

These were not his children. This was not his wife. He should be starting his own family, not engineering a takeover of Charles Rankin's, as if it were a distressed business.

At the intermission, he slipped away and called his answering service. It reported that Heidi Bruce had phoned. Lyman asked to be called on his pager in five minutes. When it began to beep, he excused himself and went to the entrance of the tent and bought a stuffed elephant for Carol's oldest and a clown for the youngest. He apologized to all of them for being called away. They all looked disappointed. He left as the tightrope walker began his act.

Lyman's answering machine was blinking as he entered the apartment. Heidi's voice came through the speaker.

"I know I can't expect you to see things my way," she said, without saying who she was. "But I don't want to see you hurt. Don't tie your future to that man. Call if you want to talk about it."

The message made him furious. She condescended to appeal to his self-interest because she assumed he was blind to the moral issues. He understood the moral issues. Working for the KGB was bad. Working for the CIA was bad, except of course if you were the marvelous Sean Gordon. Besides, Heidi was kidding herself. She wouldn't be satisfied if he rejected Bresson's offer unless he did it for the right reasons.

Lyman decided to bury himself in Charles Rankin's consolidation of Les Éditions Bresson's balance sheets. Carol had printed them out before they left for the circus. Looking them over, Lyman sighed. Rankin really had been a genius.

Spreadsheet after spreadsheet demonstrated convincingly that Bresson was broke. The reason appeared to be too much administrative overhead. The facts had been covered up by failing to account adequately for unfulfilled subscription liabilities.

When Bresson sold a subscription to one of his publications he took the cash and spent it. But he did not fully record the fact that he had a corresponding liability—the magazines and newspapers he owed his subscribers. To cover those costs, he had to sell more and more subscriptions. It was a classic pyramid game, a Ponzi scheme, and the only reason it did not collapse was that there were frequent injections of outside capital. In effect, Les Éditions Bresson was in debt three times over—to the Swiss Bank Corporation, to the Russians, and to millions of subscribers in Europe.

The bottom line for News/Worldweek shareholders was disaster. Because Richardson had run the company into the ground, News/Worldweek was not strong enough to keep the combined entity afloat when it merged with Les Éditions Bresson. Unless the Russians kept injecting capital or Bresson's empire was drastically restructured, the stockholders on the back end of the News/Worldweek deal would be getting worthless paper.

But if Bresson crashed, so what? Lyman did not care about the arbs and the institutions. They could look out for themselves. The real victim, Lyman knew, would be the small investor who bought through a discount house and didn't have a broker. Many of them would not tender their shares on time. Some, older people usually, would not even know a tender offer had been made. They would all wind up on the back end with garbage. Even the individual investor who got in on the cash portion of the deal would wind up with up to 49 percent paper when the proration was completed. Fifty-five dollars a share for 51 percent, and paper worth nothing for 49 percent, would give the shareholders a blended price of $27.50. By Lyman's calculation, that was two dollars less than the market price before the takeover started.

He picked up the phone and called Heidi Bruce. After four rings, her answering machine responded.

"This is my machine calling your machine. Yes, we do see things differently. You're worried about what happens to the national interest if Bresson succeeds. I'm concerned about what happens to the little guys if he fails. They're going to get reamed in this deal. The only way I know to prevent that is to accept Bresson's offer. I can straighten out the company so that the paper given the widows and orphans is worth something."

Lyman hung up. For the first time in his life, he felt he needed a drink. Was he really going to get in bed with that dirtbag again? Why was he responsible for making the deal whole? Lyman poured himself a tumbler of Laphroaig, but before he got the whiskey past his lips, another thought came to him. It was a much better idea, the kind of elegant solution to all problems for which investment bankers got paid huge fees. Like most conceptual breakthroughs, it was completely evident once he had thought of it. But it required two things he did not have: patience and Heidi Bruce's cooperation.

He called her number and again got her machine. "Ignore last message," he began.

27

For three days Sean Gordon had been searching through the defectors reports describing the KGB's agent of influence program, looking for anything that might shed light on Bresson or his operations. Most of the transcripts were on flimsy thermofax, the brown letters fading over the years into the beige background. The debriefings of legendary KGB defectors like Golytsin and Nosenko would soon be unreadable, their revelations only available in the sharply condensed summaries attached to each document. What kind of insight and wisdom could the CIA offer, Gordon wondered, if its understanding of the past came to be based on summaries and condensations?

He sat in a room-sized vault which had once been the inner sanctum of the CIA's legendary counterintelligence chief, James Jesus Angleton. After his fall from grace for keeping dossiers on thousands of innocent Americans, the CI staff was moved to less ominous quarters and the Inspector General took over the office. Counterintelligence had never regained its stature or influence within the Agency.

Competent and workmanlike, CI staffers kept their heads down and played by the book. They had become glorified security officers at a time when the Agency needed cunning and inspiration to deal with the worst string of intelligence disasters in CIA's history. That was why Sean Gordon had been pulled back from working on the Senate Intelligence Committee. He had been assigned to find the security breach and close it.

Not knowing where the Agency might have been penetrated, Gordon had decided to run his investigation from the Inspector General's staff—an operation too moribund and peripheral to be infiltrated by any self-respecting mole. For months, Gordon had been chasing down blind alleys. Bresson had been a diversion, something separate he had done to help Heidi. Without knowing it, she had led him to the deep penetration agent he had been searching for all along.

In the Agency's desperation to find good cover for its agents, it had broken the cardinal rule of compartmentalization. Agents were kept ignorant of each other's operations. But by providing them cover, Bresson knew of hundreds of agents and scores of CIA activities involving the most sensitive and dangerous penetrations in Europe and the Middle East. If the CIA behaved, the Soviets would let them continue. If not, the KGB would roll them up as it had so often in the last few years. How much of the intelligence obtained in these operations, he wondered, really consisted of "chicken feed,"—useless, wrong and misleading information planted on our agents by the KGB and other governments alerted by Bresson?

It was a nightmare, Gordon told himself. Our agents were in jeopardy. We didn't know what intelligence was true or false. The Agency's top officials were too dependent on Bresson to admit that he posed a threat, let alone move against him.

Bresson, Sean Gordon concluded, had more leverage on us than we could bring to bear on him. Arrest or liquidation would compel Soviet retaliation. Exposing him could provoke the KGB to blow the cover on hundreds of CIA's agents, many of whom would find their lives in jeopardy. That was why Heidi's strategy was so dangerous. He had to talk her out of it without revealing the extent of the damage Bresson had done. She would feel compelled to inform the Senate Intelligence Committee, and if they launched an investigation, the inevitable leaks would really put the fat in the fire.

Bresson's life-style made him uniquely invulnerable to intimidation. No wife or children to kidnap. No relatives to menace. No personal property to put in jeopardy. Socially, he had remained an outsider, even in France, so he could not be threatened with ostracism. And with his resources, he could buy a lot of friends.

The neutralization of Marcel Bresson had to be more subtle, Gordon decided, something self-generated. He knew firsthand that spies had psychological vulnerabilities like everyone else, in some respects even more. They constantly betrayed someone or something, and that included themselves. For that reason, they were continuously plagued by self-doubt and self-loathing, for which the only compensation was a firm ideological commitment or endless reassurance from their substitute parents—the spymaster and government who controlled them. Their personal conflicts often produced a bottomless pit of unrequited longing that they were desperate to fill.

Unfortunately, Gordon did not know enough about Bresson to exploit such vulnerabilities, if indeed he had them. For days, he had been pouring over the transcripts, reading everything on agents of influence without finding a single insight into Bresson the man. Then he paused, suddenly realizing that that, of course, was the point! Bresson wasn't a Frenchman who had been recruited as an agent of influence. He was a Russian, an "illegal agent," someone pretending to be French since the age of fifteen who did not know himself who he was or where he came from!

Gordon had been looking at the wrong material. He started back through the stack of reports, scanning the summaries for mention of "illegals." Soon he found descriptions of how illegal operations were organized, how illegals were recruited, trained and managed by Directorate S of the First Chief Directorate of the KGB and controlled through Illegal Support Officers in Soviet embassies known as "Line N." But it was two thirty in the morning before Gordon found the key, something that connected with Jayson Lyman's report on Bresson—his description of a fragment of a childhood lullaby.

A March 24, 1964, transcript of Nosenko's interrogation referred to the fact that illegals were sometimes trained from childhood. Then there was a throwaway line that would have escaped any summary or condensation: "I once heard Directorate S went so far as to find children in China." There was nothing more, except a footnote that looked like it had been added later. It referred to a Golytsin transcript of January 17, 1965.

After twenty minutes of frantic searching, Gordon found the document in a pile of transcripts he had already scanned. The passage contained what Gordon had been hoping for.

INT: Nosenko said that the KGB once recruited children in China as illegals. Why would they want Chinese children?
GOLYTSIN: Not Chinese children. Russian boys. It started during Stalin's time. Some said it was his idea.
INT: What was the point?
GOLYTSIN: Like most of Stalin's ideas, it combined paranoia with revenge. They were the offspring of the bourgeoisie who fled the Revolution. Taking away their children to work for the KGB was his idea of an exquisite punishment. He also was afraid the Chinese might recruit the children and feed them back into the Soviet Union as illegals.
INT: How did you carry out such a program in China?
GOLYTSIN: That was easy. Kang Sheng, who later became the chief of the Communist Chinese Intelligence Service, did it for us. In return, we helped them against Chiang Kai-shek.
INT: Didn't you have lots of orphans in Russia from the war?

GOLYTSIN: We had a policy against using war orphans as illegals. They were too psychologically vulnerable. Even these children we did not regard as sufficiently stable to run agents.
INT: So how did you plan to use them?
GOLYTSIN: They were just coming to maturity when I defected. I don't know specific names or assignments. It was not in my division.
INT: But you have a general idea?
GOLYTSIN: General, yes. They were to become agents of influence.

Sean Gordon folded up the transcript and put it in his suit pocket. He closed the vault door and took the elevator to the first floor. At that hour on a Tuesday morning, only the main entrance was open, and it was a long walk around the building to his car. He drove down the George Washington Parkway to Key Bridge and crossed through Georgetown. Turning left off of P Street onto 23rd, he continued up to Connecticut Avenue and then headed north several blocks to Kalorama Circle. Unable to find a parking space, he finally decided to pull into a bus stop.

At 3:45 A.M., he knocked on the door of a huge and peculiar-looking building that occupied one side of the circle. The door opened, Gordon said a few words, and then the door closed. After he stood in the street for another ten minutes with the security camera trained on him, the door opened again and Sean Gordon was admitted to the Embassy of the People's Republic of China.

The number did not answer. Heidi tried another. It was a glittering fall day in Washington, but she was holed up in her apartment trying to get the press to talk to her. She had been there for days, having called in sick to the committee. The names of reporters who were supposed to call back filled two and a half pages of her yellow pad.

From the press and the television, she could see that sentiment was building up against the News/Worldweek transaction. If she could get just one media outlet to take her story seriously, she would blow Bresson's conspiracy apart. Thus far, however, she was hovering between failure and total lack of success. The phone rang. It was probably Jay Lyman again. Instead, she heard the voice of the national editor of the *Washington News*.

"So what are you selling this time Heidi, cancer?"

"You guys have missed the story on Bresson," she said excitedly.

"Who?"

"Very funny. There's a big story here—"

"Heidi, we've already been up that hill with you. There was nothing n the other side."

"The charade at the hearing was part of it!" She pleaded. "Just listen ɔ what I have to tell you about Bresson and make up your own mind."

"Okay, I'll meet you tomorrow for a drink."

"Can't we do it today?" Heidi urged. "The tender offer closes tomor-ow and—"

"Look at our editorial page in the morning. We call our new owner verything but a rapist. If you've got worse things to say, meet me at he Class Reunion at five thirty." He hung up before she could argue urther.

There was a knock on the door.

Heidi suddenly realized that it was unlocked. In a panic, she leaped or the police lock and slammed it into place. Retreating to her bed-·oom, she picked up the phone, pressed 91, and then held down the last ligit of the police emergency number. "Who is it?" she called out.

"Sean."

Heidi started breathing again. She waited a minute to pull herself :ogether, then hung up the phone and opened the door. Sean stood :here, looking like he had not slept all night. He gestured toward the police lock.

"Nervous?"

"You look bad." She tried to ignore the question.

He would not let her. "How would you like to live with that kind of fear the rest of your life? That's what'll happen if you succeed in getting the story in the press."

"Is that why you came to see me?" she asked.

"Let's go for a walk."

They strolled in silence down the brick sidewalk on N Street toward Wisconsin Avenue. The cool autumn breeze felt good on Heidi's face. As it did once or twice each fall, the air in Washington had become crystal clear, throwing everything into sharp relief—the gingerbread details on the Victorian houses, and the slatted shutters and crisp flower boxes on the simple federal facades, the intricate brickwork on the walks and walls. Red, yellow and gold leaves swirled around them. They had strolled like this through Georgetown many times. The old homes and Sean's presence had always made her feel secure. Now he made her tense.

"I love days like this," she said moving away from him. She held out her arms and did a little turn among the falling leaves. "It's like putting on clean glasses."

"I wish you'd see what you're doing," he replied.

"Can't we just enjoy the day?"

"Frankly, no. You don't know what you're involved in. It's far bigger than we thought." His tone was somber, as though he knew he could not persuade her but had to try.

"Tell me about it."

His face said that was impossible. "If I do, will you promise not to take it to the committee?"

"You know I can't," she responded.

"What if I said I had a plan?"

"Is it the same plan Jayson's got?"

"I doubt it."

"I'd ask you to tell me about it," Heidi said.

"And if I asked you to trust me?"

"That's what Jay said."

She had stopped walking and was staring at him. He had asked her to trust him before, and always she had done so. As ever, his face was completely inscrutable. Suddenly, she felt fed up with his mystery, not knowing where he stood or often even where she could find him. Was Sean trying to protect her, or his beloved Clandestine Service? He didn't trust her, that was clear. And so she wouldn't trust him.

"I guess," she finally said, "we just have different loyalties."

28

Stockbrokers with clients owning News/Worldweek shares came to work early on October 15. Marcel Bresson's tender offer expired that evening. It would be a day of frenzy on Wall Street.

For weeks, the brokers had been sending stockholders a flood of information on the News/Worldweek deal: offers, supplemental offers, amended offers, press releases, 10Ks, 14Ds, S-20s, and when the board of News/Worldweek at last surrendered, the brokers sent out Form 14D-9, the white flag that endorsed the Bresson takeover. They had to make sure that their clients read the material, understood it, and made up their minds whether to sell. All over the country that morning, brokers were making their last phone calls, often having to explain the most basic facts to their clients.

"You own News/Worldweek stock," a broker would explain to an elderly retiree in Coral Gables, Florida, "and there's a tender offer."

"What's that?" the clients often asked.

"An offer to buy your stock. A company called Bresson USA will pay $55 in cash for fifty-one percent of the stock. Later they will trade you securities which they say are worth $47 for the rest of your shares. That's a blended priced of $50.10 if you tender now."

"What's the price on the market now?" They were not about to be fooled.

"Forty-nine seventy-five."

"You said $50.10? That's not much more."

"Before the tender offer it was $29.75. The price has risen because of the offer," the broker would explain patiently.

"Well, I don't know," was a typical response.

"If you don't tender now, you'll only be able to participate in the second step. That means you'll only get the $47 worth of securities for all your shares."

"What if I refuse to sell?" some responded adamantly.

385

"If the deal goes through, the company can force you to redeem your shares for the securities or void your stock."

In such cases, the inevitable reaction was something like, "They can't do that! It's unconstitutional! I'll take 'em to court!"

By a quarter to ten, eastern standard time, the brokers were taking Maalox with their coffee. All across the country, brokers' cubby holes were stacked with pink transmittal letters, provided by the soliciting agent, that the brokers would sign on behalf of their clients. Some desks were also piled high with bundles of News/Worldweek stock certificates sent in by those clients who insisted on holding the shares themselves. As they counted and recounted them, the brokers' fingers would turn black from the ink that came off of the certificates. Mistakes would come out of their pockets.

Even though Bresson's offer did not expire until midnight, the brokers at Gould Axewroth had to send all the transmittal letters and any stock certificates to the Reorganization Department by 10 A.M. It, in turn, was working against an 11:00 A.M. deadline to get all the letters and certificates to the Depository Trust Company, where most of the publicly traded stock in the United States was stored. After 11:00 A.M., the stockholders would have to submit Notices of Guaranteed Delivery of shares directly to Bresson's bank. They then had five days to make good on their guarantee. However, weeks could pass before Bresson paid for the stock and the transaction was complete.

In the last hours before the 11:00 A.M. deadline, Gould Axewroth's Reorganization Department was in turmoil. Folders with instructions for every account were being assembled into packages for the DTC. Stock certificates were formed up into bundles. Everything was checked, double-checked, and triple-checked. At 10:33, the transmittal letters authorizing the DTC to transfer the stock certificates and shares to Marcel Bresson's bank were placed in a heavy black suitcase. The documents, which represented $978 million in News/Worldweek stock, were then given to a bonded messenger. He strapped the case to a two-wheeled collapsible cart and rolled it three blocks through the crowds on Water Street to the DTC building on Hanover Square.

Inside the Depository Trust Company, scores of employees were logging in the letters of transmittal from brokerage houses, while others in the vaults were pulling out the News/Worldweek stock, counting it, and preparing to send it to Bresson's designated depository, the New York Irving Italian Bank. By 3:00 P.M., guards loaded a large stack of stock certificates into a Brink's armored car for the trip uptown to the bank's headquarters.

Mobilizing personnel from other offices, the Corporate Trust Department of the New York Irving Italian Bank scrambled to register the stock certificates from the DTC, the letters of transmittal arriving directly from shareholders, and the growing flood of guarantees from those who had missed the morning deadline. As the afternoon wore on, an intangible process was under way. Ownership was changing hands.

When diffused among thousands of individuals and institutions, ownership was an elusive quality of property that conferred few rights and no privileges. Ownership, in the sense of control, was a delusion unless concentrated. And as News/Worldweek stock accumulated in the trust accounts of the New York Irving Italian Bank, so did Marcel Bresson's authority to command the scores of businesses, tens of thousands of employees, and billions of dollars in assets of News/Worldweek. From all parts of the country, ownership was flowing into his hands, and with it, the power to use the company to shape the values, attitudes and opinions of the American people.

When Heidi had finished telling her story about Marcel Bresson to the national editor of the *Washington News,* Patti Page was singing "How Much is that Doggy in the Window." They sat in a booth at the back of the Class Reunion, a press hangout two blocks from the White House that featured nostalgic music from the '40s and '50s and pictures of old movie stars on the walls. Heidi knew that meeting there was not a good sign. Journalists would never parade a serious source past their colleagues at the bar.

Patti Page got through a whole chorus before the editor reacted.

"Honey, have you got anything to support this story?"

"Like what?"

"Evidence. Documents. Photographs."

Sean had the documents they had stolen from the Sommer Bank. He also had the tooth. She shook her head.

"Well, how about other sources? I'd need at least two or three to corroborate this story."

She knew Sean would be no help. Lyman was a question mark at best.

"There's the dentist in New York," Heidi said. "I can give you the address of the woman in Vienna, and you can check the archives like I did."

"What about the financial stuff?" he asked.

She hesitated. Lyman was the only possible candidate. "Will you really pursue this?" she asked him point blank.

He shrugged. "It's pretty wild, but . . . Yeah, I'll do my best."

"Then I'll try to get you another source."

As Jayson Lyman walked into Marcel Bresson's dinner party, he enjoyed watching Cooke and de Grazia spit into their drinks. The other guests in Bresson's suite at the Washington Omni included most of the takeover team: the lawyers from Skadden Fried, the PR people from McFadden Dworkin, the proxy solicitors, Sperile Beck, Maurice the accountant and Mr. and Mrs. Drew Richardson. Lyman noted Bresson's nod of approval for his having Heidi Bruce on his arm.

For four days she had refused to come. He had explained that his plan hinged on consolidating Bresson's confidence in him. He argued that her presence at the dinner would demonstrate that bygones were bygones, that he was back on the team, and that she was under control. Heidi said that dining with someone who recently had tried to kill her was medieval.

Then, at 6:30 that evening, she suddenly called his hotel to say that she had changed her mind. As they shook hands with the other guests, he found it hard to suppress the worry that she still might make a scene. Maybe he should have confided his plan to her, but he was afraid she would jump the gun and try to do it herself. She had a way of deciding that she knew best.

Heidi was not looking for trouble. She would do what Lyman wanted, and in exchange she would insist he talk to the national editor of the *Washington News*. Jayson had been as secretive as Sean about his plans, but the fact that he now seemed committed to stopping Bresson gave Heidi hope that he would help her.

She smiled sweetly as Bresson kissed her hand. Cooke and de Grazia moved in to flank him. Lyman could feel the tension in the air. Was it merely his presence?

"Everything going well?" he asked.

"I do not think so," Bresson's smile vanished. "You have seen the newspapers? The AFL-CIO ordered its pension funds not to tender their shares! We are only at forty-three percent!"

"Including Raffy?"

Cooke nodded.

A shot of hope flowed through Heidi. Bresson might lose!

"I told him everybody tenders at the last moment," de Grazia said in a tone that subordinated himself to Lyman again. "The results could come in late."

"I tried to explain," Cooke asserted himself, "that this isn't Europe. The AFL-CIO doesn't control its affiliated unions, and management has a fifty percent say in most of the union pension funds."

Bresson looked unconvinced.

"The boys are right," Lyman said magnanimously. "With the negative press of the last few days, the institutions will be extra cautious and not tender until the last minute. They don't want their stock tied up for months if something goes wrong. But it's hard to imagine what could go wrong. You've got three and a half hours to reach fifty-one percent. I wouldn't panic," Lyman said soothingly.

Heidi's heart sank. If Lyman was trying to appear sympathetic to Bresson, he was doing too good a job for her taste.

Bresson pasted on his hearty smile again and announced, "Let us all go to the table. The French ambassador loaned me his chef. He has made many courses."

He ushered them to the other end of the long living/dining area. Heidi was placed to his left. Mrs. Drew Richardson was given the place of honor at his right. Jayson was seated next to her, while Richardson was on Heidi's other side. Cooke and de Grazia wound up at the other end of the table.

As they marched through four courses and three wines, Heidi found herself largely ignored by Bresson. She had the peculiar sensation that he was treating her as an employee. Richardson proved to be the sort of man who was unable to hold a social conversation with a woman. In polite society, she knew, it was improper to ask what someone "did." In Richardson's case, it seemed that he could not conceive that she did anything worth discussing. He asked if she played golf, and when she said no, he turned to the man next to him and never spoke to her again.

Phone calls punctuated each course as the New York Irving Italian Bank reported on the percentage of News/Worldweek shares that had been tendered. After the turtle soup, the percentage stood at 45. Following the caviar torte, it rose to 47. During the quenelles, 48. By the time the midmeal sorbet arrived, the figure reached 49.5 percent. With each announcement, the party grew more spirited and Heidi more morose.

A genuine grin began to appear fleetingly on Bresson's face. Heidi thought it made him look like an eel. He motioned to the waiter to come over. A few minutes later, a five-piece orchestra began to set up in the living area.

In the middle of the truffled pigeon, de Grazia came back from the phone with an announcement. Heidi steeled herself.

"The bank reports that as of ten thirteen this evening fifty-two percent of News/Worldweek stock has been tendered to Bresson USA!"

Champagne corks popped. The band launched into "You're the Top." Drew Richardson rose and toasted Marcel Bresson's "farsighted business statesmanship." Lyman grinned and clinked glasses with the rest of them. Heidi desperately wanted fresh air, but forced herself to look pleased.

The reports kept coming—54 percent, 57 percent, 60 percent—and with each one the musicians reprised "You're the Top" and more Roederer Cristal was splattered around the table. When the count reached 64 percent, Cooke rapped on his glass and rose to speak. The band swung into the "Marseillaise."

"This is great!" Cooke exclaimed, his diction thickened by the champagne. "Congratulations! You're gonna get almost all of it! The board will have to kiss your ass. You won't have to worry about dissident shareholders. Just merge 'em out of existence." He smashed his hands together.

And the phone rang again.

"I'll take it!" Cooke gestured to de Grazia to finish his dinner.

As the rest of the table returned to congratulating themselves, Heidi watched Cooke suddenly straighten up and begin to vigorously shake his head.

"You're shitting me!" he exploded.

All conversation stopped.

"Was there any explanation?" Cooke's voice took on an edge of panic as he glanced at his watch.

"What is going on?" Bresson demanded.

Cooke turned toward the table, pressing the phone against his body as if that would keep the bad news from coming out. "It's Raffy! He's fucked us!"

"What? What?" Richardson joined Bresson.

"He's withdrawn his shares."

It took a moment for the significance of the news to sink in.

"That is impossible!" Bresson exclaimed.

"He can't do that!" Richardson echoed him.

"Yes, he can," one of the lawyers said quietly.

Heidi struggled to keep from cheering. She was going to watch Bresson crash and she knew Jayson had engineered it! She sent him an affectionate look that he ignored.

"We're back down to forty-two percent," de Grazia said in a detached way that suggested he was in shock, "and there's only forty-five minutes to the deadline."

"You've got to extend it," Cooke insisted.

"Give us a chance to revise our offer," de Grazia said in little gasps, as if he were starting to hyperventilate.

Sperile Beck spoke for the first time. "Do we have to pay the commitment fees, even if the tender offer fails?"

The word "fail" galvanized Richardson. "Has anyone talked to Raffy? Asked him why he's doing this?"

"It's a conspiracy!" Cooke declared, looking at Lyman. "He's your friend!"

"Be serious," Lyman said coldly.

"What would you do now?" Bresson directed the question to Lyman, his voice suddenly tinged with menace.

Just let these scum sink into their own muck, Heidi silently shouted at Lyman. You've done it! You stopped him! She gazed at him with eyes full of pride.

"I wouldn't extend the offer," Lyman replied calmly into Cooke's flushed face. "That would show weakness. It would look like the political campaign against you was working, and encourage the pressures to build up further. I don't think this transaction will withstand any delay"—Lyman dropped his voice—"or attention, if you get my drift."

Bresson immediately nodded.

"By the time you're back in the market with a revised offer," Lyman concluded, "the deal would be old and cold."

What's wrong with that, Heidi wondered.

"I repeat," Bresson said flatly, "what would you do?"

"Tough it out. All you need is eight points and change."

Heidi saw his strategy.

Bresson's face registered the suspicion that Lyman wanted him to fall short.

"If you don't believe me, call the bank again," Lyman said. "I'll bet the cost of this dinner that the shares are still coming in."

De Grazia ran for the phone.

"It's up to forty-three percent," he shouted. "They say there are guys with briefcases full of guarantees standing outside on the street with cellular phones waiting to be told whether to tender."

"What if they hear about Raffy's withdrawal?" Richardson asked anxiously.

"You can be sure that they already have," Lyman said. "Don't worry. If the guys with the phones are still there, that's good news."

"Maybe they're just waiting for more bad news," Cooke said worriedly.

"Forty-four percent!" de Grazia called out.

"Let us try to make ourselves comfortable," Bresson pushed back from the table. He assembled the guests in the living area. The band started to play again, but Bresson silenced them with a stroke of his hand.

Heidi sat next to Lyman on the couch. She took hold of his hand.

"Will it work?" she whispered.

"Just wait!" he whispered back. "I'll explain later."

By 11:35, the percentage stood at 45. Then it spurted to 47. For fifteen long minutes there was no new report. De Grazia hung on the phone. "They've got me on hold," he complained.

Coffee was served. Bresson took a brandy. No one spoke.

At 11:50, de Grazia shouted, "47.3."

Then, "Point eight!"

Then "Forty-eight!"

Heidi had her eyes on a large grandfather clock in the foyer. As it reached 11:55, de Grazia shouted again.

"It's crossed 48. It's 48.2!"

With each succeeding minute the decimals added up.

".6."

".8."

"Forty-nine percent!"

Two minutes to midnight. Another pause in the reports. Heidi gripped Jayson's hand. He seemed so damned relaxed!

One minute to midnight.

"49.1!"

"Point one!"

".2!"

".4!"

".8!"

The clock in the old City Hall building across Pennsylvania Avenue began to toll. Bresson looked stricken. Over the sound of the bell, de Grazia yelled, "Fifty percent!"

Then "50.5, 51.2 . . ."

"Are they too late?" Bresson asked desperately.

"No. The reports are running a little behind," Lyman said easily.

"I have won!" Bresson exclaimed in surprise. "I own News/World-week!" Bresson pulled Lyman to his feet and out of Heidi's grasp.

No! No! Heidi wanted to shout. Jayson had failed! She wanted to comfort him, convince him that going to the press was the only way. Then she realized that Lyman didn't look like he had failed. He and Bresson hugged one another while the band again struck up the Marseillaise. He was laughing, and shaking hands, and spilling champagne with the rest of them. Jayson seemed happy as hell!

Lyman could not escape feeling satisfied. They all were patting one another on the back as the Roederer Cristal flowed indiscriminately over glasses and trays and onto tables, clothes and carpets. He had called it exactly.

"We are a team, Jayson! We are a team!" Bresson repeated over and over. He smiled. Everything was going precisely as he had planned.

"Where is Miss Bruce?" Bresson suddenly wanted to know. "I wish to dance with her!"

Lyman quickly looked around. She had gone.

"She has a tough day tomorrow," he said quickly, "but she asked me to convey her congratulations."

The phone call Sean Gordon had been waiting for came at 3:15 A.M. Two rings, then two rings, then nothing. He quickly dressed in a running suit and jogged up the hill from his apartment on the Potomac River to the Mechanics and Farmers Bank on the corner of Wisconsin and M streets. His destination was the set of public phones next to the automatic teller in the parking lot.

Gordon checked his watch as he approached the intersection. Kicking aside the mounds of trash that accumulated on the streets of Georgetown every night, he slowed to a walk. He did not want to hang around for the call, for fear that some D.C. patrol car might take too great an interest in him.

He arrived at the phone bank just as the call should be coming through. Nothing happened. He gave it fifteen seconds, then moved closer to the phones. The first one had no receiver. The second had a receiver, but the cord was broken off. The third had a massive dent in it as though struck by a sledgehammer. None of them would be receiving calls that evening.

Gordon checked his watch again. He had waited too long. He started sprinting up Wisconsin Avenue, praying that he would not attract police attention. He reached the Little Tavern hamburger stand on N Street just as the phone was ringing. One of the policemen at the counter reached it first.

"Are you Kenneth?"

Gordon nodded, slightly out of breath.

"Then it's for you."

He took the phone. He dreaded giving the countersign to the voice on the line. The Chinese used such peculiar and old fashioned terms. CIA tradecraft required that countercodes fit the situation like, "That's two Jumbo burgers without onions?"

Instead, Gordon said, "The frequency is fifteen."

Both policemen were openly staring at him.

The voice on the phone replied, "Your package will arrive at JFK on China Airlines flight number nine eight one, at twelve noon. It is extremely fragile." The line went dead.

Gordon hung up the phone and turned to leave. The largest policeman stood in his way.

"Can you show us some ID?"

Gordon did not want to show his Agency identification. And he did not have to. He had dressed so rapidly he left his wallet on the dresser.

"I'm sure you'll be able to explain who you are," the policeman said, "and what 'frequency fifteen' means, when you get downtown."

Heidi did not sleep all night. She could not believe what had happened. Jayson Lyman had played her for a sucker. He had no intention of blocking the News/Worldweek deal. He just wanted to get back on board the gravy train. And she was his ticket. She was a dupe. As dawn began to lighten the dark, she finally drifted off into dreams of revenge.

She woke up after ten, feeling more determined than ever. The national editor of the *Washington News* was still on her side. It would break security, but she could show him the memos she had prepared on Bresson for the Chairman. That would give him names and places he could check out. She could reveal her role in the Sommer Bank break-in, and tell him about the killings in Vienna and Geneva. He could verify all that too. She could end up in deep trouble, but it would be worth it to get Bresson!

The morning paper was waiting at the front door. She was eager to find out how the *Washington News* had handled the climax of the takeover battle. She pulled off the rubber band and spread it on the kitchen table. For the first time in a week, the front page carried no story on the News/Worldweek deal. Coverage was confined to a small box in the business section reporting that the tender offer expired at midnight and the transaction was expected to go through. Disappointed, she flipped on the portable TV on the counter and tuned it to Cable News Network. While she struggled to make coffee, the 10:45 Business segment came on. The lead story confirmed that Marcel Bresson's tender had been successful. Lou Dobbs went on to talk about the controversy surrounding the takeover. In disgust, Heidi reached over to turn it off but stopped.

". . . that controversy continued today," added Dobbs, "as several senior editors at the *Washington News,* the News/Worldweek flagship publication, announced their resignations this morning. The *News* had been openly critical of the $8.9 billion transaction . . ."

She dashed for the phone.

"The national editor, please," Heidi said anxiously.

His secretary came on the line.

"Is he there? This is Heidi Bruce calling."

"No, he's not here." Her voice sounded strained.

"Will he be back?" Heidi asked, "or did he . . ."

"Yes!" The woman burst into tears. "He's resigned. What will happen to us?"

Heidi put the phone down without responding. She felt dead inside. That was it. Bresson had won. Nobody could or would stop him. Unless . . .

A desperate idea forced itself into Heidi's mind. She would face jail. But there would be a trial and she could explain. They would have to listen. Did she have the courage? She really had no choice. Heidi got dressed and headed for the office.

Sean Gordon did not get out of the D.C. jail until 9:30 A.M. when his assistant arrived with his wallet and a change of clothes. He still had time to meet the China Airlines flight in New York at noon. His assistant drove him across the 14th Street Bridge while he pulled off his jogging clothes and changed into a suit and tie. They arrived at National Airport at 9:52; only to be caught in a jam at the entrance. Gordon leapt out and dashed to the Trump Shuttle. They were already boarding.

"The flight's closed," the clerk said.

"I'm on official government business," Gordon waved his ID.

"Flight's closed," she repeated brightly.

"The line's still boarding. I can see them. Is it full?"

"Sir, the flight's closed!" With that she walked away, leaving Sean Gordon no one to argue with.

He thought briefly of trying to talk his way past security and onto the flight, but he did not need to be arrested again that day. Instead, he hurried back through the main terminal building and down the long corridor that led to the North Terminal and the Pan Am Shuttle. It should arrive in New York's La Guardia Airport by 11:30. That would give him thirty minutes to make the twelve and a half mile taxi ride to JFK Airport. He might still make it.

The 10:30 flight was not full, and he easily found a seat near the front so he could deplane quickly. At 10:31, the pilot came on the loudspeaker.

"Due to air traffic congestion in New York, they're holding us at the gate for a few minutes. So if you'll all just sit back and relax, we'll get going as soon as we can. Sorry for the inconvenience."

Gordon wondered if it was a tape-recorded announcement.

By 10:42, the plane finally pushed away from the gate and the pilot came back on the air. "We're now sixth for take-off. We'll be getting off the ground anytime now."

As the minutes slowly passed, Gordon tried to think of alternatives. There were none. He had to meet the plane.

At 10:51, they finally lifted off. The stewardesses served snacks. When Gordon pulled the foil top off of the orange juice, it squirted all over his tie.

The plane landed at 11:36. At the taxi stand, Gordon was assigned a taxi driver who was from Madagascar, or the Seychelles or the Maldives. Wherever it was, he spoke four words of English and ran by a slower clock. When Gordon offered him a twenty to step on it, he took the money, said, "yes, yes," and stayed in the right-hand lane. At Jewel Avenue, where the Grand Central Parkway collided with the Van Wyck Expressway, the traffic came to a halt. It was 11:52. As the two left lanes started moving, Gordon's continued to sit there. He finally lost his temper.

He got out of the cab. Then he opened the front door and yanked the driver out from behind the wheel. As he sat in the road dumbfounded, Gordon jumped back inside, pulled onto the shoulder and took off.

At 12:01, he skidded to a halt in the underground passageway outside Pan Am's international arrivals section. He opened the trunk, walked casually to the curb as if he were about to collect luggage, then quickly stepped into the terminal, abandoning the taxi in the street. Waving his CIA identification, he crashed through customs and immigration and rushed up a labyrinth of corridors to the China Airlines gate. His watch read 12:05.

No one was there. He looked around for an airline official or clerk, but they were all on the other side of a glass door. If he opened it, every alarm in the terminal would go off. He finally found a maintenance man with a walkie-talkie. For ten dollars, he agreed to check.

"The flight's been delayed at least an hour," he reported.

"We have enough for a quorum," the vice chairman said, looking around the News/Worldweek boardroom. "Shall we begin?"

With one exception, the directors were all assembled. Drew Richardson, the president of News/Worldweek, the chief financial officer, the former Secretary of State, General Linx, the president of Stickney College, and Julian Alexander, each took seats at one end of the table. Bresson placed himself at the opposite end, like an alternate chairman. His party included Lyman to his right, and Cooke to his left. Sperile Beck and Maurice the accountant had taken chairs behind him. Everyone was waiting for Raffy Nichols.

Though outwardly calm, Lyman felt increasingly tense. Raffy was crucial to his plan. He searched his mind for ways to delay the start of the meeting.

"Wouldn't it be better to wait?" he said to Bresson. "Let's not give him any pretext for more trouble."

"What trouble?" Cooke countered, "you've got the stock, break his bones."

Bresson looked at each of them. Lyman could see that he enjoyed playing them off against one another. He hoped it would be his turn when the key moment came.

"Continue," Bresson announced, siding with Cooke. Though technically a guest of the board, Bresson's control of 51 percent of the stock meant that the board now was expected to defer to his wishes.

"This, in effect, is our last real meeting as a board," the vice chairman said, "so I'd like to thank everyone for their friendship and cooperation. I can't say we achieved many of the goals we set for ourselves." He gave a rueful little laugh. "The company's being dismantled, the stockholders are getting paper. I guess our biggest accomplishment is that the directors haven't been sued!"

"You also got the top price for the company!" Cooke declared.

"I also want to thank the board." Bresson moved in soothingly, playing the good cop to Cooke's bad-cop act. "Once the merger is complete, the board will be disbanded, but I would be honored if you would all join my international advisory committee. It is composed of prominent statesmen, intellectuals and industrialists, distinguished individuals like yourselves. Of course, you would have the inconvenience of visiting Paris several times a year," Bresson put on his most ingratiating smile, "but you would be well compensated for that."

The former Secretary of State and General Linx and the president of Stickney College all nodded happily. Lyman had never seen more blatant bribery in a boardroom.

Where in the hell was Raffy, he anxiously wondered. Had he made a mistake in counting on him? Raffy wasn't a Wall Street shark. He specialized in giant rutabagas and papier-mâché ear studs. Brilliant concept, Jayson, he thought, but your execution sucks.

The vice chairman thanked Bresson profusely and moved to the agenda. "Our job today is straightforward," he said. "We have to consider, and hopefully approve, the proxy materials in front of us. They spell out the terms of the securities that Mr. Bresson is offering for the second stage of the transaction. All the financial information to support a $47 a share value is in the little booklet. We also have a fairness opinion."

"What happens after we approve it," General Linx asked. "Does it go out to the shareholders?"

"No." Lyman spoke up. "It goes to the SEC for approval first. You'll have a fairness opinion and the SEC behind you, so there's no real liability."

"If that's what you're worried about," Cooke added with a sneer.

"Are there any other questions?" the vice chairman asked.

"I can explain some of the numbers," Lyman offered, to keep the discussion going.

"They can read," Cooke cut him off.

"If there are no more questions," the vice chairman said, "I'll entertain a motion—"

Julian Alexander raised his hand. "Actually, I haven't read the proxy material all that carefully," the lawyer admitted. "Don't we have other items we could take care of and then come back to this one?"

It was a reprieve, Lyman thought.

"We've got the cold comfort letter," the vice chairman responded. "Tab B in your book. We told Mr. Bresson that we couldn't give him one, but our accountants didn't get the word. They prepared it anyway."

"What does it mean, 'cold comfort'?" the former Secretary asked.

"It assures Mr. Bresson nothing's suddenly gone wrong with the company," Lyman explained.

"Shouldn't we also be getting a comfort letter from Mr. Bresson," Alexander asked, "to back up his securities?"

The vice chairman was thrown for a moment.

"There should be one in the proxy statement," Lyman pointed out.

"Right," the vice chairman said. "Well, can I take it there's no objection to our comfort letter? If not, then it's approved. Now," he continued, "if there are no objections to the proxy . . ."

Lyman opened his mouth to say something, anything, to delay the board, and heard a loud "No! Don't do it!"

Raffy came through the door. "The board would make a big mistake approving this offer," he declared. "That's why I pulled out of the tender last night." He sat down. "They told you about that, didn't they?"

The outside directors shook their heads in surprise.

"Drew"—the former Secretary of State addressed Richardson—"I would have thought you or Mr. Bresson would have informed us of such an important matter."

"What difference does it make," Cooke asserted, "we've got fifty-one percent of the company."

"The issue is whether you're trying to steal the other forty-nine percent," Raffy charged.

"Are you questioning our integrity?" Cooke blustered.

"I'm questioning the value of the securities you're offering in this proxy. You say they're worth $47. I say bullshit. The interest rate's too low, there's no sinking fund to assure redemption. If you're not prepared to negotiate a better deal, I'll have no alternative but to sue for an appraisal."

The other outside directors looked at one another.

"You're threatening to sue us?" the former Secretary of State asked.

Drew Richardson said, "Raffy, don't be hasty."

"I'm not. Look, more than forty-six percent of the stockholders didn't tender for $55 cash. How do you think they feel about this toilet paper you say's worth $47? Think about it."

"Could we recess?" Bresson asked. "I would like to consult my advisors."

They reassembled in the hall. This was a critical moment in Lyman's plan.

"I told you last night we should have revised the offer," Cooke whined.

Lyman shook his head. "How many deals have you done, Marshall?"

"I sold Gould Axewroth!" he said defensively.

"Billy Gould did that from his oxygen tent."

"You cannot pay any more," Sperile Beck warned.

"Jayson, what do you recommend?" Bresson demanded.

"Time and momentum are still essential. You must announce board approval of the proxy at today's press conference. You need to get the SEC to start the thirty-day clock ticking to close the back end. If you haggle with Raffy, or let the board duck a vote on the proxy, the red flags will start going up."

"But what if Raffy sues for an appraisal?" Cooke challenged him.

Lyman looked at him. He was a pathetic combination of pugnacity and indecision. "Marcel, I would go in there and start out by telling Raffy he can have his appraisal without a suit. I'll tell him we have confidence in these securities."

"You?" Cooke hissed, "this is my deal now!"

"Marshall," Bresson restrained him, "It is my deal. Go ahead, Jayson."

By the time Heidi got to her office, she was overwhelmed with doubts. Yes, Lyman had betrayed her. Her chairman had rejected her. The editor at the *Washington News* had failed her. But did that justify what she was planning to do?

Maybe, Heidi thought, I should give it up. Sean still had a plan. She should be a good girl and just let him take care of it. But would he? Bresson now controlled News/Worldweek, and what had Sean done? If the situation were reversed, would he sit back and let her deal with it? Depressed as she was, Heidi had to laugh.

She picked up her phone and called him.

His secretary answered. "No, he's not here," she said.

"Can you give him a message?"

"If he calls in. He's traveling," she explained.

Traveling? She felt the fury explode within her. He wasn't doing anything! "Never mind!" Heidi slammed down the phone.

She was on her own. Reaching for the file drawer in her desk, Heidi spun the dial on the combination lock. Under "Identities," she found the envelope containing the phony letter from the *Harvard Business Review.* Then she stood up and marched down the long center corridor of the office and entered the vault.

"I'd like to see the exhibits for the terrorism hearing," she told the clerk.

"In the back," he said.

She stared at the displays for a long time. Finally she took a deep breath. "Can you help me carry some of this stuff to my desk?" she asked the clerk.

"You'll have to sign for it."

After she initialed a receipt, he carried two of the exhibits, while she took the third.

One display consisted of three huge blow-ups of satellite photographs depicting terrorist training camps in Syria, South Yemen and Libya. Heidi placed the pictures around her cubbyhole so that it was difficult to look in at her. The second exhibit was a ten-pound package of plastic explosive, with a detonator showing markings that the CIA had traced to Iran. Heidi carefully set it aside.

She placed the third exhibit in front of her and sat down. It was a two-foot square board encased in a transparent plastic box. She turned it over and unscrewed the wing nuts in the back. The plastic cover came off. She turned the board over. Fastened to the painted surface was a Glock 17 plastic handgun, made in Austria, and two 9-mm explosive bullets.

Heidi sat staring at them.

"Considering shooting somebody?"

She jumped. It was the staff director.

"God! You scared me," she said. "I was just thinking of how we need a box that opens more easily so that the Chairman could take it out. Wave it around under the nose of the president of the National Rifle Association. Like Frank Church and the poison-dart gun."

"Good idea," the staff director said, and disappeared back into his office.

Heidi tryed to pull herself together. This was crazy. What should she do? Desperately, she ransacked her mind for alternatives and found none. Sean's voice came back to her, "far bigger than we thought."

She took a small hand-held tape recorder out of her desk. Opening the battery compartment, she dumped the two AAA Energizers into her waste basket. Next, she pried the two bullets off the board and put them inside the tape recorder. They fit perfectly.

Heidi checked the time. She had to hurry, or she would miss the press conference. She put the letter and the tape recorder in her purse. The handgun was held to the board by rubber straps. They slipped off easily. She held the weapon in her hand for a moment. If felt so light. Strange that it could kill somebody. She dropped it in her bag.

Then Heidi took the time to reassemble the exhibit box and turned

t over on her desk. She also placed the case containing the explosives
on top of it. Finally, she took down each of the three-by-four inch
photographs and placed them face down on top of the other exhibits.
All staff members were required to turn their classified work upside
down when away from their desk so that outsiders coming into the
office would not see it. The photos were Secret-Codeword, and Heidi
did not want a security violation.

Sean Gordon's "package" turned out to be very old, and in a wheelchair. During the arrival delay, Gordon had arranged for a helicopter
to take them from the Pan Am terminal at JFK to LaGuardia. The
China Airlines flight landed at 1:20 and his passenger was quickly
cleared through customs and immigration. Sean Gordon calculated
that they would get to LaGuardia in time to catch the 2:00 P.M. shuttle.
But when they arrived at 1:45, the New York Helicopter staff had no
wheelchair.

Gordon waited for an agonizing ten minutes until an electric cart
showed up. Ignoring the protests of the ground personnel, he crossed
the tarmac directly to the Trump Shuttle building. They had a
wheelchair, and a flight attendant helped them up the steps to the
gangway. They were the last passengers to board the flight to Washington. The News/Worldweek press conference was scheduled for 3
P.M. Despite everything he had done, Gordon resigned himself to
being late.

Marcel Bresson came out of the boardroom with a smile that showed
all of his bad teeth. The vote on the board had been eight to one for
the proxy. Only Raffy had held out.

"Excellent work, Jayson!" Bresson slapped him on the back like a
Russian.

The other directors came out, and they all shook hands, except Raffy,
who headed for the elevator without saying anything to anyone.

Lyman waved for de Grazia, who had been waiting in the reception
area. "Get the proxy over to the SEC immediately," he said.

"The messenger's right there." He pointed to a young black man in
skin-tight shorts and a helmet standing by the receptionist's desk.

"This is the letter of transmittal, signed by Bresson." Lyman handed
it to de Grazia.

DAVID AARON

"Jayson! What are you doing? Let us have lunch! I am off my diet to celebrate!" Bresson announced.

"But you have a press conference now," Cooke reminded him.

"Oh, no," Bresson responded. "Why do I need a press conference?"

Lyman went cold inside. Without the press conference, his strategy was out the window. He had to think fast.

Cooke beat him to it. "Jayson will probably disagree with this," he said defensively, "but I think it's essential that you show up. You've still got some selling to do to get the seventy-five percent level that will let you freeze out everybody else, including Raffy. And with all the recent publicity, you've got to show them you don't have horns."

Bresson looked at Lyman, who shrugged to indicate it was his call. He was afraid to look eager.

The frown deepened on Bresson's face. "But I am hungry," he said stubbornly.

"We'll get you a sandwich," Richardson said to be helpful.

Bresson looked like the thought was poisonous. He stopped and folded his arms. Lyman forced himself to speak.

"We'll get a reservation at Jean Pierre. You can keep it short."

For a moment, Bresson looked like a willful child. "*Bien,*" he finally conceded.

Lyman coughed and hit his chest to start his heart pumping again.

As Heidi had expected, security was tight. She first had to stop at a desk to show her phony letter from the *Harvard Business Review* to get a press credential. Then she joined the crowd of reporters filling the lobby of News/Worldweek as they waited to pass into the auditorium through a metal detector. The security guards also had an x-ray machine to screen bags and briefcases.

In the taxi, Heidi had taken the pistol out of her bag and put it in the pocket of her jacket. When she reached the x-ray machine, she put her purse with the tape recorder and bullets onto the conveyor belt. She watched anxiously as it slowly moved inside. The machine had two monitors, one of which was in color to give a contrasting image. The woman operator looked carefully at both screens. The purse emerged from the other side of the machine. She was still staring at the monitor. Then she switched her attention to the next object. It had passed.

Heidi now had to go through the metal detector. She readied herself. As soon as the light flashed green, she stepped through. The bell went off.

"Put all your metal objects on here," the guard handed her a tray.

Heidi knew that the machine worked on the basis of the mass of metal passing through an electromagnetic field. While others pushed by, she took off her belt, her watch, her bracelets, her necklace and her ring. The pistol, she knew, was not entirely plastic. It had metal springs, firing pin and barrel. As she got back in line to go through the machine again, she could feel her blouse grow damp from sweat.

"Would you like to take off your jacket?" the guard held out his hand. "It's got metal buttons."

"No, that's okay!" Heidi almost shouted, and quickly stepped through the machine. The alarm went off again. Heidi was panic-stricken.

"You've got to wait for the green light!" the guard admonished her. "Try again."

This time, there was no alarm.

With her heart beating wildly, Heidi picked her bag off the conveyor and cut across the crowded foyer in search of a ladies' room.

The press loves a funeral, Lyman thought, looking out on the sea of reporters. McFadden Dworkin had set up the stage just as he had suggested: a raised dais in front of a large white screen with a podium in the center. Inspecting the lectern, Lyman was relieved to find it equipped with a slide projector and controls for the auditorium lights.

Cooke nudged him and pointed into the audience. Raffy stood surrounded by reporters bathed in bright TV lights.

"He's holding his own press conference, for Christ's sake!" Cooke exclaimed.

"It's still a free country," Lyman responded. "We'll only create a bigger story if we try to stop him."

Richardson was tapping the microphone and calling for order. Lyman placed himself beside Bresson who sat next to the lectern. Sperile Beck took the seat to Lyman's left. Cooke and Maurice the accountant were on the other side of the podium with Richardson. The other directors were seated behind them.

"If you'll all take your seats," Richardson's voice boomed over the amplifiers, "we can get started. I'm the chairman of News/Worldweek. I want to welcome you to this momentous occasion. This great firm has taken the first step toward becoming part of an historic global enterprise, created through the farsighted leadership of Marcel Bresson. It is my honor and privilege to introduce . . ."

Lyman had been through scores of such press conferences. They always followed a predictable pattern. He prayed that this one would, too.

Heidi felt relieved and furious at the same time. She was sitting in a stall in the ladies' room listening to Richardson's voice come through the walls and glaring at the gun. The bullets were in her hand, but she could not figure out how to load them. It was an automatic, but the handle was empty. She had no clip.

Maybe it was a sign, Heidi told herself. She wasn't a murderer. Then she heard Bresson's voice: "This is the happiest day of my life."

Gritting her teeth, she began to search through her purse. Finally she dumped it into her lap. A checkbook, keys, lip gloss, sunglasses, barrettes, nail polish, a change purse, note pad and assorted pencils, wads of receipts and ticket stubs, a comb, brush and address book were among the flotsam of her daily life that spilled into her skirt. Stirring through it, she found what she needed, a small, square tortoise-shell compact. It fit neatly into the butt of the gun.

Turning the pistol upside down, Heidi dropped one of the bullets into the hollow handle. It got caught at an angle and she had to use a nail file to get it to lie straight on the bottom. Then she inserted the compact into the grip and holding the weapon between her knees, pushed down on the bullet. Suddenly she realized the muzzle was pointing at her stomach. She turned the gun toward the door and pressed it down on her thigh, forcing the compact and the bullet up inside. With her left hand she pulled back the action. As she pushed it forward, Heidi could feel the bullet slide into the chamber.

Placing her purse between her feet, she opened her knees and let her belongings slide down her skirt and into the bag. She peered inside the handle of the gun, shaking it to make sure the bullet was firmly in the chamber. Then she double-checked the safety before putting it into her jacket pocket.

As she left the ladies' room, Heidi realized she would only get one shot. With resignation and determination, she vowed to make it a good one.

Bresson, slowly reading a six-page statement of bland corporate homilies in heavily accented English, had just about put the entire audience to sleep. The more he talked about "transitions," "responsibility," "evolution," "global interface" and "democratic culture," the more Lyman could see the journalists' eyes glaze over. He worried that the reporters would fail to be aggressive in the question-and-answer period. As tense as he was, even Lyman was having a hard time staying awake. Until he saw Heidi Bruce appear at the back of the hall.

Sean Gordon spent the entire flight to Washington negotiating for a wheelchair to meet the flight. Just before landing, he was informed that one would be available, but they would not, as he had requested, be allowed to take it with them.

Gordon's assistant met them at the curb with a car. Together they lifted their precious passenger onto the backseat. The assistant then got back behind the wheel, while Gordon fished through his wallet for a tip for the Eastern Airlines clerk who was pushing the wheelchair.

"Have you got change for a hundred?" Gordon asked, waving the bill under the attendant's nose.

"Just wait a minute." He turned and went inside.

Immediately, Gordon collapsed the wheelchair, stuck it in the trunk and jumped in the front seat.

"Get going," he ordered, looking at his watch. "The press conference has already started."

The guard at the entrance to the auditorium ordered Heidi to stand next to him. When the questions began, he let her go forward in search of a seat.

There was no room up front. Heidi finally found a place on the side, but it was too far from the podium, and gave her an awkward angle. Each time a question was asked, she moved, stepping on other people's feet and stumbling over their knees, trying to find a better spot. At last, she spotted a vacant chair, up close and to the left of the lectern. A Nagra tape recorder occupied the cushion. The woman in the next seat wore a credential that said National Public Radio. Heidi asked if she could move it.

"Sorry, can't you see I'm using the seat for my recorder?" she said brusquely.

"Do you think your recorder will still work," Heidi asked, "if I drop it on the floor?"

Lyman's curiosity about Heidi moving from seat to seat was eclipsed by his growing anxiety over the questions.

"Do you think you've been treated fairly by the American press?"

"What is your reaction to the resignations at the *Washington News?*"

"What are the differences between the press in Europe and the United States?"

Ad nauseum! All they cared about was themselves! The media viewed the media as the story!

What about the deal? Lyman wanted to shout. Where were the tough questions about why Raffy pulled out? Why the board failed to unanimously endorse the second step? Why 47 percent of the stockholders didn't tender? This was a love fest.

Twelve minutes of the question period had gone by. Bresson said he would only allow fifteen. And he was filibustering, answering each one as long and slowly as possible. If the right question didn't come soon, Lyman's plan would fail. Raffy was supposed to have planted the questions. Instead, this was a love feast. He thought it had been set up perfectly, but he realized he had ignored Michael McFadden's first rule of public relations, "Always count on the press to screw you."

Heidi forced herself to breathe more slowly. She felt on the verge of fainting. Could she do it? Bresson was standing right above her. Lyman was staring right through her. The questions were becoming repetitive. The press conference would be over soon. She had to act now. Heidi gripped the handle of the gun and started to draw it from her jacket.

The man in front of her stood up.

It was just the question Lyman wanted. "We were given a statement a few minutes ago," the reporter said, consulting his notebook, "by Mr. Raphael Nichols. He charged that the securities you're offering the rest of the shareholders are not worth the $47 that you claim. How do you answer his allegations?"

Lyman could see a cloud cross Bresson's face. Then he smiled.

"The board considered that question and rejected his point of view," Bresson said simply.

Don't leave it at that, Lyman wanted to yell at him, follow up! But the reporter sat down. Heidi was left standing behind him with her hand in her pocket.

"Ah! Miss Bruce," Bresson said, "you have a question? It will be the last one."

Heidi was stunned. She wanted to hide. The arrogant son of a bitch was challenging her! She saw Jayson vigorously shaking his head. Screw him. She wouldn't ask a question; she'd make a speech!

But before she could open her mouth, a man to her right shouted, "Answer the question! Why are the securities worth forty-seven bucks?"

Lyman braced himself. His whole strategy came down to this moment. He prayed that Bresson was too clever to respond himself.

"I am happy to reply. I hope you all will listen carefully, because I want all the remaining shareholders to learn of it as well. Permit me to ask the man who answered Mr. Nichols at the board meeting to give you his response. May I introduce my financial advisor, Jayson Lyman."

He stood up slowly, opened his briefcase, and took out a folder. Lyman then replaced Bresson at the lectern. He assumed his most careful and meticulous investment banking demeanor.

"The strength of any security depends on two things. One is the terms: the interest rate, the existence of special redemption features and so forth. The security being offered in this transaction is competitive in every respect with securities of comparable value."

Watching Bresson nodding his head and Lyman up there apologizing for him, Heidi wondered if she wasn't trying to shoot the wrong person.

"But there's a second and ultimately more important factor," Lyman continued, "and that's the underlying strength of the company that stands behind the security."

Bresson nodded his head even more vigorously.

"So let me tell you something about Les Éditions Bresson." Lyman snapped a switch and the auditorium suddenly went dark. The wall behind him lit up with a chart.

"This is the consolidated historical performance of the companies that make up Les Éditions Bresson."

Red and green lines snaked across the wall. Beck leaned over to Bresson and asked what they were looking at. Bresson shook his head.

"The green line represents revenue, the red line represents cost. You'll notice the red line is well above the green in every year."

"What is he doing?" Beck insisted. "Someone must stop him!" Bresson realized he was being betrayed. Desperately, he looked around in the dark for a guard.

"You may ask how a company with such a continuous deficit manages to survive," Lyman continued, "let alone make acquisitions like News/Worldweek."

There was scattered laughter in the audience. Bresson was now gesturing wildly for a security guard. Everyone was riveted to the screen. The slide changed.

"The answer is easy. Debt! You keep borrowing to cover the deficit. This is a chart of Éditions Bresson's assets and liabilities. They are in green and red respectively. Again you'll note the red above the green. Liabilities exceeding assets. In the investment banking profession," he concluded carefully, "we call that negative net worth." He snapped on the lights.

The questions came in a fusillade.

"Does that mean Bresson's bankrupt?"

"Is he offering worthless stock?"

"Is this proxy a fraud?"

"Who lends him all that money?"

Bresson turned desperately to Beck, "Tell them you guarantee me!"

Beck looked at the reporters shouting frenzied questions at Lyman. "I can't!" Beck backed off. "It could start a run on the bank!"

"But you are guaranteed!" Bresson grabbed him by the lapels.

"Are you mad?" Beck knocked his hands away. "We can't talk about that!"

Bresson leapt to his feet, tipping over his chair. He grabbed Lyman by the shoulder, yanking him away from the microphone.

"That is our joke!" he shouted over the questions. Cooke was pushing a guard onto the stage.

"Mr. Lyman thought this event would be boring," Bresson grimaced in effort to smile, "so we made up this little charade."

There was scattered uneasy laughter in the audience. The guard asked Lyman to leave the stage. Lyman knew he must behave with dignity, or he would be written off as a crazy person. He had made his point. He left Bresson alone to confront the press.

Heidi felt flooded with pride for Lyman. She wanted to rush to him, but she was trapped by reporters who had all pressed toward the stage. They were bombarding Bresson with questions.

"Silence!" he shouted. "Do not make fools of yourselves over a little joke! These charts are a fiction, I tell you! The Swiss Bank Corporation has supported me for years!" He pointed at Beck, who sat frozen in his chair. "Do you think they would do so if I were bankrupt? Do you think this distinguished board would accept a *chantage?*" He groped for the English word. "A swindle?" The directors looked dumbfounded.

The reporters began to quiet down. Heidi could see some start to nod their heads as if they were having second thoughts.

That bastard's going to get away with this, she thought wildly.

"We have created a glorious new entity," Bresson was selling hard. "Truly the first twenty first-century corporation. It unites two great democracies, France and America. I have submitted all of my financial information to the U.S. authorities. So do not take this joke as serious.

I must be careful with my Gallic humor." He forced out one of his barking laughs.

Lyman stood at the edge of the stage in amazement. The power of preconception was greater than the truth. Again the press appeared to be eating out of Bresson's hand. It was as if nothing he had said mattered. Or were they thinking they might be working for him some day? Lyman did not know what to do.

Heidi did. She climbed on her chair to get a clear view of Bresson. She felt for the gun. If she was seen, someone could easily knock her over. It would have to be all in one motion. And it had to be fast.

"I can assure you," Bresson was saying, "Bresson USA is here to stay. I may even become an American citizen."

And, Heidi said to herself, it has to be now.

As she began to pull the gun from her pocket, she heard a commotion at the back of the hall. Everyone turned. Heidi looked too.

Sean Gordon was pushing a wheelchair down the aisle. Security guards cleared the way. The person in the chair was old, very old. From the Chinese tunic, Heidi could not tell if it were a woman or a man. The crowd of reporters parted to let them through.

Bresson was still selling. "In thirty days, when News/Worldweek and Bresson USA merge, America will not be losing a great company—"

A guard put a folded note in front of him.

"—America will be gaining a great European firm," he continued talking while he opened the note. Then he stopped.

The note was in Russian, *"ZHENSCHINA V INVALIDNAYA KOLYSKA TVOYA MAT."* It said, "The woman in the wheelchair is your mother."

The audience had turned to look at him. Bresson could not speak. He stared at the woman. The ancient face gazed back at him with the clear gray eyes he could never forget. His sense of time and place seemed to be slipping away. He felt overwhelmed by a terrible and alien emotion—he wondered if it were shame.

The hostile questions started coming again, as if the press sensed he was wounded. With the clamor rising around him, Bresson staggered back from the podium, shaking his head, mute. Richardson grabbed the microphone and announced that the press conference was over.

Lyman saw Heidi over the crowd of reporters surrounding him. "I can give you a full set of documents supporting those charts," he was saying. Raffy broke through and tossed his arms around him. "We did it! We did it!" he shouted.

"It's not over yet," Lyman said, but he allowed himself a smile.

Heidi had worked her way through the throng. They stood awkwardly apart for a moment.

"I know I was taking a big chance," Lyman said, "but I didn't want to stop him, Heidi. I wanted to destroy him."

"I know. I know," she pulled his arms around her and kissed him fiercely.

When he came up for air, he asked, "My God, is that a gun in your pocket?"

"That's supposed to be my line."

He laughed and squeezed her harder. "Where's Sean? I owe him an apology."

They looked around through the thinning crowd but he was nowhere to be seen. Richardson, Cooke and the board members had disappeared.

"Maybe he's still with the old woman," Lyman suggested.

They approached the circle of reporters that had gathered around her.

Photo flashes burst on all sides, but the journalists were strangely quiet. As Jayson and Heidi approached, they could see the old woman sitting serenely in a space cleared by the security guards. She was not alone. But it was not Sean Gordon who was with her. The man kneeling at her feet was Marcel Bresson. He was showing her a pearl.

EPILOGUE

Marcel Bresson fought hard to save his empire. He denounced Lyman's revelations as a CIA plot, but apart from his own publications, the press did not take the charges seriously. French officials made a few routine anti-American comments, but the government did nothing.

Bresson demanded that the Swiss Bank Corporation fulfill its loan commitments on the News/Worldweek deal, arguing that they were fully guaranteed. But Liechtinvest suddenly went out of business and the Swiss Bank Corporation declared that neither its stockholders nor the Swiss authorities would allow it to assume a $4.3 billion obligation at a time when the solvency of Les Éditions Bresson was in question.

In desperation, Bresson tried to sell off part of his empire, but before he could get very far, the SEC announced an inquiry into his proxy statement, thus endorsing Lyman's claim that he was bankrupt. Bresson's creditors fell on him like wolves.

Bankruptcy, Jayson explained to Heidi, was like a sudden heart attack. The moment after death, the body was essentially unchanged. The bones, the muscles, the organs, the red and white blood cells, the antibodies, the DNA, remained. But when the spirit of life vanished, the body became a handful of chemicals not worth the cost of recovery.

Les Éditions Bresson continued to have plants, equipment, real estate, employees and products. However, once confidence that it could pay its bills evaporated, the company mysteriously lost value as a going concern. It would remain worthless until bits and pieces could be revived or sold as salvage.

Six days after Marcel Bresson's triumphant closing of the News/Worldweek tender offer, his aircraft disappeared from air traffic control radar screens while over the Baltic. Bresson, his mother, Sperile Beck, and Yves Coudert were listed as being aboard, along with someone named Maurice, last name unknown.

Since the tendered shares had not been paid for, the acquisition unraveled. Gould Axewroth, the New York Irving Italian Bank and the

414

Depository Trust Company worked overtime to get the stock back to the proper shareholders. Everyone remotely connected with the transaction sued everyone else.

Drew Richardson resigned from the board of News/Worldweek, and Raphael Nichols was elected chairman. He invited Jayson Lyman to join the board, and hired Gould Axewroth to carry out a restructuring and recapitalization of the company.

Billy Gould died of heart failure, but not because the Bresson deal fell through. He passed away on an operating table in Yorba Linda, California, where he had moved from the Eisenhower Center because the new hospital planned not to charge him for his transplant. Instead, he had worked out a deal whereby he would make a tax-deductible gift to the cardiology department.

Under the bylaws of Gould Axewroth, Billy Gould's stock was sold back to the firm, which paid his estate in nonvoting securities. This changed the balance of power among the partners, and at their next meeting, they forced Marshall Cooke to step down and made Jayson Lyman chairman.

Convinced he was on a roll, Jayson Lyman gave Heidi Bruce an ultimatum: marry him or else. She, of course, refused. After several weeks of tumultuous negotiations, however, the two of them finally came to terms. They agreed to reside in both New York and Washington, where Heidi was about to become staff director of the Senate Intelligence Committee. Heidi planned to keep her name, but the children would take Lyman's. There would be no prenuptial agreement.

The wedding took place in Washington on a fine November afternoon in the medieval hall of the Society of the Cincinnati, the male counterpart to the Daughters of the American Revolution. Max the Saint had arranged it, in exchange for being a member of the wedding party. As Jayson struggled into his tuxedo, Max told him stories to make him relax.

"You know," Max said, "I never finished the one about the kid whose father's so happy he's joining the family firm that he gives him half the company stock as a graduation gift from Harvard Business School."

"So how does it end?" Lyman asked, retying his bow tie for the fifth time.

"Remember how the kid and his dad are trying to decide where the young man should start out in the firm? The father suggests the mail room, and the kid says, 'Okay, but remember I've got asthma.'' So the old man suggests accounting, and again the kid agrees. But he also points out that accounting was his worst subject. He wouldn't want to make a mistake that could cost the firm a lot of money. The father sees the sense in that. So finally he proposes that his son start in the marketing department.

" 'I'd love to, Dad,' he says, 'but Uncle Herbert runs marketing, and he's hated me ever since I got into a fight at his daughter's wedding.'

"The father's stumped. Finally, he asks his son if he's got any suggestions.

" 'Sure, Dad,' the kid says. 'You could buy me out.' "

The music began and the best man, Dick Rensselaer, finished Lyman's tie. The bride was to be given away by the Chairman of the Intelligence Committee. Sean Gordon had promised to do it, but at the last moment he claimed that he had to go out of town. During the ceremony, Lyman thought he saw him in the back, standing at the top of the stairs.

Jayson and Heidi stayed a long time at the reception, eating, drinking and dancing. Finally, Lyman's mother told them that it was unseemly and that they had to go. As they prepared to run the gauntlet of rice and confetti, Raffy drew Lyman aside and gave him an envelope.

"Thanks, Raf."

"It's not a wedding present. A messenger just delivered it from the office."

Lyman noticed his worried look. He opened the envelope. The letter was addressed to Raffy as chairman of News/Worldweek:

Dear Sir,

We have the honor to inform you of our interest in purchasing the News/Worldweek Corporation. We are prepared to offer $65 per share in cash for all of the stock in the company. It is our hope that this proposal will meet with the approval of your board of directors. However, we reserve the right to present our offer directly to the shareholders of News/Worldweek.

"The favor of your response is required by next Monday.

It was signed, "Hiro Nakamura, Chairman, Ashahi Shimbun."

Jayson handed the letter back to him. "Call Carol Rankin in our M&A department," he said.

"But you can't just leave!" Raffy protested.

Lyman shook his hand and started down the steps. "Relax, Raffy," he called back, "it's only business."